Like

Some Old

Country Song

Clay and Marianne

Summer Lake Silver

Book One

By SJ McCoy

A Sweet n Steamy Romance

Published by Xenion, Inc

Copyright © 2018 SJ McCoy

LIKE SOME OLD COUNTRY SONG. Copyright © SJ McCoy 2018

All rights reserved. Except as permitted under the U.S. Copyright Act of 1976, no part of this publication may be reproduced, distributed, or transmitted in any form, or by any means, or stored in a database or retrieval system without prior written consent of the author.

Published by Xenion, Inc.
First Paperback edition January 2019
www.sjmccoy.com

This book is a work of fiction. Names, characters, places, and events are figments of the author's imagination, fictitious, or are used fictitiously. Any resemblance to actual events, locales or persons living or dead is coincidental.

Cover Design by Dana Lamothe of Designs by Dana
Editor: Kellie Montgomery
Proofreaders: Aileen Blomberg, Traci Atkinson, Jennifer Solymosi and Becky Claxon

ISBN 978-1-946220-47-9

Dedication

For Sam. Sometimes, life really is too short. Few xxx

Prologue

Clay took a slug of his beer and then peered down into the bottom of the bottle, watching the bubbles fizz and pop. He couldn't help thinking that he and the others were just like those bubbles. All of them. He looked around the dressing room.

Lawrence was standing talking to Shawnee, Matt was sitting on the sofa trying to raise a laugh and keep things light as Autumn talked up young Carson, prepping him to go out and be the warm up act for them tonight.

Clay shook his head. They were three generations of country music, if you wanted to look at it that way. He was on the home stretch of his career, as were Lawrence and Shawnee. Matt was at the zenith of his, and young Carson was just at the beginning. And they were all like the bubbles in his beer. He took another swig then watched it fizz as he set it down on the table. The bubbles rose up, caught the light, sparkled on their way to the top. Then all too soon, they reached the surface and popped. Their journey over.

He chuckled to himself, wondering what had him feeling so philosophical. He needed to pull himself together. Turn on the magic, be the guy everyone wanted to see. It wasn't as though it was just an act. That was who he was, who he'd always been. The guy everyone turned to, the guy they brought their problems to. The life of the party. He sighed. The guy who made everyone feel good, about themselves, about life. Whether it was with his songs or a kind word here and there, he knew he made people happy. So, why wasn't the magic working on himself anymore? Why did he feel empty most of the time? And why was it that these days he found himself sitting alone like this more often than not while the party carried on around him?

He knew the answer. It was because he was feeling old. He'd achieved everything he'd set out to and more in his career. He was considered the granddaddy of country music these days. He wasn't just a singer. He owned a label, brought on new talent and ran some of the biggest names in country—some of them were in this room tonight. But he'd never be a granddaddy, not a real one, not to some little boy or girl. At McAdam Records they liked to call themselves family, and in many ways, they were better than family. But with every year that went by, it tugged harder at Clay's heart that he didn't have a family of his own. He might have built a great legacy, but there was no one to leave it to. No one to go home to, no …

He picked up the bottle and took another sip. He knew better than to go down that road. He'd made his choice a long time ago. He'd chosen the love of his life and he'd given her his all. His love wasn't a woman, it wasn't even a career. It was a passion, a passion to write and sing great songs, songs that told stories that touched people's hearts. His own heart might feel like it had missed out on that one big love story, but he knew he'd been a part of thousands of other love stories. Couples danced to his songs, played them at their weddings, made love to them, curled up and cried away the lonely nights to them. He couldn't feel too badly about his own heart when he knew he'd done so much for so many others.

He told himself he couldn't feel too badly, but sometimes, on nights like tonight, he did. But then he gave himself a kick in the ass, put the smile back on his face and focused on the good stuff. There was so much good stuff in his life and he was grateful for all of it. Just because a woman had never walked into his life and stolen his heart, it didn't mean he couldn't appreciate everything else he had going for him.

He looked up at the sound of a knock on the dressing room door. The others were too busy with their conversations to notice it. "Come in," he called.

The door opened, and Laura Benson came in. Clay liked her. She wasn't a singer, she was a jeweler of all things. She'd made the engagement ring that Lawrence would soon give to Shawnee. She was a good girl, strong, ambitious, she had a good head on her shoulders. If Clay had ever had a daughter, he would like to think that she might have turned out like Laura.

"Laura." He got to his feet and went to wrap her in a hug. "I'm glad you came. I wasn't sure if you'd want to, but this guy," he jerked his head at Lawrence, "insisted we should ask you."

"I'm glad you did," she said with a smile. "This is wonderful."

"See." Lawrence grinned as he moved in for a hug of his own, only to be elbowed aside by Shawnee.

They were saying something about Laura's last night of freedom—she was here for her bachelorette party, but Clay was no longer focused on their words. His head had filled with cracks and pops and white noise, just like an old forty-five before the needle reached the first bars of the song. He was looking past them at a woman, a woman whom he felt he already knew—and not just because she looked so much like her daughter.

She met his gaze; her blue eyes felt like an ocean he wanted to swim in. The air felt thick as he reached through it to take hold of her hand. "You don't need any introduction," he said. "You're Laura's mom, and now we know where she gets her beauty from."

Her gaze was still locked with his. For a moment, her lips moved, but no sound came out. Her fingers tightened slightly around his, making him realize that he hadn't yet let go of her hand. A crazy little voice in the back of his mind was singing an old hit about never letting go.

"Thank you." Her voice reverberated through his whole body. Just two little words spoken, and he knew. They were in tune. She was the reason he'd never managed to fall truly in love with another woman. He'd been waiting. Waiting for her.

"It's a real pleasure to meet you, Mr. McAdam."

Hearing her call him that brought him back to his senses. He couldn't just scoop her up and carry her out of here, couldn't fly her away to some hideout in the mountains or even ditch the show and the others and take her out to dinner. She saw him as *Mr. McAdam.* That had to change, and he had to change it soon, but he couldn't rush her. He could already tell. She was wary. She felt the attraction, too, but she'd run if he came on too strong.

He made himself give her a friendly smile when all he really wanted to do was take her in his arms and tell her welcome home. "Please, call me Clay? All my friends do, and I have a feeling we're going to become friends."

She smiled, and it lit up the whole room, hell it felt like it lit up his heart and soul. "Very well, Clay. And you must call me Marianne."

He chuckled. "I will call you, Marianne." He knew it must sound like a cheesy old line, but it was so much more than that. He was giving her as much warning as he could that this wasn't a passing meeting. He would call her, they would see each other again. This was the beginning of something beautiful. He knew it in his heart. Even if she didn't yet.

~ ~ ~

Marianne realized she was still holding his hand, but she couldn't make herself let go. All she could do was smile and stare deep into his gorgeous brown-green eyes. The laughter lines were etched deep around them, they just added to his appeal—and they helped her feel less conscious of the lines around her own eyes.

Clay McAdam. This felt like a dream. She'd had a crush on him for more than thirty years. Now here she was, holding his hand, and he was looking at her as if he saw her, as if he knew her. She really should shake the feeling that he did know her, that he'd always known her and that she'd always known him. She mustn't make a fool of herself—or of Laura. These people were Laura's friends. Just because Marianne felt starstruck she mustn't get carried away, mustn't let herself believe that this gorgeous man really felt the same way as she did right now.

He kept hold of her hand and led her away from the others. They faded out of her awareness. To Marianne, in that moment, there was no one else in the room—no one else in the world other than her and Clay. She was vaguely aware that she shouldn't let herself get too carried away. She was just a fan, the mother of a friend at best. Clay was no doubt more used to the attention of girls Laura's age. But that awareness wasn't enough to drown out another feeling, the feeling that she, Marianne was more than just Laura's mom. She was a woman, a woman who might be the wrong side of fifty, but who had once been just as beautiful as her daughter and who wore her years well. This was a once in a lifetime opportunity to spend a few moments with a man, perhaps the only man, she'd always felt attracted to.

"How long are you in town for?"

She smiled sadly, wanting to believe that he was interested to know if she'd be here for a while, if they could see each other again, yet at the same time acutely aware that that was just wishful thinking. "Just the night. Just for Laura's party. She's getting married tomorrow. We have to go home."

"Of course, I knew that. I'm sorry." He shook his head as if to clear it. "Can I tell it to you straight, Marianne?"

She drew in a deep breath as she nodded slowly. She wanted to hear that he felt the same kind of attraction to her that she did to him, but the little voice inside her head—the one that had always tried to hold her back—prepared her instead to hear that he needed to go and get ready, that it'd been nice to meet her, but he had to go now.

His eyes twinkled when he smiled. "Don't look so scared."

She let out a little laugh. "How could you tell?"

"Maybe because I'm scared, too."

Her heart beat even faster as the humor left his eyes. "What are you scared of?"

"I'm scared at the thought of you walking out of this room and never seeing you again. I'm scared to tell you that my heart is beating out of my chest, scared that you'll notice how much my palm is sweating."

She looked down at their still joined hands.

"I said I'd give it to you straight, Marianne. I'm scared that the bolt of lightning that struck me when I laid eyes on you just now has changed my life, and even more scared that I'm not going to be able to convince you that it's real."

Her lips moved, but no words came out. She didn't know what words could ever answer him. Her heart knew. Her heart beat faster and faster to a rhythm that sang that it, too, knew that life would never be the same. Her heart wanted to say that it had found its match and wanted to beat beside him forever. She drew in a deep breath. Her mind and her mouth weren't capable of helping her heart out, so she just continued to stare at him mutely.

He gave a low chuckle. "I just scared you even more, didn't I?"

She smiled. It was impossible not to at the sound of his deep laugh. "Yes, yes you did. But not in the way you think."

"You're not scared that I'm crazy or that I'm just feeding you a line?"

She shook her head. "I'm scared because I understand what you're saying, I understand what you're feeling because I'm feeling it, too. Most of all I'm scared because there's nothing we can do with it."

"We can do whatever we want with it. We can go slowly. I'm a patient man, Marianne. Now that I know what you're afraid of, I won't give up until you believe that it's real, until you're not scared anymore. Until we're together."

Marianne looked over at the others as they all laughed at something. Her heart clenched at the thought that maybe they somehow knew what she and Clay were saying, and they were laughing at her. She shook her head. "It's not real, Clay. It's just a moment in time."

He smiled. "Isn't that all life ever is; one moment in time and then another and another until we reach the end?"

"I suppose it is, but this? This moment is an anomaly. It's not a part of your life and it's not a part of mine. We each stepped outside of our reality for a moment and saw a possibility that could have been—if we were different people who'd lived different lives."

"No. We're seeing what can be." His eyes were so earnest as he looked into hers. "I know it's crazy. I don't blame you for not believing, but would you do something for me?"

"What?"

"Can we just enjoy tonight as though a different life was a possibility? As though we're just a man and a woman who ran into each other someplace and who feel the way we feel and believe it's possible to explore it?"

She thought that over as she looked back into his eyes.

"What's the worst that could happen?"

She didn't answer that. How could she tell him that, the way she felt right now, she could fall in love with him in the space of just one evening and then have to spend the rest of her life trying to forget him.

"I feel like I waited my whole life for you, Marianne."

She nodded slowly. Ridiculous as it sounded, he was only voicing what she felt, too.

He smiled. "They're going to clear the room soon, but I'll come find you as soon as I get off stage."

She smiled back. "I'll be waiting."

At that moment a piercing whistle sounded, and they turned to look at the others—who were now all standing by the door.

"Jeez, Clay," said Lawrence Fuller. "Would you let poor Marianne go? Laura's waiting to get back to her party and you need to get ready."

Clay squeezed her and then let it go as he grinned around at them all, looking embarrassed. "Sorry, everyone."

Marianne went to join Laura as the others started to make their way out. She could feel Clay's eyes on her every step of the way. She turned back when she reached the door. It felt like that bolt of lightning struck her again when their eyes met. He smiled and addressed Laura. "Can we come find you when we get done on stage?"

"Of course, that'll be great."

Marianne felt as if she was walking on air as they made their way back out into the club. Laura and the others chatted away. Oscar, who owned the place, put his arm around her at one point and joked that Clay had been staking his claim to her. She wanted to believe that was true, but now that she was away from his warmth and his presence she was starting to wonder if she'd somehow just daydreamed the whole encounter. "I'm just a star-struck fan, and he was being kind."

Oscar laughed. "You don't seriously believe that, do you? If ever I saw a man bowled over, it was Clay just now."

She shook her head. What else could she do? "I don't think so."

The rest of the evening passed in a blur for Marianne. She smiled and made polite noises at the girls around her. She wanted to enjoy it, it was her daughter's bachelorette party, after all. But most of the time she was lost inside her head, reliving those few moments she'd spent with Clay, going back through what he'd said about them making the most of this one evening, pretending they were just two regular people— that he wasn't a country music superstar! She chuckled to herself. Maybe it was a role play game he enjoyed? She didn't think so. Whatever had been between them had felt so very real when she was with him. But it was hard to believe now that she wasn't.

She tried to bring herself back to reality. Soon, Lawrence Fuller and Shawnee Reynolds would take the stage. She'd been looking forward to seeing them. She looked up when someone tapped her on the shoulder. It was one of Clay's guys. He'd been outside the dressing room earlier.

"Ms. Benson, would you like to come with me? Mr. McAdam asked if you could spare him a few minutes."

Marianne looked around. Everyone was busy chatting, some of the younger ones were off dancing. No one was paying any attention to her. Her heart raced as she got to her feet with a smile. Why not? She'd probably never see Clay again after tonight, and she knew she'd always regret it if she didn't go. She looked around as she followed the guy down the steps. No one saw her leave, not even her sister, Chris; she was deep in conversation with Seymour Davenport. She smiled to herself; she and Chris would have some catching up to do tomorrow.

When they reached the dressing room door, the guy knocked on it and Clay answered almost immediately. "Thanks, Adam."

Marianne watched Adam make his way back down the corridor. She couldn't make herself turn back to look at Clay until he took hold of both of her hands.

"I'm not going to ask you inside."

She smiled. "Good, because I'm not sure I'd go in with you. I think we might be a little old for that."

Clay chuckled. He wasn't even sure why he had asked for her to come back here. He'd have to go out on stage soon. "I don't think we're too old, but we're not in any rush either. I meant what I said earlier, Marianne. I'm not going to give up until I can convince you that this is for real."

Her eyes were such a deep blue, they were full of emotion. She nodded but didn't speak and he understood why he'd needed her to come back here.

"You're starting to doubt already, aren't you? You went back out there and convinced yourself that what we just shared wasn't real."

She nodded again. "It's easier to believe that I made it all up. That I imagined it. I didn't manage to convince myself, though."

"Good. I know you'll have your doubts, this seems crazy to me, too. But I'm used to living a crazy life. I'm not going to give up on this, Marianne. I'll prove it to you, no matter how long it takes. There's nothing that can stop me."

"Nothing?" He saw hesitation in her eyes.

"Nothing except you telling me that it's not what you want."

She drew in a deep breath and then blew it out again. "I don't even know what this is, but I know it's what I want—I want to explore it at least. It scares me. I think we might both be crazy, but it is what I want."

He smiled and squeezed her hands. "That's what I needed to know."

Chapter One

(One Year Later)

Marianne shrugged deeper inside her jacket and shoved her hands into her pockets. The wind blowing off the lake was cold and damp. For the first time since she'd been here in Summer Lake the chill managed to seep its way into her bones. She shrugged and blew out a sigh. Maybe coming for a walk on the beach hadn't been the greatest of ideas, but she'd needed to do something in an attempt to blow the cobwebs away.

She looked up at the gray sky. The clouds hung low and promised rain. She smiled to herself. Rain was always a good thing. Even if she got caught out here and got soaked, that'd be okay. Maybe it'd wash away her blues, since the wind wasn't doing anything for the cobwebs. She walked down closer to the water and picked up a stone. It was perfect for skimming. She looked over her shoulder to make sure no one was around before skipping it across the surface of the lake. She'd had the knack for skipping stones for as long as she could remember. She used to beat most of the boys at it when she was a kid.

She started walking again. She'd been good at a lot of things—but not at the things that got you anywhere in life. She'd been a failure at marriage—hers hadn't lasted more than three years. She hadn't exactly excelled in the world of work—

though she'd always had a job and always managed to provide for her daughter and herself. Granted, they hadn't lived in the lap of luxury, but they'd never gone hungry either. She smiled as she thought about Laura. Laura could live a life of luxury now, if she chose to. She was a huge success both in her career and in her marriage. Marianne might not have been able to teach her by example, but she liked to believe that she'd instilled the right values in her daughter and in doing so had contributed to her happiness and success. That was enough. Her own life was nothing to shout about, but that didn't matter. She was at peace with herself because she'd succeeded in her most important mission—she'd equipped her daughter with the tools to go out in the world and make the best life she could.

She checked her watch. She should get back. She was meeting Chris for lunch at the Boathouse.

"Hey. You're late." Chris greeted her with a grin from her perch at the bar.

Marianne made a face. "No. I'm on time. It's just that you're early—as always."

Chris shrugged. "I suppose. I always was the punctual sister. Are we sitting here or getting a booth?"

"You know my answer to that." Marianne smiled at the girl behind the bar.

"Anywhere you like. I'll bring your menus over."

Chris picked up her drink and slid down from the barstool. "You choose, but can we at least sit somewhere where I can still see the doors?"

Marianne laughed and led her to one of the raised booths. "Will this work for you?"

Chris nodded and slid onto the bench that gave her a view of the doors and most of the restaurant, leaving Marianne to sit facing the wall—which she didn't mind at all.

The server came over with their menus and a soda for Marianne. Once the server had gone, Chris smiled at her. "Anything new to talk about?"

Marianne shook her head. They had lunch at least once every week. It wasn't as though either of them led a very exciting life, so the conversation tended to be the same—they talked about the kids and what they were up to. "No. You already know Laura's in Nashville again this week. And I already know that Dan's in San Francisco and Jack's getting broody again."

Chris laughed. "Aren't we sad, that we only ever talk about the kids?"

Marianne shrugged. "I don't think so. I think we can feel very proud of them. They're all doing great things with their lives."

"They are, but what about us? What are we doing with our lives?"

"Well…" That was a question Marianne tried to avoid. She'd had a sense of purpose when Laura was young, when she was still at home, and even when she'd gone to college. But since she'd moved to San Francisco and opened her jewelry store—and even more since she'd met Smoke and moved out here to Summer Lake, Marianne had felt lost, if she was honest.

"Exactly." Chris hadn't been looking for an answer. "We're not doing anything."

Marianne narrowed her eyes at her sister. "Uh-oh. I know you too well. That means you think we should be doing something, and you have some hair-brained idea of what it should be."

Chris laughed. "Not exactly, no. Don't worry, I'm not going to ask you to go into business with me or anything. It's just that I've been feeling like I need more purpose in my life. And I think you do, too. So, we should figure out what that purpose could be."

"I feel as though I fulfilled my purpose. I was thinking about that on my walk this morning. I raised Laura the best I could. I gave her the tools and she's putting them to better use than I ever could have imagined."

"I can't argue with that. Laura's amazing. So are my boys. But, come on, Marianne. They're all in their thirties, they're all married. We can be grandparents, but we're not central to their lives anymore. We're at the point where we step back and let them get on with it. But I still have a lot more living left to do. I'm not just this used up shell who produced decent offspring and who now just gets to wait around to die."

Marianne laughed. "You're hardly waiting around to die. You help out at the women's center. You have a full and busy social life. You help Emma and Jack out with little Isabel. You hang out with Missy's Scott more often than is reasonable for a young man to hang out with his grandma."

Chris grinned. "I know, and I love it all, but I need more. I love being part of their lives, but I'm just a minor player. I want to play a role in my own life—I want to play the starring role." Her grin faded, and she took a sip of her drink. "Does that make any sense to you, or does it just sound selfish?"

Marianne gave her sister's arm a squeeze. "It makes all the sense in the world, Chris. It's not selfish. Or maybe it is—and maybe that's what we're supposed to be? Selfish. What's wrong with being selfish? Why's it considered bad somehow to put yourself first? Why shouldn't we make our lives about ourselves?"

Chris nodded. "I don't see any reason why we shouldn't do whatever we want in life at this point—hell, we've earned it."

"We have. But what is it that you want to do?"

Chris shrugged. "I haven't figured that out yet. What about you?"

Marianne shook her head. "I haven't even thought about it. I've been happily living this quiet little life and—"

"Have you, though?" Chris cut her off. "Have you been living happily, or just living?"

Marianne met her gaze.

"I thought so." Chris nodded. "When was the last time you were happy?"

Marianne closed her eyes as her heart leaped in her chest. She didn't allow herself to revisit that memory very often. She only let herself go there when she was alone. Usually in bed at night, so she could fall asleep and dream about him. That was as it should be—he'd never been anything more than a dream—a fantasy.

Chris gave her a hard stare. "Can I guess?"

"I'd rather you didn't."

"Because you know I'll get it right and give you a hard time?"

Marianne nodded.

Chris blew out a sigh. "You're a fool, Marianne."

She nodded and swallowed around the lump in her throat. "I know."

"You're finally admitting it?"

She nodded again.

"Damn. I never thought I'd see the day. It's not too late, you know."

Marianne let out a short laugh. "Come on, Chris. Of course, it is. My window of opportunity was open for maybe a couple of months—tops. And that's a year ago now. I blew it."

Chris shook her head. "I don't think so."

"It doesn't matter either way. You asked me when was the last time I was happy. And I admit it; I was happy that night in LA when I met Clay McAdam. But just like I've done my whole life, I got scared. I decided the risk was greater than the reward. I blew it."

"You don't know that. He said the only thing that would stop him was you telling him that it wasn't what you wanted. The poor guy tried for months. The only reason he stopped was because you told Laura to make him stop."

Marianne bit down on her bottom lip. "Yep. And that's it. End of story."

"I think there's a whole lot more story to tell there. If you'd just turn the page, open a new chapter."

"No."

"You wouldn't want to?"

"I'd love to, but it's just not going to happen."

Chris smiled at her. "It could. I heard on the grapevine that he's coming here."

Marianne's heart began to race. "He's coming here? To Summer Lake? Why?"

"For his birthday party."

Marianne stared at her. She didn't know what to say, she didn't know what to think. All she knew was how she felt—and what she felt was hope. Hope that she'd get to see him again. Hope that maybe, by some miracle, he still felt the same way he had almost a year ago. And hope that she'd somehow be able to get over her stupid fears and doubts enough to trust her heart this time.

"So, what are you going to do about it?"

"I don't know that there's anything I can do. I guess I'll just have to wait and see—see if he comes, see if he even remembers me if he does come, and see if I'm brave enough to tell him I'm sorry that I lied to him."

~ ~ ~

"Isn't it a bit cold to be sitting out here?"

Clay set his mug of coffee down and turned to look up at Autumn. "Good morning to you, too."

Autumn frowned. "What's up?"

He shook his head. "Nothing, nothing at all. Can't a guy enjoy his morning joe out in the fresh air without it being a problem?"

"I suppose. Anyway ..." Autumn tapped at her phone. "I need to talk to you about Addison's tour. I ..."

He shook his head. "Tomorrow or later, but not now, Autumn. Just not right now."

She put her phone back in her purse and took a seat beside him. "What's wrong, Clay?"

He had to smile. She was a tough cookie, Autumn, but she had a heart of gold and she cared about him. "It's okay. There's nothing wrong. If anything, I'm feeling old and a little down. Nothing to worry about. I just don't want to deal with anything right now. If you need to, you go take care of it, however you see fit."

"I don't need to, Clay. It's all just stuff. Just the details of what we do. None of it matters as much as you do."

He nodded and patted her hand. "I'm fine little girl, just fine. Feeling a little melancholy, that's all."

She nodded. "Maybe you should write a song about it?"

He chuckled. "I probably should—but I ain't gonna."

She laughed. "Now I know you're feeling real. You only talk like that when shit gets real."

He nodded. "Yeah. That's the real me. The guy who didn't know how to talk fancy."

"You don't talk fancy now."

"True. I just learned enough that they don't see me for the dumb country boy I am."

Autumn pursed her lips. "You're all country, but you ain't dumb—never were, never could be, it's not in your DNA."

"No. It isn't. Don't mind me. Maybe we should talk about Addison's tour? Like I said. I'm just feeling old and maybe a little sad. Maybe work's what I need to buck me up."

"No. What you need is to find something that'll make you feel not old, something that'd make you feel happy again."

Clay shrugged. "If you come up with anything, let me know, would you? That's been my problem lately. Everything that used to make me happy now just makes me feel old—because I can't do it like I used to when I was young."

Autumn cocked her head to one side. "I'm not sure I want to know what used to make you happy."

He laughed. "I was talking about touring—it's a young man's game. After a year of it I'm beat."

"Ah, and I thought you were talking about wine and women and ..." She raised an eyebrow.

"Nope. I probably do better with wine now than I did when I was younger—since the hard stuff's too hard and the beer is too..." He stopped himself, not wanting to explain why, at fifty-five he didn't like to drink too much beer.

"And what about the women?"

He shook his head. That subject remained closed.

Autumn held his gaze for a long moment. She could break most men with that stare. He wasn't going to give in to her, though. He shook his head.

"I talked to Laura last week."

Clay pursed his lips. He knew she was trying to make him talk about it—about Marianne—but there was no point.

"Don't you want to know how she is?"

He nodded, unsure whether the *she* Autumn was referring to was Laura or her mom. Either way, he wanted to know.

"Laura is doing just fine."

He waited, willing Autumn to say more, to tell him something about Marianne.

She didn't. Instead she changed the subject completely and he had to pull himself together. "I've been thinking; what do you want to do for your birthday?"

He shrugged. "I don't know. I could have a few people over here. Drinks, maybe finger food. I don't want a full sit-down dinner."

Autumn shook her head.

"No? No, what?"

She smiled. "You can't just stay here. It's a special birthday. You need to do something special."

Clay rolled his eyes. "What kind of special?"

"You need to have a party."

"Isn't that what I just talked about?"

"No! You talked about having a few people over—like you do at least once a week when you're home. You need to have a big party. Go somewhere."

"Like where? If you already have something in mind, you might as well tell me."

She held his gaze for a long moment. "Well, like I said. I talked to Laura."

His heart started to race again. "And?"

"And she was telling me about the lodge where she got married. It sounds perfect. I thought maybe you could hold your birthday party there."

"And why would I want to do that?"

She pursed her lips. "Well, apart from the one very obvious reason that we're deliberately not mentioning, I thought you could invite all your West Coast friends and it wouldn't be so far for them to travel. You love California, and you've been missing your small-town roots. Summer Lake sounds like the quintessential small town." She sat back and shrugged. "But if you really don't like the idea …"

Clay shook his head, realizing that he was leaning forward eagerly, hoping to hear something about Marianne.

Autumn raised an eyebrow at him. She was good. "Should I tell Laura it's a bad idea?"

"Laura's the one who told me it was a bad idea."

Autumn's eyes widened, she was no doubt as surprised as he was himself. That was as close as he'd come to talking about Marianne openly in the last eight months—ever since Laura had told him that her mom had asked that he stop calling.

"Laura never wanted to tell you that."

Clay frowned. "What are you saying?"

"I'm not saying anything. It's not my place to say. I'm just going to ask you one question."

"What?"

"Did you give up because you wanted to?"

He shook his head. "You know I didn't. It was what she wanted."

"Well, you know what they say is a lady's prerogative, don't you?"

He frowned again until he figured out what she was getting at. "Are you telling me she changed her mind?"

Autumn shrugged. "I'm not telling you anything. I'm just asking a question."

Clay picked up his mug and took a swig of his coffee.

"So?"

"What?"

"Do you want me to organize you a birthday party?"

His heart was racing. Not a day had gone by that he hadn't thought about the dark-haired, blue-eyed beauty who'd stolen his heart in the space of a few minutes just over a year ago. He'd told her he wouldn't give up until she believed him that what they'd both felt was real. He had given up—but only at her request. He sucked in a deep breath. "Do you think there's any point?"

"What does it matter what I think? What do you think?"

He smiled. "I think, yeah. I think I want a birthday party and I think I want to stand face-to-face with her and make her look me in the eye and tell me she's not interested before I'll accept that I should give up."

Autumn grinned. "There you are. I wondered where the Clay I know and love had been hiding."

He smiled. "Maybe I'll go into hiding for good after this birthday party, but I guess I have to show myself one last time before I call it quits."

Chapter Two

Marianne jumped when she heard a knock on the front door. She'd been so engrossed in her book that the sound of the real world intruding startled her. She hurried out into the hallway to see who it was and smiled at the sight that greeted her through the frosted glass. Some women might be afraid to see a tall, burly looking man on their doorstep. She considered herself lucky to call him her son-in-law.

"Smoke." She greeted him with a hug. "This is a lovely surprise. Come on in. What can I do for you?"

He followed her through to the kitchen and sat down at the table with a smile. "Nothing, thanks. I just wanted to check in with you. I know you had lunch with Laura the other day, but I haven't seen you in a while."

"Aww, you might fool some people with your ways, but you're a real sweetheart, aren't you?"

He shrugged and tried to hide his smile, but Marianne knew he liked it when she called him a sweetheart—and he truly was one.

"Can I get you a drink? I made cookies yesterday."

He shook his head with a rueful smile. "You get me with those cookies every single time. I should say no, but I can't."

She laughed and placed the cookie tin in front of him then poured him a glass of milk to go with them. He might be an astute businessman and an accomplished pilot—not to mention a multi-millionaire, but Marianne couldn't help but see him as the little boy who'd grown up in a life too grand for simple pleasures like milk and cookies. She smiled to herself as he enjoyed them.

"Is everything all right?" she asked.

He nodded and wiped his mouth with the back of his sleeve before rolling his eyes. "Sorry, can you pretend you didn't just see that?"

She chuckled. "See what?"

"Thanks. Everything's fine. Laura's great. We're both loving being home at the same time for once and ..."

"And what?"

He shrugged. "I'm not good at beating around the bush. We're both looking forward to Clay's party this weekend and I want to be sure that you are. Laura's all excited that she's engineered an opportunity for you and Clay to be in the same room again. I just want to make sure that you're happy about it?"

She sucked in a deep breath and then blew it out slowly. "Thanks, Smoke. It's okay. Part of me is happy. Part of me is scared to death. I feel foolish. I feel nervous. I feel like maybe I should get sick before Saturday, so I don't have to go to the party."

Smoke pursed his lips and nodded.

"I know it must sound crazy to you. I like the man. I'm not denying that. But ..." She shook her head, not knowing how she could explain it to him. He wasn't the kind of person who would ever let doubt and fear stop him from going after what he wanted.

He smiled. "It doesn't sound crazy. Not to me. I know Laura's been telling you for weeks that you'd be crazy to pass up on a second chance—and Chris has been after you about it, too. I guess that's why I'm here. They both want what's best for you, but they don't understand how scary it is."

She nodded, touched that he understood.

"When I first met Laura—when I realized that there was something real between us—something big—it scared me so much I tried to run away from it, a couple of times. You know all about it. At least you know what I did, but I'm not sure if you ever knew why. I blew up little things so that I could run, because the thought of sticking around and going all in was way too scary. Of course, hindsight is a wonderful thing. I didn't know what I was doing at the time. It made me sad when you asked Laura to tell Clay to back off."

"Why?" Marianne's heart was racing. She hadn't expected Smoke to be so honest with her—about his feelings, or hers.

He smiled. "That night. The bachelorette party. When I heard that some guy had taken you backstage to see Clay, I got a bit over-protective. I pulled a Jack, if you like."

Marianne had to smile at that. Her nephew, Jack, did tend to go overboard in trying to protect the women in his life— especially his mom.

"Laura and I followed you backstage. I don't know what I thought I was going to do." He gave her an apologetic smile. "But what I didn't expect was to see you and Clay standing outside his dressing room, holding each other's hands, looking into each other's eyes like you were in love."

"In love?"

"Yeah. You heard me the first time. I'm not going to try to make you talk about it if you don't want to. But apparently I have good ears and big shoulders if you do."

"Aww, Smoke. Thank you. I'm not sure there's anything to say. Well, other than, thank you and you're right. That's how I felt that night but afterwards it seemed too, too… big. I got scared and then I decided I was just foolish."

"I know. But you weren't foolish. Just scared. I just wanted you to know that if *I'd* stayed scared, Laura and I wouldn't be together now."

"That's a horrible thought."

He nodded. "That thought was the scariest to me. The thought that I might miss out on the best thing that ever happened to me." He raised an eyebrow at her. "Is that a chance you want to take?"

She looked down and fiddled with her fingers. "I don't know that it would even be a good thing—let alone the best thing."

"But you do know that it has the potential to be, don't you?"

She nodded without looking up.

"Then promise me you'll at least go to the party, talk to him, give it a chance?"

She nodded again and looked up with a smile. "Thank you."

"Nothing to thank me for. I just want to see you happy." He grinned and downed the last of his milk. "If a happy wife makes for a happy life, surely a happy mother-in-law does the same?"

She laughed. "I suppose it might. So, you're just looking out for your own interests, then? Trying to sweeten up your miserable old mother-in-law?"

He got to his feet and winked. "Yeah, and I'd appreciate it if that's what you'd tell people. I'm supposed to be a grouch, you know?"

She went to him and reached up to kiss his cheek. "You're the sweetest grouch I've ever known. You're just misunderstood."

"And I like to keep it that way." He wrapped his arm around her shoulders and gave her a hug. "Seriously, though, be brave—and if you need any help with that just know I've got your back. Laura and Chris mean well but they don't understand how scary it is—I do."

"Thank you."

After he'd gone, she went and sat back down on the sofa. She picked up her book, but there was no way she'd be able to get back into it now. She looked out of the window. A gust of wind rustled through the branches of the tree in the yard, causing it to shed a shower of its golden leaves. Marianne shook her head with a rueful smile. It felt like a sign. She was in the autumn of her life, winter would arrive soon enough. Maybe she should allow herself a blaze of beautiful color before it was too late. She picked up her book again—maybe she should steer away from such fanciful thoughts.

~ ~ ~

Clay peered through the window as the jet turned onto its final approach into the Summer Lake airport. Laura hadn't been joking when she told him how beautiful it was up here. The mountains, which had seemed so small just a few minutes ago, now reached up to greet them, and as the plane touched down on the runway, they towered above. They felt like welcoming giants, huddling around to greet their new visitors.

"Ladies and gentlemen, welcome to Summer Lake. They'll be sending golf carts out to collect your baggage. It should arrive at the front desk shortly after you do." Zack's voice came through the intercom loud and clear, making Clay smile. Zack and Luke were the new pilots he'd hired just a couple of weeks ago and they were turning out to be great additions to his team.

He pressed the button in the arm of his seat. "Thanks for the ride, guys. It'd be great to see you at the party tomorrow, but your time's your own till Monday."

"Thanks, Clay," said Luke. "We'll be there tomorrow."

Clay had to smile to himself. Luke and Zack both used to work here at Summer Lake. He knew that the *we* Luke was referring to were himself and his girlfriend, Angel, who still lived here. In fact, she ran the lodge where he was holding his party. "Great," he said. "Make sure you and that little lady of yours come talk to me."

"We will."

"You going to be there, Zack?"

"I wouldn't miss it."

"Good. I might need you to spring me from a boring conversation or two."

Zack laughed. "I'll be happy to, boss."

Clay was hoping to get to know both of them better. They were good guys. He knew that much already. He hoped he was going to be able to find a way to help Luke and Angel be together more than a long-distance relationship would allow. And he was more than curious to get to know Zack's story. He was open and friendly, easy-going, but there was a certain air of mystery about him that had piqued Clay's curiosity.

He looked up at the feel of Autumn's gaze on him. "What?"

She smiled. "I was just wondering how you feel now that we're here."

He knew what she meant. She'd kept dropping hints about Marianne and what his plans might be. He wasn't sure he wanted to tell her—and he sure as hell wasn't about to tell her in front of the others. He shrugged. "Like I want to get to the lodge and get settled in, and that maybe I want to take myself for a walk this afternoon."

Autumn groaned. "Just do me a favor? If you're going to ditch these guys," she jerked her head at Adam, his security chief, "At least leave your cell phone on?"

He winked at her. "Sure thing, boss lady."

As it turned out, he didn't get chance to take himself for a walk. When they arrived at the lodge, Lawrence and Shawnee were waiting for him. Shawnee greeted him with a hug and pecked his cheek. "I'm glad you're doing this, Clay."

He nodded. "I have a birthday party every year."

She made a face at him. "Don't give me that crap. You know full well what I mean."

Lawrence grinned at him. "Don't look at me to save you. I'm glad you're here, too. Are you going to go over to see her?"

Clay blew out a sigh. "I don't know what the hell I'm going to do."

Shawnee touched his arm. "So, why don't you come on up to our room and do some brainstorming?"

"Because I was planning to take myself out for a walk. Get some fresh air and try to figure it out."

Lawrence shook his head. "Nope." He waved at Autumn. "We're hijacking him, hon."

To Clay's surprise, instead of looking irritated, Autumn grinned. "Okay. I'll get him checked in and all sorted out."

Clay scowled at her as Shawnee linked her arm through his and led him toward the elevators. "This is supposed to be my party, my weekend. I'm supposed to be able to do what I want."

"It is, and you are. But you've been shying away from what you really want for too long. So, we're going to help you with it."

Clay looked at Lawrence as they stepped into the elevator, but his old friend just held up his hands. "Sorry. I can't help you. The women have decided that you need a kick in the ass, or at least a push in the right direction. I'd be powerless to stand in their way—even if I wanted to."

"And you don't want to?"

Lawrence shook his head with a smile. "I want to see you happy and I believe that Marianne is someone who can make you happy, if you give it a chance."

Clay pursed his lips. He wasn't sure he liked this. Autumn had orchestrated this whole party just to get him around Marianne again. Laura had reassured him that it was a good idea—that her mom wasn't against it. Lawrence and Shawnee had been encouraging of the whole thing and now it seemed they were planning to do their part to make sure the opportunity didn't slip away.

Once they were inside their room, Lawrence went to the bar and raised an eyebrow at him. "What's it to be?"

"Just a soda."

Shawnee smiled. "Good man. You need to keep your head clear."

Clay had to laugh. "Why? What for? So, I can be fully cognizant of the fact that I'm about to make a fool of myself again?"

She shook her head. "No, so that you can make a couple of wise decisions."

He raised an eyebrow at her. "About what?"

"First of all, do you care about making a fool of yourself?"

He shook his head slowly. "Honestly? No, I don't. For one thing, I'm too old for that shit. And for another, I already know I won't make a fool of myself. We could have something good, something real, Marianne and I. I know it without a doubt. I see nothing foolish in pursuing that possibility. If nothing comes of it, it'll be because she doesn't want to try— either because she doesn't feel the same way, or—more likely—because she's too afraid to."

Shawnee nodded. "Good. That's the way I see it. So, there's no reason to hold back?"

Clay shot a glance at Lawrence. He felt like Shawnee was leading him somewhere; his old friend no doubt knew where she was going. But Lawrence just shrugged. "I already told you, I can't help you, and I don't want to. I'm on their side."

Clay looked back at Shawnee. "Are you going to tell me where this is going?"

She nodded and handed him a soda. "Sure. Take a seat."

He sat down and blew out a sigh. "Why does this feel like an intervention?"

Lawrence laughed. "Maybe it kind of is one. Maybe we're sick of seeing you miserable."

"I'm not miserable!"

Shawnee gave him a hard stare. "Really?"

"No. I'm not. I have you guys, I have Autumn and Summer. I have the music and …" His voice trailed off as they both stared at him. "I'm not miserable." He wasn't, was he? No. He wasn't. He had a full life. He'd achieved more than he'd ever dreamed was possible. He pursed his lips and stared back at them.

"Are you telling me, you're happy and fulfilled?" asked Shawnee.

Hmm. That was a very different question. He shrugged. "I do all right."

Lawrence punched his arm. "You do. No one's trying to take anything away from you. You're a superstar—in every sense of the word." He shot a glance at Shawnee. "No one's trying to say you're not doing well. You've done more in your lifetime than most men could achieve in ten. Damn, you can have your cake and you can eat it. It's just that ..." He smiled. "Your cake? It's great cake, but we'd like to see you have the cherry on top."

Clay had to laugh. Lawrence came up the weirdest analogies sometimes.

Shawnee laughed with him. "Yeah, I wouldn't have put it that way, but he's right. You done good, Clay. But we'd love to see you have someone to share it with. Maybe we're just born-again romantics. Since we finally got our act together," she waggled her fingers, making the huge diamond in her engagement ring sparkle as it caught the light, "we want you to know the same kind of happiness."

"Thanks, guys. I appreciate it. And I do, I plan to talk to her and to see if she's open, interested in seeing what can happen between us. But at the same time, how realistic is it? She lives here. I live in Nashville." He shook his head, feeling bad again that his pilot Luke had moved to Nashville to work for him and had to leave his girlfriend behind here. He was under no illusions about how difficult that must be.

Lawrence smiled at him. "Fortunately for you, you have your own jet—and a pilot who I'm sure would love to fly you back here just as often as you want to come."

Shawnee shook her head.

"No?" Clay asked.

"Yes, of course he's right. But I'm thinking about something bigger."

"Bigger like what?"

"Like, haven't you been bleating about wanting a vacation home?"

Clay held her gaze for a long moment.

She nodded. "This seems like a great place to me. You wanted a small town. It has everything you enjoy."

Clay looked out the window. The clouds had parted, allowing the sun to peek through and sparkle on the lake. The mountains huddled around, looking like friendly giants, welcoming and protective. "Shouldn't I see if she'd be interested first?"

"Maybe," said Shawnee. "That might seem like the logical way to go. But the Clay I used to know would go at it the other way around. He'd set himself up here first and then stick around and work on it until she was interested."

He had to smile. "I think it's about time I remembered that Clay, too."

Chapter Three

Marianne applied her lipstick and then sat back and eyed herself in the mirror.

"You've still got it, sis." Chris grinned at her.

"So, have you. You look great."

Chris gave a twirl and then patted her hair. "I do, don't I? It's just a shame for me that the guy I'm interested in won't get to see it."

"Do you have any idea when he'll be coming back here again?"

Chris shrugged. "No. I try not to ask Missy about Chance and Hope too often. Missy's nobody's fool. She knows damned well I'm only angling for information about Hope's dad."

"And I'm sure she doesn't mind telling you whatever she knows. Missy has a heart of gold."

"Exactly. And I don't like her feeling that she should be trying to get the low-down on her brother's father-in-law so that she can feed the information back to her own mother-in-law."

Marianne had to laugh. "Yeah. Since you put it like that ..."

Chris blew out a sigh. "She does let me know whatever she hears about him, but it's not as though she's ever going to hear news about how he's feeling or whether his heart has healed enough to be open to trying something new. Anyway. I'm just kidding myself. Me and Seymour is just a crazy fantasy. You and Clay—that's a different matter. That's a reality and it's a reality that should have happened the first time you met. I hope you're not going to blow your second chance."

Marianne shook her head. "I'm not. I'm looking forward to seeing him. I'm excited." Judging by the way the butterflies were swirling in her stomach, excited was something of an understatement.

"And so you should be. I'm excited for you."

"But why, Chris?" Marianne shook her head. "I mean. I know it's a lovely idea. Of course it is. But even if the feelings are real. Even if I didn't imagine the whole thing—"

"Dammit, Marianne. You didn't imagine it!"

"Okay, okay. Don't get so frustrated, and listen to me for a minute, would you?"

Chris looked taken aback. Marianne usually let her go on and get her point across, even when she was missing Marianne's point completely. But this was too important. She knew Chris cared about her, but she needed to stop blindly encouraging and listen to Marianne's very real concerns.

"Sorry, but this is important. What if I see him tonight and we both still feel the way we did? I mean, yes, it'd be wonderful, but what would it mean—really? If you look at best case scenario, it might mean we got together."

Chris grinned. "That's more like it."

"Maybe, but what would me and Clay McAdam being together look like?" Marianne felt herself going red—she could hardly believe she was giving voice to the possibility. "How could it work?"

"What do you mean?"

"I mean. He's a big country star, who when he's at home, is in Nashville—and when he's not, he's off touring the country or the world. I live here. My life is here, Laura's here, you're here. I don't want to leave here. That's reality, that's the thought that helped me be okay with the decision to tell him that I didn't want to see him again. What could we ever share?"

Chris stared at her for a long moment. "See, I guess you're more grown up than I am even now. I just want to see you get together with him. I never stopped to think about what would happen beyond that."

Marianne nodded. "I've had a long time to think about it. I had to justify to myself why I ever turned the man down." She gave her sister a rueful smile.

"Well. Do you even have to think about the long term?"

"Probably not." Marianne felt foolish now.

"Don't look at me like that. You know what I mean," said Chris. "What I'm saying is, wouldn't you rather have one kiss, one party," she waggled her eyebrows, "one night, than nothing at all? Okay, so you might not be able to figure out a forever—a happily ever after. But that's okay because you never expected one. So, why pass up on the chance of one night—or maybe it'll be one night every few months."

Marianne thought about that and then finally she smiled. "Thanks, Chris. I hadn't thought of it like that. You're so right. I should make the most of what I can have, live the moments and let the rest take care of itself."

Chris grinned at her. "Exactly. You don't think I'm holding out for a happily-ever-after with Seymour Davenport, do you?" She chuckled. "Even I will admit what a crazy idea that is. No, I'm not holding out for a forever kind of love story, I'm just hoping that he and I might get to spend some time together." She waggled her eyebrows again. "And make the most of it."

Marianne laughed. "You're so bad."

"I'm just honest about it. You can't tell me you wouldn't drag Clay off to bed given half the chance."

Marianne felt the color in her cheeks. "Of course, I would."

"Well, then. Whatever happens this weekend, make the most of it."

"I will. And I'd better start by calling Laura to let her know we're ready."

"Okay. You do that, and I'll go fix us a drink—a shot of Dutch courage before we go."

~ ~ ~

Clay looked around the hall. He had to hand it to Autumn—and to Angel—it was quite a party. The lodge was great, just grand enough to feel like this was a special occasion, even for him. Yet it was still understated enough for him to feel at home—truly comfortable. This wasn't some glitzy place and it wasn't the kitschy kind of down-home country place that some of his buddies in the industry favored. It was real, and he liked it.

Zack came to stand by his side. "How's it going, boss?"

"So far, so good, thanks."

Zack shot him a sideways glance. "Can I ask the question that everyone's wondering about?"

Clay nodded. Glad that Zack felt able to even approach the subject. "Sure."

"Is she coming?"

Clay had to laugh. "I damned well hope so."

"Me too. It seems like there'll be a lot of people disappointed if she doesn't."

"Maybe, but none so disappointed as me."

"Will you find her, if she doesn't show?"

Clay rubbed his chin. "You know what, son? I think I would. I'm too long in the tooth to waste any more time."

"Hey, I wasn't implying anything like that."

Clay grinned and grasped his shoulder. "I know, don't worry. You didn't insult me about getting old, you just helped me get clear on the fact that I want—need—to get this straight tonight. One way or another."

"Well, since you waited a year already, it's time you got a final yes or no."

"It's a yes. It was a yes the night we met, but I was foolish enough to let her go and let her doubt. When I said I need to get this straight tonight, what I meant is that I need to let her know. I'm not giving up."

Zack smiled. "Good for you."

"What about you? Is there anyone back here that you miss?"

Zack shrugged.

"What's your story, Zack?"

Zack chuckled. "My story? It's long and complicated."

"Is it about a girl?"

He shook his head. "No, it's the reason I can't afford to miss a girl. It's the reason I backed off when I met her and why she thinks of me as a friend—at least she did, until I left, and now I'm just somebody that she used to know."

Clay frowned. "Would things have worked out differently with her if you'd stayed here?"

"No."

"You sound certain."

"I am. My story wouldn't allow it."

Clay shook his head. "That's sad."

Zack shrugged. "It is what it is." He smiled. "And I don't want to be the one who makes you sad on your birthday. So, how about I go get you a fresh drink?"

Clay looked down at his empty glass. "Thanks."

Zack grinned. "And you keep your eye on the door. She has to be arriving soon."

Clay smiled and checked the entrance again. That was why he was standing here.

As he watched Zack walk away, he spotted Angel standing, surveying the room. She had a smile on her face—and she had every right to. She'd organized a great party. He made his way over to her and put his hand on her shoulder.

She jumped and then turned to him with a smile. He felt bad when that smile faded, she'd no doubt thought that he was Luke.

"I have to tell you, Angel, this is the best party I've ever had."

She stood a little straighter and beamed with pride. "That makes me very happy—for both of us."

He chuckled. "You're good at what you do. The best. You know, if I still needed an events manager, I'd hire you in a New York minute."

She looked as wistful as he'd been afraid she might.

"Unfortunately," he continued, "I don't."

She smiled. "I know, and besides, I'm not sure I'd take it. I'd love to work for you—for many reasons. But I love it here. I love this place. Ben's been so good to me. Obviously, this isn't my resort, but I've been here since before it opened. It feels like it's mine—or maybe it's me that belongs here."

Clay nodded. "I respect that. Loyalty is a rare commodity these days."

"Hey." They both turned as Luke appeared beside them. "Sorry it took me a while."

"That's okay." Clay smiled at him. He wasn't a fool. He knew young love when it was staring him in the face and he felt bad for keeping the two of them apart. "Go on, kiss her. It'll be more awkward if you don't.

Luke pecked Angel's cheek.

"You two are in it for the long haul, aren't you?"

They both nodded.

"See, neither of you needed to check in with the other before you agreed with me. There's no hesitation. You're both all in, aren't you?"

"I am." Luke came to stand beside Angel and slung his arm around her shoulders. "One hundred percent all in."

Angel looked up into his eyes. "And I am."

Clay felt bad. "And you were doing just great till I came along and screwed things up for you?"

Angel shook her head. "It's not like that. Luke's worked hard for a long time to earn the kind of job you gave him. He was never going to find a job like that here. Of course, I don't like that he left, but I'm glad that he left to work for you."

Clay's heart buzzed in his chest. When he was a younger man, he used to hope that he'd meet a woman who would love him and understand him. That he'd find someone who would care about him enough to care about his dreams and all they meant to him. He'd never found that woman, but it seemed Luke had found his.

Clay turned to look at him. "You don't find love like that more than once in a lifetime. Don't let her go." He had to look away. He felt bad that he was keeping them apart, but it only added fuel to the crazy thought that Shawnee had planted in his mind earlier. Maybe he should buy a house here. Spending more time here would allow him to pursue Marianne, to finally be true to his word and not give up on her until she believed him. It'd also mean that these two kids wouldn't have to live two thousand miles apart, and it might just give Zack another chance with the girl who only thought of him as a friend.

As he looked around the room his gaze was drawn back to the entrance again, and this time she was there. His heart thudded to a halt. She stood just inside the door with Laura. Laura was a beautiful young woman, no question about it, but Clay could only see her as a pale reflection of her mother. Marianne was so much more than beautiful. She had a presence that he could feel even from across a crowded room like this.

He looked down, startled when Angel touched his arm.

"Why don't you take your own advice? You never had a great love, did you?"

He turned to look at her. He'd been in love a couple of times. At least, he'd been in long term relationships where he'd said those words on a daily basis, but he'd never felt the way he did when he looked at Marianne. And he'd never shared anything like Angel and Luke did. "Not like the two of you have found, no."

She smiled, and though she couldn't be much more than half his age, for a moment she reminded him of his mom. "Maybe your once in a lifetime waited till now—till you'd be ready to make the time for it."

The absurdity of the moment hit him, and he smiled. He must be crazy to think he could stick around here and persuade Marianne that they could have something special. He shook his head. "She's not interested."

Angel laughed, reminding him of his mom again. It was a kind, indulgent sound, not ridicule. "I think you'll find she is. And I think you'll regret it forever if you don't go and find out."

He sucked in a deep breath and then blew it out again. She was right. Regrets weren't something he wanted to start collecting at this point in his life. "Okay. Wish me luck, but if you find me drowning my sorrows in a bottle of moonshine later …"

"We won't. Go talk to her. Let your once in a lifetime start now."

Marianne drew in a deep breath and lifted her chin. She'd learned a long time ago that looking confident made her feel more confident. Right now, she needed all the help she could get.

"Here he comes."

Laura leaned in and pecked her cheek.

"Where are you going?" Her voice came out as a squeak as Laura moved away. She needed her! Needed the moral support—and possibly the physical support, too. Her knees wanted to buckle at the sight of Clay striding toward her.

Laura squeezed her hand. "I'm getting out of the way, Mom. It's up to you what you do with it from here." She smiled and then disappeared back through the door to the hallway.

Marianne's heart was hammering in her chest as Clay closed the last few yards between them. When he reached her he looked deep into her eyes. Her heart rate started to return to normal and she smiled. It *had* been real! Now he was here, now she was in his presence again, it all made sense. It was real and it was strong and there was no point trying to deny it.

He reached for her hands and she took hold of his. He smiled, and her tummy flipped over.

"I missed you."

Tears pricked behind her eyes—what a fool she'd been! "I missed you, too. I'm so sorry."

He put a finger to her lips and shook his head. "Never be sorry. It's all working out as it's supposed to. That might sound crazy—it does to me, but I know it's true."

Marianne nodded, she knew he was right. She let go of all the regret that had come surging. There was no point being sorry for what she couldn't change any more than there was reason to hope for what she couldn't have. The only thing to do was to make the most of this moment, of every possible moment they could share.

"Will you come with me?"

She nodded again and let him lead her outside, onto the balcony. She let out a little sigh when he turned to face her and looked down into her eyes. Her heart raced, and goose bumps chased each other down her spine when he placed his hands on her hips.

"May I?"

She nodded. She knew what he was asking, but she couldn't speak. He lowered his head to hers and she closed her eyes and leaned against him as his lips brushed over hers all too briefly. He stepped back with a smile. "Do you believe it this time?"

She looked deep into his green-brown eyes and nodded. She didn't just believe it, she knew it, with every fiber of her being. They were meant to be.

He smiled. "Good, because I'm buying a house here."

"You're … what …?"

He nodded, the laughter lines creasing deep around his eyes. "You heard me right. How can we do this if I'm in Nashville?"

She swallowed, wondering if she was imagining this.

He squeezed her hand. "This is our beginning, Marianne, if you want it to be."

She squeezed back. Her head and heart were buzzing. "I do."

They both turned as a set of doors opened further along the balcony and Angel and Luke came out.

Marianne looked up at Clay; she didn't want to intrude on the young couple's moment any more than she wanted them to intrude on her and Clay's.

"I won't keep you out here long, just long enough to ask you one question," she heard Luke say. She stepped further back into the shadows and pulled Clay with her. She'd seen enough of Angel and Luke to know full well what he was about to ask, and they shouldn't be there to witness it.

Luke got down on one knee and Marianne brought her hand up to cover her mouth as she watched the happiness on Angel's face. Clay slid his arm around her shoulders and she turned to smile up at him. It felt so natural to be with him like this. They leaned against each other and watched silently. The diamond in the ring Luke held up twinkled in the darkness as he slipped it onto Angel's finger.

Clay looked down at Marianne and took hold of her hand as he stepped out of the shadows. "Congratulations," he said. They looked startled when he and Marianne stepped forward.

"I know we weren't supposed to witness that, but I'm happy to be the first to congratulate you."

"Thank you."

He slid his arm around her shoulders. "I know I'm going to make all four of us happy when I say I've figured out where I want to buy a second home."

Angel looked puzzled, and understandably a little put out that Clay wanted to talk about buying a house when she'd just gotten engaged.

Clay smiled at her. "I want to buy a house here. I know you and I will both be happy if I start spending most of my time here."

Angel's hand flew up to cover her mouth, and Marianne realized that hers had done the same thing. It didn't manage to keep in the happy tears that started to roll down her cheeks.

Clay's arm tightened around her shoulders. "Let's go inside, darlin'. Congratulations, kids. Go home. Celebrate."

He guided her to the door and once they were back inside, he closed his arms around her waist, drawing her to him. "What do you say—am I crazy or do you want to help me find a house?"

She looked up into his eyes and what she saw there made her happier than she'd known it was possible to feel. "Yes."

"Yes?" He raised an eyebrow and chuckled—that rich deep sound that did dangerous things to her insides.

She nodded vigorously. "Yes, I think you're crazy, and yes, I want to help you find a house."

Chapter Four

Clay stood there for a long few moments looking down into Marianne's eyes. She was still scared, he could tell, but she felt the magic between them, just as he did. She felt it, and it was strong enough to make her take the leap, to say yes to him. The hairs on the back of his neck stood up as a crazy thought entered his head—how long would it take for her to say yes to him in the same way Angel had just said yes to Luke?

Feeling her tense made him realize that he still had his arms around her. She wasn't looking into his eyes anymore, she was looking past him, and he knew from the look on her face that someone was approaching. She looked nervous, but he didn't feel it. He slid his arm around her shoulders and turned. He wanted whoever it was to know that they were together. Hell, probably every single person here had been rooting for them.

He relaxed a little at the sight of Lawrence and Shawnee grinning at them.

"Marianne," Shawnee greeted her with a warm smile. "It's wonderful to see you, hon."

Marianne smiled, looking a little embarrassed. Clay drew her closer into his side, wanting to reassure her.

"It's lovely to see you again, too."

Lawrence stepped forward and pecked her cheek. "Relax, sweetie. We're just thrilled to see the two of you are working it out." He nodded at Clay. "This guy's been miserable since he last saw you."

Marianne looked up at him, and he nodded. "Don't look surprised, you know how I feel."

She nodded. "I'm sorry."

He held her gaze for a long moment, wishing Lawrence and Shawnee would leave them to it. This was a conversation they should be having alone, not in front of his friends. Especially since Marianne didn't know them—other than as country music celebrities. "Don't be sorry, darlin'. It's all working out as it should—in its own sweet time."

Shawnee grinned at them. "We won't keep you. I just had to come and let you know how pleased I am." She nodded at Marianne. "I'm one of his oldest friends and I hope that I'll become yours, too."

Clay felt Marianne relax a little as she smiled back. "I'd like that."

Lawrence took Shawnee's arm. "We're going to go mingle." He met Clay's gaze. "Happy birthday, bud."

Clay chuckled as he watched them walk away. "It is a happy birthday now, best one ever."

Marianne smiled. "I'm glad you think so. It feels like my birthday."

He looked down at her. "I plan to make every day feel like your birthday, darlin'. I think we need champagne to celebrate. What do you say?"

She nodded happily, and he guided her toward the bar. He was aware of heads turning to watch them pass as they made their way through the crowded room. He was grateful for all the encouraging smiles coming their way, and even more grateful that no one else felt the need to come and congratulate them like Lawrence and Shawnee had.

Once they had their champagne, he tapped his flute against hers. "Here's to the beginning of something beautiful."

"I'll drink to that." She downed half the glass and then looked up at him. "Though I might have to switch to juice after this one."

He laughed. "You knock 'em back. It'll help you relax."

Her smile disappeared, and she looked nervous again. He knew what she must be thinking and he shook his head.

"Don't worry, I'm not trying to get you tipsy, so I can take advantage of you."

She looked embarrassed—and something else, maybe, just a little disappointed.

He raised an eyebrow at her. "Unless you want me to?"

She laughed nervously. "I can't lie and say I wouldn't like that, but ... not yet."

He nodded. "I know. I'm only playing with you." As he ran his gaze over her, the interest stirred in his pants. He liked the idea of playing with her. But there was no hurry. He was still a guy, part of him would love to hustle her out of here, up to his room and out of her dress, but that wasn't the most important consideration. He was more interested in talking to her, getting to know her. It occurred to him for the first time that, although she'd occupied his thoughts for a year now, he knew very little about her. His heart had claimed that it knew her and had waited for her all his life, but his head was trying to reassert its authority and tell him that maybe there was some talking to be done before he knew if that was true.

She was looking up at him watching his face. "Clay, I ..."

He loved the way she said his name. He wanted to ask what? But instead he waited. He already knew that she wasn't overly assertive. She was reserved, timid was too strong a word, but he somehow understood that he'd have to give her space and time to speak whatever was on her mind.

"I have to tell you right now, that I might pull a Cinderella on you at the end of the night."

He chuckled. "Your carriage has to be home by midnight?"

She smiled. "No, I don't have a curfew, but I can already feel the doubts creeping back in. It's like in LA, when we met. When I'm with you, it's so easy and natural and it feels so right. But the voice of doubt is strong, and I know that when I go home, I'm going to second guess myself again."

He looked into her eyes and brushed his thumb over her cheek. "So, don't go home. Stay with me?"

She shook her head rapidly.

"I don't mean *stay* with me. I mean stay here, you take the bed, I'll take the sofa. I've waited so long for this Marianne. I want to sit up and talk to you all night."

She smiled. "You really mean that, don't you?"

He nodded. "I do. Would I love for you to share my bed? Of course, I would. But I can wait." He trailed his fingertips down her neck and was rewarded with a shiver and two pink stains on her cheeks.

She surprised him when she let out a chuckle. "If you keep doing that, I'm not sure I'll be able to wait."

He laughed and did it again, making her turn and give him a stern look that couldn't quite hide her smile—or the desire in her eyes.

"If I get my way, Marianne, we'll have all the time in the world for that."

She nodded, her eyes serious, so that when she spoke, he wasn't sure which way to take it. "I hope you get your way."

He let his gaze run over her again, reconsidering everything he'd just said about being in no hurry. Part of him would love nothing more than to take her up to his room and have his way with her right now. The way she rested her hand on his waist told him she was feeling the same.

He stepped back slightly as he saw Laura and Autumn standing at the bar together, watching them.

"Did I say too much?" Marianne looked worried. "Was that too forward?"

He shook his head and slid his arm around her waist, drawing her into his side. "No. Not at all. You made me happy. What made me hesitate is the fact that your daughter and my as-good-as-daughter are watching us like hawks."

She followed his gaze and they both laughed as Laura and Autumn waved at them, looking both thrilled and slightly apologetic.

"We should thank them, they've worked hard to make this happen."

Marianne nodded. "And I'm grateful to them. Come on, let's go and tell them they can gloat."

Clay smiled to himself as they made their way over to the bar. He hadn't known how this would turn out and had been even less certain how Marianne would feel about the way this whole party had been engineered to get them together. He was glad that not only did she know about it, but she also seemed happy about it.

~ ~ ~

Marianne smiled at her daughter as Clay led her over to the bar. His big paw was wrapped around her hand and it made her feel safe somehow.

Laura dropped her gaze and eyed their joined hands then looked back up at her mom with a smile.

"So, we did the right thing, then?" she asked.

Clay grinned at her. "You did. Thank you. I shall be forever grateful."

Autumn grinned at him. "Now that should come in handy. I'm going to ask you to be my witness that he said that, Laura."

Laura laughed. "Okay." She met Marianne's gaze. Her eyes were full of questions, but she didn't voice them.

Marianne loved her so much, and would be forever grateful to her, too. No matter how things worked out with Clay, she was grateful that her daughter cared about her enough to go to all this trouble to give her a chance at happiness. "Thank you," seemed like the safest thing to say. She could hardly start gushing about how happy she was to have this second chance with Clay, and if she tried telling Laura how proud she was of her, she'd no doubt end up crying.

Laura nodded. She understood.

"How's it going?"

Marianne turned at the sound of Smoke's voice behind her. She smiled at him happily. "It's going well, I'm being brave."

His smile told her he was proud of her, and she was as grateful as she'd ever been that Laura had found herself such a good man. His smile changed as he turned it on Clay. "I'm glad to see the two of you together. Marianne's like another mom to me."

Clay nodded. "Don't worry. I'll be good to her."

There was an edge to Smoke's voice when he spoke again. "She deserves the very best." He turned to smile at her.

Marianne wanted to laugh. It was obvious that Smoke was doing the macho thing and letting Clay know that he'd be watching him, even though the two of them already knew each other and by all accounts were friends. She appreciated him stepping in the role of the kind of protective male she'd never had in her life.

She looked at Clay, wondering how he'd feel about it. He was smiling and he grasped Smoke's shoulder. "I couldn't agree with you more, son. I intend to give her the best—of everything."

Marianne raised an eyebrow at him, wondering what he meant by that. One part of her—the part that had already succumbed to the butterflies and champagne wanted to believe that he'd give her the best sex she'd ever known. She felt the color in her cheeks even thinking about it. Another part of her was trying to ignore the look in his eyes as he said it. That made it seem like he was talking about so much more than sex.

Laura took hold of Smoke's hand and pulled him toward her. "Don't you go pulling a Jack, will you?"

Marianne smiled to herself as Smoke scowled at her. "I'm not. I just came over to say hi." He looked at Autumn. "And to tell you that Matt's looking for you."

Autumn rolled her eyes and Clay laughed.

"What does he need?"

Smoke smirked. "I don't think he needs anything, he's just wondering where you are."

"We should go find him," said Laura.

"You should," Clay agreed. "When are you finally going to put him out of his misery, Autumn?"

Autumn blew out a sigh. "Give it a rest, Clay." She looked at Marianne. "I'm happy for your sake that you're interested in the guy everyone wanted to set you up with."

Marianne smiled. "They're trying to set you up with Matt? He seems nice."

Autumn laughed. "Oh, he seems nice. He's a pain in the ass is what he is."

Clay laughed. "When are you finally going to give in and admit it? He's only a pain in the ass because he gets to you. The only reason he gets to you is because you like him, too. Stop fighting it—give him a chance."

Autumn looked at Marianne again. "I hope you're going to be my ally in this. They all think he's a good guy. I've managed him for the last few years; he's an egotistical, trouble-causing, flirtatious, pain in my ass."

Marianne smiled at her. "I can't say anything until I know him a little bit and until I've seen the two of you together." She looked up at Clay. "All I'll say for now is that sometimes we avoid someone because we're scared of how good it might be, not how terrible."

Autumn's eyes widened, and in that moment, Marianne had a gut-feeling that she was right. Autumn liked Matt—maybe as much as *she* liked Clay—but for some reason she didn't want to go there.

Autumn shook her head. "That might have been true for you. But I assure you. It's not the case for me."

Laura took her arm and started to lead her away. "Then there's no reason not to hang out with him, is there? We should go and find him and leave Mom and Clay to it."

Smoke winked at Marianne as he followed the girls away.

"Is that what you were scared of?" asked Clay once they'd gone.

"In part, yes. Mostly I was afraid that I'd made it all up. I've been a fan of yours for years. I was afraid that what I felt around you was just what I wanted to feel. And that I'd imagined that you felt it, too. I thought maybe it was a game you liked to play with starstruck groupies. That you'd tell them that you'd been struck by lightning and they'd believe you and crawl into bed with you and ..." She stopped when she saw the look on his face.

"That's who you thought I was?"

"No." She squeezed his hand. "It's what I made up when I was trying to believe that anything was more plausible than me being the woman Clay McAdam could fall for."

He smiled. "How plausible does it seem now?"

"Very, although, to be honest, not one hundred percent."

He nodded. "I've been thinking that, too. So far all we've had is a moment, a thunderbolt—well, two. When I saw you tonight I felt the same way I did when I first saw you last year. But there's a huge gap between our eyes meeting and us riding off into the sunset together."

She looked up at him, glad and at the same time a little nervous that he felt that way, too. "You're right. We have to be realistic about it."

He smiled. "We do. Do you want to know how I think we should bridge that gap?"

"Yes."

"I think we should spend as much time as we can together. Every waking moment." He winked. "And when we're ready, all our sleeping moments, too. I've spent the first fifty-five years of my life looking for you. I don't want to waste any more time."

She raised an eyebrow. "You were looking for someone?"

He shook his head. "I wasn't. I didn't know you existed, but if I had I would have searched every corner of the earth until I found you."

"Is that just a line?"

"No, darlin'. It's no line. It's the God's honest truth. I wish we'd met thirty years ago, but I'm a believer that everything happens in its own good time. Maybe when I was younger, I wouldn't have been any good for you. Now, not only do I want to be, but I know I can be, all the man you need." He put his arm around her shoulders. "Do you want to get out of here?"

She nodded. She wasn't sure what he meant. If he wanted to go to his room, she'd go willingly. If he wanted to go for a walk, she'd do that, too. All she knew was that she wanted to be alone with him, start getting to know him better and stop wasting time on the part of her life that hadn't had him in it.

Chapter Five

Clay could feel several pairs of eyes following them as he led Marianne toward the doors and out through them. Part of him wanted to defend Marianne's honor and go back and tell them that they were only going out for a walk. Part of him wanted to prove their suspicious minds right and take her straight up to his room.

Once they were out in the cooler air of the lobby he stopped and looked down at her. "Did you bring a coat?"

She shook her head. "Well, I did, but I left it in Smoke's truck."

He nodded. "Do you want to wait here while I go grab us a couple of jackets?"

"Okay." She looked around the reception area. "I can sit over there."

"Great. I'll be as quick as I can." He strode over to the elevator and was glad it was there waiting. If he'd had more than a few moments, he would have changed his mind about leaving her down here alone and instead invited her to go up with him. Then there'd be no walk in the moonlight—and no taking things slowly. She was beautiful. He was amazed how much she turned him on. He closed his eyes as he rode the elevator and all he could see was her lean willowy body encased in a cornflower blue dress that matched her eyes.

He blew out a sigh as he stepped out of the elevator and walked down the corridor to his room, wishing he'd brought her with him. His heart was hammering in his chest as he let himself in and then rummaged in his holdall. He'd only brought one jacket, she could have that. He pulled out a sweatshirt, that'd have to do for him. The way his blood seemed to be boiling in his veins every time he looked at her, he was sure he wouldn't feel the cold anyway.

~ ~ ~

Marianne checked her watch as she paced the lobby. She couldn't make herself sit down, she was too full of nervous energy. It was only nine-thirty—too early for Clay to be leaving his party. She wondered what people must be thinking. It'd felt as though everyone there had watched them leave. Did they think he was taking her up to his room—that she was a loose woman? She chuckled to herself at the thought. It was something her mother would have said. And it was ridiculous. Granted, she hadn't known if Clay was indeed taking her up to his room, and she'd gone with him willingly. So, maybe she was a loose woman? Or she would be—for Clay—given half the chance.

She turned around and walked back toward the reception area. The girl sitting behind the desk smiled at her. Marianne nodded. Roxy. That was her name.

"Hi, Roxy."

"Hi, Ms. Benson." Roxy gave her a conspiratorial smile and shot a look toward the elevators. "How's it going?"

Marianne smiled. "It's wonderful!" It was such a relief to be able to say so—and especially to someone she didn't really know.

"Oh, that's awesome. I thought it was so cool when I heard that you're the reason Clay decided to hold his party here. He's gorgeous—but then, so are you!"

"Thank you. I'd hardly say that but thank you."

"Oh, you are! I used to be afraid of growing old, but you and Miss Chris are both living proof that you can still be beautiful when you're …" She stopped herself, looking embarrassed. "Oh, my God! I didn't mean that how it sounded. I don't mean …"

Marianne laughed. "It's okay. I'm not offended. I know what you mean. When I was your age—what are you, thirty?"

"Thirty-two."

"Thirty-two. Yes. When I was thirty-two, I thought that being fifty-four would mean being old and wrinkly and …" she shrugged, "past it, I suppose. Now that I'm there, it doesn't feel that old at all. And," she smiled at Roxy, "actually, I will take the compliment. I do feel good about the way I look. Thank you."

"It's true. You are gorgeous. I'm sorry I said it wrong the first time. You're beautiful and you have something about you that's more than just looks, it's more like elegance, or grace or … I don't know."

Marianne smiled. "I guess that would be age."

She turned at the sound of Clay's voice behind her. "She's right, you know."

Marianne cocked her head to one side.

"You are gorgeous; you're a beautiful woman in the physical sense."

The butterflies swirled in Marianne's stomach at the look in his eyes when he said *physical*. "But there's something more about you than just that. You're beautiful on the inside, too."

"Aww."

They both turned to look at Roxy, who had her hands clasped over her heart with a big sappy grin on her face.

Marianne laughed. "Shall we go for that walk?" She wanted to hear more of what Clay had to say, but she didn't need an audience for it.

He held his coat out for her and helped her into it. It was a red and black plaid jacket, shearling lined. It was way too big for her, but it was warm and cozy and best of all it smelled like him. She snuggled deeper inside it with a smile as he pulled a sweatshirt over his head.

Roxy was still watching them with that big, silly smile. "Where are you going?" she asked.

Clay frowned at her, but then relaxed. "We're going for a walk down by the water."

"Do you want me to let anyone know?"

He pursed his lips. "Only if we're not back in an hour."

He took hold of Marianne's hand and steered her toward the entrance.

"Who would she tell?" Marianne was puzzled by that.

"I have a couple of security guys. They like to babysit me when I go out. I don't think we want them along, though, do we?"

She shook her head rapidly. She hadn't considered that he might have bodyguards. "Why do you need them?"

"I don't. It's more to keep Autumn and Lawrence and a couple of other people off my back."

"Why?"

He stopped before they made their way down the steps outside the lodge. He met her gaze and then blew out a sigh. "It's no big deal. I had some trouble a couple of years ago. A woman. A fan ..."

"You had a stalker?"

He nodded. "It's kind of embarrassing."

Marianne had to smile at that. "You think you're a big, tough guy and you don't need any help protecting yourself from some crazy stalker lady?"

He nodded, looking embarrassed.

She squeezed his hand. "If it's any consolation, I'm glad you have people watching your back."

"What, you don't think I'm man enough to handle it by myself?"

She stopped walking and looked up into his eyes. "Oh, I know you're man enough." She was surprised how husky her voice sounded. It gave away the fact that she would love him to show her just how much of a man he was. She needed to get a grip. "I just hate the thought of it."

"It's okay. She went quiet a couple of years ago. Probably set her sights on someone younger."

"I'm glad she left you alone, but I hope she didn't just transfer her attention to someone else."

~ ~ ~

Clay nodded. He hoped so, too. Things had been hairy for a period of about six months, but it was all behind him now. He wouldn't be bringing Marianne outside like this if he believed there was any chance whatsoever that that crazy woman might still be around.

"It's all water under the bridge. Don't worry, darlin'. You're safe with me." He slid his arm around her shoulders and started walking down toward the lake. There was something about her that made him feel protective, like he wanted to step up and be more of a man for her. He didn't subscribe to all the macho bullshit that seemed to be so much a part of the music industry. He didn't appreciate the guys who got off on being so alpha that they couldn't see through their own ego. By the same token, he didn't appreciate the women who played to that dynamic, either. Needy damsels in distress had never done anything for him—other than lose his respect.

Marianne seemed to be thinking along the same lines he was. "Is it weird if I say I know I am—safe, with you? If I'm honest, I've never needed or wanted a man to make to me feel safe." She made a face. "Perhaps, when I was much, much younger. In fact, I'll admit, back then that's what I wanted—

and it's also how I discovered that trying to get that feeling from anyone outside of yourself can be a total disaster."

"Well, I don't think it's weird, that I make you feel safe. I have to admit that I like it, but I know what you mean. And I also know that I wouldn't like it so much if you needed me to make you feel safe."

She smiled. "Honey, I was raised in Texas, by a single momma along with a feisty sister. Where I come from, no woman ever needed a man for anything."

He had to laugh. "Well, damn and I'm glad to hear it. I guess all I can do is hope that you want me around since you obviously don't need me."

She gave him a mischievous smile. "I want."

"Well, good. I'm signing up here and now to be your plaything till you don't want me anymore." Even as he said it, he hoped that day would never come.

The look on her face gave him hope that she was thinking along the same lines, but maybe that was just wishful thinking on his part.

When they reached the bottom of the road, they followed the trail between the trees and emerged on the beach on the other side.

The moonlight sparkled on the water and Clay smiled. This place felt good. It wasn't like the South, but it had a beauty of its own. He knew he could be happy here, especially if he had a beauty of his own—the one standing right beside him.

They walked hand in hand down by the water's edge.

"I guess this is very different from your childhood in Texas."

Marianne gave him a look he couldn't decipher. "It couldn't be more different. I love it here."

"How long have you lived here?"

"Only a couple of years—not even that. Once Laura decided that this was it for her, when she and Smoke bought a house together, she started asking me to move out here. Then Chris, my sister, she moved here to be near her boys." She shrugged.

"All the important people in my life had moved here, there was no reason for me not to follow."

"There was no one important still in Texas?"

"No. I had friends, but when my best friend died there was nothing left to keep me there."

"I'm sorry."

She shrugged. "I am, too. We were friends from high school. We were neighbors, had our girls just a few months apart. The girls are still friends now. It was hard to lose Cara, but …". She shrugged. "It is what it is."

Clay had wondered whether there was still a guy she cared about, but it seemed that wasn't the case.

She looked up at him with a smile. "Sorry, you were probably trying to figure out if there are any skeletons in my dating closet and instead, I got sad on you about an old friend. I haven't dated anyone since I came here. And back in Texas, I hadn't dated anyone more than a few times in oh, probably five years."

"I didn't mean to pry."

She laughed. "You didn't even ask! I just assumed that was where you were going—and I was right, wasn't I?"

He smiled. "You were. I just find it hard to believe that a woman like you hasn't already been claimed by some lucky son of a gun."

"I never wanted to be claimed."

"And now?"

He stopped walking and tugged on her hand so that she stopped and turned to face him. "How would you feel if I tried to claim you? To make you mine?"

She looked up into his eyes. "I might feel like I was dreaming. Like I was having a silly fantasy about this guy I've had a crush on for decades."

That made him smile. Somehow, she made him forget that he was Clay McAdam, country music star, and made him feel like any regular guy who just wanted to get the attention of a woman he found incredibly attractive. "You had a crush on me?"

She smiled. "Have."

He stepped closer to her. Her eyes were shining in the moonlight and she ran her tongue across her bottom lip. He watched and closed his hands around her waist. Her arms came up around his shoulders and she looked deep into his eyes. "Is this where we have our first kiss?"

He nodded. "It is, are you ready?" She cocked her head to one side, making him smile. "I ask because this is a historic occasion."

"It is?" she asked with a smile.

He nodded solemnly. "I intend for this to be the very last first kiss I ever have."

He hadn't intended that to come out as some kind of line. He was only telling her what was going through his mind. It seemed to have a profound effect on her. She relaxed against him and her expression softened. "I'd like for it to be mine, too."

He lowered his head until his lips brushed over hers, they were warm and soft and inviting. He closed his arms around her and she pressed eagerly against him. Her body felt the same way her lips did. If anything, the invitation was even stronger, and he was grateful again that he'd brought her out here and not taken her up to his room—her body was extending an invitation he wouldn't be able to turn down.

Shivers ran down his neck as she sank her fingers into his hair. He nibbled her lower lip and she opened up for him, her tongue meeting his as he kissed her deeply. His mind vaguely hoped that this truly was his last first kiss. He hadn't kissed or been kissed like this in years. There was an exploration and an innocence, while at the same time there was a need, a deep aching physical need. The meeting of their lips, the mating of their tongues was only a precursor, a foreshadowing of the movements and promises their bodies would make just as soon as they got together.

~ ~ ~

Marianne let herself get lost in him. His arms felt strong around her—and she needed the support. Her knees felt weak from the way he kissed her. It'd been a long time since she'd been kissed—and even longer since anyone had kissed her like this. In fact, no one had ever kissed her like this. His tongue was exploring her mouth, his body was pressed, warm and hard against hers. The fact that she was wearing his coat just added to the overall impression that she was surrounded by him, getting lost in him. He was everywhere and, in that moment, he was everything—and she loved it. He sank his fingers in her hair, making her scalp tingle. She let out a little moan as shivers chased each other down her spine. This was the best kiss of her life—and it was coming at a time when she'd thought her kissing days were behind her.

When he finally lifted his head, his eyes were dark green. They were soft and intense at the same time. He planted a kiss on the tip of her nose. "Wow."

She nodded. "That's what I was thinking."

"I meant what I said earlier. Will you help me look for a house?"

Her heart raced in her chest. She'd been so caught up in the moment, she'd forgotten about the bigger picture. And the bigger picture was even more exciting and promising than the moment. She nodded. "I will."

"Thanks. I know I'm going to love it here."

"I hope so." She took hold of his hand and started walking again. "Do you think you should wait, be more cautious, before you start thinking about buying a house?"

He raised an eyebrow at her. "Do you want me to wait? Do you want to take it slowly?"

She shook her head and couldn't help the smile that spread across her face. "I don't, no. And that surprises the heck out of me. So, I'm scrambling around for the voice of reason and trying to figure out what it might say."

He smiled. "Would that be the voice of reason or the voice of caution?"

"Caution, I guess."

"And do you feel cautious—about me, about us?"

She shook her head. "I don't but I feel like I should."

"We can take this as slowly as you want, but I'm going to find myself a house here."

"You like it here that much?"

"Not yet, but I'm sure I will. I'm going to get myself a house here, because I don't feel cautious at all. I feel more certain than I've felt about anything in a long time—maybe ever. I don't want to pressure you, but I know what I want. And if I'm here I can work on convincing you to want it too."

She smiled at him. "And how might you go about convincing me?"

"Hmm." He rubbed his chin. "Well, I can bring you out for walks on the beach." He grinned. "Since I know you like my music, I can use that and serenade you."

Marianne chuckled. It seemed almost too far-fetched to think of Clay McAdam serenading her because he wanted to be with her. That really was more like the kind of fantasy she'd had when she was a teenager.

He was watching her face. "Not enough? How else might you like me to persuade you?"

She tried to hide her smile.

"What?" he asked. "You have to tell me what that look means."

She dropped her head and wouldn't meet his gaze.

He tucked his fingers under her chin and made her look up at him. "Tell me? I'll do it, whatever it is."

She shook her head, feeling embarrassed. Being around him brought her out of herself, there was no question about that, but she didn't feel ready to admit to him that the word persuasion had physical connotations in her mind.

His eyes twinkled as he smiled at her and she understood that he already knew what she meant—he just wanted to hear her say it.

She shook her head.

He ran his hand down her back and then cupped it around her butt cheek, making her look up at him in surprise. There was still a twinkle in his eyes, and there was no mistaking the desire in them. "I think I like your idea of what persuasion looks like."

She smiled. "Sorry, but I have to admit that's what came to mind when you asked how you could persuade me."

He nodded. "I'd love to, but not yet."

She nodded rapidly. "No, not yet. I didn't mean that. I didn't even think …". She was embarrassed. Did he think she was hinting that he should persuade her tonight?

He dropped a kiss on her lips. "I know. It's me. I've been in a battle with myself the whole evening. I wanted to take you to my room. I want to take you back there now. But I know better. That's not the foundation we want to build on. I think I fell in love with you the first time I laid eyes on you, Marianne, but I'm not ready to make love to you. If we were to go there now, it wouldn't be all it could be."

It felt like fireworks were going off in her chest—he thought he'd fallen in love with her the first time he saw her? That was too wonderful and at the same time too crazy a thought to let herself focus on it. The thought of him making love to her was enough to deal with. She reached up and planted a peck on his lips. "I know. I'd forgotten what it's like to feel this way. If you asked me to, I'd go with you now, but I'd rather wait."

He took hold of her hand and started leading her back up the beach. She had to laugh when he turned to her and raised one eyebrow. "How long do you think is long enough to wait?"

She shrugged. "I don't know. I think we'll just know when the time is right."

He nodded. "Or when we just can't wait anymore?"

"Probably."

Chapter Six

Clay rolled over onto his back and stared up at the ceiling. It was early; still dark outside. He smiled to himself as he thought about last night; about Marianne. He blew out a sigh and sat up, swinging his feet to the floor. She wasn't here. Part of him wished she was, that he'd brought her back with him—and started their relationship with a bang. Mostly he was glad that they'd decided to wait. In his younger days he wouldn't have given it a second thought. But then in his younger days he hadn't met a woman who had turned his head around the way Marianne had. He was older now, and wiser. He got to his feet with a rueful smile and headed to the bathroom to pee. His body was older, too. He was in good shape for a guy his age, he worked out, ran a couple of times a week, but he was slower than he had been. He wanted to take his time before he brought Marianne into his bed—and he'd take his time with her when he got her there, too.

He started up the little coffee maker and went to stand in front of the windows. The sky was starting to lighten, but it was still too dark to make out the lake and the mountains. He couldn't wait to see the view again. It'd captivated him the first time he'd come up here a couple of weeks ago, and he was loving the idea that the view—the place—was going to become a part of his life. Well, what he loved most was the thought that Marianne was going to become a part of his life and it was just a bonus that she lived in such a beautiful place.

He sat in the armchair and sipped his coffee, relieved that it was surprisingly good for hotel coffee. He'd get something more robust later, but this would do to tide him over till he was showered and dressed and ready to go.

He picked up his phone when it buzzed. It was Adam, his security guy.

Don't try sneaking off. I'll drive you over to town when you're ready.

He chuckled to himself. He knew he made Adam's life difficult at times, but they both enjoyed the game. He didn't mind conceding when he was outmaneuvered.

OK. You win this one. Be ready in 30.

Adam's reply came almost immediately.

I'll be waiting out front.

Clay finished the rest of his coffee and headed for the shower. He didn't know how Adam knew that he planned to meet Marianne for breakfast over in Summer Lake, but if Adam knew, then Autumn no doubt knew, too. He'd text her on his way over there and save her from calling him and interrupting breakfast.

He walked through the lobby twenty-minutes later, wondering if he'd get the chance to take in the view before Adam came for him. Of course, he didn't. Adam was grinning at him from the driver's seat of the rented SUV. He rolled the window down. "Top of the morning to you, boss man. You ready to go?"

Clay grinned and walked around to the passenger seat. "Morning. You're getting too good at this."

Adam grinned back and nodded at the center console where two cups of coffee sat in the cupholders. "I even managed to find us some decent joe."

"Damn, you're good."

"I do my best." He pulled away from the hotel. "And we're going to the Boathouse restaurant at the Summer Lake Resort, right?"

"You know you're right. What I want to know is how."

Adam chuckled. "I keep my ear to the ground. It's my job to know what's going on around you."

Clay took a sip of the coffee. It was good. "What's going on around me is one thing. Knowing what my plans are before I tell you? That's something else."

"And that's why you pay me so much."

Clay had to smile. It was true. The first security team he'd hired had been perfectly adequate, but he hadn't gelled well with the guys. There was nothing wrong with them, or with the service they provided. They were good, but they weren't great. To Clay that was, perhaps, the most important distinction in life. Good was ... good. But it wasn't good enough. He wanted great. He demanded great—of himself first, but of the people around him, too. Adam and his team were great. They didn't have the on-paper credentials that the other firm had, but that didn't matter. They had the real-life smarts and abilities that mattered to him.

Adam shot a glance at him as he pulled out onto the main road that followed the lake south. "Uh-oh, are you wondering if I'm worth what you pay me?"

Clay laughed. "Nope. I won't say, I was thinking the opposite—because you'll only go and raise your rates on me. But I was thinking that you're worth every penny."

Adam fixed his gaze on the road ahead. "Thanks." He nodded curtly.

"And if you could just learn to accept a compliment ..." Clay punched his arm.

"Do you want to hear any of what I learned in my research?"

Clay's smile faded. Adam and his guys checked out anyone who came into his life. It was a necessary evil of his position at this point in his career. He hated that he didn't get the chance to get to know people in a normal manner anymore—they were all vetted in advance. "Only if there's some kind of deal breaker. Marianne's special. I want to get to know her in the way a guy should get to know a woman—slowly, naturally, over time, through conversation—not through an info dump of what you learned through background checks and whatever other means you use."

Adam shrugged. "Okay. I was only asking. There's nothing to be concerned about. That's all I'll say."

"Good." Clay hadn't expected there to be.

They rode on in silence for a little while until Adam shot him a quick glance. "Are you seriously going to buy a house here?"

"Yup." Clay wasn't sure he wanted to hear about why it wasn't a good idea.

"And that's not up for discussion?"

"Nope."

Adam smiled. "Okay. I was just making conversation or trying to."

Clay smiled back. "Talk about whatever you want, but don't try to talk me out of what I'm doing here."

"Okay. But would you tell me what exactly it is you're doing?"

Clay shrugged. "I can't tell you for certain. I can tell you that I'm possibly making a huge fool of myself. On the other hand, I might be setting myself up to be happy for the rest of my life. I don't know which it is yet. All I can tell you for sure is that I'm following my heart."

"In that case, I might start looking for a place of my own up here."

"And why's that?"

Adam grinned. "Because when I first met you, I could tell you lived from your heart, not your head. I wasn't sure if I'd be able to work with that. Over the last few years, I've learned that your heart steers you better than most men's heads ever will."

Clay smiled. "Thanks. I think people go wrong when they think their mind, their intellect knows what's best. They forget to listen to their heart. I wasn't raised to pay much attention to my intellect—dumb country boys aren't supposed to have much. But you're right, my heart's done me okay so far."

"Dumb country boy, my ass!"

"It's what I was raised as."

"But not who you are. Anyway, we'll be coming into town in a couple of minutes. What are your plans? Do you know? Breakfast and then …?"

"I don't know. I'm going to play it by ear, but I don't expect to want to come back over to the lodge until after lunch. You could always just drop me off, and I'll give you a call about picking me up later."

"Nice try. I'll be around."

Clay stared out the window as Adam drove down Main Street. It was quiet, they were the only vehicle on the road. It was still too early for the stores to be open—except one. He saw a couple coming out of the bakery. The woman was cute, a blonde in her thirties, he'd guess. She was carrying a box of goodies while the guy, tall, dark and handsome, maneuvered a stroller out the door. The little one in the stroller met his gaze and smiled, waving pudgy fingers at him and making him smile and wave back. The couple looked up too, the guy looking non-too-friendly at first and then smiling and waving, too. Perhaps he recognized Clay McAdam—though Clay preferred to think it was just one of those moments of human connection—moments that didn't seem to happen for him too often anymore.

"You know them?" asked Adam.

"Nah. Not them as individuals, no. But I feel like I do know them as the young couple with their first kid, living their lives in a small town—happily."

Adam rolled his eyes as he drove on. "And let me guess, you'll be writing a song about them when we get back to Nashville?"

Clay smirked. "Maybe."

He got out of the SUV and walked around to the driver's door when Adam pulled up in the square by the restaurant. "You really can take the morning off, you know. I doubt anything bad has ever happened in this town."

Adam shrugged. "I'm inclined to agree with you. It's a cute little town. Let your guard down. Enjoy yourself. But I won't be letting mine down. There's no way I can believe that word didn't get out about your party. I'd put money on there being at least a couple of groupies and celebrity watchers up here—even if not for you, think about all your guests."

Clay nodded reluctantly. "I suppose. But I'm just going to forget that you're here."

"Good. That's supposed to be the point of having me around. You get to relax while I stay vigilant." He got out of the SUV and locked it up. "I'll go in first and you won't see me again till you want me."

Clay followed him as he pushed the doors open and enjoyed the rush of warm air that greeted them as they stepped inside.

"Good morning, Mr. McAdam."

It took Clay a moment to place the guy who came toward him, hand extended. He must have met him before because Adam nodded at him and walked on by. "Ben. Ben Walton. It's good to see you again, son." Ben owned the lodge over at Four Mile Creek as well as the Resort at Summer Lake.

"And you. I hope you enjoyed the party?"

"It was amazing. Angel's a credit to you."

Ben smiled. "She is. I'm lucky to have her. I was worried for a little while there that I might lose her to you—well, to Nashville, since Luke's there with you. But I understand she's more likely to stay put now."

Clay smiled. "News travels fast. I guess small towns are the same the world over."

Ben chuckled. "I imagine they are." He swung his arm out over the mostly empty restaurant. "Do you want to choose your spot?"

Clay looked around and pointed to a booth in the corner. "Can we take that?"

"Of course."

"And would you take a coffee over to Adam? I'm sure he'd appreciate it. If he wants to eat, put it on my tab—and tell him I don't want to see him."

Ben smiled. "Will do. Can I get you a coffee while you wait?"

"I'd love one, thanks. But I won't be waiting long." The door had just opened, and Marianne came in. She'd looked amazing last night in that blue dress that had showed off her svelte figure, but this morning she looked perhaps even more beautiful. She wore jeans with boots that came up to her knees and a cream-colored wool jacket, belted around her slender waist.

"I'll be back in a little while with your coffee," said Ben.

Marianne rubbed her hands together to warm them. Walking here hadn't been the best idea. It was colder than she'd thought out there. She checked her watch, she wasn't exactly late, just a few minutes behind. She scanned the room. It was mostly empty with only a few tables occupied. She spotted Ben making his way back behind the bar and then … there he was. She wanted to pinch herself. Was that really Clay McAdam sitting in a booth waiting for her to come and join him for breakfast? Her heart raced, and shivers ran down her spine as he lifted a hand and smiled his sexy smile. She waved back and hurried over to him.

"Good morning."

He got to his feet, and once again she felt his presence surround her. She felt warm and safe—and breathless. He was just so darned good-looking. He took hold of her hands and lowered his head to kiss her cheek. Her knees went weak as his warm breath tickled her ear.

"I missed you."

She looked up into his brown-green eyes, they were twinkling again—or perhaps they did that all the time. "I missed you, too."

She started to take off her coat and he helped her out of it, then waited while she sat. She hadn't realized that there still were men who acted like gentlemen in the old-fashioned sense.

Ben appeared and set two cups of coffee and two menus down on the table. He smiled at her encouragingly—he was such a good boy, she adored him. "Just give me a shout when you're ready."

She watched him walk away before turning back to meet Clay's gaze.

"I wondered if you might get cold feet and not show."

She shook her head. "I admit I did get to questioning myself before I went to sleep, but I just told the voice of doubt to shut up and let me enjoy it. Twelve hours isn't long enough for the effect you have on me to wear off and let me get back to thinking that this isn't real."

He smiled. "Then I guess twelve hours is the maximum I should let you go without coming back to remind you that it is real."

She laughed. "That would be nice, but it's hardly realistic is it?" Her smiled faded. "Laura said you're leaving tomorrow."

"That was the old plan."

"And what's the new one?"

"I'm going to send Autumn and the others back. They need to get back to it. I reckon I can stay here a day or two longer."

"Oh, but …". She loved the idea, but she didn't want him messing up his plans just for her.

"You don't want me to stay?" His smile told her that he knew she did.

"Of course, I do, it's not that. It's just … I don't know. I don't want to put you out. Or put anyone else out. Don't people need you back in Nashville?"

"They can manage without me. Autumn's the one who runs the show—not me. If anyone needs me, they can call me. And think of it this way—we'll be doing Luke and Angel a favor. Luke and Zack can fly the others back and then they can come back here and hang out for a few more days waiting to take me home."

Marianne smiled as she remembered Luke proposing to Angel last night. She was sure the two of them would be happy with this change of plans. "In that case, I'd be happy to help out the young lovers."

He reached across the table and took hold of her hand. "I know we're not exactly young lovers, but do you want to help me out, too? I was serious about starting house-hunting. I want to set myself up with a base here just as soon as I can. Do you know a good realtor?"

"I do." Marianne felt a little self-conscious all of a sudden. Austin had helped her find her little rental house, but she doubted Clay would be looking for a place like hers. Perhaps there was another realtor in town—one who dealt with the higher end properties—the kind she wouldn't know about. "But perhaps Ben will have a better idea. He knows everyone in this town. We should decide what we want to order and call him over."

When Clay waved Ben over, he took their order with a smile. "Can I get you anything else?"

Marianne smiled at him. Hoping he'd understand why she was asking. "Not for now, but do you know of a realtor—the kind Clay might want to help him?"

Ben looked puzzled. "You mean someone other than Austin?"

She nodded, feeling guilty. She didn't want him to think she had anything against Austin. He was wonderful. "I wasn't sure if he'd have what Clay would be looking for."

Ben smiled. "Austin works with everything, from studios to lakefront estates."

"Great. Thank you. In that case ... okay."

When Ben had gone, Clay raised an eyebrow at her. "Is there some reason I might not want to use this Austin guy?"

"No." She held his gaze for a moment and the embarrassed feeling dissolved. She smiled, happy that she felt relaxed enough with him to tell him what she was thinking. "If we're going to keep seeing each other—"

"And we are."

She smiled. "Then you're going to have to know something about me."

"I know you aren't going to tell me that you used to date Austin—you haven't dated anyone since you've been here."

She laughed. "No, it's not that. And when you meet him, you'll understand why I find the idea so funny—he's good-looking, I won't deny that, but I could be his mother."

Clay smiled. "That's a relief, though I wouldn't be surprised if a young gun like that took a shine to you."

She waved her hand at him. "Don't be silly. What I need you to know is that I might get a little hung up now and then about how different our situations are."

"Our situations?" He looked genuinely puzzled.

"Financially."

"Ahh."

She hurried on, feeling stupid now that she'd started – and she knew it was stupid. Money didn't matter to her, and if it mattered so much to him that he'd think less of her for not having much, then he wasn't the guy for her anyway. "I just ... Austin found me my house. It's nothing grand. I thought perhaps there was another realtor—one who might deal with the kind of properties you're looking for."

He nodded slowly. "And what am I looking for?"

She shrugged. "Not a little two-bed rancher in town."

He took hold of her hand again. "It's okay. I get it. I really do. When I first started singing and got around people who'd already made it big, I felt the same. I grew up with nothing. I thought those folks were going to look down on me. But they didn't. Having money or not having money doesn't say anything about who you are as a person. If you have your hang-ups about it, I get it. But do me a favor and remember that they're coming from you—not from me."

She squeezed his hand and nodded. "Thank you. I'll try. That's why I brought it up, I wanted to explain."

"Okay. Are we going to call this Austin and see if he has time for us this afternoon?"

She sat back, surprised that he wanted to move so quickly. "No?"

She nodded rapidly. "Yes. Of course. I'd love to."

He winked at her. "And you won't think any less of me if I want to look at big places—waterfront estates?"

She smiled. "No. I won't. You should find whatever makes you feel comfortable."

"Only if it won't make you feel uncomfortable."

She held his gaze for a long moment. He might have a point there. "I won't let it." If she could get used to the idea that Clay McAdam liked her, then she could surely make herself get used to spending time in a big fancy house with him.

Chapter Seven

Adam turned to look back at Clay from the driver's seat as they waited outside the gate. Beyond it stretched a long driveway. The house, standing at the end of the long driveway, was just visible through the trees. "I like this place already."

Clay nodded. He did, too. He liked the idea of having a controlled entrance—maybe it'd help Adam relax a little, though he doubted it.

"Here's Austin, now," said Marianne.

Clay and Adam both rolled down their windows and Austin smiled up at them from his car. "Hi. Sorry it took me a little while."

Clay held up a hand. "Not a problem. I appreciate you taking the time on a Sunday afternoon—and for managing to get us in to have a look."

"Well, let's get in there." He pointed a remote control at the gates which swung open silently. "Follow me." He pulled ahead and started down the driveway.

Clay looked around as they went. He had a good feeling about this place. Trees lined the driveway and off to the left he caught glimpses of the lake between them. This was the kind of house he'd dreamed about as a kid. He looked at Marianne, wondering what she would make of it.

She smiled up at him but didn't say anything.

Adam pulled up next to Austin and they all got out.

As Marianne introduced him and Adam to Austin, he was glad that she didn't seem uncomfortable. While Austin told him a little bit about the property—it was twenty acres with 600 feet of shoreline—Marianne looked around with a big smile on her face.

"Anyway, let's get inside out of the cold and let you have a look around first. If you like what you see, we can take a walk down to the water and the dock."

He unlocked the front door and Clay let Marianne go in ahead of him. He knew the minute he set foot in the hallway. He loved the place.

Marianne turned to smile up at him. She did, too. He could see it in her eyes.

"Do you want the tour, or would you rather explore by yourselves?"

Clay smiled at him. "We'd like to explore. Though, I'm sure Adam here will want you to show him every nook and cranny."

Adam nodded. "Yep, that'd be great."

"I'm guessing you'll want to start with the security system?" asked Austin.

Clay watched the two of them walk away down the hall, glad that Adam seemed enthusiastic. He hadn't yet pointed out a single issue—and that wasn't like him.

He turned back to Marianne. "Shall we?"

She nodded and looked around the entrance hall. "This is amazing already. I can't wait to see the rest of it."

Clay couldn't either. He took hold of her hand and led her through to the formal living room.

Her smile faded a little, and he knew why. It was a beautiful room, but it wasn't a place he could see himself relaxing. It had French doors that led out onto a patio but didn't directly overlook the lake. "I guess this is for entertaining," he said and tugged on her hand. He had an idea that there was something much better waiting for them. Leading through to the next room he was proved right.

"Wow!" she exclaimed.

He shook his head and grinned. "I couldn't have said it better myself. This was the family room. Floor to ceiling windows rose two stories and showcased an amazing view of the lake and the mountains beyond. The furnishings were less formal, though still elegant. A rustic dining table sat next to the far windows with a view out onto a small orchard. The whole place was open plan, with the gourmet kitchen overlooking the living area and the view beyond.

Marianne moved toward the kitchen as if she was drawn to it by some unseen force. She went around the island and stood at the sink, facing the lake. "It's amazing!" she said in hushed tones.

He had to laugh. "Is that what you'd call kitchen-worship?"

She nodded enthusiastically. "It is. I've never seen a kitchen like this. It's— " she shook her head— "indescribable. I'd love to do dishes if I got to stand here and admire that view while I did them."

He went to her with a smile. "You don't need to do dishes to get the view. You can sit on the sofa and admire it while I do the dishes."

She gave him a puzzled look. "You do your own dishes?"

He laughed. "I sure do."

"All the time?" she asked incredulously.

"Mostly. Unless I have people over and have it catered, then the caterers take care of it."

She nodded. "Sorry. I guess I just thought of you having a housekeeper or something—people to take care of you—like Adam."

She'd been a good sport about Adam driving them over here. Better than Clay had been himself, if he was honest. He'd wanted to take the SUV and leave Adam at the resort to wait for his backup to come over and collect him. Marianne had insisted that he should ride with them—that she didn't mind. And Clay knew it wasn't because she was worried about his safety so much as because she didn't want to inconvenience Adam.

"No, I have a cleaning service—I could leave the dishes for them to do, but that's not how my momma raised me."

She smiled at that. "Is your momma still around?"

He nodded. "She is. She lives in an assisted living place in Alabama. I still struggle with that idea, but that's where she wants to be."

Marianne nodded. "I'll bet she's proud of you."

He grinned. "She is. Anyway, do you want to see the rest?"

By the time they'd toured the whole house, Marianne was in love—with the house for sure, and possibly with Clay, too. Maybe she was getting carried away. But how could she not? In the space of less than twenty-four hours, he'd come back into her life, told her he wanted to become a permanent fixture in it and found himself a house so that he could be.

They met up with Austin and Adam back in the kitchen. Clay raised an eyebrow at Adam. "What do you think?"

Adam smiled. "It'd make my life a lot easier. Controlled access, video security inside and out. It's as close to perfect as I could hope to find."

"And what do you think?" asked Austin. "Do you have any questions?"

Marianne sucked in a deep breath when Clay answered. "Yeah. When can I move in?"

Austin grinned. "Right now, if you want to. The owners had it on the market for over eighteen months with no takers. I could have sold it three times if they'd been prepared to come down a little on the price, but they wouldn't budge. It was on the rental market this last season, but it didn't see much business—due to the price again. When I spoke to the listing agent after you called me, he said that the owners would accept a long-term lease or purchase offer."

Marianne shot a sideways glance at Clay. A lease would make more sense than buying the place—especially if it was overpriced. He turned and winked at her, then looked back at Austin. "Tell them I want immediate possession—however that works out. I want to stay here tonight, and I want to buy the place."

Austin grinned. "Okay. I'll tell them the immediate possession part, but I suggest we play smart over telling them that you want to buy. We could probably get them to come down a couple hundred."

Marianne bit the inside of her lip. He couldn't mean a couple hundred dollars—he must mean a couple hundred thousand! She leaned back against the counter. She didn't even want to guess what the purchase price must be.

"I'd like to go and look at the water while you boys talk business." She pushed away from the counter and made it to the double doors before Adam caught up with her.

"Are you okay?"

She nodded. "I'm fine, thanks." She smiled, feeling foolish. Only this morning she'd told Clay that she wouldn't let the whole money thing get in the way. To be fair, she wasn't letting it get in the way, she was just taking a minute to deal with the reality of quite how much money they were talking about.

Adam opened the door for her and they stepped outside. "It's a great place," he said.

She nodded, not knowing what to say to him. She set out down the path that led to the water and he fell in beside her.

"He might be loaded, but he's still just a regular guy."

She turned to look at him in surprise.

"Sorry. I should probably keep my mouth shut and my nose out of it, but I can't help it. I remember what he was like after

he met you last year and how hard he tried to see you again—
and then how much he pined when you told him to stop
calling."

Marianne's heart thudded in her chest.

"Please don't get mad at me. I know it isn't my place. But
you had to get out of there because it was all too much, right?"

She nodded.

"It's too much to think about how much money he has and
how different his life is from yours?"

She nodded again.

"But when you ignore that part, the two of you aren't
different at all, are you?"

"No."

They reached the water's edge and Adam leaned on the
railing and looked out at the water. "So, what are you more
interested in—who he is or what he has?"

She frowned. "I'm not interested in what he has at all. I'm
not a gold-digger, if that's what you're getting at."

Adam smiled. "It's not. What I'm saying is, you care about
him. You're not the kind of person who would go after him
because of his money—so why reject him because of it?"

She cocked her head to one side. "I'm not rejecting him, I
just needed a minute to process it, to …"

"To decide if you can handle it? To figure out if this is a bad
idea because you're in such different places financially."

She blew out a sigh. "I suppose. I keep trying to not let it get
in the way, but it keeps rearing its ugly head."

"I know, but I hope you can make your peace with it
somehow. I've never seen him the way he is now—the way he
is about you. He's worked damned hard all his life to be in the
position he's in now. It'd be a crying shame if his hard-earned
success were the thing that prevented him from finding real
happiness—because it scared you away."

Marianne thought about it and eventually she smiled. "I
know you're right."

"Good. I'm glad you're not mad at me. I'll help you if you like. I'll give you a nudge whenever the whole money thing comes up, but give it a shot?"

"I will. I am. You care about him, don't you?"

"I do, but don't ever tell him that."

She laughed. "I won't, though I can tell that he cares about you, too."

"But like me, he'd never admit it. He likes to keep me on my toes, make life difficult for me, but it's all just a game we play."

"Is it really just a game?"

Adam's smile faded. "No. There was a real threat a couple of years ago. It faded away, but that bothers me. I'd rather have been able to end it. This way there's always a chance that she'll resurface—in addition to the fact that we always have to be alert against new threats."

"Who was she? What happened?"

Adam shook his head and turned to look up at the house where Clay and Austin were just coming out the doors. "Nothing to worry about."

Marianne frowned. "Maybe not, but I'd still like to know."

"I'll tell you some time, but for now, just be happy. It looks like he's going to be moving in here."

Clay slid his arm around her shoulders when he reached them. "What's he bending your ear about?"

She met Adam's gaze for a moment, then smiled. "He's trying to recruit me to his side, wanting to keep you safe."

Clay scowled at Adam. "That's your job."

Adam grinned at him. "And it's in my contract that I'll use all available resources to do so."

Clay raised an eyebrow at Marianne. "You're sure you want to be on his side? He just called you a resource."

She laughed. "I know what he meant, and I'll be happy to help him."

Adam nodded at her. "We're going to make a great team."

~ ~ ~

"You're serious?" Autumn stared at him.

Clay nodded. "I thought you'd be happy. You're the one who engineered this whole party to get me up here. You were hoping Marianne and I would get together. You can't deny it."

"I'm not denying it. I'm pleased for you, I am. But …" She shook her head. "I thought the two of you would start seeing each other. That you'd come out here sometimes and that she'd come to Nashville to visit you—you know, like Laura comes every couple of months."

"You know I've been talking for a while about finding a vacation home."

"I do. And I even like the idea of you finding one here. But come on Clay, you need to give me a minute to wrap my head around all this. When we first arrived you weren't even convinced that she'd want to see you. Now you're telling me that you're not coming home with us tomorrow—that you're not even going to stay here tonight. You've found a house and you're going to move into it. How does that even work?"

He had to smile. Autumn thought on her feet, but this was all happening fast, even for her.

"Austin—the realtor—took us to see the place this afternoon. It's been on the market for a long time—for sale and for rent. It's all set up as a turnkey rental, so all I need is my toothbrush and I can move right in."

"That's a good thing—since all you brought is your toothbrush and a change of clothes."

"Yep. It's a very good thing as far as I'm concerned. I've rented the place for a month on the understanding that during that time we'll negotiate the sale."

"You're going to buy it?!"

He smiled. "I am. I love it. You will, too. I can't wait for you to see it, Autumn."

"Neither can I. I should come over tonight, we all should. I want to know where we're leaving you."

"Sorry, darlin'. Not tonight."

"But what … Ah, okay. You've already invited Marianne over?"

"I sure have."

"And she's okay with things moving so fast between the two of you?"

"She's a little wary. Understandably. But we're not kids, Autumn."

She blew out a sigh. "I know. You're a grown man and can do whatever the hell you want. If it makes you happy, then I'm all for it. I'm just playing catch up here." She stared out the window of her suite for a moment before turning back to look at him. She'd switched to business mode, he could tell by the look in her eyes. "Okay. So, you're going to stay here and play house with Marianne until, what—Wednesday, Thursday?"

He shrugged. "We're not going to play house. She has her own house. I know you think this is all happening crazy fast, but I'm just laying the foundations to be able to take it slow and do it right. She's coming over for dinner tonight. That's all. Adam's going to pick her up and drive her home afterward."

Autumn made a face. "Are you shitting me?"

He laughed. "I am not. We already discussed it. I'm in a hurry to be around her, that's all. What you need to keep in mind, young lady, is that I've never had a real relationship. It's taken me fifty-five years to find her. I want to court her, take it slowly, spend time getting to know each other."

"Wow. I don't even know what to say to that."

"Then say you're happy for me and you will support me?"

"You know I will. I'm no good at the sappy stuff. You should probably talk to Summer about that, it's not my department. But I can support you in the ways I know how. I'll take care of business. Lighten your load. Free you up to stay here and do your courting and wooing or whatever it is you bygone-era people do."

He smiled through pursed lips. "Thanks. One day you'll understand."

She shook her head vigorously. "Nope. I'm not saying I won't get married someday, but I'm not into all the romance and happy-clappy stuff. Good luck with it. Off the top of my head, you don't have anything major going on until Friday. You'll have to back on Friday though, because you have that interview with the local news station."

"I know. I'll come back Thursday. I can clear my own schedule prior to that. There's nothing you need to worry about. But do you need me for anything?"

"No. There's nothing I need you to be present for. If anything comes up we can talk."

"We can." He could tell there was something else bothering her. "Go on, spit it out."

"I don't need an answer yet, but I'll tell you what I'm wondering about—because you need to figure out what the answer's going to be."

"What?"

"What's this going to look like long-term?"

He shrugged. He didn't know the answer to that. He had hopes of how things would go between Marianne and him, but he didn't know. Even if this turned out to be all he hoped it would. Even if they ended up together permanently—married. He didn't know how it would look long term. Would she move to Nashville? Would he move here? Would they split their time between the two?

"You're right. I can't answer that yet. All I can tell you is that I'll keep you posted."

"You're damned right you will. I'm going to be calling you every day just like I always do."

He put his arm around her shoulders and gave her a hug. "It's going to turn out okay however it goes. I'm going to be fine, and I'm going to be happy."

Her eyes softened, and she planted a peck on his cheek. "I know. I worry about you, that's all. You deserve happiness more than anyone I've ever met."

"So do you."

She let out a short laugh. "And here ends our sentimental moment. You're going to start on at me about Matt. I know it, and I'm not up for it. So, you go do whatever it is you need to do to get yourself moved into your new house. I have work to do. And be warned. I'll be stopping in to see your new place before I leave tomorrow, and you can bet your ass Lawrence and Shawnee will want to come too. Have you even told them yet?"

"No. I wanted to tell you first."

"Okay, well I'll leave you to it."

Clay watched her let herself out. Autumn and her sister Summer had been like daughters to him for many years now. Summer used to sing, but she'd lost her voice and gone to live in Montana. Autumn had stepped up to run McAdam Records and she was the best thing to have happened to the label. He'd already rewritten his will to leave the company to her when he passed. He shook his head. He shouldn't be thinking about what would happen when he died—especially not now when he was starting to really live.

He picked up his cellphone to call Lawrence. He knew he and Shawnee would be thrilled for him—and probably not even surprised at how fast he was moving.

Chapter Eight

Marianne hit the play button on her answer machine when she got home. Laura teased her about still having a landline, let alone a real answering machine. It had come in handy on a few occasions, though, since she didn't always remember to take her cellphone out with her when she went.

"Hey, Mom. Will you call me when you get this message? I tried your cell a couple of times, but I'm guessing you don't have it with you. I'm hearing all kinds of crazy rumors about you and I'd like to know what you're up to."

Marianne smiled to herself and went to hang her coat in the hall closet. Didn't that make a nice change? She was the one who had people talking and Laura wanted to know what it was all about.

She picked up the phone to call her back.

"Mom!"

"Hi, sweetheart. Is everything okay?"

Laura laughed. "Don't play the innocent with me. I want to hear all about it."

"What have you already heard?" Marianne was curious to hear what rumors were flying. She was amused to think that any snippets of information about her and Clay had no doubt already been twisted into something else entirely.

Laura laughed again. "Well, the first thing I heard this morning was that you spent last night with Clay. But don't worry, I put a stop to that one before it could take hold, since we gave you and Aunt Chris a ride home ourselves. Unless— you didn't sneak back over to Four Mile after we dropped you off at home, did you?"

Marianne had to laugh. "No, I didn't. But I have to tell you— this is the funniest role reversal. I remember waiting outside your window when I thought you were going to sneak back out again."

"You had so little faith in me."

"No, I had a lot of faith that you'd do it again, since you'd already done it three times that summer."

"Hmm. Anyway, this isn't about me. This is about you. I've heard that you spent the night with him. That he spent the night with you. That you're going back to Nashville with him and craziest of all, that he's already bought a house here and asked you to move in with him."

"It is crazy." Marianne was still finding it hard to believe that they'd gone and looked at that house this afternoon and that right now Clay was moving into it and she was going over there for dinner this evening.

"Mom! You're not telling me it's true?!"

She had to laugh. "I'm not moving in with him, no. But we did go and look at a beautiful house down on the water this afternoon. And he's rented it, with an eye on buying it."

"Damn!"

"You're not happy?"

"Oh, God, yes. Of course, I'm happy. I'm thrilled for you. You know I adore him. He's a wonderful person. A good man. I'm just stunned that this is moving so quickly. How do you feel about it?"

"I think I'm a little stunned, too. I'm surprised at myself. I'm not second-guessing myself or telling myself that it's not real. I'm ... honestly? I'm excited to see where this goes."

"So am I. But Mom, I know I'm the one who kind of set you up, but I'm a little worried. What if it doesn't work out?"

"What if it doesn't?"

"I don't want you to get hurt, Mom."

"That's sweet of you. But Laura, life's a gamble. I've played it safe for far too long. I'm not getting any younger. I don't have any great expectations. All I know is that I love the way that I feel when I'm around him. It might last a week, it might last forever. But I plan to enjoy whatever moments we spend together. I'll worry about what happens afterward, afterward."

"That's brave of you."

"Sweetie, when you get to be my age, you start to realize that you don't have all that many moments left on this earth. If I don't make the most of the ones I have, I'm afraid I might die without ever really living."

Laura blew out a sigh. "You're not that old, Mom. But I know what you mean. Go out and grab life by the balls, right?"

Marianne had to laugh. "Erm, I'm not quite sure I'd put it that way, but yes I agree with the overall sentiment."

Laura laughed with her. "So, when he's coming back?"

"He's not leaving."

"He's not?"

"No. He's moving into the house as we speak. I'm going over there for dinner this evening and he's staying here until Thursday. He needs to go back for a meeting on Friday."

"And what happens after that?"

"I have no idea."

"And you're okay with that?"

"I'm more than okay with it. I'm fully aware that this might just be that crazy week I spent with Clay McAdam. Show me a woman my age who wouldn't be okay with that."

Laura laughed. "I can show you plenty of women my age who'd be very happy indeed with it."

"Exactly. Of course, I hope this is the beginning of something special, but I'll be okay if it isn't."

"Okay, then. As long as you're good."

"I'm very good."

"Okay. Well, call me if you need me, or if you want to talk, or I don't know, anything. I think I'm finally starting to appreciate how you felt when I started dating."

Marianne laughed at that. "You have no idea, young lady. I'm going for dinner with a man whom you already know and like. You, on the other hand, were riding all over hell and back with some very unsavory characters."

"Have I ever told you how sorry I am about the way I was back then?"

"No, and you don't need to. You were growing up. I was there to see you through it. That's how it's supposed to be. I'm proud of both of us for the way you turned out."

"Aww, thanks, Mama."

Marianne had to swallow around the lump in her throat. "There's nothing to thank me for. I'm going to go now, before you make me cry."

"Okay, but call me when you get home tomorrow?"

"I'll call you tomorrow, but I'm coming home tonight."

"You are?"

"I am."

"Whatever you say, Mom."

She had to laugh. "You don't have to believe me, but I know. I'll talk to you tomorrow. Say hi to Smoke for me? Oh, and tell him I'm being brave."

"Did he come see you the other day?"

"That's between him and me. Bye, darling."

She hung up with a smile and went through to the kitchen. She'd never thought she'd see the day when Laura was the one who was settled and married and was looking out for *her* as she ventured into the dating world. She wasn't sure she was venturing into the dating world. It wasn't as though she had the urge to start going out or had even wanted to find someone. She was fine by herself. She enjoyed her own company. She wasn't ready to start dating, it was just that she was ready to start dating Clay.

~ ~ ~

Clay stood back and admired his work before sliding it into the oven. He'd made Adam accompany him to the grocery store on his way back over to the house and picked up everything he needed to make his go-to casserole. It was comfort food, no two ways about it, but he wanted this evening to be comfortable. He wanted Marianne to relax with him. He wanted to connect with her as the man and the woman they were. Not as the famous singer and the woman he was pursuing. He checked his watch. Adam had gone to pick up Marianne a little while ago. He should be back with her soon. It bothered him a little that he didn't know how long it would take because he didn't know where Marianne's house was. He wanted to know. He wanted to see her in her home environment. He shook his head. He needed to be patient. It'd all happen in its own good time.

He looked around at the house. The owners had been happy to rent it to him for a month, on the understanding that they would negotiate a possible sale during that time. From what Austin had said, it sounded like they were getting anxious to sell and might come down some on the price. He wanted to own it. It felt symbolic. Renting it was great—especially getting it all organized within the space of just a few hours. Hell, he hadn't even known the place existed this morning and now here he was, preparing to spend his first evening with Marianne here.

Their first evening—not their first night. He wanted her to stay. It'd been hard not to suggest that she should move straight on in with him. But it wouldn't be right. Like he'd told Autumn this afternoon, he'd never had a love story. He'd had a lot of women—but never a love story. He wanted to walk a path with Marianne, a path that led them through all the special moments a couple experienced on their way to a lasting love. He wanted them to take their time and get to know each other. It was kind of backwards, in a way. He'd known the moment he laid eyes on her that she was the one for him. Now, a year later, he was finally getting the chance to lay all the groundwork that would make it real.

He wanted them to date each other, to get to know each other, to spend long hours telling each other their life stories. That took time. He wanted to believe that they had all the time in the world—at least the rest of their lives.

He wanted her to spend the night with him, but he wanted them to build to the place where it came as a natural part of their relationship. He didn't want it to be something that they had to go back and build a foundation under afterward.

He frowned at the sound of his cell phone ringing and went to see who it was. It was Autumn's sister, Summer. He checked his watch again. Marianne might be here any minute. But he could tell Summer he had to go when she arrived. He couldn't ignore her call.

"Hey, little girl. How's it going?"

"Clay! Autumn told me about this woman, and that you're buying a house. What's happening?"

He chuckled. "Hello yourself. I'm fine, thanks."

"Oh, stop it. That's what I'm asking—how are you? What's going on with you?"

"I'm fine. I'm happy. Happier than I've been in a long time, to tell you the truth. Marianne is on her way over here right now, so I'll have to go when she arrives, but I'll call you back soon."

"You'd better tell me something right now!"

"You already know something. She's Laura's mom; you know Laura, right?"

"I've met her a couple of times. She was at Chance and Hope's wedding."

"That's right."

"Wait a minute. So, her mom is the one you met when you were in LA?"

"That's right."

"Oh! You liked her. You liked her a lot. But then nothing came of it."

"And now something has come of it."

"What kind of something? Why haven't I heard anything about it till now?"

"Because there was nothing to tell until now. If you'd made it to my birthday party, you could have met her."

"Oh, Clay. I'm so sorry I couldn't be there."

"Don't worry. I'm only teasing you."

"Well, don't tease. Tell."

"There's nothing much to tell yet. I rented a house here. I want to stick around and see what happens."

"Wow. That's wonderful."

Clay looked over his shoulder at the security monitors. An alarm sounded as the front gate swung open and the SUV appeared. "I have to go, Summer. She's here."

"Okay. Well, say hello to her for me. Tell her I can't wait to meet her. You have to bring her up here, otherwise I'll just have to come down there."

He chuckled. "All in good time, little girl. All in good time. Give my best to Carter. I'll talk to you again soon."

"Okay. Will do. Love you, Clay. Bye."

"Bye darlin'. I love you, too."

He hung up with a smile. She and her sister couldn't be more different. Summer was so sweet and gentle, while Autumn was a tough cookie. They both had hearts of gold and they both loved him as though he was their father. And he loved them like the daughters he'd never had.

He watched on the screen as Adam brought the SUV to a halt by the front steps and came around to let Marianne out. He'd wanted to go and collect her himself, but it was better this way. He knew he'd want to take her home later, too. If she really had to go. But they'd agreed in advance that Adam should play chauffeur—to hopefully reduce the temptation for her to stay.

Marianne's heart raced as she made her way up the steps to the front door. She turned back when she realized that Adam wasn't with her. "Aren't you coming?"

He grinned at her. "Hell, no. I'll see you when you're ready to leave. Have a great evening." He didn't leave, just stood there watching her.

She turned back when the front door opened and bathed the front porch in golden light. Clay stood there smiling at her and she knew it was a moment she'd remember forever—whether this was the beginning of something special for the two of them, or whether she never saw him again after tonight. She felt as though she was flooded with the warmth and light that came from this lovely house, but mostly emanated from the gorgeous man standing there waiting for her.

She hurried to him and he greeted her with a hug. Those now familiar shivers ran down her spine as he kissed her cheek and she leaned against him. "Come on in, darlin'." He took her hand and led her inside where he helped her out of her jacket.

She felt nervous as he went to hang it in the hall closet. So far, this whole thing had been a whirlwind. None of it seemed real now that she thought about it but when he turned back and smiled at her the prospect of an evening spent in the company of this charming—and very sexy—man seemed all too real.

"Are you okay?"

She nodded.

"Are you sure?"

She nodded again. "I think it's just catching up to me how crazy this is."

He came to her and put his hands on her shoulders. "It is crazy. But if you ask me, it's crazy good."

She smiled. It was good. "Better than good. It's wonderful."

"Come on. Let's get a drink. And then you can see what you think of my skills in the kitchen."

"You cooked?"

"I did. I had to do something to keep myself busy while Adam went for you."

She followed him into the kitchen. "Whatever it is, it smells wonderful."

"I hope you'll think it tastes it, too. I can tell you it goes well with a nice merlot. Would you like a glass?"

"Thank you. I would."

When he'd poured their drinks, he led her to the sofa and waited for her to sit before taking a place beside her. He sat facing her and smiled at her. "I could get used to this."

She took a sip of her wine. "I could, too."

"Good. I was hoping you'd say that." He set his glass down on the coffee table and took hers from her to set it down, too. When he turned back to her, she knew he wanted to kiss her. He had that look in his eyes and kept glancing at her lips. She'd never been the kind of woman to make the first move, but in that moment, she couldn't help remembering what Laura had said—she should grab life by the balls and go for what she wanted. She had to bite back a laugh. She wasn't hardly going to grab Clay's balls, but she did lean toward him and cup his face between her hands. He lowered his lips toward hers and then hesitated. She reached up and closed the final gap.

It started out slow and gentle, a hesitant exploration. She could tell he was holding back, and so she stepped it up. She sank her fingers in his hair and drew him closer, sliding her tongue into his mouth. Her insides melted as he responded in kind. His arms closed around her, pressing her to his broad, hard chest. She might have taken control, but she was losing it the more the kiss deepened. His hand roved up and down her back and she pressed her breasts against him. She moaned into his mouth as his hand closed around the back of her neck. He had her, she was his.

Disappointment settled in her stomach when he lifted his head. She'd been so carried away, if he'd wanted to take her right there on the sofa, she would have willingly given herself to him.

He blew out a sigh. "It's a good thing we already told Adam that he's driving you home tonight."

She nodded, not sure that she agreed. "I suppose so, but right now I can't remember why it is that we want to take it slowly."

He smiled and clasped his hand around hers. "Because, dear, sweet, impatient Marianne of mine. Things that are built to last are built slowly, with care, over time."

Her heart raced as she looked into his eyes. "And you think that this is something that can last?"

"I do." He sat back, looking serious. "You know what I'd like to do with you right now. But instant gratification has never been my thing. The things I value most in life are the things I've worked hardest to earn. I want to earn your love and your heart."

Her heart melted a little at his words. "I don't think it'll take much hard work for you to earn them. You're already on the way." It wasn't like her to speak so plainly, but it was the truth and he deserved to know it.

He smiled. "That's good to hear. Marianne, I don't need to know all your history, I just want to know one thing."

"What's that?"

"Have you ever had a great love story?"

She shook her head sadly. "No, not a great one, not even a small, semi-love story. I was young when I met Laura's father. We were married for less than three years. After that, she was the love of my life. I've had relationships, I've loved a couple of men in my lifetime, but not in the way you think of when you think of a love story."

He nodded and squeezed her hand. "My life's been the same—except of course, that I never had children. Ever since I met you, I can't help but wonder if it never worked out with anyone else because my heart was waiting for you."

She touched his cheek. "That's a beautiful thing to say."

"It's a beautiful thing to believe, and I believe it's true."

She drew in a deep breath and slowly let it out. "It might take me quite some time before I could ever believe it."

"I understand, and I've been thinking that the only way you're going to believe it is if we live our own love story. Let's do this right. Tonight is our first date. Let's start from here, let's build something special. You know damned well that there's a part of me that doesn't want to let you leave here tonight, that wants to ask you to stay and never leave. But hopefully that day will come. Tonight, I want us to enjoy our first date. I want to get to know you better. I want to be sad when it's time for you to go and I want you to miss me until we see each other again tomorrow."

She had to blink away tears as he brushed his thumb over her cheek. "It took us more than half our lives to find each other, let's spend the years we have left enjoying each other."

"I'd love to."

"Good." He visibly pulled himself together and passed her glass to her before raising his own. "Let's drink to us and our long and happy future."

"To us." She touched her glass against his, still wondering if this was too good to be true.

Chapter Nine

On Monday morning, Clay walked down to the dock with his coffee. He sat down on the bench and smiled to himself when he saw the fish cleaning station. He hoped that it would see a lot of use next summer. He would have to get Luke or Zack or one of the local guys to teach him what lake fishing was like out here. He'd fished the creeks back home when he was a kid, but in recent years the only fishing he'd done was big sportfishing in the Bahamas with his buddies.

He looked up at the sound of footsteps coming down the path from the guest house. Adam stopped a good fifty feet away.

"Are you enjoying some solitude? Or would you want some company?"

"Sure, come and join me." Clay wasn't sure that he wanted to talk, but Adam wasn't a big talker most of the time anyway.

They sat in companionable silence for a while, each staring out at the lake lost in their own thoughts. Eventually, Clay shot a sideways glance at Adam. "You got something to say? Something to ask?"

"No." Adam gave him a rueful smile. "I guess I just wanted to check that you're okay."

"I'm so much more than okay. I'm happy. I know this must look crazy from the outside. But on the inside, it couldn't feel more right."

"I suppose if you described this situation to me, I'd say it sounded crazy but being here with you, knowing you, it doesn't seem crazy at all. I'm rooting for you. I like Marianne. I like her a lot. She's good people. You can just tell. I've been dreading the day when you would meet a woman."

Clay raised an eyebrow at him. "What? You wanted to keep me all for yourself?"

Adam laughed. "Hell no! It's just that it can be hard to accommodate a woman from the perspective of a security plan. They tend to be less predictable and more prone to not liking being told what to do."

Clay laughed out loud at that. "And you have enough of that to deal with just with me."

Adam nodded vigorously. "Marianne is really sweet and it's obvious that she cares about you and your well-being. I can't see her being the kind to ignore my advice just because she wants to go shoe shopping."

Clay rolled his eyes. Adam was referring to an incident that had happened a couple of years ago when he'd been dating a minor Hollywood celebrity. "No, she's so much more than that." He met Adam's gaze for a moment. "There's something more though, isn't there? Something that you want to talk about, want to tell me?"

Adam shrugged. "It's not anything we need to talk about today."

"But we may as well, since we're sitting here anyway. Go ahead. Lay it on me."

"It's just that we both know that it won't be long before the press gets a hold of this. And once they do, stories about the two of you will start appearing. And you already know what happens when your personal life starts getting more media coverage. It draws the crazies out of the woodwork."

"I thought that was what was bothering you. But I don't want to think about it as a problem. Sure, it will mean more work for you. You'll have to be extra vigilant and if you need to bring on more guys or need more resources then go for it. If you need to up your rates because of the increased workload, that's fine too."

Adam smirked at him. "I'm not angling for a raise and you know it. What I was trying to say is that I'm hopeful for you and I want you to be able to relax and enjoy it because the guys and I have your back."

Clay grasped his shoulder. "Thanks, Adam. I appreciate it." It meant a lot to him that he saw him as more than just a job. "So, anyway, what do you think of the guest house? I hope you like it since I predict it's going to be like home for you from now on."

"I love it, it's a great place. One thing, though…"

Clay groaned. "I knew it. I knew this was going somewhere. What's the problem?"

Adam grinned at him. "It would make both our lives easier if we could extend the security system to include monitors in the guest house."

Clay pursed his lips. He wasn't entirely comfortable with living his life in full view of all the security cameras. He was even less comfortable with the idea of people watching him at all times. He shook his head. "I don't mind if you want to set up monitors of the front gate and the driveway and front door. It would make sense for you to be able to watch who's coming and going. But I don't like the idea of your guys having a live stream of what I'm doing at home."

Adam leaned forward with his elbows on his knees and wrung his hands together. "I knew you'd say that. And I totally understand why. There's always a fine line to walk when it comes to security monitoring. I don't want to invade your privacy, you know that. But at the same time, I'm more concerned about your safety. You know I respect your privacy, you know all the team does."

"I do. But that knowledge can't override my instincts."

"Okay, fair enough. I'll go with what you're giving me. For now. How about I run exterior feeds to the guest house and while I'm at it, I'll set everything up for the in-house system, too, but won't set up screens yet."

Clay pursed his lips.

"It makes sense from a budget point of view. You know it does."

Clay nodded reluctantly. "Okay, go ahead."

"Great, thanks, I will. And now that's out of the way; what's the plan for today?"

Clay smiled. "You're going to take me into town to meet up with Marianne."

"Awesome. What do the two of you have planned?"

"You're going to drive us over to the Lodge at Four Mile Creek. I'm going to touch base with the guys over there before they leave. And then we're going to wander around the Plaza. We're going to stop in and see Laura. There's a café over there that Autumn raved about. So, we might stop there for a bite. Then, this evening, she's going to come here again."

Adam started to speak and then stopped himself.

Clay had to chuckle. "I know what you want to ask. And, yes, I will need you to drive her home again."

"Sorry. I didn't want to ask."

"It's okay. I know this must seem weird. But we're taking our time."

"And I respect the hell out of that. It just reinforces for me that she is someone special and someone who'll be around for a long time."

"I hope so."

~ ~ ~

"Well, hello, you two." Laura grinned at Marianne when they entered the jewelry store. "I didn't expect to see you over here today." She turned her gaze on Clay. "If I'm honest, I didn't expect you to still be around."

"And you mind?"

"Oh, my God! No! I couldn't be more thrilled. I'm surprised, shocked might be a better word, but it's the nicest kind of surprise."

"I'm happy to hear it. From what I understand, you were Autumn's partner in crime orchestrating this whole thing, so I was hoping that you'd be happy."

"I am. Very much so." Laura turned back to look at her mom. "I should warn you, though, Smoke was also shocked, and just a little concerned."

Marianne had to laugh at that. "Aww, that's so sweet of him."

"I don't know about sweet," said Laura. "I'm not sure I like the fact that he's been having lessons in being overprotective from Jack."

Clay raised an eyebrow. "Does he have a problem? Do I need to speak to him?"

"No!" said Laura emphatically. "It's none of his business. He doesn't get to go throwing his weight around."

Marianne smiled. Laura was so fiercely independent, she hated being told what to do by anyone. But Marianne understood and liked the fact that Smoke was looking out for her best interests. She was relieved that Clay seemed to feel the same way.

"Come on, Laura," he said. "He's not throwing his weight around. And I'm glad he thinks of it as his business. I'm glad he's looking out for your mom."

Laura nodded, grudgingly. "I know, you're right, but don't tell him I said so."

Clay chuckled. "I won't, don't worry. I'll just have a word with him and reassure him that my intentions are honorable."

Laura laughed. "Okay. So, what are the two of you up to this afternoon? Have the others left yet?"

"Yes. I caught up with them before they went. I'm free and clear for the next couple of days." He slid his arm around Marianne's shoulders. "And we intend to make the most of it."

Marianne smiled up at him. "I was thinking I could cook for you."

He raised an eyebrow at her. "I thought you enjoyed my casserole?"

"I did. I loved it. I want to reciprocate and make something for you. Maybe my famous lasagna."

Laura gave her a stern look, and she knew that her independent daughter was silently chastising her for offering to a cook for a man. Marianne didn't see it the same way. She loved to cook. She enjoyed it. She didn't see it as taking care of a man in some subservient way, like she knew her daughter did. To her, it was a way of expressing that she cared about him.

"I love lasagna." Clay grinned at her. "Are you inviting me over for dinner?"

She shook her head rapidly. That wasn't what she'd been thinking at all. She was looking forward to getting the chance to cook in his amazing new kitchen. Plus, she had no desire whatsoever to invite him into her little house. She wasn't ashamed of it. It was a lovely little place. But it was modest. It wasn't what he was used to, that was all. "No. I want to make the most of that wonderful kitchen at your house."

"She's always had a thing for fancy kitchens," Laura told Clay.

He laughed. "I kind of wondered that when we first looked at the place. I was hoping it was me that was making her go all dreamy eyed, but I suspected it might have more to do with the Sub-Zero fridge and La Cornue range."

Laura stared at him blankly, making Marianne laugh. "Laura didn't inherit my love of cooking—or anything domestic really. I can guarantee that just went straight over her head."

Laura shrugged. "I get that you're talking about fancy kitchen gadgets. And I won't embarrass my mom by reassuring you that they weren't the reason she was dreamy-eyed."

Marianne could feel the color in her cheeks, but Clay tightened his arm around her shoulders. "That makes me happy."

The door from the back opened and Maria came out. "I'm back. Do you want— Oh! Hi, Marianne." She nodded at Clay. "Mr. McAdam. I'm sorry. I didn't know."

"You're fine," said Marianne. She liked Maria. She was a good girl. Marianne knew her family back in Texas. She'd been the one who suggested that Laura should hire her. "It's lovely to see you."

"You, too." She turned to Laura. "Do you want me to take over? I can take care of the place and close up tonight, if you want to go?"

"Thanks. But they only dropped in to say hi."

Marianne nodded. "We did and we're leaving now."

"Would you and Smoke like to come over one evening?" asked Clay.

Marianne's heart sank. He was only going to be here for three evenings and she'd been hoping that she would have him all to herself. Laura looked at her before she answered. She understood.

"I mean when I come back. I have a full schedule this week," Clay added.

Laura smiled. "We'd love to. You and Mom figure out when works for you and let me know."

"We will."

A warm feeling washed through Marianne's chest when he said that; *we*. She liked thinking of them as a *we*. Even when she was married, she hadn't felt like she was part of a *we*.

Clay looked down at her when they were back out on the street. "She's a credit to you."

Marianne nodded. "She is. She's my greatest achievement in life. Don't get me wrong. I'm not trying to take the credit for all that she's achieved—that's down to her. But I am proud of the way I raised her to be her own person and to trust her judgment."

"And you have every right to be."

"Thank you. Didn't you ever want children?"

He shook his head sadly. "I did. But I was never in a situation where that was going to happen."

"I'm sorry."

"I am, too. But we all make choices in life. I chose to pursue another kind of love. My love of country music. I can't complain about the way it's treated me."

"No. You've certainly done well with it."

He smiled. "I love it. And I have to admit, there are songs I need to write soon. Songs about you, songs about us."

Her heart thundered in her chest; she didn't know what to think, or what to say. If someone had told her even a week ago that Clay McAdam would want to write a song about her, she would have laughed at the idea. Now, she couldn't wait to hear how it would go.

The next few days flew by. As Clay sat sipping his coffee on the dock on Thursday morning, he couldn't believe that he had to leave this afternoon. The time had gone by so quickly. He smiled as he stared out at the lake. He didn't want to go back. He wanted to stay here and get on with the life he'd started to build. He loved Summer Lake. It was the perfect small town as far as he was concerned. Everyone seemed to know each other—but more than that everyone seemed to care about each other. Plenty of people seemed to recognize him when he and Marianne had been out and about, but no one had bothered them. No one had even asked for an autograph. A couple of people Marianne knew had thanked him for deciding to stay here—not because of him, but because they were so pleased about what it meant for Angel and Luke. News of their engagement had spread fast. He wanted to do something for them, maybe lay on an engagement party, but he wanted to talk to Luke first. He'd get the chance to do that this afternoon since Luke and Zack were flying him back to Nashville. He checked his watch. He was meeting Marianne at the Boathouse for brunch and then they planned to take a walk before Adam drove him out to the airport where the jet would be waiting at 1:00 p.m. to take him back.

Main Street was much busier today than it had been on Sunday. He loved seeing the small town thrive. There were all kinds of quaint little stores and he noticed something for the first time—there wasn't a chain store or franchise in sight. A familiar looking blonde walking down the sidewalk caught his eye and he frowned, trying to place her.

Adam shot him a sideways glance and made a disapproving noise, making him laugh.

"Hey! I'm not looking, looking. You know me better than that. Younger women have never done it for me."

Adam pursed his lips. "I'm not saying you'd do anything, but you have to admit that bartender is a looker."

"Ah! She's the bartender at the Boathouse. I knew I'd seen her somewhere."

Adam nodded. "Kenzie, that's her name. She's a real firecracker, that one."

Clay smiled. "What, you know her? Spent some time at the bar talking to her, have you? Is that why me looking bothered you?"

"No." He sounded indignant. "I'm not such an old fart as you are, but she's a bit young for me, too. I've hung out chatting with her—and with her husband. He's part of the band at the resort. They only sing weekends during the off-season, but apparently, you're his idol. The band's good, too, by all accounts. Well, it's just a duet now. You know, if you could go listen to them one weekend when you're here ..."

Clay had to smile. Young musicians were always trying to get his attention. Adam was usually efficient—and cold—about keeping them away. "You're putting in a good word for them?"

Adam shrugged. "I guess I am. I haven't heard them, but I don't know. Chase, that's his name, he's a really good guy. He tried to be all cool and blasé and not give away that he was as excited as a little kid. But it was obvious. He was more concerned that you should be left in peace and be able to enjoy yourself here without the usual frenzy that surrounds you."

Clay nodded. He appreciated that, even though he'd never met the kid. "Okay. I'll ask if Marianne wants to come listen to them one night."

Adam chuckled. "She does. She loves them. It sounds like she's a kind of *favorite aunt* character to half the kids around here. But she's the same. She'd never suggest you should come see them either."

It felt good to be surrounded by people who wanted him to be able to live as normal a life as possible. There was no one who wanted to take advantage of what he could possibly do for them. That made a pleasant change.

Marianne held tight to Clay's hand as they walked back up the beach. This week had been wonderful. They'd had so much fun together. They'd talked and they'd laughed and cried a little, too, over people they'd lost. She felt like she knew him better than she'd known any man in her life. Though, that in itself was a little scary. How could she know him after such a short time? Her heart knew the truth. It was because they'd gone into this consciously, having decided that they wanted to be open and honest with each other. To explore and to find out if the bolt of lightning feeling they'd had in the beginning was founded in anything real. So far, it seemed that it was.

He stopped walking and tugged on her hand. She smiled as she looked up into his eyes. It seemed that they twinkled all the time—or maybe it was whenever he looked at her.

"I want you to come with me."

Her heart raced in her chest. She didn't want him to leave. She wasn't looking forward to not seeing him every day. "We already talked about that." She didn't want him to leave, but it wouldn't be right for her to go with him. She wasn't ready to step into his life there. Here, it was simple. They could hide away at his house, walk the beach, wander around town, eat at the Boathouse, and no one would bother them. She knew it would be very, very different in Nashville. She'd been able to put her life on hold for a few days. He wouldn't be able to do that. "I'm going to miss you, but I don't want to go to Nashville."

The twinkle disappeared from his eyes, and she knew what he was thinking.

"I don't mean ever; I just mean not yet. There's no hurry. You have work to do. So, do I. I need to catch up with my life. I'll miss you, but I do have other things I need to get on with, as well."

He leaned down and brushed his lips over hers. "I know. You're right. We already agreed." He smiled. "But I still wish you could come."

"Me, too. But I'll see you next time you're here."

"I'll be back by next weekend. And I'll stay for as long as I can."

She smiled. "I hope that's a long time. But you know I'm okay with however long you can spare."

He narrowed his eyes and tried to look stern. "We already discussed that, too. I'm giving the time I can spare to Nashville. This is where I want to be. Here, with you. I'll go back when I have to, but no more than I have to." He closed his arms around her and held her against his chest.

She could feel his heart beating in time with her own as she clung to him. This felt like the beginning for them, but that little voice in her head reminded her that it could just as easily be the end.

As if he sensed her thoughts, he kissed the top of her head. "I'm coming back to you, Marianne. Don't ever doubt it."

Chapter Ten

It was raining as the plane came in to land back in Nashville. Even though Clay wished he was still in Summer Lake, he still felt the old familiar warmth to be back in this town. It was quite a city these days, but to him it would always be his town. He'd come here like thousands of others had and he knew just how lucky he was to be one of its success stories.

"Welcome home," Zack's voice came through the speaker. "The tower just told us we're going to have to wait a few minutes while a 747 takes off on runway 2L, but we're still a little ahead of schedule. Autumn's already here waiting for you."

"Okay, thanks, Zack." He turned to Adam. "I thought you were taking me home?"

Adam shrugged. "So did I." His phone beeped and he checked the screen. "But apparently, Autumn is taking you over to Lawrence's and Davin is meeting me in the Suburban, and we're going to follow."

Clay blew out a sigh. "Sometimes I feel like a package being shunted around. I'm pretty sure I'm a functioning adult, though. I prefer making my decisions for myself."

Adam smirked at him. "You can't blame me this time, boss. And if you're going to try to argue with Autumn, let me know. I'd like to watch."

Clay had to chuckle. Autumn tended to take a direct approach to getting what she wanted—forceful even at times. She wouldn't cross him intentionally, but sometimes she outmaneuvered him. "Not today. I choose my battles." He frowned. "But if she thinks she can dictate how much time I need to spend here ..."

Adam laughed. "I think you're safe there. She might be a little pushy but remember she's the one who set you and Marianne up. I think tonight might be about making the most efficient use of your time here. Lawrence and Shawnee want to see you. Matt needs to talk to you. Carson could do with a little encouragement from his mentor."

"And they're all going to be there?"

"That's what her text says."

Clay blew out a sigh. "Okay. At least I know what I'm in for. I want to talk to them anyway. I need to do some writing while I'm here."

Adam smiled. "Let me guess. You're going into ballad and love song territory?"

Clay shrugged. He didn't want to admit it, but that was exactly where he was going.

Autumn whisked him away to the limo as soon as they got into the terminal. Adam looked put out that he had to wait for Davin, but he was another one who didn't like to argue with Autumn unless it was completely necessary. He'd joked with Clay before that Autumn would probably protect him more ferociously than he ever could anyway. Clay was inclined to agree with him.

"So, how was it?" she asked as Carson pulled the limo away from the curb in the pick-up area.

"It was great. I didn't want to leave."

She smiled and patted his arm. "That's wonderful. I'm happy for you Clay, really, I am."

"Good, because I'm going to be spending a lot more time there."

"And I'm happy to hear it. I've been working on some scheduling. I think I can get out there a couple of times a month, even for just a day or two. That'll save you some trips back here, though of course not all of them. I know it'll work for Luke, too and from what I can gather, Zack also has reason to want to be at the lake."

Clay remembered Zack talking about a woman, a friend, who sounded like she could be something more than that. "Great, so everybody wins, and nobody is going to be too inconvenienced?"

Autumn nodded. "Almost everyone. Matt's whining, as usual, but he can deal with it."

Clay had to laugh. "When are you going to give the poor guy a chance?"

"Pft! You already know my answer to that one, so drop it. I'm more interested in talking about a tour for Carson."

"I think it's a great idea. What do you need from me?"

"You just gave me all I need for now. If you think he's ready, then I'll make it happen."

"Great. You know you don't really need me at all anymore. You can handle it all. Any decisions like this—you know he's ready. You don't need my go ahead."

When she turned to him, her gentle smile reminded Clay that she wasn't as tough as she made out. "This wouldn't be nearly as enjoyable if it were only about me, Clay. The thing I love most about my job is that I'm running the label for you. You're right. I don't need you to hold my hand, or reassure me, but I do like to feel that we're in this together."

He smiled back. "And we are, Autumn. I love that I can relax knowing everything is in your hands." He held her gaze for a moment, wanting her to understand. He loved her and Summer like they were his own. Summer told him she loved him all the time. That wasn't Autumn's way, but he hoped she knew how much he loved her.

She nodded briefly and then pulled her phone out. "The CMA people need you to confirm by the end of the week. And I emailed you the notes about your interview tomorrow."

"I know. I've seen them."

As she rattled off a list of appointments and questions, he smiled to himself. She might not want to say the words, or to hear him speak them, but this was her way of showing love.

~ ~ ~

"Don't you dare tell me you're not coming."

Marianne laughed. "Chris, I've been out every night for a week. I want to stay home and put my feet up."

"And you can. On Saturday night. Tomorrow you're coming out with me. Bear in mind that I haven't been out in a week and I haven't seen you. I need to hear all about it."

"And I'm looking forward to telling you. Can't you come over here? I'll cook for you." Even as she said it, Marianne made a face at the thought of having to cook in her own little kitchen. She'd been spoiled at Clay's house.

"Don't try to bribe me with your cooking. I want to go out. You know I like listening to the band, and it's quieter at the moment, so we can chat with Kenzie—she's such a hoot."

Marianne sighed. "Okay. I'll go. But I'm not staying out late."

"Don't tell me you want to get home to wait for a call from Clay?"

"No. Don't be silly." She didn't want to admit that she'd probably call him before she went out. He was two hours ahead of her, so it'd be too late when she got home.

"Do you want me to pick you up?"

"Okay. But don't come early."

Chris laughed. "I can't help being punctual any more than you can help being late."

"I know. But if you come early you have to wait without complaining."

"I promise."

~ ~ ~

Clay spent the morning in the office. There was a lot to catch up on. Autumn might run the place, but he still had his work cut out for him with things only he could deal with.

"Knock, knock."

He smiled at Matt, who was standing in the doorway. "Can you spare a minute?"

"Sure. For you, any time."

"Thanks."

Matt came in and sat sideways in the armchair in the corner, swinging his legs up over the side.

Clay chuckled. "Please. Make yourself at home."

Matt grinned. "I am at home, here, with you … and Autumn."

Clay raised an eyebrow, wondering where he was going. "Do I sense a *but* coming?"

"No. No *but*, more of an *and*."

"And what?"

"And I want to know if there's anything more I can do to help out around here. Autumn's always crazy busy. You are, too, and now that you're going to be spending less time here, I just, well, I wondered if there's any slack I can pick up to help out. You've done so much for me. I'd like to be able to do something for you."

Clay smiled. Matt was a good kid. He'd had his wild years, and he'd settled down a lot recently. He'd matured, both as an artist and as a man.

"Thanks. I don't know off the top of my head. But I can tell you that I'm going to be going through my workload this weekend and figuring out how to lighten it. If there's anything I can offload onto you, I'll be happy to."

Matt grinned. "Thanks, Clay. I won't let you down."

"I don't expect you to. It'll mean you'll have to work more closely with Autumn."

Matt blew out a sigh. "We both know that's not true. It'll mean I have to take more orders, more criticism and deal with her anger more often." His smile returned. "But it'll still be worth it."

Clay laughed. "What, worth it because you're helping me out, or worth it because you'll get to spend more time with her?"

"Both."

They looked up to see Autumn standing in the doorway. She moved in stealth mode sometimes. Clay had the feeling that she might have been standing there long enough to have heard some of what Matt said. He'd swear there was the hint of a smile on her face. He hoped with all his heart that one day she'd soften up and admit to herself that she liked Matt just as much as he liked her.

~ ~ ~

Marianne wondered if coming out tonight hadn't been a mistake. Kenzie beamed at her when she and Chris approached the bar.

"Good evening, ladies. What can I get you? This first one is on me. I want to buy a drink for the woman who managed to snag herself Clay McAdam."

Marianne dropped her gaze. She hadn't considered that she might have to deal with anything like this. Chris came to her rescue, just as she'd done since they were kids.

"Thanks, Kenzie. But I'm buying my sister a drink. And you know better than to think there'll be any kissing and telling from her."

"Oh, my God! No! I didn't mean that at all." She reached across the bar and squeezed Marianne's arm. I'm sorry, sugar. I didn't mean that at all. I'm just so happy for you. And come on, I have to be honest—I'm a teeny bit jealous. I was going to say don't tell Chase that, but he already knows." She laughed. "He's probably as jealous as I am. You know Clay's his idol, right? I wasn't looking for you to tell anything about him. I'm just happy for you. And I'm happy for him. I've always loved his music and it always seemed sad to me that he didn't have a woman. I mean. Lawrence and Shawnee, they've been the on again, off again soap opera of country. But Clay? I mean, you saw in the papers if he dated someone, but there was never anything that looked like it was going anywhere. Till now. Till you."

Marianne's heart sank. She hadn't thought about it. It was true that whenever Clay was dating, it showed up in the magazines and on TV. She didn't like the idea that that might happen to her.

Chris shook her head. "You can deal with that if it happens. If you ask me, a bit of press coverage is a small price to pay."

She nodded. "I suppose. But I think I'd like to make that drink a double."

Kenzie laughed. "Coming right up."

She swiveled her barstool around, so she could look at the stage where Kenzie's husband, Chase and his band mate Eddie were getting ready to start their set. She'd have to introduce them to Clay. She knew how much they'd love that.

"Mom." She turned back around, surprised to see Laura and Smoke standing there.

"Oh, hi, darling. I didn't know you were coming out tonight."

"Neither did I," said Smoke with a scowl.

Laura laughed. "We're not stopping. Maria left some things in the store and I said I'd meet her here to give them back. How are you, anyway? I thought you were having a quiet weekend after your big week."

"So, did I." Marianne winked at Smoke. It seemed the two of them often got roped into Chris and Laura's plans when all they really wanted was a quiet night. He smirked back at her. He knew what she meant.

"What she means is that I dragged her out because I wanted to see the band," said Chris.

Laura laughed. "And what you mean is that you dragged her out because you want to hear all about it. Well, so do I." She looked at Marianne expectantly.

"It was wonderful. That's all I'm going to say."

"Good for you," said Smoke. "But don't forget, we're coming over there when he gets back."

She laughed. "I can assure you his intentions are honorable."

"Maybe a little too honorable," said Chris. "She was home by herself every night."

Marianne rolled her eyes. "That's none of your business. Or anyone else's for that matter."

Chris laughed. "Sorry. I'm just shocked."

Smoke shook his head. "I want to say I'm glad to hear it, but I think what I'd rather do is unhear it. I don't want to be a part of this conversation."

"Well, that's okay, because it's over." Marianne gave Chris a pointed look. She might tell her more later about what had happened between her and Clay, but if she carried on like that, she might not, too.

"Sorry." Chris hung her head in mock shame, but Marianne knew she wasn't sorry at all.

"Oof!" Her breath came out in a rush as someone banged hard into the back of her. She spilled her drink all over Chris and barely managed to not fall off the stool.

She turned around to see what had happened and was greeted by a very angry face. She'd expected an apology but the look she got was venomous. "I'm sorry." She bit down on her tongue. She hated that she automatically apologized to people, even when she'd done nothing wrong and they clearly had.

"You need to watch yourself." The woman spat the words at her and then turned and stalked away.

Marianne turned back to the others, speechless.

"What the fuck? Are you okay?" asked Kenzie, who had seen the whole thing. She handed Chris a bar towel to mop herself up and glared after the woman.

"I wouldn't have put it quite like that, but yes." Marianne made herself smile. It was just an accident, and some people were naturally unfriendly. She'd rather forget about it.

"I don't like that woman." Kenzie was still glaring at her as she took a seat by herself in one of the booths. "She's been here all week. I'll be glad when she goes back to wherever she came from and takes her bad attitude with her."

Smoke was frowning at the woman as well. "Has she done something like that to anyone else, Kenz?"

"No. She's been rude and mean to just about everyone who works here, but she's avoided the other guests."

"What are you thinking?" Laura asked Smoke.

He shook his head and smiled at Marianne. "Nothing. I guess you were just unlucky."

Marianne nodded. "I seem to have had a whole bunch of good luck lately. I'm certainly not going to let that little incident spoil it."

Chris slid down from her seat. "That's right, sis. Nothing's going to spoil our fun. I'll just go clean myself up and I'll be right back."

Marianne watched her make her way to the bathroom. Then shot another look at the woman who'd bumped into her so hard. She caught her breath as the woman glared back at her. She was pretty, blonde and heavyset, but there was no warmth to her. Marianne looked away quickly. Those evil eyes gave her chills.

Chapter Eleven

Marianne took her glasses off and set them down on her work desk. She was surprised at the time when she looked up at the clock. Somehow the whole morning had flown by while she worked on her jewelry. Well, her trinkets. What Laura made was real jewelry. This was just Marianne's hobby. It had been a nice little earner of a hobby for the last few years, but it was only a hobby. She was under no illusions that what she did was anything special, but there were people out there who liked the little earrings and bracelets she made. She used to sell them at craft fairs when she was still in Texas. Since she'd moved here, Chris' grandson, Scot, had set up an online store for her on a big craft site. She didn't understand any of it—other than the fact that she got an email when she got an order, and she got as many of them as she could handle.

She'd had an order for three bracelets come in yesterday, and now they were ready to go. She'd take a walk into town to the post office and mail them out after she had some lunch. She was glad she'd had work to keep her busy this morning. Clay was coming back tonight, and she was excited—more excited than it was reasonable to be at her age. Or then again, maybe not. Why did she always let that little voice put a damper on things for her? She wasn't going to let it. She shook her head determinedly as she pulled out three little boxes to put the bracelets in.

She had every right to be excited. She and Clay had talked on the phone every day, and he sent her texts now and then, telling her he was thinking of her and that he couldn't wait to come back to her. So far, she'd waited for him to text her. She didn't like to interrupt him—didn't want to make his phone beep if he was in the middle of a meeting. She looked up at the clock again. He'd said he'd be back late afternoon or early evening and that he'd call when he landed.

He'd invited her to go over to his house for dinner. A shiver ran down her spine as she wondered whether she might stay there this time. He wanted to take it slowly, so, did she. But she had no idea how long that might take. She smiled to herself as she packaged the bracelets up in a priority envelope. She'd thought they were taking it slowly when she hadn't spent that first night with him at the lodge. Last week, there had been a few moments when they'd gotten carried away and she'd hoped that he'd give in. He hadn't, though. He had a great deal of will power. She was sure that if they were both younger, they'd have gotten carried away before now. But that was kind of the point, too. They were both old enough and wise enough to take their time. Still, she wouldn't mind if he didn't want to wait any longer.

The weather was much milder today, she'd worn her jacket, but she didn't need it as she walked into town. The sun shone brightly and the last of the gold and orange leaves swirled in the breeze.

"Good morning to you." Lenny, the older woman who ran the post office greeted her with a smile. "I'm glad you only have the one today." She jerked her head at the envelope in Marianne's hand. "You only just caught me. I'm going for lunch in a minute."

"Oh, sorry." Marianne had forgotten that Lenny closed down at lunchtime.

Lenny laughed. "There's nothing to apologize for. I said I'm happy that you only have one envelope, and I'm happy that you made it in time. You need to stop that, you know."

Marianne wanted to ask, stop what? But she already knew. It was bad habit of hers to apologize even when she'd done nothing wrong. It was so much of a habit that she had to bite her lip to stop herself from saying sorry again.

Lenny winked at her. "You can do it. And from what I hear around town you need to stop being so weedy anyway. If you're going to keep seeing that Clay McAdam, you're going to have to stand up for yourself."

Marianne cocked her head to one side, not understanding.

"I don't mean against him. He strikes me as one of life's good guys. I mean against the reporters and all his jealous fans."

"Ah. I see what you mean. But I'm hoping I'll be able to avoid them all—reporters and fans alike. There don't tend to be too many of them around here, so I think we're safe."

Lenny pursed her lips as she tapped the package details in. "There might not be many yet, but the more time he spends here, the more of them there'll be. You mark my words. There was a reporter in here the other week, when he was having his big party."

"I would have thought they'd be all digital these days."

"Oh, I think they are. This one was mailing postcards— because Summer Lake is just so damn adorable, apparently."

Marianne had to laugh at the look of disdain on the older woman's face. "You've lived here all your life, Lenny. This place really is beautiful."

"That may be, but she made it sound like the whole place was made of gingerbread and straight from the pages of a fairytale."

Marianne laughed. "Don't be too hard on her, it's a magical place."

Lenny shrugged. "Never mind me. I shouldn't be such a sour puss. The reporter was nice enough, if a little over the top with her praise. I'd be more concerned about the jealous fans, if I were you. There was one woman came in, said she wanted to rent a PO Box. She wanted to see a list of all the boxes we have. She was after finding out if Clay McAdam had one. She was none too bright that one. I think she thought she'd be able to see the list of all the boxes and which belonged to who. She was put out when I told her it don't work that way."

"Why would she think Clay would have a PO Box here? That's odd. I mean if she was here because of his party, Clay didn't even know he was going to be staying at that point."

"No. This was after. Must have been midweek last week. She was a real piece of work. I hope she's left by now."

Marianne did, too. She didn't want some creepy fan hanging around. It bothered her, though. How could she have known that Clay had stayed here—that he hadn't left with the others?

"You all right?" asked Lenny.

"Yeah, sorry. I'm fine." She handed over a ten-dollar bill.

Lenny shook her head. "You're going to have to work on that. You should practice banning the word sorry from your vocabulary for a week."

Marianne smiled. "I'll try. I'll let you know how I'm doing the next time I come in."

Clay grasped Luke's shoulder as they walked across the tarmac to the FBO building at Summer Lake airport. The last meeting he'd had scheduled this morning had cancelled, and he'd decided to come back early. They'd landed a couple of hours earlier than he'd planned, but he sure wasn't going to complain about that.

"It's good to be back, huh, kid?"

Luke grinned at him. "It sure is. You know I'm rooting for things to turn out great for you and Marianne."

Clay chuckled. "Oh, I know it. You wouldn't mind if I moved here permanently, would you?"

Luke shrugged. "You know my answer to that. This is where Angel is, so it's where I want to be. All I can do is make the most of whatever time we get to be here."

Clay nodded. "I know. And like I told you, I don't plan to go anywhere or even think about doing anything before next Monday. Well, I don't plan to go anywhere then either, but you and Zack will have to get back to Nashville for April and Matt."

"I know. And don't get me wrong. I love that, too. I took the job with you because I want to fly. It'd be great to be able to spend more time with Angel than I expected, but I still love to fly."

"And so I'm trying to work out the best of both worlds."

Luke shot him a grateful smile. "Thanks."

Adam, Davin and Zack met them out in the parking lot. They'd brought Clay's bags around on one of the golf carts and Adam was loading them into the back of the same SUV they'd rented when they were here last week.

Luke and Zack both came to shake Clay's hand. He'd had Adam rent two vehicles for them this time.

"I know what he's doing, but what are you going to do with yourself until Monday?" he asked Zack.

Zack grinned. "Not a lot. I'll be catching up with old friends and hanging out, I guess. He looked over at the rental cars. It was decent of you to do that, but I brought my truck back here when I realized that we're still going to be spending time here."

"Okay but keep it if you want it." Clay felt bad that both pilots had given up their apartments here when they came to Nashville to work for him. Luke wasn't worried. He'd been about to move in with Angel anyway, but he still didn't know what Zack's situation was.

"Let's get going," said Adam.

Clay raised an eyebrow at him. "Are you the one who gives the orders these days?"

Adam made a face at him. "Only if you want me to fit in everything that's on your list for this afternoon."

Clay smirked at him. "Sir, yes, sir!" He turned about and winked at Luke and Zack before he climbed into the passenger seat of the SUV.

"Are you sure you don't want to call Marianne first?" Adam asked as he pulled out the parking lot.

"No. I want to surprise her." Clay smiled to himself. He'd told her he wouldn't be here until late afternoon. He was hoping that she'd be as happy as he was that he'd managed to get here earlier.

"Okay then."

He frowned at Adam. "What's the problem? You don't think she'll be happy to see me?"

"No. Of course she will. It's not that. It's just that …"

"What?" Clay couldn't even guess what his problem might be.

"Well, she's never invited you over to her place, has she? If it weren't for me, you wouldn't be able to find it even. I feel like I'm betraying her trust by taking you there."

"Betraying her trust? What, she trusts you not to bring me to her house?"

Adam let out a short laugh. "No. It's just, well, you know what she's like. She sees a big difference between where you're at financially and where she is. She's made enough excuses to me about her *small, modest house, that really isn't much, but is all she needs,* that I know she feels a little embarrassed maybe? It's none of my business, I know. But I don't want her being caught unexpectedly in her little house, and I don't want you messing up and getting this week off to the wrong start."

Clay sucked in a deep breath and let it out slowly. "Thanks, Adam. I guess, in my eagerness to see her I didn't think about any of that."

"And that's understandable. I might be saying too much and interfering where I shouldn't."

"No. You're looking out for her—and for me, and I appreciate that."

"So, what do you think? Should I take you to the house first?"

Clay shook his head. Adam might have a point, but if Marianne was uncomfortable about him seeing her home, then he believed that they should get it over with sooner rather than later. It didn't need to be an issue, and like so many things it wouldn't be if they just dived right in and dealt with it. "No." He fished his cellphone out of his pocket and started to dial her number, then thought better of it. "No. I'm just going to land on her doorstep and hope that makes her happy enough to not worry about the rest."

~ ~ ~

Marianne put the vacuum cleaner back in the closet and breathed a sigh of relief. Cleaning wasn't her favorite pastime, but she always felt better when it was done. It'd been important to her to get it all finished up today, because she didn't know how much time she'd be spending here over the next few days. She was hoping that she'd be at Clay's, or out and about with him.

She frowned, remembering her conversation with Lenny at the post office earlier. All she could do was hope that Lenny was wrong; that reporters and fans wouldn't start coming up to the lake to find him. She wanted him all to herself and those were the last kinds of people she wanted intruding on their little bubble.

She looked up at the sound of a car pulling up in the driveway. It was Adam, she knew it was. She'd grown used to that sound last week. She'd listened out for it every evening when he came to pick her up to take her over to the lake house. She went into the front room and stopped when she saw the SUV—and Clay getting out of it. Her heart started to race and she looked around wildly. She didn't want him to see the place. At least everywhere was clean and tidy, since she'd just got done cleaning.

She closed her eyes and drew in a deep breath. She was being ridiculous. He wasn't here to see the state of her house. He was here to see her—and he was early! Once she was over her initial, irrational panic, her heartbeat soared again—thrilled that he was here. She rushed to the front door and greeted him with a smile.

His hand was raised, about to press the doorbell. He grinned at the sight of her. "Hey, darlin'."

"Clay!" She stepped toward him and he closed his arms around her. She wanted to melt into his warm embrace. She leaned against him and looked up into his eyes. He brushed his lips over hers.

"I missed you."

"I missed you, too. I didn't expect you until later. I'm not ready, I ..." She looked down at herself, realizing for the first time that she was still in her scruffs, her hair tied up in a ponytail with wisps escaping around her face. "I'm a mess."

He chuckled, the low deep rumble that reverberated through her and did strange things to her insides. "You're the most beautiful mess I've ever seen." He reached up and touched her cheek. "You're gorgeous."

She held his gaze. "You're the gorgeous one."

He shook his head. "I'm just lucky that you're attracted to the grizzly old bear look."

She laughed. "You're no grizzly, and we both know I'm not the only one who finds you attractive. I have millions of women who agree with me about just how gorgeous you are."

"There's only one woman whose opinion matters to me, and that's you." He looked over his shoulder and they both watched a couple of kids coming down the street.

She might not be thrilled at the idea of showing him her house, but it was preferable to keeping him out here, kissing on the doorstep in full view of the neighbors. She took hold of his hand and drew him inside, closing the door after them.

He leaned back against the wall in the hallway and winked at her. "I like it. And what are you going to do with me now?"

She laughed, half embarrassed, half wishing she could take him upstairs and show him what she'd like to do with him. "I was trying to save your reputation. There were people coming out there."

He let his gaze travel slowly over her. "Would it harm your reputation if there were people coming in here?"

Her tummy flipped over, and an electric current zapped through her. Her nipples tingled as he let his gaze linger on her breasts. This was new. Last week he'd only talked about how they shouldn't get physical yet, now his eyes and his words were telling her that he wanted to. She chewed on her bottom lip. She didn't know what to say, but she needn't have worried. No words were necessary as he drew her to him. He was watching the way she was chewing her lip and moistened his with his tongue before he lowered his head to her. "I'm not going to be able to hold back so much this time, Marianne," he murmured as his lips came down on hers.

He wasn't joking either. There was no hesitancy about this kiss, he claimed her mouth and kissed her deeply. His hands ran down her back and closed around her ass, making her moan. He held her against his erection and she couldn't help it, she rubbed herself against him, wanting more—so much more.

When he finally lifted his head, he looked down into her eyes. "I couldn't stop thinking about you the whole time I was gone."

She nodded.

"I couldn't stop thinking about what I want to do with you."

She nodded again. Her mind was flitting randomly, unable to process the strength of the desire that was coursing through her veins. A few moments ago she'd been worried about what he might think of her house—now all she could think about was whether she could resist taking him to her bed right this minute.

He made the decision for her when he straightened up. "Do you want to bring an overnight bag?"

She nodded. "Give me a few minutes?"

He smiled and dropped a kiss on top of her head. "I'll give you all the time you need."

Chapter Twelve

Clay poured them each a glass of merlot and took them back through to the living room. Marianne was standing in front of the windows, looking out at the lake. He gave her a glass and rested his hand on her shoulder.

"Are you okay?"

His heart buzzed in his chest when she smiled up at him with those beautiful blue eyes. "I'm more than okay. I'm wonderful."

"I'd have to agree with that. You are wonderful."

She dropped her gaze. "Thank you."

"Would I be right if I guessed that you don't like compliments?"

She looked up at him again. "I suppose. It's probably more that I'm not used to getting them."

He shook his head. "Well, you'd better get used to it. You're a beautiful woman, Marianne." He couldn't resist letting his gaze wander over her for a moment, but he forced himself to stop so he could look into her eyes. "You're beautiful, and you're warm and kind. You're everything I could want in a woman, and I want you." He'd meant that he wanted her in his life, that he wanted to be with her, but the way the words came out belied that fact that he wanted her. He wanted her now.

There was no mistaking the desire in her eyes as she looked back at him. "I want you, Clay."

He sucked in a deep breath. How long had he intended to wait? He didn't know. He couldn't remember. All he knew was that they'd waited long enough. Waiting any longer would be wrong. He wanted this to happen only when it felt natural, and right now it felt like the most natural thing on earth to take her hand and lead her up the stairs to his bedroom.

He closed the door behind them, took the glass from her hand and set it down on the dresser then came back and put his hands on her shoulders. "Are you sure?"

She nodded breathlessly. "I've never been more sure of anything in my life, Clay. I want you to make love to me."

Hearing her say it made him ache even more for her. He cupped her face between his hands and kissed her deeply. She made needy little noises as she kissed him back. Noises that turned him on so much he wanted to throw her down on the bed, push up her skirt and give it to her deep and hard right this minute. He forced himself to take it slowly, letting his hands roam over her while he kissed her.

It seemed she too was impatient. Her fingers fumbled with the buttons on his shirt. She managed to unfasten them all and push the shirt off his shoulders without breaking the kiss.

He stepped back with a smile. "Now, see, that's not fair. He shrugged out of the shirt and enjoyed watching her face as she looked him over. He stayed in good shape, and her eyes told him she appreciated it.

He brushed two fingers over her lips and then trailed them down over her chin, down her throat and let them rest between her breasts. Her breath was coming slowly as she watched him unbutton her blouse and take it off. She was in good shape, too. He couldn't take his eyes off her bra. It wasn't anything lacy or silky, it was simple, white, cotton, and it turned him on more than any bra he'd seen before.

She didn't wait for him. She reached behind her and unhooked it, then let the straps fall down and took it off. His hands reached out of their own volition and closed around her breasts. Her pale skin looked so delicate, her dark nipples so inviting.

She moaned as he teased them with his thumbs, then sank her fingers in his hair when he dropped his head to taste them each in turn. Her nipples responded to him eagerly, standing as taut peaks, hard under his tongue. He was hard, too, and he didn't want to wait a minute longer. He walked her back to the bed until her legs hit it and she sat down. He made short work of getting rid of his jeans, and she sat and watched, wide eyed.

When he stood before her in his boxer shorts, Marianne had a crazy urge to reach out and touch him, to close her fingers around him and bring him to her mouth. She bit her lip, he might love that—it might surprise the hell out of him. Instead she crawled up the bed till she was sitting back against the pillows. He could come to her—he should lead the way, this first time at least. Hopefully there would be plenty more times when she'd be able to rediscover her adventurous side.

He smiled at her and pushed his boxers down. She bit her lip at the sight of him—standing tall. She could feel the heat pooling between her legs in anticipation of him arriving there. Except, he couldn't get directly there. She still had her panties on—she still had her skirt on! Darn, she wasn't a very good seductress, was she? The fact that she hadn't had much practice in years didn't feel like much consolation.

He came to sit beside her and looked into her eyes. "Are you still sure?"

She had to laugh. "I'm sure I want you, but I'm also sure I'm messing this up. You're all ready to go, and I'm still half dressed."

He chuckled and the sound of it reverberated through her in the way that had already become familiar—except this time the reverberations all seemed to settle between her legs. "Don't you worry your head about that, darlin'. I can take care of that." He kneeled between her legs and pushed her skirt up around her waist. She sighed when he caressed her inner thighs with his big, surprisingly rough hands. He slipped one finger inside the leg of her panties and she clenched in anticipation.

"Maybe you're all ready, too?"

She nodded; to her surprise, she was wet and ready. He ran his finger over her entrance and she wished he'd get rid of the panties and replace his finger with his cock.

Instead, he lowered his head and mouthed her through the thin cotton.

"Clay!" she gasped.

His tongue sought her opening and pushed at it, then he pulled the panties aside and tasted her. She closed her eyes and grabbed two fistfuls of sheet. His tongue dipped inside her, making her moan. She wasn't going to be able to take much of this. To her relief he stopped, but the relief was short lived as he sucked on her clit and flames of white heat seared through her.

"Clay! Please! I want … I want …You!" Maybe one day she'd be brave enough to tell him that she wanted to feel his cock deep inside her.

He understood and lifted his head to smile at her. "Soon, darlin." He lowered his head one more time and this time his fingers rested at her entrance as his tongue swirled over her. She floated higher and higher as the pleasure mounted inside her, then she screamed his name as he thrust his finger deep inside her and she let go. He worked her mercilessly as her orgasm carried her away. She hadn't been sure if she could still come like that, but the floodgates had opened and a tidal wave of pleasure crashed through her.

When she was finally spent, he withdrew his hand and came up to kiss her lips. She could taste herself on him, and that sent an aftershock through her. He cupped her breast in his hand. "Are you warmed up?"

"Overheated more like! That was amazing, Clay."

He smiled. "That was just the opener." He took hold of her hand and brought it down to touch him. He was so hard, so hot, her breath caught in her chest at the thought that soon he would be inside her. "Do you want this?"

She nodded, her breath shallow and her mind a little hazy. "I should take off my panties."

He shook his head. "I like them on." He kneeled between her legs and looked down at her, bunching her skirt around her waist. "I like feeling as though we couldn't even wait to get you properly undressed."

She nodded and swallowed hard as he caressed her breast with one hand. His hardened fingertips were deliciously rough against her delicate skin. He took hold of himself with his other hand and she reached up to close her fingers around him, stroking the length of him. Her breath was ragged now; she wanted him so badly. He understood what she wanted, as he did so often, and lowered himself to her. He hooked his fingers inside her panties, pulling them to the side so that the tip of him could nudge inside her.

He held her gaze and she nodded, needing him to … and he did. He thrust his hips hard and they both gasped as he buried himself inside her. "Marianne," he breathed. "My Marianne."

Her heart felt as though it might burst out of her chest hearing him say that. She'd always loved being in his presence, now she was surrounded by his presence, but he was inside her, too. He moved slowly at first and she was grateful. He was big. He filled her and stretched her as he moved, drawing back, pushing deeper, his hips pumping against hers. She moved with him, welcoming him inside her. A crazy thought flitted through her mind that she was welcoming him home.

She brought her arms up around his back and clung to him. He felt like her home—the one she'd been searching for all her life.

He looked down into her eyes as he thrust deeper and deeper and she held his gaze, feeling as though the conversation their eyes were having backed up the one their bodies were having. They were giving themselves to each other, claiming each other as their own as they moved. He slid his hand in between them and rested his thumb against her clit, increasing the pressure in just the right place each time he thrust into her.

"Oh … oh …oh …. Clay!" She gasped. He was going to make her come again and she couldn't believe it. She'd thought this time would be to get him there, she'd had her … "Oh … I … I …"

He smiled grimly and pushed deeper and then she felt him tense, he was going to, too. And he did. "Marianne!" He gasped as he found his release deep inside her. His orgasm triggered hers and she let herself go, gasping along with him as they carried each other away. Stars exploded behind her eyes as their bodies melded together. She'd been a sensual woman in her younger years, but she'd never experienced a coupling like this. It was more than purely physical, more than just some starry-eyed *making love*. She felt as though they were becoming one, in every sense.

When they lay still, he lifted his head and smiled at her. "Can I say it now?"

She panicked for a moment. Wondering what was coming. "Say what?"

He brushed his lips over hers. "I love you, Marianne."

Tears welled up and she felt one roll down her cheek. "I love you, Clay."

~ ~ ~

After they made love that first time, something shifted. Clay wasn't sure if it was something inside of him or something between them. If he was pushed, he'd say it was both. He'd had his share of women over the years—more than his share, especially in his early days in the music industry. Over the years the thrill of constantly being pursued by beautiful women had worn off. As he'd grown as a man, he'd learned that he was looking for something more than sex. He was a guy, he wouldn't deny that a hot body and a woman who knew how to use it wasn't something he enjoyed, but then he enjoyed cotton candy, too. It was enjoyable in the moment, but it didn't satisfy you in anything more than a momentary way— and it left you feeling like shit afterward.

As he got older the hot bodies had become nothing more than a visual pleasure. He enjoyed looking but even the desire for a quick hit of adrenaline and endorphins wasn't enough to make him act on his interest, most of the time.

He'd been physically attracted to Marianne the moment he laid eyes on her. She was a beautiful woman. Her face, her blue eyes, her long dark hair and her long lean figure all drew him to her. She was no bouncing twenty-something, but they didn't have even the physical appeal they once had anyway. With Marianne, there was something more, something deeper. Her beauty shone from inside her. There may be a few crow's feet around her eyes, but they added to her beauty and those eyes shone with a kindness and a compassion that drew him in.

He poured himself a cup of coffee and took it to sit in the armchair by the window. Marianne was in the shower. He smiled. They'd had a fun time in there yesterday morning, but today she'd wanted to take her time in there, wash her hair, do whatever else it was she needed to do that he didn't need to witness. He smiled. They could have their fun. They could make love. But they were grown-ups—something he'd never thought he'd want to be. And this—what they shared—it was real. It meant he could appreciate when she wanted her time alone to do her thing, just as she could appreciate when he needed to put his glasses on and sit and catch up with emails and work. She bustled happily in the kitchen while he talked on the phone with Summer earlier. He'd given her her space and taken himself off to his office when Laura had called her.

Maybe normal relationships reached this level of ease and comfort for younger people, too. He didn't know. He'd never found out. Whether it was their age that made this so special or the fact that he'd finally reached a place in life where not only was he comfortable with this kind of intimacy, but he truly craved it, didn't matter. All he knew was that he'd found in Marianne not only the woman he wanted to spend the rest of his days with, but the woman whom he knew he could make happy and be happy with.

He smiled at the sight of her coming down the stairs in a robe with a towel wrapped around her head. Her inner beauty was the most important thing to him, but it didn't hurt that her outer beauty made his heart race, too.

He got to his feet. "You need coffee before you get dressed?"

She smiled. "Guilty as charged."

He went to the kitchen and poured her a mug. "I'm glad you're as much of a caffeine addict as I am."

She reached up and planted a kiss on the tip of his nose. "Ditto. I don't think I could make this work if you disapproved of me coming to get a hit before I even get dressed in the morning."

He closed his arms around her, loving the feel and the smell of her, all damp and coconutty against his chest. "We'd be able to make this work no matter what, you and me, darlin'. We're meant to be."

She looked up into his eyes. "I believe that, Clay. I really do."

"I just wish I'd found you sooner."

She shook her head sadly. "So, do I. But I choose to believe that this is how it's supposed to be. Maybe when we were younger it wouldn't have worked. Maybe we needed to each become the people we are today in order for this to be so perfect."

He smiled. "You're probably right. You usually are."

She chuckled. "And when I was younger, I might have needed you to tell me I was always right, and you might have resented that. And we might have had the kind of marriage that so many people seem to have."

He raised an eyebrow at her. "You used to need to be right all the time?"

She shook her head with a laugh. "No. I was just joking. You know how some men bitch that their wife always has to be right."

"Ah. Okay. I can't imagine you being like that."

"Neither can I. I went too far the other way. I mostly keep my opinions to myself and buckle when someone else has a stronger one."

"Why?"

She shrugged. "I supposed I recognize that some people need to feel that they're right about things or they get upset, or worse angry and I can't deal with that, so it's easier to let them go on thinking they're right."

He rested his chin on top of her head. "Can you do me a favor, darlin'?"

"What's that?"

"Don't ever do that with me. Call me out on my bullshit? I won't get angry at you. And if I get upset, it'll soon pass. It'd upset me more to think that you weren't being honest with me about what you really think. It'd create a distance between us that I don't want. I want us to always be as close as we are right now."

He felt her nod. "I'm not going to promise, but I will promise to try. It's scary, you know?"

"I understand." He sighed. He did understand, but he wanted

. . .

She stepped back and looked up at him. "I think I'll be okay to do it with you. You make me feel safe."

That made his heart happy. "And I'll try to always make you feel safe. I won't let anything bad happen to you—and I sure as hell won't ever be something bad to you."

"I know." She sipped her coffee. "I trust you."

"I trust you." He smiled as he said it, realizing that trust was something that had always held him back in previous relationships. He didn't trust women, generally.

Chapter Thirteen

"I can drive myself," Marianne told Adam. "You should stay here and keep an eye on him." She jerked her head toward Clay's office door.

Adam shrugged. "Davin's in the guest house. He'll be fine. He wanted me to take you."

"Okay, I suppose we'd better get going then." She was going to meet Chris for their weekly lunch and on the way back she was going to stop in at her house and collect some of her jewelry making supplies. She'd had a couple of orders come in this morning and she needed to get to work on them.

Adam dropped her off outside the restaurant. "I'll be around."

"Thanks, but you don't need to lurk nearby, it's only me. It's not Clay."

"I'll be nearby." He repeated it so adamantly that it made her stop and think.

"Are you saying that I need you around?"

"No. I'm saying that I like to be around. It's what I do. I've driven you here. This is my job—and apart from that, it's what I enjoy doing. You won't know I'm around unless you need me. So, go and enjoy your lunch." He smiled. "And say hi to Chris for me."

Marianne had to smile at that. Chris loved to tease Adam whenever she saw him. The two of them had built quite a rapport. "I will, though if she knows you're here, she'll probably make a game out of trying to find you."

Adam chuckled. "That's another reason you won't know I'm around."

Marianne left him and made her way into the restaurant where, of course, Chris was waiting for her. "I'm not late," she said as she approached the high-top table where Chris was sitting.

"I didn't say a word, in fact, I'm impressed. You're a couple of minutes early."

Marianne smiled. "That's because I didn't get here under my own steam. Adam brought me."

Chris looked around. "Is he coming in?"

"No, but he sends his regards."

"Oh, I thought he might be staying close now."

Marianne frowned. "Why now?"

Chris' eyes widened. "I would have thought it'd make sense, now that you and Clay are public."

Marianne sat down. "What do you mean—we're public? We're no more public than we were before."

"Uh-oh. Don't tell me that you two have been so caught up in your own little bubble that you haven't seen?"

"Seen what?" Marianne's heart was racing.

"There's a big article about the two of you online—you know that In-Country website?"

"What does it say?"

"Nothing much, just that Clay has found himself a new woman." She smiled. "You come off well, if that's any consolation. They talk about you as elegant and mysterious. That you might be older than the women he's usually seen out with, but that the two of you look great together—that he might finally have found his match."

Marianne pursed her lips. "Elegant and mysterious?"

Chris nodded. "They also called you a *mature* beauty, but I wasn't sure if you'd want to hear that or not."

Marianne laughed. "I'll take it. It's better than old and unattractive."

Chris gave her a stern look. "You are neither of those things."

"I'm not saying I am, but in comparison with all the perky, young beauties you often see guys like Clay with …" She shrugged. "There weren't any photos, were there?"

Chris nodded. "Just one. It's not bad. Taken from a distance, of the two of you walking down by the water."

Marianne shuddered at the thought of someone watching them. Taking their photo without them even knowing. It gave her the creeps.

"Try not to think about it. I don't imagine much will come of it, since you're both hidden away up here for now. It won't get really crazy till you go to Nashville with him."

"I don't want to go there."

Chris rolled her eyes. "Maybe not, but it looks like the two of you are getting serious. I'm the one checking on your house every day, remember. Though I'm wondering how much longer you'll keep the place."

"For a long time yet. Yes, I've stayed with him for the last ten days, but he'll have to go back to Nashville soon, and I'll have to go home."

"Will you? Why? Why wouldn't you just move yourself into his house at the lake? And by the way, I heard you're having Smoke and Laura over for dinner. I'm still waiting for my invite—and I don't mind if it's just for coffee. I need to see the place."

Marianne nodded. "I'll talk to him. I feel kind of weird about that. We're living there as though we're a couple and it's our place, but I'm very aware of the fact that it's his place. So, inviting people over feels strange."

"You invited Laura and Smoke."

"I didn't. Clay did."

"Hmph."

Marianne had to laugh. "I'm sure he'll invite you, too when he sees you."

"Only if you don't invite me first."

"Okay, so how about you come over for coffee on Friday morning?" Marianne decided that there was no reason she shouldn't invite her sister over. That was her hang-up and she didn't believe for a moment that Clay would have a problem with it.

"I'll be there." Chris grinned at her. "And good for you. It's nice to see you being bold and making decisions instead of waiting for someone else's go-ahead."

"Thanks. I know I need to work on it and being with Clay helps. He's so...supportive." She smiled. "He makes me feel safe—safe to be me."

Chris rolled her eyes. "I'm happy for you, really, I am. I couldn't be happier, but you're making me so jealous right now."

Marianne laughed. "Sorry. What about you? Have you heard anything about Seymour lately?" She felt bad that she hadn't asked about her sister's romantic interest since Clay had been here.

"No." Chris sighed. "I saw him on the news last week when the stock market fell. But I haven't heard anything about him coming here to visit. Short of convincing Missy that she should go and visit her brother—and take me with her—I'm not sure that I'll ever see him again."

"Aww. I don't believe that. I have to hope that something will work out—just like it has for me."

Chris smiled at her. "Either way, I can live vicariously through you. I'm just so happy for you. And I can't wait to come over there."

They both looked up as a woman walked by their table and perched at the next one over. She gave Marianne a withering glance.

Chris frowned at her. "Is that the woman who knocked into you and made you spill your drink on me?"

Marianne nodded. "Yep. I couldn't forget that face—I know, I've tried." She looked over at the bar and was relieved to see Kenzie working. "Let's go and see Kenzie, shall we?"

Chris gave her a puzzled look but followed her to the bar.

"Hey, ladies. Sorry I was just on my way over to you."

"No problem." Marianne smiled at her. "We're not rushing you, it's just …" She glanced back over her shoulder and was unsettled to see the woman still staring at her. "Is that the woman who bumped into me a couple of weeks ago?"

Kenzie glanced over without moving her head. "Shit. She's back. She's trouble, that one."

"What's her deal?" asked Chris.

"I'll be damned if I know," said Kenzie. "Is she causing you a problem?"

"Only by making me feel uncomfortable," said Marianne. "Would you mind if we move to a booth?"

"Of course not. I'll bring your drinks and menus over—the usual?"

"Yes, please."

Marianne looked around as she and Chris made their way to a corner booth. She felt silly. But that woman made her uncomfortable enough that she'd be happier sitting away from her in the relative privacy of a booth.

Chris sat down on the side where she could still see the woman and glared at her. Marianne was relieved to no longer be able to see her.

~ ~ ~

"What do you think?" Clay looked over the dinner table. He was pleased with himself. It'd been a long time since he'd cooked for dinner guests. He liked to cook, but he usually had his dinner parties catered. He hadn't wanted to do that tonight, though. Laura and Smoke were family. Well, they were Marianne's family and he hoped that, by extension, they might come to see him that way, over time.

Marianne came to him and kissed his cheek. "I think if you weren't such a good singer, you could have been a great chef."

He chuckled. "I want it to be good—you know?"

"I do, and I appreciate it. Thank you."

He smiled. "You're welcome, but it's not just for you. It's for me as well. I want them to feel comfortable here— comfortable with me. I'm hoping this is just the first of many dinners we'll all share."

She smiled up at him. "I hope so, too."

He slung his arm around her shoulders. "We're on our way, aren't we?"

"We are."

He held her gaze for a moment. "Is it too soon to ask you to stay?"

She laughed. "I'd say it's too late. I've been staying here for a couple of weeks now."

"That's not what I mean. You know I have to go to back to Nashville on Sunday. How would you feel about staying here while I'm gone?" He could feel the tension in his shoulders as he waited for her to answer. It was a big step. He didn't want to rush her.

After a few moments, she smiled. "I'd like that." She looked around. "This place already feels like home to me. I don't know if it will when you're not here, but I guess I'll find out."

"I told you. I'd love for you to come with me."

She shook her head. They'd had this discussion a couple of times already. "You know I don't want to do that. Not yet, maybe not ever. That's your life there in Nashville. It's your work and your business and your people—people who aren't like me. I don't belong there."

He shook his head and blew out a sigh. "And I've told you, that's not how I see it. I want to share my life with you. Every part of it. I love being here with you, but I don't want or need to compartmentalize. I want you to get to know my friends there. They're just like you. They're good people. You'd like them if you gave them a chance."

"I already do like them. It's not that. I just feel like I wouldn't fit in there. And when you go back, it's to work. You don't need me hanging around, getting in the way."

"You wouldn't be getting in the way, you'd be—" His phone started to ring, cutting off what he'd been about to say. It was Adam.

"What's up?"

"I thought you'd want to know that I just buzzed Smoke and Laura through the gate."

"Thanks. And Adam, will you do me a favor and come over here later? I'll give you a shout when we're ready, but I want you to show Smoke the security system. Marianne's going to be staying here while we're gone."

"Sure thing. Just let me know when you want me."

Clay hung up and turned back to Marianne. He leaned down and brushed his lips over hers. "They're here, so I'll drop it for now. I respect that you don't want to come this time, but I'm not going to stop trying. I want you in every part of my life, Marianne."

She reached up and touched his cheek. "And I'd like to be— one day. But there's no rush, is there?"

"I suppose not. Come on, let's go and greet them."

It felt good—right somehow—to stand at the top of the steps outside the front door with her as they watched Smoke's truck come to a stop. He put his arm around her shoulders as they watched them get out and wave up at them. He had a crazy vision of Christmas time, with Smoke and Laura arriving with their kids and Autumn and Summer arriving with Matt and Carter and kids of their own. He'd never had a family but standing here with Marianne like this gave him hope that he might yet.

Smoke grinned at him as he and Laura trotted up the steps.
"You look like Lord and Lady of the Manor standing there like
that."

Marianne waved a hand at him, before pulling him in for a
hug. "Don't be silly, we're just happy to see you arrive."

Smoke kissed her cheek before turning to Clay and shaking
his hand. "And we're happy to be here, thanks for inviting us."
He handed Clay a bottle of merlot with a smile. "It's not the
most original gift, but we could hardly bring you something
other than wine."

Clay took it with a smile. "Thanks." He looked at the label, it
was one of the best Hamilton-Groves produced. "Wow.
Thank you."

Smoke shrugged, and Laura leaned in to hug Clay. "Thanks
for having us over."

He hugged her back, grateful that she'd come into his life
through Lawrence and Shawnee. If she hadn't, he would never
have met Marianne. "Thanks for coming. Though, in the
future I hope we won't need to do the whole formal thing. Just
drop in. Your mom's here. Why wouldn't you? Anyway, come
on in."

Once they were in the living room, Laura gave her mom a
questioning look. "Is this where I need to come to find you
now, then?"

Clay was pleased when Marianne smiled. "It is. We've
decided that I'm going to stay here when Clay goes back to
Nashville."

Clay shot a glance at Smoke. He smiled but looked as though
he was concerned. He'd have to pull him aside later and see if
he couldn't alleviate those concerns. He wanted the two of
them to be happy about this, and relaxed that it was right for
Marianne. He truly believed it was and so he wasn't worried
about convincing them.

~ ~ ~

Marianne enjoyed every moment of that evening. It was wonderful to see Laura laughing with Clay in the kitchen. She was proud of the way she'd raised her daughter, but if she had one regret it was that she'd never known what it was like to have a father, or even a father figure in her life. Seeing her with Clay, made Marianne hope that maybe it wasn't too late for her to have that.

Smoke came and put his hand on her shoulder. "It's good to see you happy."

"Thank you. And thank you for the reminder to be brave. There have been lots of little things come up, things that I could have let get in the way, but I didn't. I keep remembering what you said about not using little things as an excuse to run away."

Smoke smiled at her. "I'm glad it helped." His smile faded. "And you don't think there are any big things—real reasons that this might not last?"

She shook her head. "No. I don't. Why? Do you? Are you seeing something that you don't like?"

"No. It's not that at all. I like Clay. He's a great guy. I was just concerned that there are going to be pressures and difficulties of being with him—just because of who he is. Have you thought about that?"

She blew out a sigh. "I have, and I'm trying to manage it by avoiding it. He's asked me to go to Nashville with him—but I don't want to. I don't want to be part of that side of his life."

Smoke pursed his lips. "You don't want to—or it's just too scary?"

She let out a little laugh. "Okay, so maybe I'm working my way up to being brave about that one."

He nodded. "It's okay to take your time about it, but I don't think you should discount the possibility. Even if you don't go there, I'm sure that part of his life will find you here, sooner or later—if it hasn't already."

She frowned. "What do you mean by that?"

"Nothing." He shook his head. "Nothing really, just that I'm sure there'll be reporters and ..." He let his words trail off and held her gaze as if he expected her to fill in the blank.

She didn't know what he was getting at. "And what? What are you trying to say?"

He smiled. "I don't know. I guess I'm just probing too hard to see if you have any doubts—and you don't, do you?"

She smiled. "I really don't. It'll take me some time, but I'm confident that he's worth it, that we're worth it,"

"Then I'm happy for you. You know I only want to see you happy."

She reached up and planted a kiss on his cheek. "You're a good man, Smoke. I'm so glad she found you."

Laura came to join them at that moment, carrying a tray of liqueurs. "Don't you go stroking his ego, too hard, Mom. He's too big for his britches already."

Marianne had to laugh at the way Smoke scowled at her and snaked his arm around her waist. "There's no chance of my ego getting out of hand with you around, lady."

She turned and looked up into his eyes. "That's right, there isn't, you big Neanderthal."

Clay came to Marianne and kissed her cheek. "They're great together," he murmured, "but I'm glad we don't need to compete with each other the way they do."

Marianne leaned her head against his shoulder. "Me too. And it's not just because we're older and wiser it's just that that's not who we are, is it?"

He smiled down at her. "No. We don't need to compete, we just complement each other—perfectly."

Chapter Fourteen

"Chris is coming over at ten-thirty, is that right?"

"Yes, though knowing her she'll probably be early," Marianne answered with a smile. They were sitting in the little nook overlooking the lake, drinking their coffee. It was a morning routine that Clay had grown used to and come to love already.

"In that case, I'm going to get started as soon as we're done here. I have a bunch of phone calls I need to make and some contracts I need to sign and send back to Autumn."

"Don't feel you need to stop work for Chris." Marianne smiled. "She's my sister. I'd like to think that her popping over will become something normal. We don't need to stop everything else and make a big deal out of it."

"I know. But since this is the first time she's been, I'd like to make an effort. I mean, when you think about it, it is a big deal. We're at the stage in our relationship where I'm meeting your family." He smiled. "I know I've met her before, but this is different. I want to make a good impression. I want her to see that you're happy here—in this place, but more importantly with me."

She reached across the table and gave his hand a squeeze. "Thank you."

He smiled. "I might just join you both for an hour and then get back to it. I'm sure she'll want you to herself to question you and tell you what she thinks."

Marianne laughed. "Believe me, Chris would have no qualms about telling you what she thinks. Though, she probably will want to interrogate me."

"I can believe that. Oh, and I forgot to tell you that Smoke might drop over this morning as well."

"What for?"

"I wanted to have Adam show him the security system. We had such a good time when they came for dinner that it got too late. So, he said he'd come back this morning."

Marianne made a face. "Can't I just leave everything turned off while you're not here? It's not as though anyone's going to come after me."

"No. There's nothing to worry about, but I told you I'll keep you safe, and I plan to. The system is easy enough to manage. You already know how to open the gate and check the monitors. I want Adam to show Smoke a couple more things."

"Like what? Is it stuff I should know? I mean, I'm the one who's going to be here, not Smoke."

He really didn't want to worry her, but he didn't know how she'd feel about Smoke being able to view the security camera footage from his phone. His need to be honest with her overrode his desire to not worry her. "Adam's going to set him up so that he can log into the system without needing to be here—from his phone."

She chuckled. "Okay. Well, I suppose that's not something I'd ever be able to figure out on my phone. If it'll make you happy, then I'm fine with it."

"Good, and if you want to learn how to use it, you know Adam would be happy to teach you."

"I'm sure he would. But I don't think there's much point. You know what I'm like. It's all I can do to remember to take my phone out with me."

He frowned. "I know, and I hope you're going to work on that. I'd like to be able to call you while I'm gone."

"I will, I'll try to remember." She blew him a kiss across the table. "It's different now that I have a reason to want it with me."

His phone rang. He'd hoped they could finish their coffee before his work day intruded. It was Autumn.

"Take it," said Marianne. "And seriously, don't worry if you're not finished by ten-thirty. Chris and I will be fine."

He squeezed her hand and got up. "Good morning, Autumn," he answered as he made his way to his office.

"Morning. Are you ready to start? I know I'm a little early, but I've got a crazy day ahead."

"Yep, I'm good. Fire away, what do we need to deal with?"

"Not too much. Most of it can wait until you're here on Monday. The first thing I need to know is whether Marianne is coming with you?"

"No. I haven't managed to change her mind—and why does it matter?"

Autumn blew out a sigh. "Because most of the press requests we're getting are about her—at least, about you and her. I have a list as long as your arm of interview requests."

"No. Not happening. Just keep putting them off."

"It's getting harder, Clay. Since that article ran on In-Country, everyone wants the scoop. We could get some great coverage and I know I could broker a good deal. If you grant one of the mags an exclusive, we could use it as bargaining power to get coverage for Carson's tour kicking off."

"No." Clay forced himself to breathe deeply. He couldn't be mad at Autumn, she was only doing what she did, but his relationship with Marianne was far more important to him than any amount of good press. "You tell them this is off-limits."

"Totally?"

"Yep."

"Do you think that's realistic?"

He didn't, but he wished it was.

"We both know it isn't." Autumn didn't wait for his answer. "I respect where you're coming from, but can I make a suggestion without getting my head bitten off?"

"I didn't bite your head off."

"I know, but I don't want to piss you off. I understand. But you need to be realistic."

"So, what's the suggestion?"

"That while you're back here next week, you give an interview—maybe a couple, and you ask that the press and the public respect your privacy on this one. Tell them that yes, there is a new woman, and that you're hoping it's going somewhere—I mean they're already speculating like crazy. So, you confirm the big detail, but ask them to leave you in peace while this is in its embryonic stages."

"I could do that."

"You could. You know what they're like. If you try to keep them out, they get worse. If you invite them just a little way in, they'll wait respectfully until you give them more."

"You're right—as always. Go ahead and set it up. I don't mind who you choose."

"Okay. I'm on it."

"Thanks."

They spent the next hour and a half going over the contracts she needed him to sign. It didn't seem so long ago that contracts had to be signed in real ink and hand-couriered to their destination. Life was so much easier now that he could just type his name in and hit send.

"What time are you getting back on Sunday?" Autumn asked when they were through.

"Evening. I'll text you before I leave. Though, on second thought, I might text you once I'm home—I don't need you hijacking me the minute I land again."

She laughed. "Don't worry, you're safe this time. It's just that Summer and Carter are coming. You know they'll want to see you."

"That's great. It'll be good to see them. Do you all want to come over to the house—say, around seven?"

"Let me check with them? I told them you wouldn't be here until Monday. I knew you'd want a chance to get settled back in."

"I do—but you guys don't count as visitors."

"Okay. I'll let you know."

"Thanks." He looked up at the sound of the front door opening. "I need to go—unless there's anything else?"

"Nothing that can't wait. I'll see you Sunday."

"And we'll no doubt talk again in the meantime. See ya."

Marianne had managed to get a good hour done on her jewelry. She loved the room Clay had helped her set up as her craft room. She'd been worried at first about what he might think of her work. She'd be the first to admit that it wasn't a big deal, she made a nice little income, but it seemed so trivial. He knew what Laura did—she was known internationally for her high-end, high-priced jewelry. But Clay had been so sweet. He'd told her that her stuff was just as important—and much more accessible to people. He'd made her feel good about what she did. He'd even compared her trinkets to his songs. People bought her jewelry either for themselves or to give as gifts. It made people smile and brought a little happiness into their day—just like his songs did. That was a bit of a stretch, but he'd meant it. He wasn't just trying to talk her up. She'd believed that people like him probably looked down on the little things in life. But he didn't look down on anyone or anything. He found meaning in most things—of course, she probably should have known that just from his songs. He'd become such a big artist not only because he had a great voice, but because he sang out about the little things that meant that the most in life.

She looked up with a start. It was almost ten-fifteen. If she knew Chris, she'd be here any minute. She got up and went through to the kitchen to start making coffee. She smiled when she saw the security monitor come to life. Chris' car was at the gate. She didn't get the chance to open it. Adam must have been keeping an eye out, too. She watched the gate swing open then went to the front door to wait.

Chris bounded up the steps with a big grin on her face. "Oh, my goodness! I knew this was going to be some big fancy place, but this is something else! I hope you're not going to get too snooty to talk to me now that you're living here."

Marianne greeted her with a hug. "Don't be silly."

"I'm only pulling your leg. It's more like I hope you'll get snooty enough to enjoy living here."

Marianne smiled. "I love it already. It doesn't feel snooty. Yes, it's fancy, but it feels so homey and welcoming. Come on in. You'll see what I mean."

She closed the door behind them and Clay greeted them in the hallway. "Chris! It's good to see you. Let me take your coat."

Chris made big eyes at Marianne as Clay helped her out of her coat then turned around to smile at him. "Thank you. You must be one of the last gentlemen left."

He shrugged. "I can't help it, it's how my mamma raised me."

Chris laughed. "I just wish she'd raised another one like you."

He smiled. "Sorry, I don't have a brother I can introduce you to, but I'm sure if you come to Nashville, I have some music brothers who'd love to meet you."

Marianne laughed. "Don't tempt her. She'll be right there."

Chris nodded enthusiastically. "I like that idea."

"What about Seymour?"

Chris shrugged. "Even I know that one day I'm going to have to give up on that dream."

Clay linked his arm through hers and winked at Marianne. "Come on through to the kitchen and tell me about this dream—and about this Seymour. Who is he?"

Marianne busied herself making coffee and setting out a plate of cookies, while Clay and Chris took a seat at the island.

"I didn't know there was a guy," said Clay.

"There isn't. Except in my imagination."

"Who is he?"

Chris made a face. "You have to promise not to laugh when I tell you."

Clay made a cross over his heart. "I do solemnly swear that I will not laugh. You have to remember that I was the guy who had held this crazy dream for over a year that I might some day get together with the beautiful woman I met one night in LA."

Chris grinned at Marianne. "Oh, he's good. I can see why you're so charmed. He's a real sweet-talker, isn't he?"

Marianne laughed. "He is, but he's for real. He's not just thinking up the right words—he actually means them."

"Aww." Chris patted Clay's arm. "He's a keeper, sis."

A flood of warmth spread through Marianne's chest; she thought so, too.

"I'm glad I have your approval but come on. I want to know your story."

"It isn't much of a story. It started that same night that the two of you met. Remember you promised not to laugh? Well, while you and Marianne were busy sweeping each other off your feet, I was feeling the same way about Seymour Davenport. We met. We talked. We hit it off instantly. And at the end of the night, we said goodbye and I've never heard from him again."

Clay looked sad. "Seymour's a good guy."

Chris looked at him in surprise. "You know him?!"

"I've met him a couple of times. You know I do a lot of charity work with Oscar Davenport?" he asked Chris, but shot a glance at Marianne, too. She knew about his children's charity, but it wasn't something they'd talked about much yet.

She and Chris both nodded.

"Well, Seymour's Oscar's uncle. I've met him at a few functions. He's a good guy." He looked at Chris. "You know his wife died?"

"I do. We talked about her. My husband died, too."

"I'm sorry."

Chris shook her head. "It was a long time ago, and a very different story. And the only reason I mentioned it is because Seymour and I connected because we understood that about each other. There's a big difference, though. Seymour has never gotten over it. When we talked, he thought he might be ready to try something new, but his silence since tells me that he wasn't."

Clay nodded sadly. "Maybe he will be, further down the line."

Chris smiled. "Maybe, or maybe not. Anyway, I'm not supposed to be here to dump my sad tale of unrequited love on you." She turned around and looked at the living room and out the windows to the lake. "I'm here to take a nosey at your place, and damn! is about all I can say."

Clay laughed. "I hope that's a damn of approval?"

"You bet it is. This place is wonderful."

Clay smiled at Marianne. "We like it."

The warmth in her chest intensified. She loved it when he talked about them as a we.

Chris smiled at her. "I can see why. I can also see you both being very happy here."

"Me, too," said Marianne.

"Me three," added Clay with a smile. His phone rang, and he gave them an apologetic look. "It's Adam. Would you excuse me for a moment, ladies?"

They watched him go and then Chris turned back to her. "Marianne, he's perfect! You've got yourself a good 'un there."

Marianne smiled happily. "I know. I'm glad you like him."

"You already knew I did, but seeing you here together?" She shook her head and turned away to look out the windows. When she turned back, Marianne was surprised to see tears in her eyes. "It's wonderful. I couldn't be happier for you, sis."

~ ~ ~

Clay popped his head back into the kitchen. "I need to go down to the guest house. Adam needs to show me something. You ladies enjoy your coffee and catch up, I'll be back."

Marianne smiled at him reassuringly. She was trying to let him know that she didn't mind him dipping out on them— even though he'd said he'd hang out with her and Chris. This was important, though. Adam had told him that Smoke was here—and was asking some disturbing questions.

His heart raced as he pulled on his coat and headed out the back door. He jogged down the path to the guest house, hoping that he'd misunderstood what Adam had said. He could only hope that he was jumping to the worst conclusion—and was wrong.

He knocked on the door when he got there. Adam always teased him about that, but this was where Adam was living, and it wasn't in Clay's nature to just burst in, even under these circumstances.

Adam opened the door and showed him through. "Come on in, Smoke's in the kitchen."

"Is it her?" asked Clay.

Adam blew out a sigh. "I believe it is."

"Shit!"

Smoke met his gaze. "What do we do?"

Clay looked at Adam. "Something. Something has to be done. It was bad enough before—and I didn't even take it too seriously then."

"Don't I know it." Adam scowled at him.

Clay looked at Smoke. "How seriously can a grown man take being stalked by a woman? When it's the other way around, yeah, I can see it. But it's not as though a woman's going to be able to kidnap me, or rape me or something is it?"

"When will you get it into your head that even a five-foot, one-hundred-pound woman, can kill you just as dead as a six-five, two-hundred-fifty-pound guy can? If she's carrying a gun, or some other weapon, you are in danger. Why can't you see that?"

Clay shrugged. "I suppose I can, but I can't feel threatened by it. But it isn't just about me anymore, is it?"

Smoke shook his head. "It doesn't look that way. I didn't think too much of it when she shoved Marianne in the Boathouse—"

"She what?" Clay shook his head in disbelief. "When was this? Why haven't I heard about it?" He glared at Adam.

"This is the first I've heard about it." Adam gave him an apologetic look.

"Because it seemed innocent enough at the time," said Smoke. "It was while you were back in Nashville last time. Marianne was out with Chris. Laura and I ran into them, we were all having a drink at the bar and this woman knocked into the back of Marianne—hard enough to make her spill her drink all over Chris—and to shake her up. It seemed strange. She wasn't apologetic—she seemed angry. But I wrote it off as just someone having a bad day. It was only when I saw her again last night—and Kenzie told me she's trouble, and that she's been here on and off since your party, that I started to wonder. I managed to get a picture of her with my cell phone since I knew I was coming over here this morning."

"Can I see?" asked Clay.

Smoke held up his phone and Clay's heart sank when he saw the same blonde, with the same crazy eyes who'd caused so much trouble a couple of years ago. He blew out a sigh and looked at Adam.

"The restraining order's still in place."

Clay rolled his eyes. "Like that's going to help."

Adam shook his head. "We have to cover the legal bases first."

"I know, but all I'm interested in is how do we make sure she can't get near Marianne? I want to take her back to Nashville with me, but she doesn't want to come."

"She can stay with us while you're gone," suggested Smoke.

"Or we can leave Davin here with her," said Adam. "And remember that this woman hasn't started anything yet."

Clay scowled at him. "And we're not going to wait until she does start, before we get smart about it. I want to step things up. I'll try again to persuade her to come with me, but if she won't …" He looked at Smoke. "Do you think she'd come stay with you?"

Smoke shook his head. "I don't, but I can try."

Clay didn't know what to do for the best. There was a fine line to walk between keeping her safe and making her unhappy—he knew it all too well. "If she won't come, you're staying here with her." He looked at Adam. "Davin can come with me."

Adam pursed his lips, but he knew better than to argue.

Chapter Fifteen

Marianne looked up at the sound of Chris calling her name. "Down here." She got to her feet and waved.

Chris made her way down the path and came to sit beside her on the bench on the dock. "Are you okay?"

"I'm fine." Marianne smiled. "I love it down here by the water."

"It's a bit cold to be sitting out here for my liking, but I suppose by the time it warms up I wouldn't want to sit here either."

"Why?"

"Mosquitoes like the way I taste, remember?"

"Oh, of course. I didn't think about that. I hope it's not going to be too buggy down here. I've been looking forward to sitting here and reading in the summer."

"You'll have to get Clay to build you one of those screened in porches."

Marianne shrugged. She didn't know how she felt about asking Clay to build something for her. At least, Chris didn't pick up on what she was thinking and give her a hard time about it. She had something else on her mind.

"How are you feeling about the stalker woman now?"

Marianne blew out a sigh. "I've been trying not to think about it. It doesn't scare me. But it kind of pisses me off, you know?"

Chris raised an eyebrow.

"Well, it isn't right that some unknown person can affect how you live your life. I don't want to stay holed up here. I don't want to have to look over my shoulder whenever I go into town. It isn't right that you should have to give up your time to come and stay here with me."

"I didn't have to. I wanted to. I still think you should have gone with Clay and I hope you will in the future. He wants to share that part of his life with you—and if you're going to be together, then I don't see why you wouldn't want to. But since you're such a stubborn mare, it makes sense that I should stay with you." She smiled. "And we have Adam, too."

"I know. You're right about all of it. But I can't think about any of that when I'm just plain grumpy this morning and I'm angry at that woman and the power she has over us."

Chris nodded reluctantly. "I know. Hopefully nothing bad will come of it and it will just be an inconvenience, but you have to admit that you can't just ignore the possible threat."

"I can't, but I almost want to find her and antagonize her, bring it to a head and see what she's going to do."

"Why in hell's name would you want to do that? You've got half a dozen people dedicating their time to keeping you and Clay safe from her—and you want to find her and bring it to a head? Why?"

"I would have thought that was obvious. It seems perfectly logical to me. As long as we're successful at keeping her away, then the threat will never end. Nothing can be done about her, until she does something."

Chris frowned. "You want her to do something? Like what?"

"I don't know. I know I must sound like the crazy one. But I don't want to live like this. I don't need Adam breathing down my neck. I don't need you babysitting me. I don't need to be looking over my shoulder every time I leave the house. And most of all I don't want to have to worry about Clay every single day."

"I'm not so worried about him. He's harder to get to."

"Is he, though? Is he really? I know Davin's good but Adam's the best. And he insists that I'm Adam's number one priority now. Clay's in the city. He has to go to the office and go to meetings and interviews. He's an easier target than me pottering around here with Adam."

"So, what are you saying?"

"That I'd like to confront her. If she tries to do something to me, Adam will be nearby. He'll be able to help before anything too horrible happens."

"No way are you going to put yourself in that kind of situation. You have no idea how dangerous she is."

"If she were that dangerous, she would have tried something by now, wouldn't she?"

"What did she do before? Why did Clay take out a restraining order against her?"

"She followed him everywhere. Left notes on his pillow in his hotel room. Left notes inside his car."

"Inside?"

Marianne nodded. "I know, right? That was before he hired Adam. Adam's managed to keep her at more of a distance. They thought she'd given up."

"What does she want?"

"She says she loves him and that they're meant to be. She's just waiting for him to come to his senses and understand that."

"Great. So, Clay isn't just being a gentleman having Adam watch you. She's probably more of a threat to you than she is to Clay. She loves him—she no doubt hates you."

"Yeah. I couldn't understand how someone could look so evil that night she bumped into me at the restaurant. She glared at me like she hated me and wanted me to die." She shuddered as she remembered the evil look the woman had given her.

"Yeah," said Chris. "Because she does hate you and want you to die." She blew out a sigh. "I'd be staying as far away as I could, if I were you."

"I know that seems like the right thing to do, but when will it ever end? It seems to me that I need to bring it to a head. Then she can be arrested and put away."

"Or you could get hurt or killed."

"No."

"Yes! That's a very real possibility. You're taking this too lightly, sis. I understand your frustration, I do. But you need to be careful. Promise me you won't go looking for trouble?"

"Not today."

Chris scowled. "Don't get cute with me. I'm serious."

"I know, and I appreciate it. But I can't promise you."

"Okay, well then I'm going to be sticking to you like glue."

Marianne smiled. "I thought you already were. I haven't managed to shake you off in almost a week, so I guess it won't make much difference."

~ ~ ~

Clay was glad to get back to the house. He loved this place, he just hoped that Marianne would, too—when he finally got her to come here with him.

It'd been a long day and he still had to work tomorrow morning before he could go back to her.

"What are your plans for the evening?" asked Davin when they got out of the car.

He shook his head. "As little as possible. I'm going to call Marianne and pour myself a strong one. I don't feel like cooking—do you want to organize some kind of delivery for us?"

"Sure—any preferences?"

Clay smiled. "Soul food, whatever you think. You know the best places in town."

Davin smiled back. "Sure thing, boss. You want a good down-to-earth, nothing fancy, fill-your-boots and leave you needing forty winks kind of thing?"

"That sounds about right."

"I'll put a call in and let you know when it arrives. I'll be in the back if you need me."

"Thanks, Davin." Sometimes, when he was home alone, he asked the guys if they wanted to hang out with him. They were good company to watch a movie or shoot some pool with. Tonight, all he wanted was to call Marianne and then chill out.

He went into the kitchen and poured himself a large bourbon then pulled his phone out.

"Hey, how are you?" Marianne answered.

"Better for hearing the sound of your voice, darlin'. How was your day?"

"It was okay. I did some work this morning, then Chris and I went to the post office to mail them out. We had lunch in town."

"Did you go to the Boathouse?" He hated that she was there, in the same town as that crazy woman, and he wasn't there with her.

"No, we had a sandwich at the bakery. Chris needed to check in with some of her ladies at the women's center, so we just went next-door to the bakery when she was done."

"Okay."

"I wish you wouldn't worry so much."

"I can't help it. I've put you in this situation. All I want is to take care of you, and instead I've put you in danger."

"Do you really think she's dangerous?"

He sighed. "We've talked about this before. It's not a risk I want to take. She might be a harmless crazy. But what if she's not? I know all your arguments, because I've used them myself. I used to tell Adam all the things that you tell me—that she's probably harmless, that I don't want her to dictate what I can and can't do. But I finally understand where he's coming from. I didn't care enough about taking risks when I was the only one affected. Now that you could be in danger, I'm all about being safe rather than sorry. I'll be home tomorrow afternoon. It'll be different when I'm there." He hesitated but decided to say it. "It'd be different if you'd come here with me."

"And maybe I will next time, but not because I'm scared. I've been doing a lot of thinking and you're right; if we're going to be together, then I can't say I don't belong in one part of your life. I need to get over it and go there with you, meet your friends and … I don't know, be part of it."

He couldn't help the smile that spread across his face. "Thank you. That means the world to me."

"Thank you for wanting me to be part of it."

"I want you to be part of everything from here on out. Marianne, I love you. You're my future."

She didn't say anything for a long moment.

"If you want to be," he added.

"Oh, Clay. I do want to be. I want that more than anything else in the world."

"So, do I. And I think we need to start thinking about how to make it happen."

"What do you mean?"

He smiled. "We'll talk about it tomorrow. What are you and Chris up to this evening?"

She chuckled. "Chris has invited Adam to join us for dinner later."

"That's good." He liked the idea of Adam being in the house with them. "Well, you guys have fun and I'll call you before I take off tomorrow."

"Okay. What are you going to do this evening?"

"Davin's organizing supper for us and then I think I'll turn in early and read. It's been a long day and I need to unwind. I'm not complaining that I have other things to do at bedtime these days, but I've missed reading at night."

"Every time I think you couldn't be more perfect, you come up with another reason to adore you."

He laughed. "What do you mean?"

"I'm the same. I usually manage to read a few chapters each night before I fall asleep—but like you said, we've been busy with other things since I moved in here. I love that you read in bed, too."

"What, so that we can have a new night-time ritual?"

She chuckled. "No, because there's nothing sexier than a man who reads."

He had to laugh. "I'll take the compliment that I think is intended. But I'll also be testing your statement—there has to be something sexier."

He could hear the smile in her voice. "We'll have to try things out and see, then, won't we? I can tell you that a man who sings might be another top contender for the title."

He nodded. He'd been working on a song for her this week, but he didn't want to tell her that yet. "That's good to know."

"Okay, well, Chris just got back. I'll let you go."

"Okay, darlin'. I love you. I'll see you tomorrow."

"I love you, too, Clay."

~ ~ ~

Marianne hung up and went to the kitchen, where she could hear Chris was unpacking groceries.

"I don't need to ask. That was Clay on the phone, wasn't it?"

"What makes you think that?"

"The big goofy smile on your face and the dreamy look in your eyes."

Marianne waved a hand at her. "Stop it! I'm not that bad!"

Chris laughed. "Oh, but you are. If it wasn't so sweet, it'd be ridiculous."

Marianne shrugged. "It is what it is, and it's wonderful."

"I agree. It is wonderful to see you so happy. I only have one question."

Marianne met her gaze, wondering what was coming.

Chris laughed again. "I want to know what the wedding's going to be like. I mean, do women who get married at our age still do the whole dress thing? And if you do, will it be white? Am I too old to be a bridesmaid? I think my answer to that is yes—but if that's what you want, I could force myself—just don't ask me to wear pink?"

Marianne laughed out loud. "Oh, my, God! Are you serious?"

Chris nodded vigorously. "You can't tell me that's not where this is headed?"

Marianne's heart was racing. She hoped it was. She shrugged.

"Oh, come on! The guy's nuts about you. You're nuts about him. It's going to end in wedding bells, there's not a doubt in my mind. So, you may as well quit being coy about it and start thinking about what you want."

"I'm not being coy about it. I'm too busy enjoying the moments we share. I haven't stopped to think too hard about where it's going."

Chris pursed her lips.

"I'm not denying that I'm hopeful that this is forever. We've talked about it since the very beginning, but because we started out in such a strange way—as if everything was a foregone conclusion from the moment we met—we decided to back off and just see what happened as we let things take their course and develop naturally."

"I know. And what's naturally developing is that the two of you are in love and plan to stay in love till the day you die. And when that happens, people tend to get married."

Marianne had to smile. "They do. And I hope we do."

Chris smiled back at her. "There. That wasn't so hard, was it? I only needed you to admit it."

"Okay, I admit it. And I'll also tell you that the reason that I looked so dreamy-eyed as you put it, when I got off the phone with him was that he just told me that I'm his future."

Chris grinned at her and swiped at her eyes. "That makes me happier than you know."

"Me, too." Marianne wanted to tell Chris that she hoped the same would happen for her soon. But she knew Chris would only brush it off. And besides, it didn't seem right.

Chapter Sixteen

"And you're sure you don't mind if I take the week off?" asked Luke.

Clay grasped his shoulder. "I'm one hundred percent sure. You need to make the most of Angel having time off and take a little break. I don't plan to go anywhere, and if something comes up, I'll figure it out."

Zack nodded. "If we need to fly, I can get one of the guys from the flight school to fly right seat with me."

"See?" Clay smiled at Luke. "Go, take a vacation with your lady. We'll be fine."

"Okay, thanks. I'll have my phone with me if you need me."

Clay and Zack watched him cross the parking lot to his truck.

"Do you have any plans for the next couple of weeks?"

"Nothing much," said Zack.

"Will you catch up with that friend of yours?"

Zack raised an eyebrow.

"The girl?"

"Probably. Though why I do it, I don't know."

"What do you mean?"

Zack shook his head. "It's a long, complicated story that I don't need to bore you with. I should go see if Davin's having a problem getting the car."

They'd just landed back at the Summer Lake airport and were waiting inside the FBO building for Davin to bring the car around.

"He'll be here soon enough. If I know him, he's checking the SUV inside, out and underneath before he brings it around here."

Zack nodded. "I wish you didn't have to go through this. I mean, you sing songs and make people happy, for God's sake. Your life shouldn't be under threat because of that. It's not as though you're in a war zone, or—" He stopped himself. "Sorry. I don't mean to rant. It just pisses me off. Has Adam gotten any closer to finding her and ending this since we've been gone?"

"No. There's not much he can do. It's all defensive measures. There's a restraining order against her—she can't come within a hundred yards of me. But that's about the only protection the law can afford."

Zack didn't look impressed. "That's bullshit. You should be able to do something. Do you mind if I look into it?"

"Sure. I'll take any help I can get." He met Zack's gaze. "As long as it's legal."

Zack chuckled. "I won't stray outside the law, I promise. But I can tell you that the law can be stretched and twisted and used for your benefit. You don't have to sit and wait for something bad to happen before you can prosecute."

"And you're speaking from experience?" Clay was intrigued about what Zack was getting at. He'd known for a while that Zack had some mysterious past that he didn't talk about, but this conversation was making him want to find out exactly what that past was.

"You could say that. Don't worry. I've never been in trouble with the law, but I have had some experience with it."

"You used to be a lawyer?"

"No." Zack looked out through the windows. "Looks like your ride is here."

"Okay. I'm going to get home to my lady. See what you can dig up? But remember it's my name—and my ass—on the line."

Zack nodded. "I wouldn't do anything that could cause you any trouble, Clay. You have my word. I might not be able to do anything. But I don't see any harm in me digging around a little to see what I can come up with. Do you mind if I talk to Adam and see what he can give me to get started with?"

"Sure. Thanks, Zack."

When he was out in the SUV, Clay looked back at Zack through the windows. He liked him. He somehow knew he could trust him, but he was still a little uneasy about what methods he might want to use to put an end to the stalker problem.

Marianne sat in front of the mirror in the bedroom and finished putting her makeup on. She didn't wear much but liked to at least make an effort when they went out. She was thrilled that tonight—Saturday night—they were going to the Boathouse to meet up with the kids.

Clay came to stand behind her. He rested his hands on her shoulders and met her gaze in the mirror. "You're so damned beautiful."

She turned her head and kissed the back of his hand. "Thank you. Not so long ago, I would have brushed you off, or made an excuse or a joke. But you make me feel beautiful. So, all I can say is thank you."

He dropped a kiss on the top of her head. "Thank *you*. You saying that tells me just how far we've come. I know it hasn't been that long, but at our age, how long does it take?"

"Does what take?" She thought she knew what he meant, but she wanted to be sure.

"To know. To know that not only is this what we both want, but that it's right. That we're right for each other. That there's no need to spend any more time dancing around the edges of it."

She held his gaze and waited for him to spell it out more clearly.

He smiled. "I'm ready to tell you that I want to spend the rest of my life with you, Marianne."

She reached up and grasped his hand tightly. "I feel the same way." Her heart was racing as she wondered if this was it. Was he going to ask her to marry him?

Apparently not. He squeezed her hand and then let go. "That's all I needed to know." He stepped back. "I'm going to run downstairs and check in with Adam and Davin."

She nodded. Part of her was disappointed that this hadn't been the moment, but mostly she was happy in the belief that the moment when he asked her to marry him would come—and that it wouldn't be too far away.

When they arrived at the Boathouse, Davin pulled up in front of the entrance and Marianne, Clay and Adam all got out.

"I'll find a spot and then come join you."

Clay nodded before he closed the door.

He took hold of Marianne's hand and Adam held the door open for them to go inside. She'd been looking forward to this evening. Laura and Smoke often came in here on a Saturday night to have dinner and listen to the band play with their friends. They'd invited her and Clay to join them and she was looking forward to introducing him to her two nephews, Jack and Dan, and their wives Emma and Missy.

She looked around and soon spotted them sitting at a long table with several more of their friends. Chris was sitting on the end next to Dan and she waved them over.

"Uh-oh," said Adam. "Do we have a whole bunch of hangers on because they know Clay's coming?"

Marianne smiled at him. "No. The kids all like to hang out together. Some of them aren't here, but when the whole gang makes it, there are about twenty of them."

"That's a relief." Adam smiled. "I thought some might just be here to see Clay."

"No." Marianne smiled at Clay. "You're safe. Any interest in you is because they care about me. They don't want to hang out with the famous guy—they more likely want to interrogate the guy who's dating Laura's mom."

Clay smiled back at her. "In that case, I'm open to all questions. These kids are important to you, aren't they?"

She nodded. "Come on. I'll introduce you. We'll start with my nephews, Jack and Dan."

They reached the table and she smiled around at everyone. "Hey. As I'm sure you know, this is Clay." He nodded and smiled at them. "And this is Adam." Adam raised his hand and they smiled and murmured greetings.

"Take a seat," said Chris. "There's no way you can have a real conversation while you're both standing there. Come sit down." She patted the space beside her and nodded at Adam.

Marianne gave Jack a stern look as Clay sat down beside him. She didn't want him pulling his over-protective, man-of-the-household routine.

To her relief, he winked at her and shook his head slightly.

Clay looked at him and then at Emma and back again. "Do you guys have a little girl?" he asked.

Emma beamed at him. "We do. Isabel. We saw you a couple of weeks ago. You were driving through town and she waved at you."

"That's right," said Clay. "I thought it was you. Isabel is a little cutie. She made my day when she caught my eye and smiled and waved like that."

Marianne relaxed when Jack smiled. If there was way to bypass his more aloof side, it was to talk about Isabel. He was such a proud daddy.

"It was weird," he said. "She looked up when she saw the SUV coming and it was like she recognized you. Like she was happy to see an old friend."

Clay grinned. "Well, maybe someday I'll be like an old friend—to you guys and to her."

Jack cocked his head to one side but didn't comment.

Marianne wasn't surprised that Missy, Dan's wife, was the one who picked Clay up on it. "Do you plan to stay here long enough for that to happen?"

Clay smiled at her. "I plan to grow old and die here—with the occasional trip back to Nashville, of course."

Emma put both hands over her heart and smiled at Marianne. "Oh, that's wonderful. I'm so happy for you."

Smoke leaned forward and caught Marianne's eye and she nodded. He smiled and nodded back before Laura caught hold of his collar and made a face at him. She gave Marianne a questioning look, but Marianne didn't get a chance to respond.

Clay slung his arm around her shoulders and smiled down at her. "Thank you. I'm a happy guy myself."

They all looked up when Ben arrived to take their drink orders. "Hey." He looked a little concerned. "It's good to see you, but I wasn't sure if you'd want to be here."

Clay shrugged. "We still have a life to live. And Adam's here and Davin will be in a minute too."

Ben nodded. "Have you seen Zack?"

~ ~ ~

"Not since we landed back here." He wanted to ask Ben why he wanted to know, but he decided it'd be better to wait until he could speak to him alone.

Fortunately, Ben seemed to understand that. "Okay. I was wondering if he was coming tonight." But the look on his face said that wasn't what he'd been wondering at all.

"Has anything else happened with that woman?" asked Jack.

"No," said Clay. "But don't worry. I'm not taking any chances." Marianne had told him on a couple of occasions how protective Jack was. Clay wanted to reassure him. He didn't feel defensive—he was happy that Marianne had someone else looking out for her.

Jack nodded and looked at Adam. "What's your take on it all?"

Adam shrugged. "I'm not taking any chances. And I'm trying to make sure these guys don't take any either."

Clay didn't like the undercurrent in the look Marianne gave Adam. He'd have to ask her about that later. For now, he just smiled. "We're not, we're being careful. We're hanging out in a busy place with a whole bunch of friends and having fun. I even suggested that you and Davin should join us tonight."

"That's true. I should be thankful you're working with me."

Ben took their drink orders and left them to study their menus. Clay had already decided that he wanted the ribeye. He was more interested in studying the guys in the band as they set up their gear for the night.

Marianne followed his gaze. "Do you mind if I introduce you to them properly later? They're both very nice. And I know they think you're amazing."

"Of course." Clay had been introduced to them on a couple of occasions, but only in passing. He knew one of them was married to the girl who worked behind the bar. He always felt weird meeting fellow musicians. Some of them were starstruck, and others were almost competitive. He didn't know where these two guys would fall. They hadn't approached him in the starstruck way yet, but they'd acted friendly toward him. He hoped they'd be as easy-going as most people around here seemed to be. It'd be nice to be able to talk music with them. In Nashville, his whole world revolved around it, but there was no one here who knew much about it.

It was a great evening. Clay felt right at home. He'd known Laura for over a year, and he knew that she was good people.

He'd expected her friends and cousins to be good people, too.
But he hadn't been prepared for the atmosphere he found
himself in. There were some very different characters sitting
around that table. But they were obviously bonded by strong
friendships. It was obvious that this group cared for each other
a great deal; they looked out for each other. There was a lot of
laughter and good-natured teasing. He loved that they included
Marianne as one of them—and Chris, too. And by extension,
he felt himself being drawn into their circle. There wasn't any
feeling that they were *the oldies,* intruding on the young folks'
night out.

They'd finished eating by the time the band started up. Clay
smiled as he listened to them. They were good. Talented. He
looked forward to talking to them.

As he brought his beer up to take a swig, he caught Missy
watching him. He held her gaze for a moment. She struck him
as being a little pistol. He liked her, but there'd be no putting
anything past her, he was sure. He raised an eyebrow at her.

She wrinkled her nose at him and then smiled. "Sorry. I don't
mean to be rude. I was just wondering what you think of
them. How this must all seem to you. I mean, it's not exactly
what you're used to, is it?"

He smiled back. "It's not what I get to do much in Nashville
anymore, no. But I love this. The guys are good—very good.
I'm not just saying it. I'm looking forward to talking to them.
If anything, that was the part of this evening I wasn't
particularly looking forward to. It can be hard to be polite to
people who are trying but who aren't there yet."

Missy laughed. "I get the idea that you're being polite about
that, and you have to be nice to people who suck and think
they don't."

He winked at her. "I wouldn't say that."

"Of course, you wouldn't; you're too diplomatic."

Clay looked back at the stage. "I don't need to be diplomatic
about those two. They're good. You're right, this isn't what

I'm used to, but I'm enjoying it. It's great. I was concerned that you all might see tonight as having oldies crash your party, but you don't, do you?"

Missy grinned. "Nope. If you stick around here, you'll learn that about Summer Lake—the generations all party together; always have, always will."

Marianne leaned her head against his shoulder and he put his arm around her. For some reason, what Missy said made him even more eager to put down roots here and become a part of this place.

~ ~ ~

When Davin pulled up in front of the house, Marianne waited for Clay to come around and open her door. It'd taken some getting used to, but he liked to do it and she loved that he was such an old-school gentleman.

He took hold of her hand as they started up the steps, but they both stopped at the same moment when they saw it. Adam must have sensed there was something wrong. He jumped out of the passenger door just as Davin started to pull away.

"Wait!"

Clay put his arm around Marianne and hurried her back to the SUV while Adam rushed up the steps and pulled the note off the front door.

Marianne's heart was racing.

"Are you okay, darlin'?"

She nodded. "I'm not scared! I'm angry. How can she do this? How can she get away with it?"

Adam came back down, looking angry.

"What is it?" Marianne asked. "What does it say?"

He shook his head. "Just the same thing." He met Clay's gaze.

"How did she get in here? What happened to the alarm system? Shouldn't we have known?"

Adam nodded. "We should. I'm sorry. I don't know what failed, but something did."

"What does it say?" asked Marianne again. She needed to know.

Clay shook his head at Adam, but she glared at him. "This affects me, too. I know you want to protect me, but I need to know."

Clay nodded at Adam reluctantly.

"Are you sure?

They both nodded.

"Okay. It says: I still love you, Clay. I forgive you. She has led you astray, but I'll take care of her."

Clay's arm tightened around her shoulders.

"Is she crazy?" asked Marianne. "And I mean, in the clinical sense? Do you know anything about her? Is she maybe someone who needs help?"

"Obviously," said Adam grimly.

"And have you looked into what might be possible there?"

All three of them turned to look at her as if she was the crazy one.

"I mean. Does she have family? Should she be in some kind of institutional care somewhere?"

"My job is to look out for you and Clay, not for her and her well-being." Adam looked angry.

"Yes, but maybe the best way to take care of us would be to get her taken care of—in the way she needs?"

Clay looked down at her. "You're something else, do you know that?"

"I'm looking at this differently than you've all been doing, but only because I'm a woman. I see a person—who obviously has big problems. All you see is a threat."

Clay nodded. "You're right." He looked at Adam. "Is there a different way we can approach this?"

Adam nodded. "There is. In fact, I think Zack might have already started down that road."

"Good. But what do we do tonight?"

Marianne looked at him. "I don't think there's anything we can do tonight, let's turn in and see how we can deal with it tomorrow."

He shook his head. "I mean, where are we going to turn in? We're not staying here. Not until we know how she got this far and can't do it again."

"She didn't get inside the house. Surely we're safe in there?"

"I'm not taking any chances."

Marianne opened her mouth, ready to argue, but Adam beat her to it.

"I think Marianne's right. If she'd been able to get in, the note would have been inside. How about Davin and I stay the night? We're going to be up all night anyway going through the system and finding out how she got past it."

Clay looked like he still wanted to say no, but after a moment the tension left him, and he nodded. "Okay."

Chapter Seventeen

Clay sat in his office, staring out the window at the lake. The weather out there suited his mood. Right now, the sky was dark and looming gray clouds looked like they'd bring rain. Not ten minutes ago, the sun had been shining, glinting off the lake. It was changeable to say the least. Just like he felt.

His mind kept skipping around. He'd been thinking about Marianne and their future—and the little meeting he had set up with Laura and Smoke and Jack. That made him smile. He didn't have any doubts that it would go well. Still, his smile faded. Nothing had come of Adam and Zack's efforts to find and put a stop to his stalker. That was a cloud that hung over him constantly. Adam and Davin had been staying in the spare rooms on the main floor since they'd found the note. He'd rather go back to Nashville, but Marianne was adamant that they shouldn't let the woman force them out of their home. He'd felt the same way when it was just him. This whole thing had just been an inconvenience before. But now that he had Marianne, the thought of anything happening to her was too much to face. He'd be prepared to sacrifice liberty in the name of security when it came to her—but she wouldn't hear of it.

His phone rang, startling him from his thoughts. He smiled when he saw the name on the display.

"Lawrence!" he answered. "How's it hanging?"

Lawrence laughed. "More than it's standing these days, but it can still stand up for itself when it wants to."

Clay laughed with him. "Too much information, thanks."

"Well, since I rarely get to speak to you these days, I thought I might as well tell you everything."

"And I want to hear everything—everything except your old man problems."

"And I thought you loved me."

Clay laughed. "You know I do. So, what's up?"

"Nothing. Just haven't heard from you for a while and I wanted to check in. What are you up to? Are you happy? Have you popped the question to the lovely Marianne yet? Are you going to bring her back here any time soon—or do Shawnee and I need to come out there again?"

"That's a lot of questions. I'm getting work done—I've been writing again. I am happy—very happy. I haven't popped the question yet—but I'm going to. And if I had my way, I'd bring her back there today, but she doesn't want to go. So, yeah. I'm going to need you two to come out here again soon."

"Hmm. Do I need to fill in the blanks myself?"

"Go ahead."

"As far as work goes, I'd guess you're doing whatever paperwork Autumn makes you do, and that's about it. You're writing, but not much—because you don't have me there to write with. You're happy means that things between you and Marianne are going great. You haven't popped the question yet because you're building up to it—and you want me and Shawnee there when you do. Am I right?"

"You are."

"But what about Marianne not wanting to come here— what's that about? I thought she'd gotten used to the idea and was willing to come and give us a try?"

"She is, but …" He hesitated.

"But what? Is there a problem?"

"Not between us, no. But you remember that stalker?"

"Oh, shit! She's not resurfaced has she?"

"Yup. And apparently she still wants me and is threatening to *take care* of Marianne."

"Shit! And Adam can't do anything?"

"Not within the law." He knew what Lawrence's response to that would be.

"The law can be an ass. It's supposed to protect you and if it can't, you need to take things into your own hands. I bet there's a bunch of stuff Adam would happily do if you gave him the go ahead."

"Probably, and I know you think I'm too soft. But Marianne brought something up that none of us had thought about. What if the woman just needs help? What if the quickest and easiest way to get her off our backs would be to get her help?"

"I can tell you the quickest, easiest way to get rid of her."

"I know, I know, but ...." Clay shook his head. "Maybe I could have solved this years back if I'd thought of it then. Instead of playing chess with her, trying to stay one step ahead of her and her trying to stay one step ahead of Adam and the law. What if we'd just found a way to bring her in and get her help. There's nothing we can do against her until she commits a crime—and I don't want to wait for that to happen."

"Too damned right. If she has her sights set on Marianne, then you need to take care of her fast. You know how I'd take care of her—and she'd never cause you another problem my way. But how could you take care of her in terms of getting her help?"

"Adam's looking into it. He's going to reach out to any family we can find. Maybe they'll be able to get her committed or something. I don't really know, but I'm hopeful."

Lawrence blew out a sigh. "You know I prefer a more direct approach, but surely there's something you can do to put a stop to her?"

"Not until she does something. We went through it all last time. Trespassing, is all we have against her."

"But didn't you say she's threatened Marianne? I know there's not much you can do when she's just following you around declaring undying love—but now that she's stepped it up to threats? That has to be a criminal act, right?"

Clay nodded. "You're probably right. I'll talk to Adam."

"Good and the sooner the better. Because my last guess is that you haven't popped the question to the lovely Marianne yet because you don't want to with all this hanging over you."

"Yeah, I wasn't sure if you'd understand that."

"I don't. I think you're a damned fool! You finally met the woman you've waited your whole life for and you're going to let some crazy bitch spoil it for you? You're going to wait and waste time that you could be married—I mean, how many years have you got left, old man? And how many years might this drag out for?"

"When I ask Marianne to marry me, I want it to be perfect. I don't want anything hanging over our heads."

"You and I both know, there's no such thing as perfect. It'll be the best you can make it and no better. Just like everything in life. And if you think about it, isn't this whole business bringing you closer together? Seems to me that we humans are strange creatures. We're better when we're facing adversity. It makes us stronger and draws us closer. You and Marianne are in this together, fighting a common enemy. Why would you want to wait until that's over before you make her your wife?"

Clay smiled "You're right. I hadn't thought of it that way, but you're absolutely right."

"Aren't I always?"

Clay laughed. "I don't know about that."

"So, when are you going to ask her?"

"I'm going to talk to Laura and Smoke and Marianne's nephew Jack—you'll like him. I wanted to run it by them—it's not as though I can ask for her father's permission, but I want to make sure that her family is happy about it. But then I was going to wait and see how all this played out."

"And what do you think now? How soon are you going to ask her?"

"How soon can you get here?"

~ ~ ~

Marianne packed up her jewelry and tidied everything away. She was getting more orders and she knew that things would only get busier as the holiday season approached.

She looked up at the sound of a tap on the door. "Come in."

The door swung open and Clay stood there, smiling at her. "Are you nearly done?"

"I'm just packing up. Are you finished for the day?"

He nodded and leaned in the doorway. He was so darned handsome he took her breath away.

She went to him and slid her arms around his waist. "How did I get so lucky?"

"I ask myself that same question every day. I'm the lucky one here."

She shook her head but decided not to argue with him. He'd done so much to show her that he loved her, that he thought the world of her. And she was finally at a place where she was happy to believe him. If he thought he was lucky that he'd found her, then she was happy with that.

He rested his chin on top of her head. "You believe me now, don't you?"

"About what?"

"About what I said the first night we met. That we're meant to be."

She nodded. "I do. I think I kind of believed it all along, but there were so many little things that were hard to believe. I needed time to get past them."

"I know. Words could only take us so far. You have to live it before it becomes real."

She smiled up at him. "And now it is real; I couldn't be happier."

"This is the beginning for you and me, darlin'. I feel like we've laid the groundwork, proved to ourselves and to each other that this is everything we hoped it might be and now we get to live our happily ever after."

"I agree that we've laid the groundwork, but I don't think it'll be smooth sailing from here on out. Do you?"

"No, I doubt it. But Lawrence said something the other day that really made me think."

"What?"

"He said that we—humans in general—do better when we're faced with adversity. That we step up and become stronger."

Marianne thought about that for a moment. "I'd have to agree with him. When you have to fight for something, you value it more."

He cocked his head to one side. "We haven't had to fight for us."

"No, but we've had to wait—most of our lives—for this. I think that counts, too."

He nodded. It seemed there was something else on his mind.

"What are you thinking?"

"I'm thinking about this whole situation with the stalker."

"Yeah. You could call dealing with her an adversity we have to face together."

"It is, but do you think it's brought us closer? Or do you think we would have done better if she'd never shown up?"

Marianne thought about it, then she nodded. "I suppose, in a way, she's done us a favor. Her being around has shown me how much you care about me. I think it's shown you that I see things a little differently than you do. And it's taught us both that we can disagree—about going to hide in Nashville or whatever—and respect each other's viewpoint." She nodded again. "I wouldn't have chosen to have her around, but I think Lawrence is right. A bit of adversity has been good for us. And it will probably continue to be. Adam said they can't track her down."

"Yeah. I was hoping that maybe they'd be able to find her and find some family member who was willing to take responsibility for her and get her hospitalized."

"Maybe it'll still happen. In the meantime, I guess we just remain vigilant but don't let her run our lives."

"That's all we can do. And on a different subject. Do you want me to make you dinner?"

She smiled. "I don't mind cooking."

He laughed and took her hand. "I think we're going to need some outside adversity if the worst argument we ever have is over who gets to cook."

~ ~ ~

After dinner they sat on the sofa to watch a movie. Clay wrapped his arm around her shoulders and she leaned her head against him. He blew out a happy sigh. Life was good. All he wanted now was to make her his wife.

She looked up into his eyes. "Was that a good sigh?"

He dropped a kiss on her forehead. "The best kind. I'm relaxed and happy and at peace." He wasn't quite totally at peace, he doubted he could be until something was resolved. But he was as close as he could be under the circumstances and it felt good.

"When do you have to go back to Nashville?"

That caught him off guard. Autumn had asked if he be could be back a week from Monday. He knew he should, but he didn't want to. "Not until you go with me."

She blew out a sigh of her own, and it didn't sound like a happy one. "You know how I feel about letting that woman drive me out of here."

"I'm not asking you to go because of that. I'm asking you to go because I want you there. I want you with me, in every part of my life—and you did say you'd come."

"And I will. I just ..." she sighed again. "I suppose that whole situation gets to me more than I realize. I want it to be over—resolved. I want to go with you because that's what we both want—not just because you worry about leaving me here."

"I know. I understand. But I do want you to go." He could hardly tell her that this time he wanted her to go with him because he was hoping that they'd have some big news that he wanted to share with his friends there. Even as he thought about it, he realized that he might be walking her into another kind of adversity there. Once word got out that they were engaged—assuming that she said yes—the press would be all over them. "Autumn has asked if I can go back a week from Monday."

"Okay. I'll think about it. I'd have to bring my work with me if I come."

"That'd be great. We can set you up a craft room at the house."

She nodded but didn't look too thrilled.

"You'll love it when you get used to it."

"I'm sure I will, but I don't want to think about it right now." She curled her arm around his waist and leaned toward him. "In fact, I can probably think of a good way to distract you from thinking about it, too."

She was right. He was already distracted as she stroked her hand over his chest. And he wasn't sure he knew where Nashville was anymore when she trailed it back down and started to unfasten his jeans. His cock sprang to life as she slipped her hand inside his pants and closed her long, slender fingers around him.

He lowered his mouth to hers and she kissed him eagerly while she worked her hand up and down the length of him. It felt so good, but he couldn't lose himself to the pleasure. He kissed her deeply and then raised his head and reluctantly removed her hand.

She gave him a questioning look, but he got to his feet with a smile. "We need a bed," was all he said. He didn't want to add that they didn't need to be doing that in front of a wall of windows when there was no knowing if there was someone out there watching them.

Chapter Eighteen

By midweek, Clay had taken care of all the details. Laura and Smoke were thrilled. Jack had been pleased to be included in his kind-of request for Marianne's hand. From what Clay understood, Jack had stepped up to the be the man of the family when his dad died. At seventeen he'd made himself responsible for his mom, Chris, and his Aunt Marianne and cousin Laura. Clay had to like the guy for that.

He'd spent what seemed like hours on the phone with Autumn and was grateful that she was the one organizing flights and accommodation for the Nashville contingent. Summer and her husband, Carter, were coming down from Montana. That had worked out better than he could have expected since Carter's buddy, Chance, also had family in Summer Lake. He and his wife, Hope, had offered Summer and Carter a ride in their plane with them, so that was taken care of. And he was hoping it might make Chris happy since Hope was Seymour Davenport's daughter.

He'd told Marianne that he was going into town this morning to do some shopping, but he knew she didn't believe him. She knew he was up to something, he just hoped she didn't know what it was.

She came downstairs looking fresh from her shower. He went to her and closed his arms around her. "I love you."

She gave him a shrewd look. "I love you, too. But if you're hiding something from me, I wish you wouldn't. I thought we were going to be open and honest with each other?"

His heart sank. He did want to be open and honest with her—about almost everything—but he also wanted to be able to plan a surprise for her. He brushed his hand over her cheek. "There's nothing to worry about."

She pursed her lips. "I'd rather be able to decide that for myself. What is it? Is that woman back? Has she done something?"

"No. It's not that. There hasn't been sight or sound of her in a while."

"What is it then?"

He smiled. "I'm not going to lie to you and say it's nothing, but can you trust me when I tell you that it's something good? I'm planning a little surprise for you, that's all."

She relaxed against him. "I'm sorry. I don't mean to be all suspicious. You're doing something nice and I'm going and spoiling it."

"You aren't. But will you trust me on this one? I hope you're going to be happy about it."

"Can you give me a clue?"

He chuckled. "Okay. I will." He could give her a clue that might actually help him out. "Since you don't want to go to Nashville yet, I wanted to bring a little bit of Nashville to you."

"What do you mean?"

"Well. Lawrence and Shawnee and Autumn and Matt and young Carson are all used to me being around there most of the time. I wanted to see them and for them to get to know you, so I've invited them all here—oh, and Summer and Carter, too."

He eyes widened. "When?" She looked around the house. "Do we have room for all of them? I'll have to get the guest rooms ready and ..."

"Slow down. I wouldn't do that to you. I wouldn't invite them to stay here without asking you. They're going to be staying at the resort. Ben let me rent one of the big cabins down by the water. It's private enough, they'll be fine there."

"Oh, okay." She looked relieved. "But we can have them all over for dinner on Saturday night?" She smiled. "We could cook together."

"You know I like that idea, and one day soon we will cook for them, but maybe we'll start with just Lawrence and Shawnee. I think you'll get along well with Shawnee. But this weekend we can all go to the Boathouse for dinner. It'll be easier, and I think they'll enjoy it. I know Chase and Eddie will be thrilled to play in front of all of them. Matt said he might even get up on stage with them. He met them on the night we met."

She nodded. "Okay. So, they're all coming for the weekend, but staying at the resort, and we're just going to meet up with them—I don't need to do anything?"

"Not a thing. Just hang out and get to know them. How does that sound?"

She smiled. "It sounds lovely. I'll look forward to it."

"Good." He glanced up at the clock. "But I still need to go into town to finish making the arrangements. Do you need anything?"

"No. I'm fine, thanks. You know Chris and I are going over to the plaza to have lunch with Laura? I might be gone before you get back."

"Okay. I'll have Davin go with me. Adam can go with you."

"Okay."

He was grateful that she'd stopped protesting about always having one of the guys go with her. He just wished that it was no longer necessary. Adam had come up with nothing in his attempts to track the stalker down. Zack had been cagey when Clay had asked him if he'd managed to discover anything—

Clay could only guess that he hadn't but didn't want to admit as much.

Marianne smiled at Laura across the table. She loved coming over here to have lunch with her daughter and sister. The café was lovely. It felt very cosmopolitan to her. She knew Laura didn't see it as anything special, and she loved that. It reminded her how well she'd done by her daughter. She might still be aware of her own very humble beginnings, but she'd set Laura up so that she felt at home anywhere in the world. She went to London every couple of months and worked with the world's top designers. She'd made rings for some of the world's wealthiest people and most famous celebrities. Marianne smiled to herself. She made the engagement ring that Lawrence Fuller had given to Shawnee Reynolds. That one was probably the one Marianne was happiest about. If Lawrence hadn't asked Laura to make that ring, she herself would never have met Clay. She shuddered at the thought. She couldn't imagine her life without him in it anymore.

"What's up with you?" asked Chris.

Marianne smiled. "Nothing. I'm just thinking about how far we've all come."

"A long way," said Laura.

"And your journey's only just beginning," said Chris.

Marianne was surprised to see Laura shoot Chris a warning look.

"It feels like it is. I mean, I think I've done well so far in life. I raised you and set you on the right path, but when I came here, I thought I was set to live out a quiet little life and hope that maybe one day you'll change your mind and give me grandbabies. Now I'm at the beginning of a whole new chapter."

Laura laughed. "I've never said never about babies, there's time yet."

Chris raised an eyebrow at her. "Do I sense a mellowing in your attitude, young lady? I'm sure you've always said never."

"No. I've always been firm about not yet, if ever, that's all. And besides, this is about Mom's new beginning. Not me." She smiled at Marianne. "I always wanted you to have a love story of your own. And now you do. I'm so happy for you— and so happy that it's Clay. It was going to take someone special, or he would have had a rough time from me—and Smoke. But Clay is one of the best men I've ever known."

Chris grinned at her. "So, you won't mind having a stepdad?"

Marianne was again surprised at the look Laura shot at Chris. She hoped that it wasn't because she would mind. Maybe it was, and if so, she didn't want to get into it now and spoil their lunch. "Stop teasing, Chris. It's not as though that's something we even need to think about yet."

To her surprise, Chris gave them an apologetic smile. "Sorry. You're right. I just get a bit carried away. I'm excited for you. Remember, I have to live vicariously through you."

Marianne was happy to be able to change the subject. "Well, Clay told me this morning that some of his friends are coming into town this weekend. Summer is coming from Montana— and she's coming with Chance and Hope."

Chris' eyes lit up. "Oh! I didn't know that."

"Why would you?" asked Laura sharply.

Marianne was going to have to ask her later if she had a problem with Chris lately. Instead of answering her in the same tone, Chris looked apologetic again—there must be something going on between the two of them. She hoped they could leave it be while they enjoyed lunch. She'd be glad for it to be over if they were going to carry on like this.

She looked over to the counter where Adam was sitting, sipping a coffee. He caught her eye and winked. He was a good man. She liked him. She just wished that he'd been able to track down the stalker and stop her somehow. She'd disappeared after the note on the front door, but in some ways that seemed worse. She might leave them alone for weeks or months or she might come back at any moment—and do who knew what.

"Who are you smiling at?" asked Chris. She turned to look and waved at Adam. "Isn't he lovely? Don't you have any single friends left, Laura? He'd be a good catch for someone."

Laura shook her head. "He seems like a nice guy, but I'm not sure his job would fit too well with being in a relationship."

Marianne nodded. She'd asked Adam if he had anyone special, but he'd said the same thing Laura had.

She watched him answer his phone and look around. He slid down from his seat and went to the door. She was surprised to see Zack come in and stand inside the doorway talking to him for a few moments before leaving again.

Adam avoided her gaze on his way back to his seat. She'd have to ask him later what that was all about.

~ ~ ~

The weekend took forever to arrive—or at least, it felt that way to Clay. All he wanted was for Marianne to say yes to him. He wanted to make her his wife and he wanted to share the joy with his friends and her family.

First, he wanted her to have the chance to at least get to know his friends a little. He didn't want her to have to share their moment with people who still felt like strangers to her. He'd been disappointed when Autumn had called him yesterday afternoon and told him that they wouldn't be able to make it until this morning. But that was the kind of thing that happened in their line of work.

Zack had called him a few minutes ago and told him that they'd landed and Autumn and Lawrence and the rest of them were on their way over to the resort.

Marianne came to join him in the kitchen. "Was that them?"

He nodded. "It was Zack to let me know that they've landed. I'm sure the others will be calling soon."

His phone rang again, and he gave her a rueful smile.

"Hey, Lawrence, you made it?"

"We did. We're on the way to the cabin now. What's the plan?"

"I thought we'd give you chance to get settled in and then come over there to see you." He'd told Marianne that she wouldn't have to do a thing, and he knew that she'd feel she had to if she knew they were coming over to the house.

"Sounds good to me. Want to come in about an hour?"

"Yep. We'll see you then." He hung up and smiled at Marianne. "I said we'd go in about an hour—is that okay?"

"It is. I'm glad we don't have to wait too long, I'd only get nervous."

He landed a kiss on her lips. "There's nothing to be nervous about. I promise you."

Clay let out a low whistle of appreciation when they pulled up in front of the cabin. "Wow. Ben said it was nice—and private—but I didn't expect this."

Marianne nodded. "This end of the resort is really nice. Well, it's all nice, but down here all the cabins are more like mansions and most of them have their own little beaches. I used to take my walk through here last winter when it was quiet."

Clay smiled at her explanation. He'd had a momentary pang of jealousy that maybe she'd stayed here with some other guy before he met her.

"Are you okay?"

He smiled. "I'm wonderful, darlin'. Look— Autumn's out on the front porch waiting for us."

Autumn waved as they got out of the SUV.

Clay took hold of Marianne's hand. He knew she was a little nervous about this and he wanted to do everything he could to let her know he was right there with her. He was grateful to Autumn as she stepped forward and hugged Marianne. That was a special effort for her; she wasn't much of a hugger.

"Hi. It's great to see you again. I know you're going to get swamped when we go in there, but I was watching out for you so that I could catch you for a minute first. I just want to say thank you for making this guy so happy. He's been like a dad to Summer and me, and we always hoped he'd find someone who could make him happy one day."

Marianne hugged her back. "Thank you—for being so welcoming, and for working with Laura to give the two of us another chance."

The door flew open and Lawrence's voice came booming out a second before he did. "Autumn Breese! You sneaky little …" He made a face at Autumn and came straight to Clay and wrapped him in a bear hug. "You should have called to say you were here—then that little madam wouldn't have gotten the jump on us." He turned to smile at Marianne. "There you are. It's so damned good to see you again."

Clay wondered how she'd react when Lawrence wrapped her in a bear hug, too. She didn't seem to mind and hugged him back with a big smile. "It's nice to see you, again, too."

Shawnee had followed him out and pushed him aside. "Never you mind that big oaf, you'll get used to him." She hugged Marianne and then held her at arm's length. "Damn. You are just as beautiful as I remember. You're going to have to share your workout routine with me. But no. On second thought, just say you'll have lunch dates with me? I could starve myself and work out seven days a week and I'd never have a figure like yours."

Marianne chuckled. "I'd love to have lunch with you."

Shawnee smiled. "It's a date—hopefully we can make it a regular date once you get this guy to bring you to Nashville with him." She came and kissed Clay's cheek. "All you need to do is get her to town." She turned back to Marianne. "Once you get there, we'll have so much fun you won't want to leave. We can have lunch and go shopping. I'll show you the sights."

Marianne nodded. "I'd like that. Thank you."

Matt came out next and grinned at Marianne. "It's good to see you again. Thanks for inviting us up here. I love this place. I wouldn't mind having a little cabin of my own up here."

Autumn rolled her eyes. "Only because he thinks he'll get to see more of Chance that way."

Clay laughed. Matt had had something of a man-crush on Chance for a couple of years now. "Leave him alone, Autumn. And are we going to stand out here all afternoon, or are you going to invite us in?"

Once they were inside, Lawrence pulled Clay aside while Autumn and Shawnee commandeered Marianne.

"So, is this it? Did you get everything figured out? Is today the big day?"

Clay nodded happily. "Yep."

Lawrence frowned— "And do you think it's wise?"

Clay's smile faded. "Of course, I do. Are you telling me that you don't?"

"Don't look like that. I only mean, is it wise to ask her tonight? In public like that?"

"It's not going to be in public. We're all going out for dinner *afterward.*"

"Ahh. Good deal. I was worried. Especially with the problems you'd had."

Clay shook his head. "No. I'm not like you. I don't need TV cameras and the whole world watching."

Lawrence smiled. "I know. You're the classy one. Shawnee tells me all the time I should be more like you. But she doesn't mean it."

Clay laughed. "No. She doesn't. She probably just wishes you weren't so much larger than life sometimes."

Lawrence shrugged. "That's my charm. I am what I am."

~ ~ ~

Marianne glanced over at Clay and Lawrence talking. Not so long ago it would have been a big deal to be in the same room as them. She would have been starstruck. Now what she saw was the man she loved talking to his best friend.

Shawnee touched her arm. "Please say you'll come to Nashville? I know it means the world to Clay that you should, and on a selfish note, those two are like that all the time. I can't wait to have you there and for us to be able to do our own thing."

"I will come. I'd like that, too." She wasn't just being polite. Shawnee struck her as someone she'd like to be friends with.

"And don't forget me when you get there," said Autumn. "Everyone thinks I'm this robot who works all the time, but I'd like to get some girlfriend time, too."

Marianne put her arm around Autumn's shoulders and gave her a squeeze. She could tell by the look on Shawnee's face that people didn't usually treat Autumn that way. But Shawnee wasn't a mother, she didn't see what Marianne saw—she didn't see a girl putting on a brave face because she'd never had any other choice. Marianne would happily volunteer to be a safe place for Autumn, a friend with whom she could feel safe to take off her armor. "I'll look forward to it, very much."

They all looked up as the door opened. Marianne recognized Autumn's sister, Summer Breese, immediately. She'd been a huge star for a few years, but had retired and moved to Montana where she'd married the man who followed her in. Even Marianne couldn't think of a different description for Carter Remington than a brick outhouse. He wasn't quite as tall as Clay, but he was stocky, solid muscle. He made Summer look even smaller and more delicate than she was.

Summer ran to Clay and he picked her up and swung her around. Marianne's heart warmed at the affection between them. When Clay put Summer down, Carter shook his hand and embraced him warmly. Carter looked bashful to Marianne. He might look like a big bull, but she got the impression he was more of a sweet lamb underneath.

Clay brought them over to her and came to stand beside her. "Marianne, I'd like you to meet Summer and Carter."

She didn't get the chance to speak before Summer came and flung her arms around her. "It's so great to finally meet you."

"And you."

Carter shook her hand and held her gaze. "It's a pleasure, ma'am."

Marianne warmed to them both immediately. She'd wondered if Summer could really be as sweet as she'd come off in the press. It seemed that she was, and Carter was just a big sweetie. She could see herself growing to love them and Autumn. They might not be Clay's daughters by blood, but they were in every other sense.

In just a couple of hours she understood what Clay had meant, that his friends were people she would like. She loved them already.

Clay came to find her in the kitchen where she was talking with Summer and young Carson. She'd heard him on the radio a few times and knew that he was Lawrence's nephew. She'd thought that he was along for the trip because he was family and that maybe Lawrence had made him come. It turned out that he loved hanging out with them. He was here because he loved his *Uncle* Clay and wanted to see him. Apparently, he knew Laura from her visits to Nashville, too.

"Are you ready to go, darlin'?"

She wasn't. She could happily stay here with them; this was fun.

Her expression must have told him that because he chuckled. "Don't worry, you'll get to see your new friends again later, but we need to go home and get changed."

She smiled at him. "Okay. We can go. As long as this isn't over. I'm having far too much fun."

Summer smiled at her. "Me, too. But we need to go back to our cabin and get changed soon."

Shawnee came over to join them. "Can you believe this, Marianne? For once it's the guys who are saying it's time to wrap it up. We'll just have to continue this party later."

Chapter Nineteen

Clay went into his office while Marianne showered. Everything was ready. He couldn't have been more pleased with the way this afternoon had gone. Marianne had gotten along with them all better than he could have hoped. He had a feeling that she and Shawnee would become fast friends—and he could see Chris joining them to make a threesome to be reckoned with. He smiled at the idea. He hoped that it would help make Marianne feel as much at home in his world as he already felt in hers.

He picked up his phone when it buzzed with a text. It was Laura.

What time can we come?
I'm too excited!

He smiled as he texted back.

Whenever you like. She said she'd be ready in 15.

Laura's reply came back in seconds.

Then tell everyone at least half an hour!
You should know that by now!

He laughed as he tapped out his answer.

I did. I thought you'd like to be here first.

He wondered what she'd have to say to that. Her answer warmed his heart.

And that's just one of many reasons you're perfect for her. See u in 20.

He put his phone away with a smile. He looked forward to Laura being his ... what? Step-daughter. That seemed such an alien concept. He thought of step-kids as being much younger. Laura had been his friend before he'd ever met Marianne. The title didn't really matter; what mattered was that they were becoming family.

~ ~ ~

Marianne checked herself over in the mirror. She looked good. It was important to her that she should tonight. Shawnee was so glamorous, she didn't want to feel dowdy by comparison. She smiled at her reflection; she knew she could wear jeans and a t-shirt if she wanted to and Clay would still see her as the most beautiful woman in the room.

She checked her watch. She needed to get a move on. When they'd come back from visiting the others at the resort, she'd thought they had plenty of time before they went back out to meet them this evening, but Clay had told her that he had a little surprise lined up and asked if she could be ready by six. It was five till six now. She wasn't going to be late.

She fastened her favorite bracelet around her wrist. It was one of her own designs. It might not be anything like all the bling that Shawnee wore, but she wasn't trying to compete. She was more interested in being herself and wearing a reminder of how she wanted to live.

When she got to the bottom of the stairs Clay came to her with a big smile on his face. There was so much love in his eyes she could feel it washing over her.

"You're beautiful."

"Thank you. So are you."

She turned to look through the window as a movement caught her eye. Her heart started to race in a not so pleasant way. "There's someone out there!"

Clay smiled. "Don't worry. It's Laura and Smoke."

She frowned. "Why? I thought we were meeting them at the Boathouse with everyone else later?"

He shrugged. "They wanted to come here first. Shall we go and let them in?"

Marianne went with him to the front door. She was a little put out; she'd been hoping that whatever surprise he had for her meant that they'd get to spend some time alone together before they went out. Still, she was always happy to see her daughter.

She was even more surprised when Clay opened the door and she saw Laura and Smoke weren't the only ones. Lawrence and Shawnee were getting out of an SUV. Summer and Carter pulled up in a truck which Autumn and Matt climbed out the back of. Chris' car was already parked over by the guest house. She looked up at Clay.

He smiled. "I knew if I told you they were coming it'd be work for you, even though you didn't have to. I figured this way would be a nice surprise."

She smiled back at him. He was right. She was glad they were all here and that they'd get to meet each other and see the house, but she would have been in a panic trying to have things ready if she'd known they were all coming. She rested her head against his shoulder for a moment. "Thank you."

Clay waited for a while. He wanted all the initial chatter and introductions to be over, before he gathered everyone around. He loved seeing them all here—the fact they were in the home that he shared with Marianne and the fact their two families were becoming one. Though, most of them weren't strangers.

Summer and Carter already knew Smoke and Laura. Laura knew everyone. Chris had that way with people where she became friends with them as soon as she spoke to them. Young Carson was a little quieter than the rest, but Smoke was chatting with him. It was going well.

Marianne came to stand beside him after having chatted with Shawnee for a while. He dropped a kiss on her lips and then raised an eyebrow at her. "Did I do good?"

She nodded happily. "You did. This is lovely. Thank you."

His heart started to race in his chest. This was it. It'd taken him fifty-five years to get to this point—and for fifty-four of them he'd doubted he ever would. It'd taken the woman standing before him to make him want to be married. To make him want to share his life with someone. And now that he'd found her, he wanted to share every day, every moment with her.

"This is how I want our life to be, darlin'. You and me, making our home here—"

"And going to Nashville sometimes, too," she interrupted.

He chuckled. "I thought you'd warm to that idea once you knew these guys as people and not just as singers."

"I'm sorry, I was so wary at first. I'm over it now."

He nodded. "You were wary about me at first, too. But I know you're over that."

"I am. I just want to live out the rest of our days together."

He sucked in a deep breath and blew it out slowly. "Good, because there's something I want to ask you."

He picked up a fork from the island and tapped it against his glass. "Guys …"

The chatter around the room turned to silence.

~ ~ ~

Marianne's heart started to beat so hard it felt like it might burst out of her chest. As every pair of eyes turned toward her and Clay, she knew why they were all here. Her eyes started to fill with tears before he spoke another word.

She clung tightly to his hand as he got down on one knee before her. Her other hand came up to cover her mouth as she tried to hold in the happy tears that were already starting to roll down her cheeks.

"Marianne," he began.

She nodded vigorously. He didn't need to say another word. Her answer was, yes! It'd always been yes.

He chuckled. "Give me a minute here, would you? There's a few things I'd like to say."

She nodded.

"Marianne. I've loved you since the moment I laid eyes on you. I didn't believe in love at first sight until that night in LA. But the moment I laid eyes on you, I knew."

Marianne had to swallow back a sob. Her doubts and fears had cost them a year that they could have been together if she'd been brave enough to believe him and take the risk.

He shook his head; he knew what she was thinking. "It might have taken us a little while longer to get to this point than I would have liked, but what matters is that we're here now. Love at first sight is an amazing feeling. But love that lasts a lifetime is even more amazing. On that first night, I believed we could have that kind of love. Now, a year later, I know we do. I love you with all of my heart and soul. And want to spend the rest of my days loving you and making you happy. I want to love you, honor you, cherish and protect you. The way you love me makes me a better man. I want to strive every day to deserve your love. Please, say that you'll be my wife and that we can walk through the rest of our days together? Will you marry me?"

Marianne couldn't help it. Her yes came out on a big sob. "Yes." She tried again, but her shoulders were shaking as the sobs wracked her body.

Clay got to his feet and put his arm around her shoulders. He looked worried sick. "Are you okay, darlin'?"

"Yes! I'm sorry. This is ridiculous." She sniffed. "I'm happier than I've been in my whole life, but I can't stop bawling."

He pulled a ring box out of his pocket. "Maybe this will make you smile?" He opened the box and held it up for her to see.

It brought a fresh wave of tears. It was beautiful! It was obviously one of Laura's rings, but it was modeled after one she'd designed herself years ago that Laura had loved. Her own version had been made with a large cubic zirconia. This one was a beautiful diamond. He slid it onto her finger and closed his arms around her. As she pressed herself against his broad, hard chest, she was vaguely aware of applause and shouts of congratulations. The others crowded around them, slapping Clay's back and hugging her. It all seemed to go by in a daze, she was too busy floating on air to be a part of the reality.

Laura waited until all the others were done and then she came and linked her arm through Marianne's. "Congratulations."

Another tear rolled down her cheek. "Thank you." She held her hand up. "And thank you for this. I didn't even know you remembered it."

Laura's eyes shone. "I've never forgotten it. I was only little, but I remember when you made it and I remember asking you why you wore it when you weren't married. You said that just because you didn't have a husband shouldn't mean you couldn't wear a nice ring." She smiled. "Of course, I figured out later that it was to stop guys from hitting on you at the diner. When I was little I used to pray that one day you would have a husband and when I got older I promised myself that I'd make you a real version of that ring. You're so talented, Mom. It's beautiful."

Marianne had to swallow hard to keep herself from bawling. Clay closed his arm around her shoulders. "I'm just grateful that I get to be your husband—and that I finally gave Laura reason to make you your ring."

"Thank you. Thank you both."

Laura reached out and touched the bracelet on her wrist. "I'm glad you're wearing that."

Marianne smiled at her. "It's a reminder of how I want to live my life." She looked up at Clay. "It's going to be my motto for our life together."

He leaned down to take a look. "What does it say?" He smiled when he read it.

"Live the moments," said Marianne. "And I intend to. Every single one of them."

~ ~ ~

Clay made his way to the bar. He could see the Boathouse becoming his new favorite hangout. It was a great place. Half the people here were either friends or relatives, and the rest were easy-going and either didn't recognize him and the others or were too busy having a good time of their own to care.

Autumn came to stand beside him. "Congratulations."

"Thanks. You like her, don't you?"

Autumn gave him one of her rare, gentle smiles. "I like her a lot. I'm looking forward to spending more time with her."

"Hey!" The blonde bartender, Kenzie, greeted them with a smile. Clay liked her; she struck him as a tough cookie with a heart of gold—a lot like Autumn. "I hear congratulations are in order. What can I get you? It's on me."

"Thanks. I'll get them. I'm getting a round in, but I appreciate it."

"Next time then."

"I'll take you up on it. Marianne and I will come in one afternoon before it gets busy, sit at the bar, maybe your Chase will want to join us?"

Kenzie grinned at him. "You can bet your ass he will."

Autumn smiled at her and then at Clay. "Maybe I should stick around for this and invite Eddie and his fiancée too. They're good."

"Please do," said Kenzie. "Can you imagine how happy they'll be if I get them a date with the two of you?"

Clay laughed. "Consider it done. We're leaving on Monday, but as soon as we get back, we'll drop in and set something up."

"And give me enough notice so I can get here," said Autumn.

Clay took the drinks back to the table and left Autumn chatting with Kenzie. She'd only heard the band warm up so far. He wouldn't be at all surprised if she wanted to talk seriously about them by the end of tonight. She'd have to wait though. He didn't plan to hang around here talking music at the end of the night. He planned to take Marianne—his fiancée—home and make love to her, and then maybe start making wedding plans.

She wasn't at the table when he got there. He looked around wondering who she was off talking to. It seemed that everyone in the place wanted to stop them and congratulate them.

He frowned when he couldn't see her. Davin was over near the doors. He looked around again. Adam was stationed between the stage and the ladies' room. Maybe she was in there.

Chris came and touched his arm. "Congratulations, again. I have to tell you, you have good taste. I've known her all her life and she's the best person I know."

Clay put his arm around her shoulders and gave her a squeeze. He liked Chris. "Thank you. She's the best person I know, too. I know how lucky I am."

Chris grinned up at him. "Good, just don't ever forget it, because you'll have me to answer to if you do."

He laughed with her, but he knew she was only half joking. "Don't worry. I plan to look after her for the rest of her days.

I'll never hurt her, and I'll do my best to protect her from any hurt."

~ ~ ~

Marianne was glad to step inside the cool of the ladies' room. She was overheated from all the excitement. She was so happy. Everyone was so happy for her. Clay was so wonderful. And he was going to be her husband! She stepped into one of the stalls, believing that this must be the happiest night of her life.

When she stepped out again, she feared it might be the last night of her life.

The woman stood just inside the doorway. Her back against it. If looks could kill, then Marianne knew she'd no longer be breathing. Pure evil was the only way to describe that look.

"You can't have him; he's mine."

Marianne went from overheated to chilled to the bone as the woman took a step toward her.

"He needs me. He just doesn't know it yet." She came closer still. "You're weak. He won't miss you when you're gone."

Adrenaline surged in Marianne's veins. "I'm not weak." The sound of her voice matched her words. Even to herself she sounded strong and composed.

The woman paused, but then came forward another step. She looked Marianne up and down as if sizing her up. She froze when she saw the ring on her finger. "Nooo!" She screamed and threw herself forward, gauging her nails down the side of Marianne's face, then grabbing her hand, trying to remove the ring.

That act was enough to push Marianne to action. She'd been frozen to the spot, wondering how she could get out of there. Now she knew she couldn't—not without a fight. She curled her hand into a fist, first to keep the ring on her finger, but also to use to try to push the woman away.

It didn't work as she grabbed a handful of Marianne's hair and somehow, they both ended up on the floor. She saw stars as a fist landed in her face.

"You can't have him!"

Marianne hit back and scrambled across the floor, trying to get to the door. The woman grabbed hold of her ankle just as she got to her feet. "You're too weak."

For some reason that enraged Marianne. "I am not weak!" She knew that too many people in her life had believed she was weak just because she was timid. They weren't the same thing and if there was a good time to prove that—to herself as much as anyone else—that time would be right now. She looked around desperately to see if there was anything she could use as a weapon. Of course, there wasn't.

She managed to get back to her feet, but the woman got up, too, and came at her again. This time Marianne was ready. She grabbed hold of her and used her own momentum to swing her against the door. The breath rushed out of her lungs and she stood, stunned for a moment. Marianne was stunned, too, but she came to her senses and grabbed hold of the woman's arm. She twisted it behind her and pushed it up her back, making the woman gasp.

"Let go of me!"

"No way!" Marianne knew this was just a momentary advantage, but she didn't know what to do next.

The woman screamed again, sounding like a savage animal.

Marianne twisted her arm higher up her back and tried to figure out how she could open the door and get out without setting her loose.

Fortunately, she didn't have to figure it out. The door flew open and Adam and Clay came barreling in, almost knocking them over.

Adam took hold of the woman and Clay came straight to Marianne. "Are you all right, darlin'?" He touched her face,

which made her remember the scratches—which now stung
like hell.

She leaned against him, trembling from head to toe now it
was over. "I'm okay."

Adam was hustling the woman out of there, but she got in
one last scream before she went. "Nooo! He's mine!"

Clay closed his arms around Marianne. "I'm so, so sorry
darlin', I said I'd keep you safe."

She looked up into his eyes. The relief came out as laughter.
"I am safe. It's okay, and best of all?"

He raised his eyebrows. "There's a best to this?"

She nodded. "There is—now it can be over. Whether she
gets help or gets put in jail, I don't really care anymore, but
surely they can do something now?"

"They better damned well had, and if not I'm putting
Lawrence on it."

"What do you mean?"

"Nothing. All that matters is that you're okay. I should have
been able to protect you, though. You needed me, and I wasn't
here. I'm so sorry."

She tucked her fingers under his chin and made him look
into her eyes. "Clay, there's nothing to be sorry for. In a way,
I'm glad this happened. She told me I was weak, which
reminded me that I'm not. She tried to take the ring—and
there was no way in hell I was going to let that happen."

"I'm proud of you, that you fought her off, but you shouldn't
have to. You needed me to take care of it before now, and I
didn't."

She planted a kiss on his lips. "I told you before, I was raised
in Texas, by a single momma. Where I come from, no woman
ever *needed* a man for anything. Want—that's a different
matter. But that woman reminded me who I am—that I'm
powerful in my own right. I love you, I want you, but I don't
need you to make it all right for me."

He dropped a kiss on her lips. "I get it. You're not only beautiful, you're strong, too. You're not going to be my little lady, you're going to be my equal and my partner."

She nodded. "And I'm going to love you with all my heart for the rest of my days."

"Just as I'm going to love you."

He lowered his head and she reached her arms up around his neck. He held her close against his chest and kissed her deeply. They only stopped when the bathroom door opened. Marianne looked up to see all their friends and family crowding around the doorway, looking worried.

Laura laughed. "You guys! Aren't you a little old to be making out in the bathroom?"

Marianne had to laugh, and the sound of Clay's deep, sexy chuckle mixed with it.

"We were just taking a moment," said Clay.

"Everything's okay now," Marianne reassured them.

He hugged her into his side, and she rested her head against his shoulder, knowing that her words were true. Everything was okay now that they were together with no more threats on the horizon. They could step into their future without looking over their shoulders. And they could live the hell out of all the moments they had left;

;

A Note from SJ

I hope you enjoyed Marianne and Clay's story. Please let your friends know about the books if you feel they would enjoy them as well. It would be wonderful if you would leave me a review, I'd very much appreciate it.

There are so many more stories still to tell and quite honestly, I don't know where I'm going next! As you may have noticed, there are several new couples angling for a book at the lake. There are also a few old friends still waiting to get married. The Nashville folks are pushing Clay and Marianne to the forefront, and there is a bunch of cowboys growing very impatient in Montana. That's without even thinking about Grady who would like the Hamiltons series to be at least five books long. And Spider, from the Davenports series—he's no millionaire but he so deserves his own book and will get one.

If you know me at all, you'll know that planning and organization are not my strong suits. However, I intend to spend the next few weeks mapping out what I'm going to write next year – yulp! I'll let you know when I figure it out.

In the meantime, check out the "Also By" page to see if any of my other series appeal to you – I have a couple of freebie series starters too so you can take them for a test drive in ebook format from all the major online retailers. You can find all the information you need on that on my website.
www.sjmccoy.com

If you'd like to keep in touch, there are a few options to keep up with me and my imaginary friends:
The best way is to Join up on the website for my Newsletter. Don't worry I won't bombard you! I'll let you know about upcoming releases, share a sneak peek or two and keep you in the loop for a couple of fun giveaways I have coming up :0)

You can join my readers group to chat about the books on Facebook or just browse and like my Facebook Page.

I occasionally attempt to say something in 140 characters or less(!) on Twitter

And I'm always in the process of updating my website at

www.sjmccoy.com

with new book updates and even some videos. Plus, you'll find the latest news on new releases and giveaways in my blog.

I love to hear from readers, so feel free to email me at AuthorSJMcCoy@gmail.com.. I'm better at that! :0)

I hope our paths will cross again soon. Until then, take care, and thanks for your support—you are the reason I write!

Love

SJ

PS Project Semicolon

You may have noticed that the final sentence of the story closed with a semi-colon. It isn't a typo. <u>Project Semi Colon</u> is a non-profit movement dedicated to presenting hope and love to those who are struggling with depression, suicide, addiction and self-injury. Project Semicolon exists to encourage, love and inspire. It's a movement I support with all my heart.

> *"A semicolon represents a sentence the author could have ended, but chose not to. The sentence is your life and the author is you."*
>
> - Project Semicolon

This author started writing after her son was killed in a car crash. At the time I wanted my own story to be over, instead I chose to honour a promise to my son to write my 'silly stories' someday. I chose to escape into my fictional world. I know for many who struggle with depression, suicide can appear to be the only escape. The semicolon has become a symbol of support, and hopefully a reminder – Your story isn't over yet

Also by SJ McCoy

Summer Lake Silver

Clay and Marianne in Like Some Old Country Song

Seymour and Chris in A Dream Too Far

Ted and Audrey in A Little Rain Must Fall

Izzy and Diego in Where the Rainbow Ends

Manny and Nina in Silhouettes Shadows and Sunsets

Teresa and Cal in More than Sometimes

Russ and Ria in Like a Soft Sweet Breeze

Summer Lake

Love Like You've Never Been Hurt

Work Like You Don't Need the Money

Dance Like Nobody's Watching

Fly Like You've Never Been Grounded

Laugh Like You've Never Cried

Sing Like Nobody's Listening

Smile Like You Mean It

The Wedding Dance

Chasing Tomorrow

Dream Like Nothing's Impossible

Ride Like You've Never Fallen

Live Like There's No Tomorrow

The Wedding Flight

Fight Like You've Never Lost

Summer Lake Seasons

Angel and Luke in Take These Broken Wings

Zack and Maria in Too Much Love to Hide

Logan and Roxy in Sunshine Over Snow

Ivan and Abbie in Chase the Blues Away
Colt and Cassie in Forever Takes a While
Austin and Amber in Tell the Stars to Shine
Donovan and Elle in Please Don't Say Goodbye

MacFarland Ranch
Wade and Sierra in The Cowboy's Unexpected Love
Janey and Rocket in The Cowgirl's Unmistakable Love
Coming soon:
Deacon and Candy in The Sheriff's Irresistible Love

Remington Ranch
Mason
Shane
Carter
Beau
Four Weddings and a Vendetta

A Chance and a Hope
Chance is a guy with a whole lot of story to tell. He's part of
the fabric of both Summer Lake and Remington Ranch. He
needed three whole books to tell his own story.
Chance Encounter
Finding Hope
Give Hope a Chance

Love in Nashville
Autumn and Matt in Bring on the Night

About the Author

I'm SJ, a coffee addict, lover of chocolate and drinker of good red wines. I'm a lost soul and a hopeless romantic. Reading and writing are necessary parts of who I am. Though perhaps not as necessary as coffee! I can drink coffee without writing, but I can't write without coffee.

I grew up loving romance novels, my first boyfriends were book boyfriends, but life intervened, as it tends to do, and I wandered down the paths of non-fiction for many years. My life changed completely a few years ago and I returned to Romance to find my escape.

I write 'Sweet n Steamy' stories because to me there is enough angst and darkness in real life. My favorite romances are happy escapes with a focus on fun, friendships and happily-ever-afters, just like the ones I write.

These days I live in beautiful Montana, the last best place. If I'm not reading or writing, you'll find me just down the road in the park - Yellowstone. I have deer, eagles and the occasional bear for company, and I like it that way :0)

Made in United States
Orlando, FL
18 September 2023

37052073R00133

M000083468

Virtues of Soy

A
Practical
Health Guide and Cookbook

Written and Cover Illustration
by

Monique N. Gilbert

Universal Publishers
USA • 2000

The information contained in this book has been obtained by the author
from sources believed to be reliable, accurate and true. The author does
not intend to diagnose, dispense medical advice or prescribe the use of diet
as a form of treatment for illness without medical approval. The intent is
only to offer health and cooking information to help you understand the
benefits of soy and soy-based products and how to incorporate them into
your diet and lifestyle. In the event you use this information without a
health practitioner's approval, you are prescribing for yourself, which is
your right. However, the publisher and author assume no responsibility.

Virtues of Soy:
A Practical Health Guide and Cookbook

Copyright © 2000 by Monique N. Gilbert
Cover Illustration Copyright © 2000 by Monique N. Gilbert

All rights reserved.
No part of this book may be reproduced or transmitted in any form or by
any means, electronic or mechanical, including photocopying,
recording, or by any information storage and/or retrieval system without
permission from the author.

monique@chef.net

Universal Publishers/UPUBLISH.com
USA • 2000

ISBN 1-58112-706-5

www.upublish.com/books/gilbert.htm

This book is dedicated to Michael Tagrin.
My devoted husband, lover, best friend and soul mate.
You showed me the value of patience, perseverance and
the importance of integrity.
Thank you for your encouragement, enthusiasm, love and support.
You helped me make this book, and so much more in my life, possible.

This book is also dedicated to my parents,
Marianne and Warren Gilbert.
My mother gave me a passion for cooking and discovering different
cuisines, and my father, ambition and a thirst for knowledge.
Thank you both for all your love and support.

Each, in their own special way,
influenced my life and inspired my actions.

TABLE OF CONTENTS

INTRODUCTION

Soy is an extremely versatile and nutritiously packed legume (bean) which promotes good health and vitality. Current research suggests soy foods can ward off heart attack, stroke, various cancers, osteoporosis, menopausal symptoms, diabetes and kidney disease. These medical conditions and diseases are widespread and approaching epidemic levels throughout our Western society. Yet soy is still a mystery to many Americans. Therefore, I feel it is my mission to educate and enlighten everyone interested in this glorious bean.

This book will examine the many *Virtues of Soy*. Not only will it describe the benefits of soy nutrition, it will also teach you how to incorporate soy into a health promoting diet. There are three very good reasons why you may want to learn how to make your own soy foods. First of all, soy can protect and enhance your overall health. Secondly, preparing your own soy foods is much more economical than buying it ready made. Finally, good old-fashioned home cooking is usually tastier, more varied and more nutritious than most commercially prepared foods.

The first part of this book discusses the background and nutritional breakdown of soy. It also details how and why soy positively affects the various health problems mentioned above. All this information is presented in a question and answer format, with references for each section provided at the end of the book. If you have any medical condition, please consult your doctor before making any dietary changes.

The second part of this book explains how to deliciously prepare soy-based products like tofu, textured soy protein, soy flour, tempeh, miso and soymilk. I have included 169 of my favorite original kitchen-tested recipes. Follow the recipe instructions carefully at first. Once you are sure of the cooking process and flavor, you can begin to experiment on your own and make adjustments to fit your own taste. Cooking should be a magical and creative event that provides enjoyable nourishment, so have fun with it.

I have been learning about and using soy for more than ten years, and would like to share with you the knowledge that I have gained along the way. The soybean has a very long and interesting past, with a very promising future. Soy and soy-based products possess many unique qualities. Because soy foods contain components that provide health benefits beyond basic nutrition, I consider soy as culinary medicine. Once you become informed about soy's many attributes and uses, you will be more apt to include it into your diet as well. By doing this, you too can reap soy's benefits and enjoy a happy healthy long life.

1

CHAPTER 1: SOY CULINARY HISTORY & DIETS

Recent studies show evidence that adding soy to your diet makes good nutritional sense and provides many health benefits. The Mayo Health Clinic newsletter reports rates of heart attacks, cancer and osteoporosis are far lower in Asian cultures where soy is the main source of protein. This has fueled the current interest in, and increased research of, soy. However, considering soy foods as culinary medicine is not a new concept. China has been extensively cultivating and using soybeans as a source of food and medicine for 5,000 years. So important are soybeans to the Chinese that they're considered one of the five sacred foods for health and well being, along with rice, wheat, barley and millet.

How can I know that soy foods are not just one of the latest health food fads, in the news today and forgotten by tomorrow?

While soy may be considered a new health food in the United States, soy and soy-based products actually have a long and extensive culinary history. More than 3,000 years ago farmers in Manchurian China began cultivating the wild legume to grow upright, and made soymilk from the beans. Around 2,200 years ago, in Han Dynasty China, soybeans were first fermented to make douchi, the predecessor of soy sauce and miso. Soy began to be fermented to make miso (soy paste), shoyu (soy sauce) and tempeh (a soybean cake invented in Indonesia). During this time, the Chinese also ate and considered steamed green soybeans (edamame), roasted soynuts, doufu (soy curd) and soybean sprouts highly nutritious.

Several hundred years later, during the sixth and seventh centuries, the Japanese began adopting many aspects of Chinese culture including the processing of soybeans into doufu (which became known in Japan as tofu). Japanese monks refined and exclusively made tofu and miso until the tenth century.

During the seventeenth century, the flourishing spice trade in the Far East brought soy sauce and tofu over to Europe. Soy sauce became a popular and widely traded commodity at this time.

Benjamin Franklin introduced tofu to America. He discovered it while living in France in the late 1700's. Samuel Bowen was the first to bring the soybean to America for cultivation. By 1767, soybeans were being grown in Savannah, Georgia, processed into soy sauce and sold to England. During the civil war soybeans were even used to make a facsimile of coffee.

In the 1930's, the United States began to explore and develop soybean varieties through hybridization. By the 1940's, the United States Department of Agriculture (USDA) promoted soy to be grown as a green vegetable. To supplement protein requirements and help civilians through the food rationing of World War II, people were encouraged to plant soybeans as part of their victory garden. During this time, canned soybeans were also available in grocery stores. After World War II, farmers found soybean oil to be a growing market for their crops. Grocery stores began selling soy oil, pure or blended, under the generic name vegetable oil. Every part of the soybean found a use.

By the late 1950's, soy flour, soy grits and 70-percent soy concentrates had been perfected. Soy flour became an added ingredient in many bakery goods. By 1960, a 90-percent soy protein extract had been produced. During the 1960's, *Baco-bits*, a non-meat bacon substitute, became America's first commercially successful soy-based product. By 1970, the first soy protein with the texture of meat was developed and marketed as Textured Vegetable Protein (TVP).

In 1980, tofu appeared in U.S. supermarkets. Health food stores and Asian food markets were no longer the only suppliers of tofu. Americans were introduced to *Tofutti* in 1982, the first popular non-dairy ice cream using a blend of tofu, soymilk, and other soy proteins. The mid-1980's marked the beginning of the ready-made and frozen second generation soy foods, like soy-based hotdogs, burgers, cold-cuts and entrees.

During the 1990's, the USDA allowed up to 30 percent of soy in school lunch meats like hamburgers and chicken patties. A few schools were allowed to offer 100 percent soy foods through a la carte menu. There, students were able to buy whatever combinations they wanted, not just USDA approved meals.

By the year 2000, federal officials concerned with the amount of fat in school lunches, dropped their restrictions on how much soy could be used in all federally subsidized meals. They allowed schools and day care centers to increase the amount of soy added into their standard meals to 100 percent. Schools could now serve completely meatless entrees consisting of tofu, veggie-burgers and other soy-based products as meat substitutes. During that same year, the federal government also updated its Dietary Guidelines for Americans, which for the first time, recommended soy products. The new guidelines included soy-based beverages (soymilk) with added calcium in the dairy group, as well as, tofu and soy-based burgers in the meat and beans group.

Today, a much wider variety of soy-based foods can easily be found on grocery store shelves. Food manufacturers have introduced more than two thousand new soy-based products to the American marketplace since 1985, and the number is ever increasing as each day goes by. Besides the traditional soy foods like tofu, soy sauce, miso and tempeh, soy also comes in other forms, known as modern soy foods. These include soy flour, textured soy protein (textured vegetable protein), soy meal, soy concentrates, and soy isolates. A second generation of soy foods based on

3

traditional and modern soy products has blossomed. These processed foods include soy-based burgers, hotdogs, cold-cuts, frozen entrees, soy cheese, soy yogurt, soy ice cream, pocket sandwiches, snack bars and soy protein powders, just to name a few. Many mainstream grocery stores are even prominently displaying soy products right alongside traditional food items. Americans have such a diverse selection of soy products to choose from in today's marketplace, that soy foods are definitely here to stay.

What sparked so much interest in soy and soy-based products?

Demographic studies from around the world suggested that soy products and their constituents are partly responsible for the lower rates of chronic diseases and conditions in different populations. Many Asian societies traditionally use soy and soy-based products as their primary source of protein. After noticing dramatically lower rates of heart disease, cancer, osteoporosis and menopausal symptoms in many of these Asian cultures, researchers began to increase their focus on soy.

Chinese researchers have shown that people who eat a traditional Asian diet have lower blood cholesterol levels and are much less likely to suffer the physical symptoms of heart disease. The American Journal of Epidemiology published a study noting that people in China and Japan historically have had lower rates of breast, colon, rectal, lung, stomach, prostate, endometrial and ovarian cancers. Studies of Chinese and Japanese women reveal that they have one-fifth the rate of breast cancer of U.S. women. When comparing dietary habits to bone health, Asian women tend to have a lower incidence of osteoporosis than American women. Population studies also disclose that Asian women have fewer hot flashes and other menopausal symptoms than their American counterparts. About 85 percent of North American women report experiencing hot flashes, while only 25 percent of Japanese women report the same.

However, what researchers find most compelling is that the cancer mortality rates in Asian countries are much lower than in the United States. Countries which consume large quantities of soy in their diet also have very low rates of cancer death, even though many of them have high rates of smoking. In Japan, the mortality rate from breast cancer is only one-fourth, and the death rate from prostate cancer one-fifth, that of the United States. Interestingly, the rate of getting prostate cancer is the same for both Japanese and American men; however, the rate of death from prostate cancer is far lower in Japan than in the United States. In Asia, prostate cancer often does not develop into any life-threatening condition, while in the U.S. and other Western countries, it more often develops into an advanced and aggressive form.

4

What exactly is the typical Asian diet, and how is it different from the standard American diet?

Soy foods are used in many Asian countries like China, Japan, Taiwan, Korea, Indonesia and Vietnam. While the Chinese have been using soy the longest, the Japanese have been using the widest variety of soy products. The typical Asian diet is high in fruits, vegetables, rice, green tea and soy. Protein is mainly derived from soybeans, tofu, miso, soymilk, tempeh and many other soy-based products. This type of diet is low in meat, fat and dairy products, with a moderate amount of fish. Meat is used more as a condiment than the main course. The quick method of cooking, characteristic of Asian cuisine, also plays an important role in the Asian diet. Steaming and stir-frying reduces the amount of fat needed to prepare foods, and allows foods to retain much of their nutrients.

In contrast, the standard American or Western diet is high in meat, dairy, potatoes, starches, sugar, soda, fast foods and junk foods. Beef, pork, fish and poultry are the main sources of protein. This type of diet is low in fiber and high in saturated fats and cholesterol. Deep-fried foods, such as french fries, potato chips and onion rings, are popular but very unhealthy. This method of cooking causes foods to absorb a high amount of fat, and the oils used to deep-fry are not always the best. Often vegetables are overcooked, causing them to lose many of their nutrients. The quick method of eating, characteristic of American dinning, also plays an important role in the Western diet. The convenience of ready made and processed foods often provides a lot of calories with little nutritional value.

What makes researchers believe that a soy rich diet is the cause of the health differences between Asian and Western populations?

Researchers have been studying soy's health benefits for more than 30 years. Results from various population-based studies demonstrate that soy products have a protective effect against many chronic diseases and health problems. Research on diet's role in heart disease and cancer has found the plant-based diets in many lesser developed societies are the healthiest, so long people get enough to eat. Countries where soy consumption is high have relatively low rates of prostate and breast cancer compared to the United States and European countries, where soy consumption is low. Over 20 studies involving Asian participants found that consuming just one serving of soy daily is associated with a reduced risk of breast, prostate, colon, rectal, lung, and stomach cancers. One study in Japan even showed that men who consumed tofu five times a week had their risk for prostate cancer reduced by 65 percent.

5

Migration studies also supports the theory that a soy-based diet protects against many major health problems. When people from Asian countries move to Western countries, like the United States or Australia, and take on a Western diet, their health starts to change. They begin to have the same chronic diseases, conditions, and rates of death typically seen in these Western countries. Chinese research shows that when Chinese people move to Western cities, such as San Francisco or Sydney, their arteries make the changes which lead to heart disease. By adopting a Western diet and lifestyle, they increasingly begin to suffer the physical symptoms associated with this disease. Migration studies also disclose that when Japanese men move to Hawaii and take on the typical low-soy American diet, their death rate from prostate cancer increases to the same level as American men.

Since the early 1990's, well over 1,000 research articles have been published on soy and how it positively affects cholesterol levels, the cardiovascular system, cancer, osteoporosis, and menopause. Researchers concluded that diet and lifestyle factors, not genetics, are primarily responsible for the health differences between the two cultures.

What kind of diet do researchers recommend to promote and maintain good health?

According to the American Institute of Cancer Research (AICR), the smartest strategy to promoting good overall health is to eat a balanced, predominantly plant-based and nutritionally-dense diet. Most of your daily calories should come from vegetables, fruits, whole grains and beans, especially soy.

Take advantage of the highly developed food distribution system, which allows a vast array of fruits, vegetables and other plant foods to be available throughout the year. Eat less fat and more fiber. Make plant-based foods the largest part of every meal. Limit the amount of animal-based foods, such as meat and dairy products, which are loaded with saturated fat and cholesterol. Use olive oil or canola oil instead of butter or margarine to reduce your intake of saturated fat and hydrogenated fat. Moderate your consumption of fried, salted and smoked foods. Eat portions to satisfy hunger, not to clean the plate. The AICR recommends these steps to help protect against several cancers, lower the risk of heart disease and promote good health. Soy and most soy-based products meet these dietary guidelines. They are low in saturated fat, high in fiber, and contain many other important nutrients which offer protection from health problems like heart disease, stroke, cancer, osteoporosis, diabetes and kidney disease.

The National Cancer Institute (NCI) links one-third of all cancer deaths to diet. They state that we can reduce the risk of cancer and other chronic diseases through dietary means. Both the AICR and the NCI believe in the benefits of eating a plant-based diet, rich in soy foods. They feel it is reasonable for most of us to include soy products, like tofu, soymilk, tempeh and textured soy protein, as part of a healthy diet. If nothing else, soy can be an excellent and complete alternative protein source when decreasing your consumption of meat and dairy products.

However, researchers do not want people to consider soy as a magic bullet to counteract bad eating habits. They don't want people to rely on adding just one or two soy products to their diets while continuing to eat foods high in saturated fat and cholesterol. Nor do they advise people to consume large quantities of soy supplements to try to achieve soy's health benefits. Balance, moderation, and variety are the keys to a healthy diet. Nothing should be excessively consumed. Loading up on any one food or nutrient is never wise. Each soy-based or plant-based product provides a different chemical composition. The best way to take advantage of these various beneficial nutrients and compounds, is to adopt good eating habits which include a wide assortment of nutritionally-dense foods.

CHAPTER 2: NUTRITIONAL & BENEFICIAL COMPOUNDS

Soy foods are nutritional powerhouses, providing many essential nutrients the body needs every day. Soy and soy-based products contain all three macro-nutrients the body needs in large amounts to function properly, namely protein, carbohydrates and fat. They also contain many micro-nutrients that the body needs in small quantities to maintain good health. These include vitamins and minerals, as well as beneficial compounds like phytochemicals and antioxidants.

Soybeans and most soy-based products are high in protein, dietary fiber, and a variety of micro-nutrients and phytochemicals. Low-fat complex carbohydrate soy foods, like textured soy protein and soy flour, offer protection against colon, rectal and pancreatic cancers due to their high content of fiber, vitamins, minerals and phytochemicals. These products along with tofu, tempeh and soymilk, can lower cholesterol and the risk of heart disease; reduce the risk of some breast, ovarian and prostate cancers; prevent osteoporosis and diabetes; and ease many menopausal symptoms.

Which particular vitamins and minerals are found in soy foods?

Soy foods contain a wide array of vitamins and minerals. They are very good sources of vitamin E and many of the B vitamins, especially niacin, pyridoxine (B-6) and folacin (folic acid). Vitamin E is needed for muscle development, red blood cell protection, blood clot prevention, male potency and various other bodily functions. It works with selenium in strengthening capillary walls and protecting tissue against the oxidation of LDL cholesterol (the bad cholesterol). Vitamin E is an antioxidant that helps maintain a healthy heart. It also has been linked with slowing the aging process.

Niacin is essential for healthy skin, digestive track, nervous system and the production of sex hormones. Pyridoxine (B-6) helps the body process amino acids and enhances the immune system. Blood levels of this vitamin naturally decline with age. It is necessary for macro-nutrient metabolism, energy conversion and weight control. Folic acid (folacin) is needed for cell growth and reproduction. It functions with vitamins B-12 and C in breaking down proteins and making hemoglobin (a compound in the blood that carries oxygen from the lungs to the cells and carbon dioxide away from cells and back to the lungs). Folic acid also helps make hydrochloric acid in the stomach (which is required for digestion), stimulates the appetite, and slows the graying of hair.

Soy foods are also loaded with the minerals iron, zinc, potassium, copper, magnesium and calcium. Iron is needed for healthy red blood cell production. It is vital for the formation of hemoglobin and myoglobin (a compound that causes muscle tissue to be red in color and able to store oxygen). Zinc aids digestion, the metabolism of protein, prostate gland function and the body's healing process. Potassium helps control the activity of nerves and muscles. It is also one of the important minerals that help regulate blood pressure. Copper works with vitamin C to form elastin and aids the formation of red blood cells. It is needed for good bones, hair color and skin. Magnesium works with calcium and phosphorus for the healthy maintenance and formation of bones and teeth. It is a catalyst in the utilization of macro-nutrients, essential for the production and release of energy. Magnesium is also important for proper nerve, heart and muscle function, healthy arteries, and mental alertness.

While soybeans have a modest amount of calcium, tofu is an excellent source of this important mineral, when it is processed with calcium sulfate (gypsum). Calcium is necessary for the development of strong and healthy bones and teeth. It also helps nerve signal transmissions, muscle contractions, blood clotting, and heart function. A healthful diet with adequate calcium is crucial in achieving peak bone mass in children and young adults and maintaining bone health during adulthood. Individuals who do not store enough calcium throughout their lives have an increased risk for developing osteoporosis. Recent findings show calcium may also help relieve menstrual cycle discomfort. Other soy products, like soymilk, have added extra vitamins and minerals, like vitamin D and calcium, to boost their nutritional profile. To see if you are getting a calcium-rich soy food, check the list of ingredients and the Nutrition Facts label.

I keep hearing how some fats are good for you and some are bad. I thought all fats were bad and should be eliminated from the diet. What makes a fat good or bad?

The body needs a certain amount of fat in the diet. It stores fat to serve as a quick energy source and to protect important organs. However, all fats and oils are high in calories. Fats provide 9 calories for each gram contained in food, while protein and carbohydrates each provide only 4 calories. While fat is necessary and essential for proper health, some types of fats are damaging to the cardiovascular system.

Artery-clogging fats that increase blood cholesterol include saturated fat and trans fat. Saturated fat mainly comes from animal sources like meat and dairy products, but it can also be found in coconut and palm oils. Trans fat comes from hydrogenated vegetable oils, like margarine and vegetable shortening. Both saturated fats and trans fats stay solid at room temperature.

A more heart healthy fat is unsaturated fat, generally found in vegetables. This type of fat includes both monounsaturated and polyunsaturated fats. Monounsaturated fat is found in olive, canola and peanut oils. These oils are liquid at room temperature but start to thicken when refrigerated. This type of fat is considered the healthiest for your heart and body. Avocados and nuts also contain monounsaturated fat. Polyunsaturated fat is found in soybean, corn, safflower and sunflower oils. These oils are liquid at room temperature and in the refrigerator. This type of fat is considered the next healthiest fat that does not clog arteries.

However, when unsaturated vegetable oils are manufactured into solid form, they turn into trans fats. This type of fat is commonly called fully or partially hydrogenated vegetable oil in a food's list of ingredients. Trans fats are found in hundreds of processed foods, usually to protect against spoiling and to enhance flavor. Restaurants tend to use a lot of trans fat (hydrogenated vegetable oil), especially for frying.

Trans fats are even worse for the cardiovascular system than saturated fats. Researchers have conservatively calculated that trans fats alone account for at least 30,000 premature deaths from heart disease every year in the United States. Recent studies indicate that trans fats drive up the body's LDL, the bad cholesterol, even faster than saturated fats. High levels of cholesterol has been linked to heart disease and stroke.

Diets high in fat, particularly saturated fat, also promotes breast, colon, endometrial, lung, prostate and rectal cancers. Therefore, saturated fats and trans fats are the only fats that we should strive to eliminate from our diet. Replace these fats with monounsaturated and polyunsaturated fats. The American Heart Association recommends that daily fat intake should be less than 30 percent of total calories; saturated fat intake less than 8-10 percent of total calories, and cholesterol less than 300 milligrams per day.

What kind of fat is found in soy foods? Are soy foods high in fat?

Soybeans and most soy products contain no cholesterol and virtually no saturated fat. The fat found in soy foods is mostly polyunsaturated and high in essential fatty acids, especially Omega-3. Our body cannot produce essential fatty acids, but we need them for correct growth and functioning. Omega-3 is necessary for proper brain growth and development. Tests have shown Omega-3 fatty acid can help lower blood cholesterol levels and inhibit the growth of tumors. Evidence also suggests Omega-3 can reduce the risk of cardiovascular disease, hypertension, arthritis and diabetes.

The actual fat content in soy foods varies considerably. Some soy-based products like textured soy protein and defatted soy flour contain next to no fat, because processing methods extract the fat from these products. Other soy foods do contain fat, like tofu, tempeh, soy cheese, soy yogurt and soymilk. However, low-fat varieties of these soy products are also available. Some second generation soy products can be high in total fat or contain trans fat (hydrogenated oil). Always read the Nutrition Facts label and list of ingredients to find out the amount of, and the type of, fat contained in any particular soy food. Avoid all foods that have fully or partially hydrogenated oil in its ingredients.

Are soy foods a good source of fiber?

Yes, soybeans and many soy-based products are excellent sources of fiber. According to the American Heart Association (AHA), fiber is important for the health of the digestive system as well as for lowering cholesterol. Dietary fiber is a transparent solid carbohydrate that is the main part of the cell walls of plants. It is nondigestible, but provides the bulk needed for proper functioning of the stomach and intestines. Fiber promotes healthy intestinal action and prevents constipation by moving bodily waste through the digestive tract faster, so harmful substances don't have as much contact with the intestinal walls. Both the AHA and the National Cancer Institute recommend that people consume 25 to 30 grams of fiber a day.

Whole soybeans and foods made from whole soybeans, such as soy flour, textured soy protein and tempeh, are extremely rich in fiber. Some soy foods, like tofu and soymilk, contain very little fiber due to the way they are processed. Tofu, for example, leaves most of its fiber behind in processing when the milk is squeezed from the soybean. A fiber-rich diet is very important in reducing the risk of getting heart disease, certain types of cancer and diabetes.

I keep hearing so much about the benefits of soy protein. What makes soy protein so good?

The soybean is the only vegetable offering a complete protein profile. Soy protein is of the highest quality, equal to that of meat and dairy products, but without the cholesterol and saturated fat. It can be the sole source of protein, without causing any nutritional imbalance. Our body breaks down protein into individual amino acids, which form helpful antibodies and enzymes for our bodies. Amino acids are necessary for proper growth, development, health and maintenance. Of the twenty-two amino acids we require, our body produces only fourteen. These are called nonessential amino acids. The remaining eight are called essential amino acids, which must come from the foods we eat.

Soy protein provides all eight of these amino acids, making it a complete protein. Besides having a higher quality protein, soybeans also have a higher amount of protein than other beans. Soybeans have 35 to 38 percent of total calories coming from protein, while other beans only have about 20 to 30 percent. However, not all soy foods contain the same amount of protein. Extra firm and firm tofu, for instance, has more protein than soft or silken tofu because they contain less water. Read the Nutrition Facts label on soy foods to determine the protein content.

Soy protein also contains a high concentration of the phytochemical compound called isoflavones. Soy isoflavones possess a myriad of biological properties that can benefit the body. Chemists at the USDA found that the isoflavones in soy protein help certain cells screen out error-prone messages before they can do any damage to the body. Therefore, scientists have attributed most of soy's positive health effects to its unique combination of protein and isoflavones.

What are phytochemicals? Are isoflavones the only phytochemical contained in soy?

Phytochemicals are a large collection of chemical compounds found only in plants (phyto means plant). Many hundreds of these bio-active plant chemicals are found in dietary sources. Phytochemicals have become a catchall term for the vast array of chemical substances found naturally in beans, fruits, vegetables, nuts, seeds, grains, herbs and spices.

Soybeans contain a variety of phytochemicals. They are the only food source with nutritionally significant amounts of one important class of phytochemical called isoflavones. While low levels of isoflavones can be found in chick peas and other legumes, soybeans are unique because they have the highest concentrated amount of this beneficial compound.

The phytochemicals in soy show tremendous potential to fight disease on several fronts. Researchers have discovered that isoflavones protect against errant cell signals that can spark illness. Isoflavones have been shown to help prevent the buildup of arterial plaque which leads to atherosclerosis (hardening of the arteries) and heart disease. These compounds help to reduce breast cancer by blocking the cancer-causing effects of human estrogen, and fight osteoporosis by stimulating bone formation. Evidence also suggests that isoflavones decrease many of the symptoms associated with menopause and PMS.

Laboratory studies reveal that soy contains several other phytochemicals that also impede or prevent the development of cancer, like protease inhibitors, saponins, and phytosterols. Protease inhibitors have been shown to slow the rate of cancer division in cells, saponins may prevent cancer cells from multiplying, and phytosterols seem to block estrogen.

How do isoflavones offer protection against major health problems?

A great deal of research indicates isoflavones have many beneficial and protective health effects. In various experiments, isoflavones have been found to lower cholesterol, possess anti-cancer activity, inhibit bone resorption and relieve many menopause symptoms. Studies suggest soy isoflavones account for approximately three-fourths of this protection, while soy protein is responsible for about one-fourth. Isoflavones are a type of phytoestrogen, or plant hormone, that resembles human estrogen in chemical structure yet are weaker in their estrogenic activity. Researchers have identified at least twenty different phytoestrogens. These weaker compounds mimic human estrogen at certain sites in the body, providing many health benefits that enable the body to stay clear of disease.

Researchers believe isoflavones act much like human estrogen in lowering cholesterol and reducing the risk for coronary heart disease. These phytoestrogens also offer protection against the detrimental effects that the stronger version of this hormone has on the body. Isoflavones can compete at the estrogen receptor sites with the estrogen naturally produced by the body. Their binding action blocks the more potent estrogen from exerting their full effect. Since high blood levels of estrogen are an established risk factor for breast cancer, weaker forms of estrogen may provide protection against this type of cancer.

Isoflavones also play an important role in maintaining and protecting bones. Some significant studies conducted at the University of Illinois concluded that consuming soy isoflavones can increase bone mineral content and bone density. By preserving bone health while increasing bone mass, researchers noted the potential role of soy isoflavones in preventing, and possibly even reversing, the effects of osteoporosis. Other studies suggest soy isoflavones can also be an alternative to estrogen replacement therapy for relief of mild menopausal symptoms.

The two primary isoflavones found in soybeans are genistein and daidzein. Researchers think that these are the particular compounds responsible for soy's beneficial and preventative properties. Studies over the past decade indicate that genistein dampens the communication from a cell's surface to its interior, filtering out the undesirable signals. Chemists discovered that genistein appears to calm cell circuits so that they are less receptive to errant chemical signals which come from poor diets or harmful environmental factors. This over-active or defective cellular signaling leads to many chronic diseases.

Evidence also shows that genistein inhibits the growth of cells that form artery-clogging plaque. In addition, genistein has also been found to hinder numerous breast and prostate cancer cell lines. In fact, the National Cancer Institute is even considering using the genistein found in soy as a cancer drug. Genistein acts against cancer cells in a way similar to many common cancer-treating drugs. Scientists believe that the body has certain enzymes that convert normal cells to cancer cells. Some cancer drugs

13

restrain these enzymes, and genistein has been shown to do the same.

Other studies signify that genistein and daidzein help promote strong and healthy bones. Researchers found that genistein suppresses the activity of osteoclasts, which are the cells that help the resorption of bony tissue in the bone regeneration process. Nutrition experts believe that daidzein prevents bones from breaking down. Interestingly, daidzein is very similar to a drug widely used in Europe and Asia to treat osteoporosis. When the body metabolizes this drug, it actually breaks down to form daidzein. Scientists are now developing and testing a synthetic version of daidzein for the treatment of osteoporosis in the United States.

All these findings suggest eating soy foods, natural sources of the isoflavones genistein and daidzein, can protect you against heart disease, cancer and osteoporosis. Soy isoflavones can reduce hyperactive cellular signaling, mimic the hormone estrogen, exhibit antioxidant capabilities, and perform other functions that enhance overall health.

How do isoflavones act as antioxidants?

Antioxidants are compounds that prevent or repair damage to cells caused by pollution, sunlight, and normal body processes. These elements cause oxidation in our body, which produce dangerous chemical compounds called free radicals. These compounds are highly reactive and have the potential to damage DNA, causing mutations that can result in the malignant transformation of cells. Free radicals can easily cause harm to the immune system, whose cells divide often. They may also be responsible for some of the changes of aging.

We can help the body in its ability to scavenge and destroy free radicals, before they cause harm, by supplying it with natural substances that act as antioxidants. These substances block the chemical reactions that generate free radicals in the first place, and destroy the ones that have already been formed.

Many laboratory studies have documented the strong antioxidant properties of soy isoflavones in the fight against heart disease. Oxidation, the same process that leads to rust on metal, causes fats to harden and form the blockages that damage arteries. Isoflavones incorporate into lipoprotein particles, such as LDL, and protect them from oxidation. This antioxidant effect can reduce the onset of atherosclerosis by decreasing LDL accumulation in blood vessel walls.

A reduced level of oxidative damage is also associated with a decreased risk of cancer. Research has found that the antioxidants in soy foods efficiently and effectively protects cells from free radical damage while boosting the immune system. This, in turn, helps to prevent cancer and premature aging.

Which soy foods are the best sources of soy protein and isoflavones?

Researchers believe that the least amount of processing and the closer to the whole soybean the better. Edamame, roasted soynuts, tempeh, textured soy protein, soy flour and soy protein powders are the best sources of both soy protein and isoflavones. The next best sources are tofu and soymilk. Researchers claim it's the combination of isoflavones and soy protein that provide the major health benefits. However, all soy foods differ in their content of protein and isoflavones, and some products contain little to none of these compounds. For instance, soy sauce has very little soy protein with no isoflavones, and soybean oil contains neither of these healthful substances.

Overall, traditional and modern soy foods are better providers of soy protein and isoflavones than many second generation products. Because of their processing methods, products like soy-based burgers, soy hotdogs, soy sausages and other meat replacements, may not be significant sources of isoflavones. Products made from alcohol extracted soy protein concentrate have lower quantities of isoflavones because this method removes most of these compounds. Second generation products such as soy hotdogs, soy burgers, soy cheese, soy yogurt, soy ice cream and soy isolate powders do provide soy protein. However, competition with other ingredients and various processing methods can affect the quality and the amount of their isoflavones. Additionally, many soy supplements are not very reliable sources of these beneficial compounds either. When concentrated into a pill form, the process can also destroy these healthful substances.

How much soy protein and isoflavones do researchers recommend consuming per day?

Researchers recommend consuming a soy rich diet that provides at least 25 grams of soy protein and 30-50 milligrams of isoflavones daily. Scientific studies have shown that 25 grams of soy protein a day in the diet is needed to produce a significant cholesterol lowering effect. The U.S. Food and Drug Administration (FDA) recently gave food suppliers permission to use labels on soy-based foods claiming a link between eating soy and a lower risk of heart disease.

To qualify for this health claim, a food must contain at least 6.25 grams of soy protein per serving. This amount is one-fourth of the effective level of 25 grams per day. A serving generally equals 1/2 cup of cooked soybeans, tofu, textured soy protein or tempeh, or 1 cup of soymilk. Foods eligible for the FDA health claim include soy beverages (soymilk), tofu, tempeh, soy-based meat alternatives, and some baked goods. Products that carry the claim must also meet the requirements for low fat, low saturated fat, and low cholesterol content. Foods made with the whole soybean may also qualify for the health claim if they contain no additional fat, only that present in the whole soybean.

In Asian countries, the usual daily intake of isoflavones is about 30 to 50 milligrams. This is equivalent to about one to two servings of soy foods a day. Since the Asian population has significantly lower incidences of heart disease and cancer, experts believe this is a sensible and reasonable goal for most Americans trying to maintain optimum health.

The Third International Symposium on the role of soy in preventing and treating chronic disease noted recent studies showing increased amounts of soy isoflavones and protein can offer cardiovascular and bone protecting benefits to postmenopausal women. A daily dietary inclusion of 60-70 milligrams of isoflavones and 40 grams of soy protein had a positive impact on LDL-oxidation, HDL-cholesterol and significantly reduced bone turnover in healthy postmenopausal women.

Because of the variety of soy foods available, it is possible to consume soy protein and isoflavones at all meals and snacks throughout the day. Use the following table of average soy protein and isoflavone content to help create your own daily combinations. Keep in mind these examples of common soy foods are just averages based on comparing numerous reports and product Nutrition Facts labels. Some of these products may not have the soy health claim on their label, because they may not fit the fat criteria. However, they still can help you reach 25 grams soy protein and 30-50 milligrams of isoflavones daily.

Soy Product	Serving Size	Isoflavones	Protein
Textured Soy Protein	1/2 cup (4 oz.) cooked, 1/4 cup dry	55-60 mg	16 g
Tofu	1/2 cup (4 oz.)	35-40 mg	11 g
Roasted Soynuts	1/4 cup (1 oz.)	55-60 mg	16 g
Tempeh	1/2 cup (4 oz.)	55-65 mg	19 g
Soymilk	1 cup (8 oz.)	25-30 mg	10 g
Soy Flour	1/2 cup (3 ounces)	50-60 mg	16 g
Soy Protein Powder	1/3 cup (2 scoops)	60 mg	18 g
Whole Soybeans	1/2 cup (4 ounces)	55-60 mg	14 g

What is the best way to consume soy products to get the most health benefits?

Research indicates it is best to spread out the intake of soy products throughout the day. Incorporating small amounts of soy into most meals and snacks, rather than loading up on it all at one sitting. The health claim on soy food labels is approved for one-fourth of the recommended daily amount of soy protein. The FDA does not expect people to consume all 25 grams of soy protein in one meal. Additionally, a series of studies designed to determine how the body absorbs and utilizes soy isoflavones, concluded that the absorption of isoflavones from food may be saturable. This means once these compounds reach peak levels, the body is unable to absorb any more at that time, and any additional intake of isoflavones is wasted and eliminated. Peak concentrations of these compounds are generally seen between 4-8 hours after dietary intake. Most of the isoflavones daidzein and genistein are excreted from the body within 24 hours. Based on these findings, the optimum way to maintain a steady concentration of soy isoflavones in the blood, is by regularly ingesting small amounts of these compounds throughout the day.

Many health experts discourage people from jumping prematurely to supplements. Instead, they want people to learning how to incorporate soy foods into a balanced diet. When soy is in food form, it is also in combination with other nutrients and compounds that contribute to its many health benefits. They believe soy's cholesterol-lowering effect cannot be achieved by just popping a couple of isoflavone pills. The FDA health claim is for soy protein in food form. The scientific studies for lowering cholesterol were not done using only isoflavones extracted from soy protein. Researchers do not believe isoflavones alone can lower cholesterol as effectively as in combination with soy protein. Studies indicate that when isoflavones are removed, the same cholesterol-lowering effect is not achieved. Therefore, researchers have concluded that isoflavones and soy protein work best together.

If soy isoflavone pills are taken for bone health or reducing menopausal symptoms, researchers advise taking these supplements along with foods containing soy protein. This way the benefits of both forms of soy can complement and enhance each other.

Finally, even with a hectic or fast paced lifestyle, you can still take advantage of soy's healthful qualities. Soynuts, soy protein powders and nutritional soy protein bars are quick and easy sources for soy's beneficial compounds. Because these soy products require no cooking and are portable, they are good alternatives for those who don't have time to cook or travel frequently.

CHAPTER 3: HEART DISEASE, STROKE & CHOLESTEROL

According to the American Heart Association (AHA) and the FDA, coronary heart disease is the leading cause of death in the United States, killing more people than any other disease. Coronary heart disease causes heart attack and angina (chest pain). The AHA ranks stoke as the third most fatal disease in America, causing paralysis and brain damage. Heart disease and stroke have become major health problems in most developed countries, and are rapidly increasing in prevalence in many lesser developed countries. This is mainly due to the influence of the animal-based Western diet, which is high in saturated fat and low in fiber. The AHA calculates that there are over 1 million new and recurrent cases of coronary attack each year in the United States. Approximately 12 million victims of angina, heart attack and other forms of coronary heart disease are still living. They also estimate that about 600,000 Americans suffer a new or recurrent stroke each year, with more than 4 million stroke survivors alive today.

While many risk factors, such as cigarette smoking and hypertension (high blood pressure), contribute to the risk for coronary heart disease and stroke, lipid abnormalities are the most significant factors. The FDA claims that high levels of total cholesterol and high levels of low density lipoprotein (LDL) cholesterol are the largest risk factors for these killers. About 20 percent of Americans, almost 40 million adults, have high blood cholesterol levels of 240 mg/dL or higher. Approximately 32 percent of Americans, nearly 59 million adults, are considered borderline with levels from 200 to 239 mg/dL. Studies done on people 20 years old and over show that more women than men have total blood cholesterol of 200 mg/dL or higher beginning at age 50.

What exactly is cholesterol and how does it contribute to coronary heart disease and stroke?

The AHA states that cholesterol is a substance found in all animal-based foods and fats. (Plant-based foods do not contain cholesterol.) They also say that the human body constantly makes cholesterol, mostly in the liver and kidneys. In our body, cholesterol is most common in the blood, brain tissue, liver, kidneys, adrenal glands and the fatty covers around nerve fibers. It helps absorb and move fatty acids. Cholesterol is necessary to form cell membranes, for the making of vitamin D on the surface of the skin and the making of various hormones, including the sex hormones. It sometimes hardens in the gallbladder and forms into gallstones. High amounts of cholesterol in the blood have been linked to the development of cholesterol deposits in the blood vessels, known as atherosclerosis. Cholesterol, and other fats, can't dissolve in the blood. They have to be transported to and from the cells by special carriers of lipids and proteins called lipoproteins. There are several kinds of lipoproteins, but the ones to be most concerned about are low density and high density lipoproteins. Low density lipoprotein (LDL) carries the bulk of the cholesterol in the blood, and has a central role in the atherosclerotic process. LDL penetrates the walls of blood vessels and arteries feeding the heart and brain, where they are oxidized by free radicals and accumulate as a gruel-like material that blocks the blood vessels. When this plaque-like material leaks into the blood vessel, it can cause a blood clot (thrombosis). Thrombosis can lead to a stroke if the clot goes to the brain, or a heart attack if the clot blocks a coronary artery. A high level of LDL cholesterol reflects an increased risk of heart disease and stroke, which is why LDL cholesterol is often called the bad cholesterol.

High density lipoprotein (HDL) only carries approximately one-third to one-fourth of the blood cholesterol in our body. HDL cholesterol has a protective effect, preventing LDL oxidation and removing cholesterol that accumulates in the blood vessel walls. Medical experts believe HDL carries cholesterol away from the arteries and back to the liver, where it is eliminated from the body. They also suspect HDL removes excess cholesterol from atherosclerotic plaques and slows their growth. A high level of HDL seems to protect against heart attack and stroke, which is why HDL is known as the good cholesterol.

Cholesterol is measured in milligrams per deciliter of blood (mg/dL). Total blood cholesterol is the most common measurement of cholesterol. It is the number you normally receive as test results. Knowing your total blood cholesterol level is an important first step in determining your risk for heart disease and stroke. An important second step is knowing your level of good HDL cholesterol in relation to total cholesterol. Some doctors use the ratio of total cholesterol to HDL cholesterol. The goal is to keep the ratio below 5 to 1, with the optimum ratio at 3.5 to 1.

Triglycerides are also often measured when testing for cholesterol levels. Triglycerides are the chemical form in which most fat exists in food as well as in the body. Calories ingested in a meal and not used immediately are converted to triglycerides and transported to fat cells to be stored. Hormones regulate the release of triglycerides from fat tissue so they meet the body's needs for energy between meals. Elevated triglycerides are linked to the occurrence of coronary artery disease and may be a consequence of other diseases, such as untreated diabetes mellitus. Saturated fats and trans fats are the chief culprits in raising blood cholesterol and triglyceride levels. Ingesting animal-based products and hydrogenated fats can significantly increase both of these levels.

How does soy and soy-based products effect cholesterol?

Generally, the consumption of vegetable proteins will result in lower serum cholesterol levels than animal proteins. Research confirms that soy's protein and isoflavones are the active components responsible for its positive cholesterol lowering effects. A recent study in the Archives of Internal Medicine found that when people added soy to their diet, their high levels of LDL cholesterol dropped 6 to 10 percent. Statistics from 38 human clinical trials noted that soy protein decreases serum (blood) concentrations of total cholesterol, LDL-cholesterol, and triglycerides, while at the same time, increases concentrations of HDL-cholesterol.

Soy's protein and isoflavones inhibit cholesterol oxidation by reducing LDL susceptibility to oxidize. Oxidized cholesterol undergoes structural changes, which cause fats to block and damage arteries. Reducing the susceptibility of LDL to oxidize also reduces the risk of coronary heart disease and stroke. The isoflavone genistein represses the growth of cells that forms the plaque which lines, and eventually clogs, the arteries. New findings indicate that isoflavones cannot lower cholesterol by themselves. They must be ingested along with soy protein to work.

Based on evidence from more than 50 independent studies, the FDA concluded that incorporating at least 25 grams of soy protein a day into the diet can substantially lower both total and LDL-cholesterol levels. Heart experts generally agree that a 1 percent drop in total cholesterol can equal a 2 percent drop in heart disease risk. But, to get the full heart-healthy impact of soy protein, its ingestion must coincide with a diet low in saturated fat, trans fat and cholesterol. A report in the New England Journal of Medicine, based on 38 studies, noted that eating three servings of any soy product a day lowers cholesterol levels by 9 milligrams. As little as 25 grams of soy protein per day can reduce total blood cholesterol levels by 10 to 15 percent, enough to significantly cut the chances of a heart attack or stroke in people with high cholesterol. In these studies, researchers also found that the more soy was added to the diet, the more the levels of cholesterol went down. Eating a greater amount of soy protein, about 47 grams a day, reduced the bad LDL cholesterol levels by 13 percent and triglycerides by 10 percent.

Studies at the University of Toronto demonstrate soy's effect on cholesterol is fast. Over a two one-month period, Canadian researchers were able to considerably reduce the levels of LDL cholesterol in healthy middle-aged men and women by replacing the meat in their diets with soy substitutes, vegetables and beans. All these findings demonstrate the power of soy foods in the fight against cholesterol, and may explain why heart disease is so rare in countries where soy consumption is much higher.

Are there any other positive effects that soy has on the cardiovascular system?

Yes, regular consumption of soy has many important protective effects upon the cardiovascular system. Soy provides antioxidants, reduces the plaque that clogs arteries, decreases blood clotting, improves blood pressure and promotes healthy blood vessels. These factors can reduce the risk of hardening of the arteries (atherosclerosis), stroke, heart attack, and high blood pressure (hypertension).

Soy isoflavones have antioxidant properties which protect the cardiovascular system from LDL oxidation. Oxidized LDL cholesterol accumulates in the arteries as patches of fatty buildup which blocks the flow of blood, resulting in atherosclerosis. Genistein inhibits the growth of cells that form this artery clogging plaque. Arteries damaged by atherosclerosis usually form blood clots (thrombosis).

Soy's protein and isoflavones can reduce the risk for blood clot formation. Soy protein decreases platelet aggregation or clumping, an early step in blood clot formation. Genistein also inhibits the formation of blood clots. These blood clots can lead to a stroke (brain attack) or heart attack. According to the American Heart Association (AHA), stroke is a leading cause of serious chronic disability in the United States.

The AHA states that high blood pressure also directly increases the risk of stroke and heart attack. About 20 percent of the U.S. population, around 50 million Americans over the age of 6, has high blood pressure. Of those with high blood pressure, nearly 32 percent do not even know they have it. A double-blind, randomized, placebo-controlled study in men and postmenopausal women shows that the soy isoflavones daidzein and genistein are able to substantially improve and reduce blood pressure.

Studies show soy isoflavones also have health promoting effects on blood vessels. Blood vessels damaged by atherosclerotic plaque tend to develop spasms, or inappropriate clamping down, when exposed to stress. This further decreases blood flow though the partially blocked vessel and can aggravate angina or brain symptoms. Soy proteins and their isoflavones restore normal reactivity to damaged blood vessels, protecting them from these abnormal spasms.

CHAPTER 4: CANCER

Cancer is not just one disease. It is a general term that refers to a group of diseases characterized by the uncontrolled growth and spread of abnormal cells. These cancer cells usually invade and destroy normal tissue cells. There are more than 150 different kinds of cancer.

A cancer tends to spread to other parts of the body by releasing cells into the lymph system or blood stream. If the spread is not controlled, it can result in death. Many different factors can cause the development of cancer. These include external factors such as viruses, too much exposure to sunlight or x-rays, cigarette smoking, and chemicals in the environment; as well as internal factors like hormones, immune conditions, and inherited mutations. When exposed to a carcinogen, it often takes more than ten years before a cancer is detectable. The most common sites for cancer are the skin, lung, prostate, breast, colon, uterus, mouth and bone marrow.

According to the National Cancer Institute (NCI), cancer is the second leading cause of death in the United States, exceeded only by heart disease. More than 500,000 Americans die from some form of invasive cancer each year. Over 1.2 million new cases of cancer are diagnosed annually in the United States alone. Many are curable if found in the early stage. The NCI estimates that approximately 8.4 million Americans alive today have a history of cancer.

Scientific evidence suggests up to one-third of the cancer deaths in the United States are related to diet and nutrition, and can be prevented. According to the American Institute of Cancer Research (AICR), eating right, staying physically active, watching your weight and not smoking can reduce your cancer risk by 60 to 70 percent.

Can eating soy and soy-based products help reduce the risk of getting cancer?

Yes, eating a healthy diet is one of the most critical factors in preventing cancer. Unlike hereditary risks, which a person cannot change, diet and lifestyle are completely within a person's control. As previously stated, medical research indicates that proper diet and nutrition can influence up to 70 percent of all preventable cancers, and 35 percent of cancer deaths in America.

Today there is growing evidence linking a soy-rich diet to cancer prevention. Eating a plant-based diet, rich in soy and a variety of fruits, vegetables, legumes and minimally-processed complex carbohydrates, can greatly reduce your risk of getting certain cancers. Plant foods, which include soy foods, are established cancer protectors because they are loaded with fiber, vitamins, minerals, antioxidants and phytochemicals.

The NCI has identified 5 different chemical classes of anti-carcinogens in soybeans. These include isoflavones, phytosterols, phytates, saponins and protease inhibitors. However, most of the research and interest in soy has focused on the isoflavones, primarily genistein and daidzein. Soybeans are also high in phenolic acids, many of which are also anti-carcinogens. Collectively, these compounds explain soy's theorized anti-cancer effects.

The AICR claims isoflavones, protease inhibitors and saponins protect against the development of various cancers. AICR studies suggest that the isoflavones genistein and daidzein inhibit the growth and spread of many types of cancer. Genistein, in particular, stops the growth of cancer cells by interfering with the enzyme activity that convert normal cells to cancer cells. It acts against hormone dependent cancers, like breast and prostate cancers, by inhibiting the growth of both estrogen dependent and independent cells.

Researchers at the University of Minnesota found that genistein also interferes with the process by which cancer cells and tumors receive nutrients and oxygen. It is thought to act against cancer similar to common cancer-treating drugs. Genistein may even increase the effectiveness of certain cancer fighting drugs, and can be beneficial against some cancer cells which are resistant to pharmacologic treatment. It can suppress growth in estrogen receptor-negative tumors, which typically don't respond to anti-estrogen drug therapies. More than 100 studies on a variety of cancer cells have demonstrated the effectiveness of genistein.

Research at the University of Illinois reveals that soy isoflavones can slow the growth rate of cancerous tumor cells while leaving healthy cells alone. This research also suggests saponins do the best job of protecting cells from cancer-starting activity.

Nutrition experts recommend as part of a healthy diet, consuming natural food sources of soy isoflavones instead of taking isoflavone pills. This is because soy foods usually contain all these potential anti-cancer agents, while supplements contain only one. People with cancer should discuss soy intake with their doctor before making any dietary changes.

What types of cancer has soy been most effective in preventing?

Populations who regularly consume soy foods have less cancer of the breast, prostate, lung, colon, rectum, ovary, uterus and stomach. A number of factors may account for the reduced breast and prostate cancer rates seen in Asian people, one being that their high soy consumption starts at birth. Recently, most of the research has been specifically directed toward soy's relationship and effect upon breast and prostate cancers. However,

23

evidence that soy intake may reduce the risk of other cancers, like colon and uterine, is at least as strong.

Results from recent studies indicate high-fiber protein-rich soy-based products, such as textured soy protein and tempeh, help in preventing and treating colon cancer. Small amounts of soy protein, consumed daily for a year by people diagnosed with colon cancer or precancerous colon polyps, appeared to cause changes in how colon cells divide and reproduce. These changes reduced the likelihood of recurrent tumors or polyps.

Studies conducted at the Cancer Research Center of Hawaii found increased intakes of soy in the diet may reduce the risk of endometrial cancer (cancer of the uterus). Researchers found that the women who ate the highest amounts of phytoestrogen rich foods, like legumes, tofu and other soy-based products, had a 54 percent reduction in endometrial cancer risk, compared with those who consumed the least amounts. When isoflavones attach to the estrogen receptors on tumor cells, they prevent the body's far more potent natural estrogen from doing so, thereby producing a protective effect against hormone-related cancers.

How does soy effect breast cancer?

The low breast cancer mortality rates in Asian countries, and the presumed anti-estrogenic effects of isoflavones, have fueled speculation that soy may reduce breast cancer risk. Breast cancer is a malignant tumor of breast tissue, the most common cancer among women in the United States, excluding skin cancers. First symptoms include a small painless lump, thick or dimpled skin, or nipple withdrawal. As the tumor grows, there may be nipple discharge, pain, ulcers, or swollen lymph glands under the arm. According to the American Cancer Society, breast cancer is the second leading cause of cancer death among women, after lung cancer.

Studies show American women are five times as likely to get breast cancer than Chinese and Japanese women. Asian women generally consume from 10 to 50 grams of soy protein per day while American women basically consume only around 1 to 3 grams per day. This translates to 20 to 80 milligrams of isoflavones consumed per day by Asian women compared to less than 5 milligrams per day for U.S. women.

A recent study found that soy consumption was associated with about a 50 percent decreased risk of breast cancer in premenopausal women. One of the risk factors for breast cancer is believed to be an excess exposure to estrogen over a lifetime. Estrogen is a naturally occurring female reproductive hormone. Before the body can use estrogen, it must bind to proteins called estrogen receptors. Findings from various studies and experiments suggest isoflavones can serve as anti-carcinogenic

24

estrogen receptor blockers. Phytoestrogens, which include isoflavones, have similar properties to human estrogen, but are much weaker. Because plant estrogen has a chemical shape very similar to human estrogen, it can fit into the receptor sites on breast tissue where the endogenous estrogen usually attaches. This prevents the more powerful human estrogen, which can promote cancerous tumors, from binding to these receptors.

Estrogen is produced during the menstrual cycle. The more often a woman menstruates, the greater her exposure to estrogen. This is why women who start menstruating early and stop late, who have short menstrual cycles, or never had children are believed to have an increased risk of breast cancer. Other risk factors include a family history of breast cancer, being overweight, diabetes, high blood pressure (hypertension), and possibly traditional hormone replacement therapy (HRT).

Daily ingestion of soy protein can produce a significant change in the length of a woman's menstrual cycle. A British study found that women who were given 60 grams of soy a day had longer cycles. Asian women, who ingest more soy on a daily basis, generally have longer menstrual cycles than American and European women. Longer cycles lead to less exposure to estrogen during a woman's lifetime, putting her at a lower risk of breast cancer than women with shorter cycles.

Lifelong exposure to estrogen can encourage breast cancer cells to multiply. During a woman's monthly cycle, her breast tissue's cell division rate is four times as great immediately after ovulation, as during the follicular phase before ovulation. A lengthening of the menstrual cycle, especially in the follicular phase, may protect women against breast cancer. Furthermore, the isoflavones genistein and daidzein also appear to influence cancer development by inhibiting the growth and formation of cancerous cells and tumors. Evidence shows that soy may prevent the new blood cell and blood vessel growth (angiogenesis) which is needed to support tumor proliferation. Angiogenesis in breast tissue is thought to be a sign that breast cancer may follow.

Will a soy rich diet reduce the risk of breast cancer in every woman?

No, to say that soy can reduce the risk of breast cancer in all women would be irresponsible. There are too many unknown factors when it comes to cancer. For instance, there is more than one type of breast cancer; more than one cause, and more than one type of mammary cell affected. A woman goes through four stages of life where her body chemistry, known to affect mammary conditions, are widely different. Also, there are various undocumented diet, lifestyle and environmental factors in many of the populations studied. With this in mind, healthcare professionals have established two different recommendations for women when it comes to soy consumption. One for women without breast cancer and one for women with, or at high risk for, breast cancer.

Women who do not have estrogen receptor positive breast tumors, and who do not have a strong family history of breast cancer, may eat all the soy they wish. For these women, the weak soy estrogen may actually protect against breast cancer by fitting into the receptor sites on breast tissue where estrogen usually attaches. Thus, preventing the more powerful human estrogen from attaching and starting the cancer causing process.

However, women with or at risk for estrogen stimulated cancers are cautioned to limit their intake of soy until researchers know for sure that plant estrogen will not stimulate their cancer to grow. Although plant estrogen is much weaker than human estrogen, there is a concern that any form of estrogen may stimulate tumor development in these women.

Women on Tamoxifen therapy are also urged to limit their consumption of soy-based products. Tamoxifen, a drug sometimes given to breast cancer patients, is similar to the soy isoflavone genistein. Both are able to combat tumors that contain estrogen receptors, both work on estrogen-positive and negative cells, and both work by attaching to estrogen receptor sites. In order to get the most benefit from Tamoxifen, it is recommended that the intake of weak plant estrogen be restricted.

While there have been no studies to confirm these assumptions, until there is documented proof that phytoestrogens will not contribute to cancers, doctors will continue to be cautious and recommend restricting foods with these compounds. Again, this applies only to women who are in the risk groups mentioned above. These women should consult their own doctor about soy consumption. Scientists are only beginning to understand the potentially powerful health benefits of soy. They are continually working to formulate what may be protective in soy, and what may not, realizing that not all cancers are the same.

Does soy have an effect on male hormone-related cancers, like prostate cancer?

Yes, soy appears to have a positive effect on male hormone-related cancers, like prostate cancer. In fact, a recent study of Seventh Day Adventists in California found that men who regularly drank at least one cup of soymilk a day, reduced their risk for prostate cancer by 70 percent.

The prostate is one of the male sex glands, located just below the bladder, partially surrounding the urethra. It makes fluid that becomes part of the semen. Cancer of the prostate is found mainly in older men. As men age, the prostate may get bigger and block the urethra or bladder, causing difficulty in urination or sexual functions. This condition can be a result of benign prostate enlargement or prostate cancer. The symptoms for both are similar. General symptoms include a weak or interrupted flow of urine; painful, burning or frequent urination, especially at night; blood in the urine, or nagging pain in the back, hips, or pelvis.

According to the American Cancer Society, prostate cancer is the most common cancer among men in the United States, besides cancers of the skin. They also state that prostate cancer is the second biggest cancer killer of older American men, after lung cancer. Doctors usually determine a man's prostate health by rectal examination and PSA testing. The PSA test is a diagnostic blood test that measures the amount of prostate specific antigen the prostate gland is producing. This antigen is a small protein molecule that normally combines the seminal fluid. It is almost nonexistent in the blood stream of men without prostate cancer, but becomes persistently elevated in men with prostate cancer. The higher the PSA level, the greater the likelihood of cancer. A recent study suggested that men with a rising PSA level may benefit from ingesting soy-based products on a regular basis. During a 6-month trial, soy appeared to decrease the rise in PSA levels, compared with a placebo group.

American men are almost five times as likely to die of prostate cancer than Japanese men. According to the American Prostate Society, population studies show that Japanese men do get small prostate tumors. However, their high consumption of soy-based products, like tofu and soymilk, apparently delays the onset of cancer and slows the growth of their tumors. While they may have a relatively high incidence of latent prostate cancer, their mortality rate from this disease is infinitesimal compared to American men. Except when they immigrate to the United States and take on an American diet, then Japanese men end up having the same death rate from prostate cancer as their American counterparts.

An examination of prostate cancer deaths in 59 countries shows that diet is strongly linked to mortality from this disease. This international study concluded that death from prostate cancer is positively associated with the affluent Western diet which is high in animal-based products, fat and alcohol consumption. Conversely, intakes of cereals, nuts, seeds, fish, soybeans and soy-based products are negatively associated with prostate cancer mortality. Researchers did not determine whether fish had a protective effect, because the men who ate the most fish also ate the most soy. Both fish and soy contain omega-3 fatty acids, which has been shown to inhibit the growth of tumors. What this international study did determine was that the men who ate the most soy products were the least likely to die of prostate cancer.

Researchers found that the ingestion of animal fat (saturated fat) may increase the risk for prostate cancer, and other hormone sensitive cancers, by raising sex hormone levels. Prostate cancer is linked with testosterone levels, and is often treated by cutting the production of this hormone, either surgically or chemically. Clinical evidence points to the beneficial role of soy in reducing hormonal levels.

Researchers attribute isoflavones with soy's cancer protective effects, because they influence cell growth and regulation. Soy isoflavones tend to concentrate in prostate tissue and may prevent prostate cancer by inhibiting its growth during the initial phase of the disease. Results from a study at Harvard University Medical School indicate that soy can drastically reduce tumor growth and its spread to other organs. The substances found in soybeans appear to block the development of blood vessels (angiogenesis) needed by the tumors, causing them to starve to death.

CHAPTER 5: OSTEOPOROSIS

According to the National Osteoporosis Foundation, osteoporosis (which literally means porous bones) is a disease characterized by a loss of normal bone density, thinning bone tissue and the growth of small holes in the bones. This disorder causes spinal pain, especially in the lower back; loss of body height, bone mass and strength; and various bone deformities. Osteoporosis especially thins and weakens bones in the hip, spine, and wrist to the point where they break very easily. Osteoporosis is called the silent disease because symptoms are often not noticed until it is too late. People can lose bone over many years and not know they have this disease until a bone breaks.

The National Institutes of Health's National Institute on Aging (NIA) estimates about 25 million Americans have osteoporosis, with 80 percent being female. While most of the attention has focused on preventing and reversing osteoporosis in women, researchers realize that osteoporosis affects men as well. One out of two women and one in eight men over age 50 will have an osteoporosis-related fracture. It occurs most often in women who have a family history of osteoporosis, experience an early menopause, or who have small body frames. When women go through menopause, their levels of the female hormone estrogen drops. Lower hormone levels can lead to bone loss and osteoporosis. Men generally have less risk of getting osteoporosis because they do not have the same kinds of hormones. However, when men become inactive, paralyzed, alcoholic or take steroids, they have a greater risk of developing this disease.

Osteoporosis can strike at any age, but the risk increases as you get older. After about age 30, bones stop growing and absorb less calcium. There is a decrease in bone formation and an increase in bone breakdown. As people advance in years, it becomes more important than ever to maintain optimum levels of calcium in the bones. Women and men lose 1 to 3 percent of their bone mass each year after the age of 50. As life expectancies increase, osteoporosis may become even more prevalent unless preventive measures are taken.

The NIA believes osteoporosis is preventable. A person's diet and lifestyle both greatly influence bone loss and osteoporosis. Dietary factors include your consumption and absorption of calcium, vitamin D and magnesium, as well as your amount of protein, sodium and alcohol intake. While lifestyle factors refer to your level of physical activity and exercise, and the act of smoking.

When comparing bone health to dietary habits, research indicates that Asian and vegetarian women have a lower incidence of osteoporosis than Western and omnivorous women with a similar calcium intake. This result may be attributed to soy protein, replacing animal protein, in the diets of many Asian and vegetarian women. Dietary composition appears more important than the total amount of calcium intake, because certain types of foods may actually interfere with the body's ability to absorb calcium. Doctors at the University of Pennsylvania School of Medicine found that excessive meat and salt consumption causes calcium to be lost through the urine. For every 1 gram increase in animal protein ingested, the body losses an average of 1.75 milligrams of calcium in the urine. Medical evidence shows that 7,000 milligrams of calcium enters and exits bones every day. The ability to retain calcium is particularly important as bones are in a continuous state of turnover and remodeling.

The amount and type of protein in the diet both have an important impact on calcium absorption and excretion. Even if a person takes in enough calcium, more calcium might be lost when eating high amounts of animal-protein. Researchers believe that the sulfur amino acids, cysteine and methionine, increase acid loads, which leads to increased calcium loss in an animal-protein diet. Eating plant-based proteins like that found in soy adds calcium, magnesium and isoflavones to the diet which the body can more readily absorb.

How does soy reduce the risk of getting osteoporosis? Can it reverse the devastating effects of this disease in people who already have it?

New research suggests eating soy foods is an easy way to build strong bones, lower the risk of osteoporosis, and possibly reverse the effects of this disease in those afflicted. Researchers note that soy increases bone density while at the same time improves bone quality. Evidence indicates that soy may work in three ways to protect the health of bones.

First, many soy foods, such as tofu, textured soy protein, tempeh and fortified soymilk, are rich in calcium that the body can easily absorb. The daily value for calcium is 1,000 mg for adults and children age four or older. If the Nutrition Facts label on a soy product states calcium is 15%, then the amount of calcium for one serving is 150 mg. Tofu made with calcium sulfate (gypsum) has nearly 130 mg calcium per 1/2 cup. Tempeh has about 100 mg calcium per 1/2 cup. Regular soymilk has around 80 mg calcium per cup, while fortified soymilk has up to 300 mg per cup.

Secondly, soy protein helps enhance calcium retention in the body. When people eat soy protein instead of animal protein, they excrete far less calcium in their urine. By helping the body retain calcium, soy reduces the risk of getting osteoporosis.

Thirdly, the isoflavones in soybeans prevent bones from breaking down. Two types of cells, osteoclasts and osteoblasts, are responsible for the continuous turnover process of bone reformation. Osteoclasts break down bone, and osteoblasts build it. Until the age of 30, when bone mass peaks, osteoblasts prevail in bone building. After this age, osteoclasts begin to dominate. Bone breakdown starts outpacing bone formation, resulting in a decline in bone density. The soy isoflavones, daidzein and genistein, have been shown to suppress the activity of osteoclasts.

A study conducted by the Division of Nutritional Science, at the University of Illinois in Champaign-Urbana, found that post-menopausal women with a high concentration of soy in their diet had stronger bone health. Results from the study showed significant increases in both bone mineral content and bone density in the lumbar spine of women with a high soy diet. These results indicate the potential role for soy isoflavones in maintaining bone health and improving bone quality. Additional studies by the Department of Human Nutrition and Dietetics, at the University of Illinois in Chicago, found that soy protein may also be a natural therapy for osteoporosis sufferers.

In a three-year study of Chinese women, conducted at the Chinese University of Hong Kong, scientists discovered that foods high in soy isoflavones and soy protein can significantly reduce bone loss in pre-menopausal women. In this study, researchers reported strengthened bone mass in women aged 31 to 40 after ingesting soy foods, which contained isoflavones. The research team also revealed that the amount of soy protein in the diet appears to relate to the rate of bone loss. Increased intakes of soy protein seemed to slow the loss of bone mass in these women. The study concluded that soy consumption can minimize bone loss, increase bone strength and is an important dietary factor.

Other studies have found that a soy-rich diet can offer bone protecting benefits to women in periods of estrogen deficiency. These studies indicate that reduced bone turnover was evident after only 4 weeks, and substantial after 12 weeks of dietary intervention with an isoflavone-rich diet.

Much attention has focused on preventing and possibly reversing the effects of osteoporosis. The search for bone-building drugs and therapies continues. So far, researchers have identified several naturally occurring bone-specific growth factors in soy, and are investigating their use as drug treatments for osteoporosis. In the meantime, including more soy and soy-based products into your diet will allow you to take advantage of soy's bone preserving phytochemicals and nutrients.

CHAPTER 6: MENOPAUSE & OTHER FEMALE CONCERNS

Menopause is generally the period ending the female reproductive phase of life. The end of menstruation naturally occurs with the decline of monthly hormonal cycles between the ages of 45 and 60. It may stop earlier in life because of an illness or hysterectomy. Over time, the ovaries gradually lose the ability to produce estrogen and progesterone, the hormones that govern the menstrual cycle. As the production of estrogen decreases, ovulation and menstruation happen less often, and eventually stops. Variations in the circulating levels of the hormones occur as the levels of estrogen rapidly decline. Some of the general symptoms of menopause experienced by many American women are hot flashes, night sweats, insomnia, irritability, mood swings, headaches, anxiety, depression, bone loss, vaginal dryness, urinary tract infections, incontinence and fatigue. These symptoms are often controlled with estrogen replacement therapy (ERT), but will stop in time without this hormonal treatment.

Doctors also routinely prescribe estrogen and progesterone, known as hormone replacement therapy (HRT), to replace the hormones lost during menopause and to prevent osteoporosis. Both HRT and ERT protect women from heart disease and stroke as well. The risk of getting these diseases drastically increases with the decline of estrogen. According to the American Heart Association, women account for more than 60 percent of stroke fatalities in the United States. Other health risks associated with the loss of estrogen include an increased risk of ovarian and colon cancer; periodontal (gum) disease and tooth loss; and cataract formation. A study reported in The Lancet suggests that estrogen replacement may even protect women against Alzheimer's disease. However, experts do not know all the risks associated with long term use of HRT or ERT. Concern over the potential risks of these therapies is causing many women to explore natural ways to address the decrease in estrogen production that accompanies aging.

Can soy help relieve the symptoms associated with menopause?

Yes, soy has been found to relieve many menopausal symptoms. On going research on soy's protein and isoflavones, conducted at Physicians Laboratories in North Carolina, indicate that soy protein can help to relieve menopausal symptoms like hot flashes, night sweats, fatigue, and vaginal dryness. Researchers also recommend soy for other benefits, like preventing heart disease, stroke, breast cancer, osteoporosis and diabetes.

A major study of soy at Wake Forest University School of Medicine indicates that 20 grams of soy protein a day can help reduce hot flashes, irritability and the sleep problems some menopausal women experience. Additional studies at Wake Forest University Baptist Medical Center in Winston-Salem, N.C., show that the phytoestrogens in soy protein may be just as effective as traditional estrogen replacement drugs at limiting the formation of atherosclerosis, a leading cause of heart disease and stroke. Scientists have shown isoflavones function similarly to HRT and ERT, without producing the risks associated with these traditional treatments. Even though they are only one-hundredth to one-thousandth as potent as human estrogen, because of their similar structure, isoflavones can help offset the drop in estrogen that occurs at menopause. Eating soy foods, which are rich in isoflavones, may offer women a more natural way to treat mild menopausal symptoms. Studies report that when women added soy to their diets, their hot flashes reduced by almost 40 percent.

Medical experts say that while soy may affect the frequency and intensity of hot flashes, it may also work better for some women than others. Women who consume a lot of soy in their diet generally have fewer hot flashes than those who do not. Population studies show that Japanese women are much less likely to experience any of the symptoms associated with menopause. Since each woman reacts differently to soy, they recommend that women try it for themselves to see if incorporating soy into their diet works for them. Eating at least two servings a day for six weeks is enough time to see if you are getting positive results. These experts suggest that soy can decrease overall menopausal symptoms by 25 percent, making it a great alternative for women who suffer from mild symptoms. However, for women who experience severe or unbearable menopausal effects, a better choice may be traditional HRT since it can decrease overall symptoms by 65 percent.

Which soy products work best at relieving menopausal symptoms, and how much is needed to produce any effect?

Researchers are still studying the effects of soy to determine which products achieve the best results, and the optimal amounts needed to get the most health benefits. So far, they have identified isoflavones as the active ingredient in soy which helps lessen many of the menopausal symptoms. The best forms of soy are those with the highest amount of isoflavones in them, like whole soybeans, tempeh, textured soy protein, soy flour, soynuts and some soy protein powders. The next best would be tofu, soymilk, miso and various second-generation products. However, the actual isoflavone content has to be high enough to be able to help lessen symptoms. Some processed soy foods made from soy protein concentrate, like soy hotdogs, have very little isoflavones due to their processing method. Other soy products, such as soybean oil and soy sauce, contain no isoflavones in them at all.

Preliminary evidence suggests, as little as 20 grams of soy protein a day can help lessen the hot flashes and curb the estrogen fluctuations that occur during menopause. According to the North American Menopause Society, 60 to 90 milligrams of isoflavones a day can improve menopausal symptoms and reduce cholesterol levels. A recent study on phytoestrogens found that menopausal women who took daily supplements of soy protein, containing about 75 mg of isoflavones, for 12 weeks had a 45 percent decrease in their hot flashes. Many women report a notable reduction in their hot flashes and night sweats when they take in half a cup of soy products a day. Australian researchers also found that women who consumed 1/2 cup of soy flour daily felt a significant reduction in their menopause symptoms.

Many doctors are recommending soy to their patients not only for relieving hot flashes, but for other important mid-life factors, like high cholesterol levels and weight gain. Some women gain 10-20 pounds around the time of menopause. Women who want to lower their cholesterol levels and weight should eat less meat, less saturated and trans (hydrogenated) fats, and shift to a more vegetarian style diet. Soy foods fit nicely into this approach because they are excellent sources of high quality protein, isoflavones, essential fatty acids and dietary fiber, with less fat than most animal-based foods.

Can soy also help relieve symptoms of PMS?

Yes, soy appears to also help relieve many premenstrual symptoms. Premenstrual syndrome (PMS) is characterized by anxiety, mood swings, difficulty concentrating, lethargy, nervous tension, irritability, weight gain, food cravings, fluid buildup, nausea, headache and breast tenderness. The Mayo Clinic Women's Healthsource, estimates 30 to 40 percent of women have symptoms severe enough to impair their daily activities. These symptoms are generally a result of the fluctuating estrogen levels each month in the days just before the start of the menstrual cycle. Symptoms generally begin from 7 to 14 days before menstruation, and end within 24 hours after the cycle has begun. As the estrogen level drops in the second two weeks of a woman's cycle, the body starts accumulating fluid. This usually leads to weight gain and breast tenderness. To reduce the fluid buildup, nutritionists suggest to drink plenty of water, reduce the amount of salt intake, and increase the amount of fruits, vegetables and soy products in the diet.

Including foods high in soy protein and isoflavones, like textured soy protein, tempeh, soynuts and soy flour, into your daily diet can lessen the intensity of many PMS symptoms. Soy provides natural plant estrogen, which help regulate hormone levels. Isoflavones bind to the body's estrogen receptors and supplement the effects of estrogen when levels are low.

Consuming soy products that are high in calcium and magnesium, like tofu and soymilk, can also help alleviate many PMS symptoms. The American Journal of Obstetrics and Gynecology reported a study which found that 1,200 milligrams of calcium taken daily reduced the physical and psychological symptoms associated with PMS by almost 50 percent. Another study reported in the Journal of Women's Health found that 200 milligrams of magnesium a day produced a 40 percent reduction in fluid retention, breast tenderness and bloating.

Can soy cause problems during pregnancy or interfere with fertility?

Results from two studies suggest that a diet high in soybeans during pregnancy and breast-feeding may have a subtle but long-term impact in helping children develop normally. However, many medical experts express concern that these results might lead pregnant women to overload on soy, especially in supplement form. They stress the need to choose soy foods, such as soymilk, tofu and soynuts, which contain isoflavones, and warn against the pill versions of soy. The American Dietetic Association believes scientists don't have enough information about the effects of isoflavones extracted from soy products and processed into pill form.

A few preliminary studies have suggested eating large quantities of raw or undercooked soybeans may have a negative effect on fertility and possibly developing fetuses. Until scientists know more, pregnant women and those having difficulty conceiving may want to reduce their exposure to estrogen rich foods, like soy, and not take any isoflavone supplements. They should only consume, in moderation, fully cooked soy foods or fermented soy products, like tempeh and miso.

Demographic studies show that women from Asian countries have fewer health problems associated with hormones than American women. One reason for the health benefits displayed by these cultures is the fact that their high soy consumption starts before birth and continues throughout their lifetime. Researchers theorize it is this early exposure to soy which is really beneficial. That early soy consumption may assist in the proper development of the mammary cells in girls before puberty. Evidence also suggests that the earlier a person starts eating soy foods, the greater their lifelong resistance to cancer. This implies that later soy consumption may not be as protective to women as lifelong consumption. However, even though it has been shown that the earlier soy is introduced into the diet the better, women who incorporate soy into their diet later in life will still receive a benefit from doing so. Additionally, if women begin consuming soy foods in their childbearing years, it would provide this early protection to their offspring.

Generally, Asian women have not shown detrimental effects from eating soy foods before, during or after pregnancy. Therefore, we can surmise that a well balanced plant-based diet with a moderate amount of soy would be safe for pregnant and nursing American women. However, if in doubt, discuss soy consumption with your doctor or pediatrician to find out if it is right for you and your baby.

CHAPTER 7: DIABETES & KIDNEY DISEASE

The American Diabetes Association (ADA) defines diabetes (medically called diabetes mellitus) as a complex disorder mainly caused by the failure of the pancreas to release enough insulin into the body. A defect in the parts of cells that accept the insulin may also lead to diabetes. Normally, when the body breaks down complex carbohydrates it produces glucose. Cells need insulin to absorb glucose. Insulin is a hormone produced in the pancreas that converts sugar, starches and other foods into energy. Natural insulin may be present in diabetics. However, their cells may not recognize it, and thus cannot absorb glucose. This inability to produce enough insulin or utilize existing insulin in the body, results in high sugar levels in both the blood and urine. Diabetes often runs in families. The most common symptoms are the need to urinate often, increased thirst, weight loss, and increased appetite. Diabetes may negatively affect the eyes, kidneys, nervous system, extremities, blood vessels and skin. Infections are common and hardening of the arteries often develops. Diabetic complications due to these effects include blindness, kidney failure, amputations, heart attack, stroke and impotence.

According to the ADA, diabetes is a chronic and incurable disease. With its complications, diabetes is the seventh leading cause of death (sixth leading cause of death by disease) in the United States. About 16 million Americans have diabetes mellitus. Particularly troubling is that more than a third of these individuals do not even know they have the disease. The two most common categories of diabetes are Type 1, affecting 5-10 percent of Americans with diabetes, and Type 2, affecting 90-95 percent of American diabetics. Type 1 diabetes primarily targets children and young adults, and requires treatment with daily injections of insulin. Type 2 diabetes generally has an onset later in life, usually after the age of 40. This form of diabetes often develops in overweight adults who do not exercise regularly, and in people with low HDL or high triglycerides. Often people with Type 2 diabetes have no symptoms. Doctors often treat Type 2 diabetics with changes in diet and exercise, or a combination of these and oral medications.

Both Type 1 and Type 2 diabetics have an elevated risk for heart disease, stroke, high blood pressure, disorders of the nervous system, amputations of the extremities, blindness, impotence and kidney disease. According to the ADA, more than 75 percent of Americans with diabetes die of some form of heart or blood vessel disease. Diabetics are two to four times more likely to have heart disease or suffer a stroke. Up to 21 percent of all individuals with diabetes will develop kidney disease. Diabetic kidney disease is the most common cause of kidney failure or end stage renal disease, a condition which requires dialysis or a kidney transplant in order to live. Impotence due to diabetic kidney disease or blood vessel blockages, afflicts approximately 13 percent of Type 1 diabetic males and 8 percent of Type 2 diabetic males. Medical reports indicate diabetic men over the age of 50, have impotence rates as high as 50-60 percent.

Modifications in diet are critical to help keep diabetes in control, and possibly prevent its onset. The ADA has revised its eating guidelines for diabetics over the past few years. The simpler food system focuses on eating smaller portions of food regularly throughout the day to keep the blood-sugar level steady. Smaller, more frequent meals will also allow for a wider variety of food intake. Food content should consist of 50-60 percent of total calories coming from complex carbohydrates, 10-20 percent from protein, and 20-30 percent of daily calories from fat. The ADA also recommends this dietary guideline for non-diabetics as a preventive measure and a way of promoting good overall health.

Can soy help prevent diabetes, or treat any of the symptoms and conditions that develop as a result of having diabetes?

Yes, the use of soy for the prevention and treatment of diabetes was first suggested in 1917 by Dr. Harvey Kellogg. Since then, researchers have continued to support the benefits of substituting soy protein for animal protein, in the diet of diabetics. They have especially focused on soy's role in normalizing blood glucose, serving as a rich source of soluble fiber, reducing cholesterol levels, as well as preventing and treating diabetic kidney disease.

Researchers have found that diabetics who consume soybeans have less glucose in their urine. This indicates that their cells are better able to absorb glucose. Scientists believe a high fiber, high complex-carbohydrate diet may help enable cells to recognize the insulin in the bloodstream. The soluble fiber in many soy products, like textured soy protein, tempeh and soy flour, helps the body regulate glucose levels by producing a smaller and slower rise in blood glucose. Soy foods also seem able to slow the absorption of glucose into the blood stream. This is helpful in allowing insulin time to work effectively. Keep in mind that the amounts of fiber contained in different soy products vary significantly. Tofu and soymilk, for instance, have virtually no fiber content at all. Read the Nutrition Facts label to find out if a particular soy product is high in fiber.

Research into soy's effect on diabetes also found that by reducing cholesterol levels, soy protein helps to prevent and control some of the complications of diabetes. In particular, the devastating conditions like atherosclerosis, heart attack, stroke, and kidney disease.

For those at risk for diabetes, or with a family history of diabetes, health professionals recommend taking precautionary steps to prevent the onset of this debilitating disease. Implementing healthy lifestyle and dietary changes can achieve this goal. You can easily increase your activity level by taking a daily walk, or improve your dietary profile by restricting animal protein intake while increasing soluble fiber and soy protein consumption.

How can a soy-protein rich diet help diabetics maintain their kidney health?

Diets high in protein generally make healthy kidneys filter at a higher rate, and can accelerate the progression of kidney disease. Diets low in protein have been shown to have beneficial effects on kidney function. However, diabetics who substitute soy-protein for animal-protein in their meal plans are better able to preserve their kidney health. Evidence shows the type of protein in soy foods does not have the same negative impact on kidney health as animal proteins do. A soy-protein rich diet may actually protect people with diabetes from developing diabetic kidney disease.

Diabetic kidney disease is progressive, often taking several years to develop. In the kidney, many tiny blood vessels act as filters to remove wastes, chemicals, and excess water from the blood. In diabetic kidney disease these blood vessels are damaged. They become leaky and protein begins to spill into the urine. Eventually, these damaged filters are destroyed, putting more stress on the remaining filters. This creates a cascade effect by causing the remaining filters to become damaged. When the entire filtration system breaks down, the kidneys fail to function. The ADA calls this end-stage renal disease. Preventing diabetes-related kidney problems begins with good control of blood glucose levels, controlling blood pressure, and regular screening by a health care professional.

Research continues to focus on the role a soy-protein rich diet has in preventing the onset of diabetic kidney disease. Individuals at risk for developing this disease, secondary to their diabetes, should try to incorporate at least one or two servings of soy foods into their daily diet. Research has shown that a plant-based diet decreases the workload of the kidneys, and may help prevent and treat diabetic kidney disease. Soy foods may also help avert kidney damage by normalizing the glomerular filtration rate (GFR) and protein excretion in the urine. The GFR is the rate by which the kidneys filter waste products from the body, and is often used as a clinical marker to measure kidney health.

All these findings suggest that soy's type of protein and soluble fiber content can help diabetics control their glucose levels, blood pressure, cholesterol levels, protein excretion and kidney filtration process. However, even though soy provides many health benefits, as with any medical condition, those with diabetes or kidney disease should always consult their physician before making any kind of dietary changes.

CHAPTER 8: OVERVIEW OF SOY FOODS

This book focuses on the traditional and modern soy-based products like tofu, textured soy protein (textured vegetable protein), tempeh, soy flour, miso, soynuts and soymilk. These soy foods are more nutritionally complete than most second generation soy products because they are less processed. However, something needs to be done to make them taste better. Unlike second generation products, these soy foods are rather bland when eaten on their own. For instance, eating a plain block of tofu wouldn't have much flavor, nor would it be very enjoyable. The trick is to spice it properly and combine it with other foods. Tofu absorbs the flavor of whatever is added to it. Textured soy protein, tempeh, and soy flour have similar flavor needing qualities as tofu. Soymilk also tastes best when added with other foods or flavorings rather than drinking it plain.

Generally, nothing needs to be done to prepare second generation soy products. They are mostly ready made, just heat and eat. However, their convenience comes at a higher cost. The vast majority of these second generation soy foods are less nutritious and more expensive than the traditional and modern soy-based products.

Asians, vegetarians, and health enthusiasts have known for years that foods rich in soy protein are excellent and wholesome alternatives to meat, poultry and other animal-based products. In recent years, as more Americans pursue healthier lifestyles, the consumption of soy foods has risen steadily, bolstered by scientific studies showing various health benefits from these products. This book will teach you how to make traditional and modern soy foods taste good. The better these foods taste, the more apt you will be to include them into your daily diet. The more soy you eat and enjoy, the more health benefits you will obtain from doing so.

For those reluctant to try soy foods for fear that it will taste bad, I recommend adding small amounts of soy to your daily meal plans. Start with one or two recipes at a time. Then, when you become familiar with soy's various tastes and textures, you can add more soy to your diet. Once you become familiar with the recipes contained in the following chapters, you will be better able to substitute soy-based products for animal-based products in your favorite family recipes.

Because many soy foods have a mild or even neutral flavor, like tofu, soymilk, textured soy protein and tempeh, you can add soy to most recipes and barely know it's there. For example, tofu can easily be substituted for ricotta cheese or low-fat cream cheese in lasagne, casseroles or dips. It is one of the most versatile of the soy-based products because of its bland taste. Soymilk can be used in place of any form of cows' milk called for in a drink or recipe. Textured soy protein is a great high quality protein substitute for ground beef or ground pork. It can completely or partially replace ground meat in recipes, to reduce saturated fats and cholesterol in your diet. Add soy flour to any bread, muffin, cake, burger or gravy recipe to boost its protein content. Miso makes a wonderful soup starter and can be used instead of salt in many recipes. Tempeh is a terrific meat alternative and one of most easily digestible soy foods. Because tempeh is fermented, it does not require a long cooking time. Making it ideal for people in a hurry to cook something hearty and satisfying in a short amount of time.

In summary, soy's health benefits are just beginning to be fully understood. Scientists are continuing to research soy and its constituents to discover exactly how they work. To date, soy's isoflavones, protein, and soluble fiber content has proven to be the most advantageous against heart disease, stroke, certain cancers, osteoporosis, menopausal symptoms, diabetes and kidney disease. The positive effects of these powerful nutrients and phytochemicals will increase soy's role as culinary medicine. This, in turn, will allow soy to be more accepted and integrated into the mainstream Western diet of the future. In the meantime, you can begin to take an active role in preserving and improving your own health by understanding why soy and soy-based products are beneficial, and learning how to incorporate these foods into your daily diet.

Where can I purchase soy foods?

The more popular soy foods such as tofu, soymilk, soy cheese, soy sauce, soybean oil, soy-based burgers, breakfast patties and other meat alternatives, can be found in most U.S. supermarkets. As each day goes by, regular supermarkets are offering more and more soy-based products.

The greatest variety of traditional, modern and second generation soy foods can be found at natural health foods stores. These stores carry the widest selection soy products, like tofu, tempeh, soy flour, whole soybeans, textured soy protein, soynuts, soymilk, soynut butter, cold-cuts, soy yogurt, soy-based burgers, hotdogs and various frozen entrees and desserts.

Asian food stores carry most of the traditional soy products like tofu, tempeh, miso, soy sauce and whole soybeans. Many soy foods can also be found at gourmet markets, as well as through mail order catalogs and online websites.

I thought there was only one type of tofu. However, when I go to a health food store or an Asian store, I see so many varieties I don't know which one to choose. What is the difference between them all?

Tofu is available in various forms and degrees of firmness, from extra firm to silken soft. Each degree of density is intended for a separate culinary use. The extra firm and firm tofu varieties are very dense and solid because they contain less water. These densities hold up the best when stir-fried, grilled, sauteed or baked. Extra firm and firm tofu are also higher in protein and calcium than other forms of tofu. Tofu made with calcium sulfate (gypsum), is a great source of easy to assimilate calcium. Soft tofu is good for blended recipes, like dips and spreads. However, firm and extra firm tofu can also make excellent high-protein dips and spreads. They just need to be blended in a food processor longer (a full 1-2 minutes).

Silken tofu is a Japanese-style form of tofu with a silkier texture than the regular Chinese-style tofu. It is available in various densities from firm to soft. It has a very smooth creamy consistency and a strong taste, for tofu. Silken tofu can be pureed for soups, desserts, dressings or fruit smoothies. It can also replace sour cream in many dip recipes. Silken tofu is generally sold in special vacuum-packed 12 ounce containers, which can be stored unrefrigerated until opened.

Regular Chinese-style tofu is usually sold in 16-oz. water-packed plastic packages which must be stored in the refrigerator. Once opened, refrigerate any unused portion and change the water daily. Tofu can also be frozen up to three months. Freezing will change its texture, making it chewier. It is also sold in powder form at many Asian food stores. Tofu is easy to digest; cholesterol-free; rich in protein, isoflavones and calcium; low in calories and low in sodium. Making it one of today's most versatile and healthful foods. (See p. 181)

What is the difference between the various forms of soymilk?

Soymilk comes unfortified and fortified, regular or low-fat, organic or non-organic. It is available in a variety of flavors, like plain, chocolate or vanilla. Soymilk is most commonly sold in special aseptic containers which do not need refrigeration before opening. However once opened, it does need to be refrigerated and should be used within a week to ten days. This form of soymilk is the richest in flavor. Also, since it can be stored for an extended period of time without refrigeration, it is ideal for emergencies, camping or traveling.

More recently soymilk has become available in quart and half gallon containers in the dairy case, which does need refrigeration before and after opening. This form of soymilk is lighter in flavor because more water is often used in its processing. Soymilk is also sold in powder form. However, it is often very sweet because sugars have been added to the mix.

All these varieties of soymilk can be used cup-for-cup in place of cows' milk. Serve soymilk with hot or cold cereals, or use it to make delicious drinks, desserts, soups, sauces and baked goods. (See p. 179)

What is the difference between textured soy protein (TSP) and textured vegetable protein (TVP)?

Textured soy protein (TSP) is a product description while textured vegetable protein (TVP) is a product name. TSP usually refers to products made from textured soy flour. The term can also be applied to textured soy protein concentrates and spun soy fiber. Textured soy flour is made by running defatted soy flour through an extrusion cooker, creating various forms and sizes. (The defatted soy flour is compressed until the structure of the protein changes.)

TSP contains about 70 percent protein and retains most of the soybean's dietary fiber and isoflavones. It is sold dried in granular and chunk style. When hydrated it has a chewy meat-like texture. TSP is widely used as a meat extender or meat substitute. Textured Vegetable Protein (TVP) is one of the more popular brands of TSP. Archer Daniels Midland Company owns the rights to this product name. *(See p. 181)*

Can I use soy flour the same way as I use wheat flour?

No, soy flour should be combined with wheat flour for baked goods, burgers, sauces, gravies, and soups. Because it lacks gluten and has a rather strong taste, soy flour should not completely replace wheat flour. Soy flour adds moisture to baked goods and can be used as an egg substitute. However, since soy flour is gluten-free, yeast-raised breads made with too much soy flour can become dense in texture. To make sure your muffins, cakes, pancakes, yeast breads and quick breads are light and nutritious, only replace 15-20 percent of the total flour with soy flour. Due to its strong flavor, in other recipes, such as burgers, soups and gravies, replace no more than 30-40 percent of the total flour with soy flour.

Soy flour is usually made from roasted soybeans ground into a fine powder. There are basically three kinds of soy flour: natural or full-fat, which contains the natural oils found in the soybean; defatted, which has the oils removed during processing; and lecithinated, which has had lecithin added to it. Soy flour is very high in protein, about two to four times that of wheat flour. It is also lower in carbohydrates than other flours. While all soy flour gives a protein boost to recipes, defatted soy flour provides more protein than natural or full-fat soy flour. *(See p. 179)*

I keep hearing that miso is so healthy, how should I use it?

Miso is a rich, salty condiment characteristic of Japanese cooking. The Japanese use this fermented soybean paste to make miso soup and to flavor an assortment of other foods like sauces, dressings, marinades, spreads and dips. Miso comes in dozens of varieties, that range in color from ivory to almost black, and in flavor from mildly sweet to very salty.

Because of its strong and distinct flavor, a little goes a long way. Miso is usually used sparingly to enhance flavor in cooking, much like most condiments. Generally, the lighter color miso is milder in flavor than the darker color miso, which has a very intense taste. The lighter and milder varieties are usually used in dressings, dips and spreads. The darker and stronger tasting varieties are usually used in soups, sauces and marinades. *(See p. 177)*

What exactly is tempeh, and what is the difference between the many varieties available?

Tempeh, originally developed in Indonesia, is a fermented soy product made from cracked soybeans inoculated with beneficial bacteria cultures. It is a rich source of high quality soy protein and isoflavones. Tempeh comes in many varieties. It can be made with either 100 percent soybeans, or soybeans combined with one or more grains like rice, millet, or barley. When tempeh is made with soybeans and grains, it tends to mellow the flavor. Each grain, and grain combination, adds a subtle difference to the tempeh's taste.

Tempeh made only with soybeans has the highest amount of soy protein and isoflavones. The more grain that is added to the tempeh, the lower its protein and isoflavone content. Whatever variety you choose, tempeh is still one of the easiest ways to get lots of protein and isoflavones in a minimally processed soy food. The fermentation process actually allows tempeh's nutrients to be more easily assimilated and absorbed by the body.

All varieties of tempeh can be used the same way. They can be stir-fried, sauteed, crumbled, stewed or baked to make many kinds of dishes and sandwiches. Tempeh doesn't need to be cooked very long, making it one of soy's best fast foods. Its nutty flavor and meaty texture allow it to be a wonderful sandwich stuffer. Just add a little soy sauce or liquid hickory smoke seasoning to enhance its flavor and lightly brown in a skillet. Tempeh is one the most nutritious and easily to prepare of all the traditional and modern soy foods. *(See p. 180)*

CEREALS

Hot Creamy Brown Rice Cereal

1/2 cup uncooked brown rice
1-1/2 cups water
1/2 teaspoon salt
2/3 cup soymilk
1 tablespoon maple syrup (or 2 teaspoons sugar)

1. In a coffee grinder or grain mill, grind 1/2 cup brown rice to a course ground. Do not over grind rice into a powder like consistency.
2. Heat water to a rolling boil, add salt and maple syrup (or sugar).
3. Slowly stir in ground rice. Continue stirring for a minute to avoid lumps. Bring back to a boil. Then add soymilk, reduce heat and let simmer for 5 minutes, stirring occasionally.
4. Turn off heat and let sit for 1-2 minutes. Then stir well and serve. Adjust thickness and sweetness at table by adding more soymilk and sweetener. Serve with juice and toast, or a Soymilk Biscuit.

Makes about 3 cups (2-3 servings)

Hot Creamy Millet Cereal

1/2 cup uncooked millet
1-1/2 cups water
1/2 teaspoon salt
2/3 cup soymilk
1 tablespoon maple syrup (or 2 teaspoon sugar)

1. In a coffee grinder or grain mill, grind 1/2 cup millet to a medium grind, but don't over grind millet or it will become too powder like.
2. Heat water until it begins to boil, add salt and maple syrup (or sugar).
3. Very slowly stir in ground millet, continue stirring for a minute to avoid lumping. Bring back to a boil. Then add soymilk, reduce heat and let simmer for 5 minutes, stirring occasionally.
4. Turn off heat and let sit for 1-2 minutes. Then stir well and serve. Adjust thickness and sweetness at table by adding more soymilk and sweetener. Serve with juice and toast, or a Soymilk Biscuit.

Makes about 3 cups (2-3 servings)

Hot Creamy Oats Cereal

1 cup water
3/8 teaspoon salt
1 tablespoon maple syrup (or 2 teaspoons sugar)
1 cup old fashioned rolled oats
3/4 cup soymilk

1. Heat water to a rolling boil, add salt and maple syrup (or sugar).
2. Add rolled oats. Bring back to a boil. Then add soymilk, reduce heat and let simmer for 5 minutes, stir occasionally.
3. Turn off heat, cover with a lid and let sit for 1-2 minutes. Stir and serve. Adjust thickness or sweetness by adding more soymilk or sweetener. Serve with juice and toast, or a Soymilk Biscuit.

Makes about 3 cups (2-3 servings)

Soynut Raisin Granola

4-1/2 cups uncooked old fashioned rolled oats
1/2 cup honey
2 tablespoons canola oil
2 tablespoons water
1 tablespoon applesauce, unsweetened
1/4 teaspoon salt
1/2 cup chopped soynuts
1/2 cup raisins

1. Mix together honey, oil, water, applesauce and salt. Pour this mixture over oats, and mix thoroughly to coat all the oats.
2. Preheat oven to 275°. Lightly oil a cookie sheet with canola oil. Spread oat mixture out onto a cookie sheet.
3. Bake at 275° for 35-40 minutes or until lightly browned. Stir oats every 10-15 minutes to ensure even browning.
4. Then remove from oven, stir in soynuts and raisins. Let granola cool on cookie sheet, stirring often to breakup chucks and prevent clumping. Store in a jar or plastic bag. Serve with soymilk, juice and toast.

Makes about 6 cups (6-8 servings)

Cheesy Mushroom Omelet

2 eggs - from all-natural grain fed, cage free hens
2/3 cup sliced mushrooms (4-5 medium mushrooms)
1/4 cup soymilk
2 teaspoons nutritional yeast
3/8 teaspoon salt

1. Whisk together eggs, soymilk, 1 teaspoon nutritional yeast and 1/8 teaspoon salt. Set aside. Slice mushrooms.
2. Heat a pan over medium heat. Add 1 teaspoon canola oil, mushrooms and 1/4 teaspoon salt. Saute 2 minutes, until mushrooms produce a liquid. Then stir in 1 teaspoon nutritional yeast, remove from pan and set aside.
3. Add 1 teaspoon of canola oil to heated pan. Pour egg mixture into pan and let sit until egg mixture begins to get firm. Then gently lift sides with a fork or spatula to allow the uncooked portion of egg mixture to flow underneath. Turn heat down, cover with a lid, and let cook for 2-3 minutes, until eggs begin to puff up. Then carefully flip over omelet.
4. Add mushroom filling, carefully fold in half. Divide into two and serve. Great with juice, toast and a Country Soy Sausage.

Makes 2 servings

Rich Scrambled Eggs

2 eggs - from all-natural grain fed, cage free hens
5 tablespoons soymilk
1/2 tablespoon nutritional yeast
1/8 teaspoon salt
dash of black ground pepper

1. Whisk together eggs, soymilk, nutritional yeast, salt and pepper.
2. Heat pan over medium heat, add 1 teaspoon canola oil. Test pan's heat before adding eggs. Add a drop of egg mixture to pan. If it gets firm right away, pan is properly heated. If not, wait a minute and test again.
3. Pour egg mixture into pan, let sit for 1-2 minutes. Then begin pulling eggs from outer edge of pan towards the center, until eggs get firm. Turn down heat, cover with a lid and let sit 1-2 minutes to allow eggs to puff up. Then flip eggs over, take off heat and serve. Great with juice, toast and Country Soy Sausage.

Makes 2 servings

Shiitake Scrambled Eggs

2 eggs -from all-natural grain fed, cage free hens
6 tablespoons soymilk
1/2 tablespoon nutritional yeast flakes
4-6 small dry shiitake mushrooms
1/8 teaspoon salt
dash of black ground pepper

1. Whisk together eggs, soymilk, nutritional yeast, salt and pepper. Rinse shiitake mushrooms. Using a pair of scissors, cut thin strips of mushrooms. Let mushrooms soak in egg mixture for 5 minutes.
2. Heat a pan over medium heat, add 1 teaspoon canola oil. Test pan's heat before adding eggs. Add a drop of egg mixture to pan. If it gets firm right away, pan is properly heated. If not, wait a minute and test again.
3. Pour egg mixture into pan, let sit for 1-2 minutes. Then begin pulling egg mixture from outer edge of pan towards the center, until eggs begin to get firm. Turn heat to low, cover with a lid, and let sit 1-2 minutes to allow eggs to puff up. Then flip eggs over, take off heat and serve. Great with juice, toast and Country Soy Sausage.

Makes 2 servings

PANCAKES

Blueberry Pancakes

1 cup unbleached bread flour
1 tablespoon baking powder
1 tablespoon sugar
1/2 teaspoon salt
1 teaspoon canola oil
1/2 cup soymilk
1/2 cup water
2 teaspoons pure vanilla extract
1/8 teaspoon ground cinnamon
1/2 cup fresh blueberries

1. Mix together flour, baking soda, salt, sugar and cinnamon.
2. Add canola oil, soymilk, water and vanilla. Mix until there are no lumps.
3. Wash blueberries, cut each in half, and stir blueberry halves into batter.
4. Heat and oil a skillet with canola oil. For each pancake, drop about 2

tablespoons of batter into the well oiled skillet.
5. When pancakes bubble and are lightly browned on one side, flip over. Lightly brown other side, then remove from skillet and put on a plate.
6. Use a big soup pot lid to cover pancakes until done cooking all of the batter. This will keep pancakes warm and supple. Serve with maple syrup and a Country Soy Sausage.

Makes 8-10 pancakes (2-4 servings)

Cornmeal Pancakes

1/2 cup cornmeal
1/2 cup unbleached bread flour
4 teaspoons baking powder
1 tablespoon sugar
1/2 teaspoon salt
1 teaspoon canola oil
1/2 cup soymilk
1/2 cup water

1. Mix together cornmeal, flour, baking soda, salt, and sugar.
2. Add canola oil, soymilk and water. Mix to a smooth consistency.
3. Heat and oil a skillet with canola oil. For each pancake, drop about 2 tablespoons of batter into the well oiled skillet.
4. When pancakes bubble and are lightly browned on one side, flip over. Lightly brown other side, then remove from skillet and put on a plate.
5. Use a big soup pot lid to cover pancakes until done cooking all of the batter. This will keep pancakes warm and supple. Serve with maple syrup, scrambled eggs and a Country Soy Sausage.

Makes 8-10 pancakes (2-4 servings)

Plain Soymilk Pancakes

1 cup unbleached bread flour
1 tablespoon baking powder
1 tablespoon sugar
1/2 teaspoon salt
1 teaspoon canola oil
1/2 cup soymilk
1/2 cup water

1. Mix together flour, baking soda, salt, and sugar.

2. Add canola oil, soymilk, and water. Mix until there are no lumps.
3. Heat and oil a skillet with canola oil. For each pancake, use about 2 tablespoons of batter. Drop batter into the well oiled skillet and gently form into round pancakes.
4. When pancakes bubble and are lightly browned on one side, flip over. Lightly brown other side, then remove from skillet and put on a plate.
5. Use a big soup pot lid to cover pancakes until done cooking all of the batter. This will keep pancakes warm and supple. Serve with maple syrup and a Country Soy Sausage.

Makes 8-10 pancakes (2-4 servings)

Soy Millet Pancakes

1/2 cup ground millet
1/2 cup unbleached bread flour
1/4 cup soy flour
4-1/2 teaspoons baking powder
1 tablespoon sugar
1/2 teaspoon salt
1/2 cup soymilk
1/2 cup water
1 teaspoon canola oil
1 teaspoon pure vanilla extract

1. In a coffee grinder or grain mill, finely grind uncooked millet to a flour like consistency. Mix together the ground millet, bread flour, soy flour, baking soda, sugar and salt.
2. Add soymilk, water, canola oil and vanilla extract. Mix until there are no lumps.
3. Heat and oil a skillet with canola oil. For each pancake, use about 2 tablespoons of batter. Drop batter into the well oiled skillet and gently form into round pancakes.
4. When pancakes bubble and are lightly browned on one side, flip over. Lightly brown other side, then remove from skillet and put on a plate.
5. Use a big soup pot lid to cover pancakes until done cooking all of the batter. This will keep pancakes warm and supple. Serve with maple syrup and a Country Soy Sausage.

Makes 10-12 pancakes (2-4 servings)

Soy-Rich Pancakes

1 cup unbleached bread flour
1/4 cup soy flour
1 tablespoon baking powder
1 tablespoon sugar
1/2 teaspoon salt
1/2 cup soymilk
1/2 cup water
1 teaspoon pure vanilla extract

1. Mix together bread flour, soy flour, baking soda, salt, and sugar.
2. Add soymilk, water and vanilla extract. Mix until there are no lumps.
3. Heat and oil a skillet with canola oil. For each pancake, drop about 2 tablespoons of batter into the well oiled skillet.
4. When pancakes bubble and are lightly browned on one side, flip over. Lightly brown other side, then remove from skillet and put on a plate.
5. Use a big soup pot lid to cover pancakes until done cooking all of the batter. This will keep pancakes warm and supple. Serve with maple syrup, juice and a Country Soy Sausage.

Makes 2-4 servings, 8-10 pancakes

POTATOES

Potato Tofu Hash

5.3 ounces tofu - diced (1/3 of a 16-ounce block firm tofu)
3 cups potatoes - diced (3 medium or 4 small potatoes)
1 cup onion - diced (1 large onion)
1-1/2 tablespoons canola oil
3/8 teaspoon salt
1/8 teaspoon turmeric
1/8 teaspoon black ground pepper

1. Dice tofu into 1/4 to 1/2 inch cubes. Peel and dice potatoes into 1/2 inch cubes.
2. Heat 1 teaspoon canola oil, add diced tofu, turmeric, 1/8 teaspoon salt and a dash of pepper. Stir until all cubes are thoroughly coated and get a nice yellow color. Saute tofu until golden brown and firm. Set aside.
3. Heat 1 tablespoon canola oil, add diced potatoes, black ground pepper and 1/4 teaspoon salt. Stir to coat all the potato cubes with oil, salt and pepper. Cover with a lid and allow to steam for 3-5 minutes. Uncover

51

for a minute before flipping potatoes over, this will prevent any sticking. Then flip potatoes, cover and steam another 3-5 minutes. Uncover and flip potatoes again. Keep flipping until all potatoes are golden brown.

4. When potatoes are golden brown, mix in tofu cubes and push to one side of the pan. Add 1/2 teaspoon canola oil and diced onions to empty side of pan. Stir and cook onions until translucent, then mix thoroughly with potatoes and tofu. Salt and pepper to taste. Serve with juice and toast or a Soymilk Biscuit.

Makes 2-4 servings

TOASTS

Baked Walnut Cinnamon Tofu Toast

5.3 ounces tofu (1/3 of a 16-ounce block)
1 tablespoon maple syrup
1 tablespoon applesauce - unsweetened
2 teaspoons vanilla
2 teaspoons canola oil
1 teaspoon cinnamon
1/2 teaspoon salt
1/2 cup soymilk
1/4 cup walnuts
6 large pieces of bread (pp. 60-69)

1. In a food processor add tofu, maple syrup, applesauce, vanilla extract, canola oil, cinnamon, and salt. Combine until smooth and creamy.
2. Add soymilk and blend mixture again. Then add walnuts and grind processor just to break up the walnuts.
3. Preheat oven to 375°. Oil a baking sheet with canola oil.
4. Cut bread slices in half diagonally. Coat one side with half the tofu mixture. Place bread slices, coated side down, onto the baking sheet. Then spread the rest of the tofu mixture on the other side.
5. Bake for 10 minutes. Flip over bread slices, and bake for another 8-10 minutes or until lightly browned. Serve with maple syrup and a Country Soy Sausage. Freeze any leftovers and reheat in microwave or toaster-oven for 1-2 minutes. These Baked Walnut Cinnamon Tofu Toasts freeze very well and make a great healthy alternative to store-bought toaster pastries or frozen waffles.

Makes 4-6 servings

French Toast

6 slices Light Wheat Soymilk Bread (p. 62)
2 eggs - from all-natural grain fed, cage free hens
1/2 cup + 1 tablespoon soymilk
2 teaspoons canola oil
1 teaspoon sugar
1/4 teaspoon salt

1. In a bowl first beat eggs, then add soymilk, sugar and salt.
2. Cut bread slices in half. Quickly dip in egg mixture to coat the outside. Don't let bread sit in egg mixture too long, or it'll become soggy.
3. Heat canola oil in a large skillet. Place egg dipped bread slices in pan. Cook for about 2 minutes, until lightly browned. Turn over and lightly brown other side. Serve with maple syrup and a Country Soy Sausage.

Makes 2 servings

French Vanilla Toast

6 slices Light Wheat Soymilk Bread (P. 62)
2 eggs -from all-natural grain fed, cage free hens
1/2 cup + 1 tablespoon soymilk
2 teaspoons canola oil
1 teaspoon sugar
1 teaspoon pure vanilla extract
1/4 teaspoon salt
Pinch of nutmeg (less than 1/8 teaspoon)

1. In a bowl first beat eggs, then add soymilk, vanilla, sugar, salt and a pinch of nutmeg.
2. Cut bread slices in half. Quickly dip in egg mixture to coat the outside. Don't let bread sit in egg mixture too long, or it'll become soggy.
3. Heat canola oil in a large skillet. Place egg dipped bread slices in pan. Cook for about 1-2 minutes, until lightly browned. Turn over and lightly brown other side. Serve with maple syrup, juice and a Country Soy Sausage.

Makes 2 servings

Seeded Soy Rye Toast with Tofu Cream Cheese

4 slices Seeded Soy Rye Bread (p. 63)
4 tablespoons Tofu Cream Cheese (p. 88)

1. Lightly toast Seeded Soy Rye Bread in a toaster-oven.
2. Spread about 1 tablespoon Tofu Cream Cheese over each slice. Cut toasted slices in half at a diagonal and serve.

Makes 2 servings

Super Soy Honey Wheat Cinnamon Toast

4 slices Super Soy Honey Wheat Bread (p. 67)
2 tablespoons canola oil
2 tablespoons sugar
1/2 + 1/8 teaspoon ground cinnamon
A pinch of salt

1. Sprinkle 1/2 tablespoon canola oil on each slice of bread.
2. Mix together sugar, cinnamon and a pinch of salt. Sprinkle this mixture over the oiled slices of bread.
3. Lightly toast bread in a toaster-oven, until cinnamon sugar begins to caramelize. Remove from toaster, cut each slice in half at a diagonal and serve.

Makes 2 servings

Toasted Bagels with Tofu Cream Cheese

2 bagels (pp. 57-59)
4 tablespoons Tofu Cream Cheese (p. 88)

1. Slice bagels in half. Place cut side up in a toaster-oven and lightly toast top side only.
2. Spread about 1 tablespoon Tofu Cream Cheese on each bagel half and serve. Also great with some jelly or fruit preserves on top as well.

Makes 2 servings

CHAPTER 10: BREADS, PIZZA, BURGERS & PATTIES

QUICK BREADS

Soy Cornbread

2/3 cup cornmeal
1/2 cup unbleached bread flour
3 tablespoons soy flour
1/3 cup sugar
1 tablespoon baking powder
1/2 teaspoon salt
3/4 cup soymilk
2 tablespoons water
1-1/2 tablespoons canola oil

1. Combine cornmeal, bread flour, soy flour, sugar, baking soda and salt.
2. Add soymilk, water and canola oil. Mix to a smooth consistency.
3. Preheat oven to 350°. Oil an 8 x 8 inch baking pan with canola oil. Evenly spread out batter in baking pan.
4. Bake for 10 minutes or until top is golden brown, sides begin to pull away from pan and a tooth pick inserted in center comes out clean.
5. Let cool for 5 minutes. Then cut cornbread into 8 triangular pieces (make 4 cuts - first make 2 cuts to quarter bread, then make 2 more cuts from corner to corner, to cut each quarter in half) and serve. Excellent with chili, soup, salad or rice and beans.
Makes 8 pieces (4-8 servings)

Soymilk Biscuits

1 cup sifted unbleached bread flour
1 tablespoon baking powder
1/2 teaspoon salt
1 teaspoon sugar
1 tablespoon canola oil
1/2 cup soymilk

1. Sift flour into a bowl. Mix in baking powder, salt and sugar.
2. Mix in 1 tablespoon canola oil. Sprinkle oil into flour and stir. With your thumb and pointer, pinch oil lumps in flour to help distribute it.
3. Fold in soymilk by adding 1/4 cup of soymilk and gently folding dough over, then add another 1/4 cup of soymilk and fold again. Mix gently

55

until dough begins to hold together. Don't over mix dough or it will become tough; the less mixing, the lighter the biscuit.
4. Preheat oven to 350°. Lightly oil a baking sheet with canola oil. Sift flour onto baking sheet, make sure surface is well coated.
5. Spoon out 2 large or 4 small balls of dough and sift flour on top. Carefully roll sides of dough balls on floured surface to make balls round. Then form into biscuits by gently pressing down on top of dough ball with fingers.
6. Bake at 350° for 8-10 minutes. Serve with honey, jelly, maple syrup or fruit preserves.

Makes 2-4 biscuits (2-4 servings)

Whole Wheat Soymilk Tortillas

1 cup whole wheat flour
1 cup unbleached bread flour
1/2 cup soymilk
1/2 cup water
1 tablespoon canola oil
1 teaspoon salt

1. Mix together bread flour, whole wheat flour and salt. Add canola oil and pinch into flour using thumb and pointer.
2. Add soymilk and water, mix well. When dough forms into a ball, turn out onto a vinegar cleaned and floured surface. (Pour vinegar on work surface, spread around with your hands, and wipe off with a dry cloth or paper towel. Then dust surface with flour so dough doesn't stick.)
3. Knead dough for 1-2 minutes. Form into a long roll and cut into 12 pieces. Fold over each piece until they look like a round ball.
4. Using a rolling pin, roll out each ball from center to edges. Flour top of dough, turn over and roll again. Repeat this step until dough forms a 7-8 inch round tortilla. Make sure to use plenty of flour so the dough does not stick to anything.
5. Place one tortilla at a time in a heated un-oiled skillet. Turn over when tortilla becomes a bit stiff and forms air pockets (use a fork or spatula). Lightly cook other side. Make sure not to brown or burn tortilla or else it will become hard and brittle. Tortillas should be firm yet soft and pliable. Tortillas can be stored in the freezer. When ready to use, either set out on a plate to thaw, or microwave for 30 seconds or until soft.

Makes 12 large tortillas (3-4 servings)

YEAST BREADS - BAGELS

Soymilk Bagels

2-1/4 teaspoons active dry yeast (1 package)
3 tablespoons sugar
2 teaspoons salt
1 cup soymilk
3/4 cup water
4 cups unbleached bread flour
1/2 cup whole wheat flour
2-4 tablespoons sesame seeds or poppy seeds

1. Mix together active dry yeast, sugar and salt in a large bowl or pot.
2. Mix together soymilk and water. Heat liquid to 110°F, use a thermometer to measure temperature. If water is too hot, it will kill the yeast. If water is too cold, yeast won't activate. Pour liquid over yeast, sugar and salt. Stir to dissolve yeast. Let sit for 5 minutes or until yeast begins to rise up to the surface and becomes frothy, this means yeast is activated.
3. Mix in bread flour and whole wheat flour. Keep mixing until dough forms into a stiff ball, becoming elastic and smooth. Cover and let dough rise for 20 minutes.
4. Clean a work surface using vinegar. Pour vinegar on surface, spread around with your hands, then wipe off with a clean dry cloth or paper towel. Vinegar is used because it is a non toxic acidic cleaner.
5. Once work surface is dry, liberally flour it so dough won't stick. Turn dough out onto floured surface. Dust the top of dough with some more flour so it won't stick to your hands. Knead dough for 2-3 minutes.
6. Cut dough into 12 portions. Form each portion into a round ball. Take a dough ball and poke a hole through the center of the ball, using your thumb and pointer. Then carefully work your fingers through the hole. Gently shape dough ball to make a 1-1/2 inch hole in the center. Dust with flour and place on a floured surface to rise. Do this step for all 12 dough balls. Let sit to rise for 30 minutes.
7. In a 4 quart pot, add 8 cups water, 1 tablespoon sugar and 1/2 teaspoon salt. Bring to a rapid boil. Then turn heat down to medium-high.
8. Preheat oven to 375°. Oil a baking sheet with canola oil and sprinkle with sesame seeds and/or poppy seeds.
9. Carefully pick up a bagel using a spatula and place into the slightly boiling water. Cook 3 bagels at a time. Cover pot with a lid and cook for 3 minutes. Then take off lid and let cook for another 3 minutes. Using a spatula or slotted spoon, remove bagels from water and place

57

on the oiled baking sheet. Sprinkle top of bagels with sesame seeds, poppy seeds, or both. Repeat this step until all the bagels are boiled.
10. Bake bagels at 375° for 15-20 minutes, or until lightly golden brown. Remove from oven and let bagels cool on a wire rack.
Makes 12 bagels

Super Soy Bagels

2-1/4 teaspoons active dry yeast (1 package)
3 tablespoons sugar
2 teaspoons salt
1 cup soymilk
3/4 cup water
3-1/2 cups unbleached bread flour
1/2 cup whole wheat flour
1/2 cup soy flour
2-4 tablespoons sesame seeds or poppy seeds

1. Mix together active dry yeast, sugar and salt in a large bowl or pot.
2. Mix together soymilk and water. Heat liquid to 110°F, use a thermometer to measure temperature. If water is too hot, it will kill the yeast. If water is too cold, it won't activate yeast. Pour liquid over yeast, sugar and salt. Stir to dissolve yeast. Let sit for 5 minutes or until yeast begins to rise up to the surface and becomes frothy. This means yeast is activated.
3. Mix in bread flour, whole wheat flour and soy flour. Keep mixing until dough forms into a stiff ball, becoming elastic and smooth. Cover and let rise for 20 minutes.
4. Clean a work surface using vinegar. Pour vinegar on surface, spread around with your hands, then wipe off with a clean dry cloth or paper towel. Vinegar is used because it is a non toxic acidic cleaner.
5. Once work surface is dry, liberally flour it so dough won't stick. Turn dough out onto floured surface. Dust the top of dough with some more flour so it won't stick to your hands. Knead dough for 2-3 minutes.
6. Cut dough into 12 portions. Form each portion into a round ball. Take a dough ball and poke a hole through the center of the ball, using your thumb and pointer. Then carefully work your fingers through the hole. Gently shape dough ball to make a 1-1/2 inch hole in the center. Dust with flour and place on a floured surface to rise. Do this step for all 12 dough balls. Let sit to rise for 30 minutes.
7. In a 4 quart pot, add 8 cups water, 1 tablespoon sugar and 1/2 teaspoon salt. Bring to a rapid boil. Then turn heat down to medium-high.

8. Preheat oven to 375°. Oil a baking sheet with canola oil and sprinkle with sesame seeds and/or poppy seeds.
9. Carefully pick up a bagel using a spatula and place into the slightly boiling water. Cook 3 bagels at a time. Cover pot with a lid and cook for 3 minutes. Then take off lid and let cook for another 3 minutes. Using a spatula or slotted spoon, remove bagels from water and place on the oiled baking sheet. Sprinkle top of bagels with sesame seeds, poppy seeds, or both. Repeat this step until all the bagels are boiled.
10. Bake bagels at 375° for 15-20 minutes, or until lightly golden brown. Remove from oven and let bagels cool on a wire rack.

Makes 12 bagels

Whole Wheat Soymilk Bagels

2-1/4 teaspoons active dry yeast (1 package)
3 tablespoons sugar
2 teaspoons salt
1 cup soymilk
3/4 cup water
3 cups unbleached bread flour
1-1/2 cups whole wheat flour
2-4 tablespoons sesame seeds or poppy seeds

1. In a large bowl or pot, mix together active dry yeast, sugar and salt.
2. Mix together soymilk and water. Heat liquid to 110°F, measure temperature with a thermometer. If water is too hot, it will kill the yeast. If water is too cold, yeast won't activate. Pour liquid over yeast, sugar and salt. Stir to dissolve yeast. Let sit for 5 minutes or until yeast begins to rise up to the surface and becomes frothy, this means yeast is activated.
3. Mix in bread flour and whole wheat flour. Keep mixing until dough forms into a stiff ball, becoming elastic and smooth. Cover and let rise for 20 minutes.
4. Clean a work surface using vinegar. Pour vinegar on surface, spread around with your hands, then wipe off with a clean dry cloth or paper towel. Vinegar is used because it is a non toxic acidic cleaner.
5. Once work surface is dry, liberally flour it so dough won't stick. Turn dough out onto floured surface. Dust the top of dough with some more flour so it won't stick to your hands. Knead dough for 2-3 minutes.
6. Cut dough into 12 portions. Form each portion into a round ball. Take a dough ball and poke a hole through the center of the ball, using your thumb and pointer. Then carefully work your fingers through the hole.

Gently shape dough ball to make a 1-1/2 inch hole in the center. Dust with flour and place on a floured surface to rise. Do this step for all 12 dough balls. Let sit to rise for 30 minutes.

7. In a 4 quart pot, add 8 cups water, 1 tablespoon sugar and 1/2 teaspoon salt. Bring to a rapid boil, then turn heat down to medium-high.
8. Preheat oven to 375°. Oil a baking sheet with canola oil and sprinkle with sesame seeds and/or poppy seeds.
9. Carefully pick up a bagel using a spatula and place into the slightly boiling water. Cook 3 bagels at a time. Cover pot with a lid and cook for 3 minutes. Then take off lid and let cook for another 3 minutes. Using a slotted spoon or spatula, remove bagels from water and place on the oiled baking sheet. Sprinkle top of bagels with sesame seeds, poppy seeds, or both. Repeat this step until all the bagels are boiled.
10. Bake bagels at 375° for 15-20 minutes, or until lightly golden brown. Remove from oven and let bagels cool on a wire rack.

Makes 12 bagels

YEAST BREADS - LOAVES, BUNS & ROLLS

Honey Oat Soy Bread

1-1/2 cups water
2-1/4 teaspoons active dry yeast
2 tablespoons sugar
1/2 tablespoon salt
1/2 tablespoon extra virgin olive oil
1 tablespoon honey
1 cup soymilk
4 cups unbleached bread flour
2-1/3 cups oat flour
2/3 cup soy flour

1. Heat water to approximately 110°F, use thermometer to measure temperature. If water is too hot, it will kill the yeast. If water is too cold, yeast won't activate.
2. In a big bowl or 4 quart pot, mix together active dry yeast, sugar and salt. Pour in warm water and stir to dissolve dry ingredients. Let stand for a few minutes until yeast starts rising up to the surface and appears frothy. This means the yeast is activated.
3. Add soymilk, extra virgin olive oil and honey. If not using honey in recipe, replace with an equal amount of sugar. Then stir in unbleached

bread flour, oat flour and soy flour one cup at a time. (Oat flour can be made by placing rolled oats into a coffee grinder and grinding it until it forms a fine powder, or purchased at a heath food store.) Use a big spoon and mix by hand, or use a food processor with a dough hook. Keep mixing until the dough forms a ball and becomes elastic. This is the gluten which gives the bread its body and texture.

4. Cover bowl or pot with a plate or lid so dough does not dry out and form a skin. Let stand in a warm spot, out of cold drafts, for about an hour or until dough doubles in size.

5. Clean a work surface (bread board or counter top) using vinegar. Pour vinegar on surface, spread around with your hands, then wipe off with a clean dry cloth or paper towel. Vinegar is used because it is a non toxic acidic cleaner.

6. Once work surface is completely dry, liberally flour it so dough won't stick. Turn dough out onto the floured surface. Dust the top of dough with some more flour so it won't stick to your hands.

7. Knead dough for a few minutes. Fold edges toward center, press down, and give dough ball a quarter turn. Repeat this step 3-4 more times.

8. Divide dough into 2 pieces. Keep dough pieces floured. If dough begins to stick to your hands or surface, sprinkle with more flour.

9. Form dough pieces into loaves. Fold dough pieces into thirds, press down and give a quarter turn. Repeat this step 2 more times. Then pinch bottom seam using thumb and pointer.

10. Oil pans with extra virgin olive oil. Lightly flour pans so bread won't stick to pan. This light dusting also ensures thorough coverage of oil, because flour only sticks to the oiled surface of pan. Any spot with no oil is where the bread will stick, making it difficult to get out of pan.

11. Place loaves seam side down into pans. Press each loaf in pan from center to edges, using a fist. Let sit and rest for 15-20 minutes.

12. Then score the top of loaves with 3 diagonal cuts about 1/8 inch deep using a sharp knife or pair of scissors. Do not score too close to the edge of pan, leave a 1 inch margin from the sides of pan. When bread rises, the surface will tear, scoring is controlled tears. You can put any pattern you want on the loaves, just make sure the score is not deeper than 1/8 inch. Let loaves stand and rise for about another 40-45 minutes, or until dough doubles in size.

13. Preheat oven to 400°. Bake breads for 30-35 minutes. When breads are a nice golden brown, remove breads from oven. Breads are done when they easily come out of the pan and have a hollow sound when you thump the bottom of the loaves.

14. Place loaves on a cooling rack. Cool 10-15 minutes before cutting.

Makes 2 loaves

Light Wheat Soymilk Bread

1-1/2 cups water - 110°F
2-1/4 teaspoons active dry rapid rise yeast - 1 package
1-1/2 tablespoons sugar
1/2 tablespoon salt
1 cup soymilk
1/2 tablespoon canola oil
1/2 tablespoon honey
2 cups whole wheat flour
4 cups unbleached bread flour
1 tablespoon sesame seeds

1. Heat water to approximately 110°F, use a thermometer to measure temperature. If water is too hot, it will kill the yeast. If water is too cold, it won't activate yeast.
2. In a big bowl or 4 quart pot, measure out active dry yeast, sugar and salt. Pour in warm water and stir to dissolve dry ingredients. Let stand for a few minutes until yeast starts rising up to the surface and appears frothy. This means the yeast is activated.
3. Add the soymilk, honey and canola oil. If not using honey in recipe, replace with an equal amount of sugar. Then stir in the whole wheat and unbleached bread flour, one cup at a time. Use a big spoon and mix by hand, or use a food processor with a dough hook. Keep mixing until the dough forms a ball and becomes elastic. This is the gluten which gives the bread its body and texture.
4. Cover bowl or pot with a plate or lid, so dough does not dry out and form a skin. Let stand in a warm spot, out of cold drafts, for about an hour or until dough doubles in size.
5. Clean a work surface using vinegar. Pour vinegar on surface, spread around with your hands, then wipe off with a clean dry cloth or paper towel. Vinegar is used because it is a non toxic acidic cleaner.
6. Once the work surface is completely dry, liberally flour it so dough won't stick. Turn dough out onto floured surface. Dust the top of dough with some more flour so it won't stick to your hands.
7. Knead dough for a few minutes. Fold edges toward center, press down, and give dough ball a quarter turn. Repeat this step 3-4 more times.
8. Divide dough into 2 equal pieces. Keep dough pieces floured. If dough begins to stick to your hands or surface, sprinkle with more flour.
9. Form dough pieces into loaves. Fold dough pieces into thirds, press down and give a quarter turn. Repeat this step 2 more times. Then pinch bottom seam using thumb and pointer.

10. Oil pans with canola or extra virgin olive oil. For a lighter crust use canola oil, for a flavorful hearty crust use extra virgin olive oil.
11. Lightly flour pans so bread won't stick to pan. This light dusting also ensures thorough coverage of oil, because flour only sticks to the oiled surface of pan. Any spot where there is no oil is where the bread will stick to the pan, making it very difficult to get the loaf out of pan.
12. Sprinkle sesame seeds on bottom of oiled and floured pans. Then place loaves seam side down into pans. Press each loaf in pan from center to edges using a fist. Let sit and rest for 15-20 minutes.
13. Then score top of loaves with 3 diagonal cuts about 1/8 inch deep using a sharp knife. Don't score too close to the edge of pan, leave a 1 inch margin from the sides of pan. When bread rises, the surface will tear, scoring is controlled tears. You can put any pattern you want on the loaves, just make sure the score is not deeper than 1/4 to 1/8 inch. Let loaves rise another 40-45 minutes, until they double in size.
14. Preheat oven to 400°. Bake breads for 30-35 minutes. When breads are a nice golden brown, remove them from the oven. Breads are done when they easily come out of the pan and have a hollow sound when you thump the bottom of loaves.
15. Place loaves on a cooling rack. Let cool 10-15 minutes before cutting.

Makes 2 loaves

Seeded Soy Rye Bread

2 cups warm water - 110°F
4-1/2 teaspoons yeast (2 packages)
6 tablespoons sugar
1/2 tablespoon salt
2 tablespoons caraway seeds
1 tablespoon extra virgin olive oil
2 teaspoons Dijon mustard
1 cup soymilk
4 cups unbleached bread flour
2-1/2 cups rye flour
1 cup soy flour

1. Heat water to about 110°F, use a thermometer to measure temperature. If water is too hot, it will kill the yeast. If it's too cold, yeast won't activate. In a big bowl or pot, measure out yeast, sugar, salt and caraway seeds. Pour in warm water, stir to dissolve yeast and let sit for 5 minutes.

2. When yeast rises up to the surface and appears frothy, stir in extra virgin olive oil, Dijon mustard and soymilk. Then add bread flour, rye flour and soy flour. Mix with a big metal spoon by hand or with an electric dough hook until dough becomes smooth, elastic and forms into a ball (about 3-5 minutes).
3. Cover with lid or plastic wrap and let rise in a warm place for 1 hour or until dough doubles in size.
4. Oil 2 loaf pans with extra virgin olive oil. Then lightly flour the pans to ensure proper oil coverage and prevent breads from sticking.
5. Clean a work surface using vinegar. Pour vinegar on surface, spread around with your hands, then wipe off with a clean dry cloth or paper towel. When completely dry, liberally flour the work surface.
6. Punch dough down and turn out onto the floured work surface. Knead dough for 2-3 minutes then divide in 2 equal portions. Press dough into a 6 x 9 inch rectangle and roll up lengthways (start at 6 inch side and roll up the 9 inch length). Pinch the ends and place seem side down in loaf pans and punch dough down into pans.
7. Let rise for 15-20 minutes, then using a sharp knife or a pair of scissors, score three diagonal slashes about 1/8 inch deep and 3 inches long. Let rise another 40-45 minutes, or until dough doubles in size.
8. Preheat oven to 400°. Bake breads for about 30-35 minutes. Breads are done when they easily come out of the pan, are golden brown and have a hollow sound when you thump the bottom of the loaves.
9. Cool on a wire rack for at least 15 minutes before cutting.

Makes 2 loaves

Sesame Seed Soy Wheat Buns

2 cups water - 110° F
2-1/4 teaspoons active dry rapid rise yeast - 1 package
1-1/2 tablespoons sugar
1/2 tablespoon salt
1/2 tablespoon canola oil
1/2 tablespoon honey
1 cup soymilk
2 cups whole wheat flour
4 cups unbleached bread flour
1 cup soy flour
6 tablespoons sesame seeds

1. Heat water to approximately 110°F, use a thermometer to measure temperature. If water is too hot, it will kill the yeast. If water is too

cold, yeast won't activate.
2. In a big bowl or 4 quart pot, measure out active dry yeast, sugar and salt. Pour in warm water and stir to dissolve dry ingredients. Let stand for a few minutes until yeast starts blooming to the surface and appears bubbly. This means the yeast is activated.
3. Add the soymilk, canola oil and honey. (If not using honey in recipe, replace with an equal amount of sugar). Then stir in whole wheat and unbleached bread flour. Mix by hand with a big metal spoon, or use a food processor with a dough hook. Keep mixing until the dough forms a ball and becomes elastic.
4. Cover bowl or pot with a plate or lid, so dough does not dry out and form a skin. Let stand in a warm spot, out of cold drafts, for about an hour or until dough doubles in size.
5. Clean a work surface using vinegar. Pour vinegar on surface, spread around with your hands, then wipe off with a dry cloth or paper towel.
6. Once work surface is dry, liberally flour it so dough won't stick. Turn dough out onto floured surface, and dust the top with some more flour.
7. Knead dough for a few minutes. Fold edges toward center, press down, and give dough ball a quarter turn. Repeat this step 3-4 more times.
8. Divide dough into 16 pieces. Keep dough pieces floured. If dough begins to stick to your hands or surface, sprinkle with more flour.
9. Form dough pieces into a snake like shape, about 1-1/2 inches wide and 4 inches long. Knot pieces into a simple knot. Hold piece in left hand between thumb, pointer and middle finger. Let piece drape over back of pointer and middle finger. Grab piece with right hand, bring it around hand and back up to thumb. Remove pointer and middle finger, and push tail end through the hole. (Like knotting a sock or rope; drape it down, bring it around, cross it under and push it through.) If piece sticks to your hands, roll it into some flour.
10. Oil 2 baking sheets with canola or extra virgin olive oil. Lightly flour baking sheets, so buns won't stick, and sprinkle 1-1/2 tablespoons of sesame seeds across bottom of each baking sheet.
11. Place 8 buns on each baking sheet with about 1/2 to 1 inch space in between. Sprinkle 3 tablespoons sesame seeds on top of buns (1-1/2 tablespoons per baking sheet, or about 1/2 teaspoon of sesame seeds per bun). Lightly press top of buns to set seeds into dough.
12. Let buns rise for about 1 hour or until dough doubles in size.
13. Preheat oven to 400°. Bake buns for 15-20 minutes. When buns are a nice golden brown, remove from oven.
14. Take buns off baking sheet and place on a cooling rack. Cool 5-10 minutes before serving.
Makes 16 buns

Soymilk Poppy Seed Rolls

1-1/2 cups water - 110°F
2-1/4 teaspoons active dry rapid rise yeast - 1 package
1-1/2 tablespoons sugar
1/2 tablespoon salt
1/2 tablespoon canola oil
1/2 tablespoon honey
1 cup soymilk
2 cups whole wheat flour
4 cups unbleached bread flour
1/2 cup poppy seeds

1. Heat water to approximately 110°F, use a thermometer to measure temperature. If water is too hot, it will kill the yeast. If water is too cold, yeast won't activate.
2. In a big bowl or 4 quart pot, mix together active dry yeast, sugar and salt. Pour in warm water and stir to dissolve dry ingredients. Let stand for a few minutes until yeast starts blooming to the surface and appears frothy. This means the yeast is activated.
3. Add the soymilk, canola oil and honey. (If not using honey in recipe, replace with an equal amount of sugar). Then stir in whole wheat and unbleached bread flour, one cup at a time. Use a big spoon and mix by hand, or use a food processor with a dough hook. Keep mixing until the dough forms a ball and becomes elastic.
4. Cover bowl or pot with a plate or lid, so dough does not dry out and form a skin. Let stand in a warm spot, out of cold drafts, for about an hour or until dough doubles in size.
5. Clean a work surface using vinegar. Pour vinegar on surface, spread around with your hands, then wipe off with a clean dry cloth or paper towel. Vinegar is used because it is a non toxic acidic cleaner.
6. Once work surface is completely dry, liberally flour it so dough won't stick. Turn dough out onto floured surface. Dust the top of dough with some more flour so it won't stick to your hands.
7. Knead dough for a few minutes while adding 1/3 cup of poppy seeds. Sprinkle some poppy seeds on top of dough ball. Fold edges toward center, press down, give the dough ball a quarter turn. Sprinkle some more poppy seeds on dough ball, fold, press and turn. Repeat this step 3-4 more times, until the poppy seeds are well combined into dough.
8. Divide dough into 16 pieces. Keep dough pieces floured. If dough begins to stick to your hands or surface, sprinkle with more flour.
9. Form dough pieces into a snake like shape, about 1-1/2 inches wide

and 4 inches long. Knot pieces into a simple knot. Hold piece in left hand between thumb, pointer and middle finger. Let piece drape over back of pointer and middle finger. Grab piece with right hand, bring it around hand and back up to thumb. Remove pointer and middle finger, and push tail end through the hole. (Like knotting a sock or rope; drape it down, bring it around, cross it under and push it through.) If piece sticks to your hands, roll it into some flour.

10. Oil a baking sheet with canola or extra virgin olive oil. Lightly flour baking sheet so rolls won't stick. Place rolls on baking sheet with about 1/2 to 1 inch space in between. Sprinkle the rest of the poppy seeds on top of rolls. Use about 1/2 teaspoon of poppy seeds per roll for the top sprinkle. Lightly press top of rolls to set seeds into dough.

11. Let rolls rise for about 1 hour or until dough doubles in size.

12. Preheat oven to 400°. Bake rolls for 15-20 minutes. When rolls are a nice golden brown, remove from oven.

13. Take rolls off baking sheet and place on a cooling rack. Cool 5-10 minutes before serving.

Makes 16 rolls

Super Soy Honey Wheat Bread

2 cups water - 110°F
2-1/4 teaspoons active dry rapid rise yeast - 1 package
1-1/2 tablespoons sugar
1/2 tablespoon salt
1 cup soymilk
1/2 tablespoon canola oil
1 tablespoon honey
4 cups unbleached bread flour
2 cups whole wheat flour
1 cup soy flour
1 tablespoon sesame seeds

1. Heat water to approximately 110°F, use thermometer to measure temperature. If water is too hot, it will kill the yeast. If water is too cold, it won't activate yeast.

2. In a big bowl or 4 quart pot, measure out active dry yeast, sugar and salt. Pour in warm water and stir to dissolve dry ingredients. Let stand for 4-5 minutes, until yeast rises up to the surface and appears frothy.

3. Add the soymilk, canola oil and honey. Then stir in unbleached bread flour, whole wheat flour and soy flour, one cup at a time. Use a big

spoon and mix by hand, or use a food processor with a dough hook. Keep mixing until the dough forms a ball and becomes elastic. This is the gluten which gives the bread its body and texture.

4. Cover bowl or pot with a plate or lid so dough does not dry out and form a skin. Let stand in a warm spot, out of cold drafts, for about an hour or until dough doubles in size.

5. Clean a work surface using vinegar. Pour vinegar on surface, spread around with your hands, then wipe off with a clean dry cloth or paper towel. Vinegar is used because it is a non toxic acidic cleaner.

6. Once work surface is completely dry, liberally flour it so dough won't stick. Turn dough out onto floured surface. Dust the top of dough with some more flour so it won't stick to your hands.

7. Knead dough for a few minutes. Fold edges toward center, press down, and give dough ball a quarter turn. Repeat this step 3-4 more times.

8. Divide dough into 2 equal pieces. Keep dough pieces floured. If dough begins to stick to your hands or surface, sprinkle with more flour.

9. Form dough pieces into loaves. Fold dough pieces into thirds, press down and give a quarter turn. Repeat this step 2 more times. Then pinch bottom seam using thumb and pointer.

10. Oil pans with canola or extra virgin olive oil. For a lighter crust use canola oil, for a flavorful hearty crust use extra virgin olive oil.

11. Lightly flour pans so bread won't stick to pan. This light dusting also ensures thorough coverage of oil, because flour only sticks to the oiled surface of pan. Any spot where there is no oil is where the bread will stick to the pan, making it difficult to get the loaf out of the pan.

12. Sprinkle sesame seeds on bottom of oiled and floured pans. Then place loaves seam side down into pans. Press each loaf into pan from center to edges using a fist. Let sit and rest for 15-20 minutes.

13. Then score the top of loaves with 3 diagonal cuts about 1/8 inch deep using a sharp knife or pair of scissors. Don't score too close to the edge of pan, leave a 1 inch margin from the sides. When bread rises, its surface will tear, scoring is controlled tears. You can put any pattern you want on the loaves. Just make sure the score is not deeper than 1/4 to 1/8 inch. Let loaves stand and rise for about another 40-45 minutes, or until dough doubles in size.

14. Preheat oven to 400°. Bake breads for 30-35 minutes. When breads are a nice golden brown, remove them from the oven. Breads are done when they easily come out of the pan and have a hollow sound when you thump the bottom of the loaves.

15. Place loaves on a cooling rack. Cool 10-15 minutes before cutting.

Makes 2 loaves

Whole Wheat Soymilk Bread

1-2/3 cups water - 110°F
2-1/4 teaspoons active dry rapid rise yeast - 1 package
1-1/2 tablespoons sugar
1/2 tablespoon salt
1 cup soymilk
2 teaspoons canola oil
2 teaspoons honey
3-2/3 cups whole wheat flour
2-2/3 cups unbleached bread flour
1 tablespoon sesame seeds

1. Heat water to approximately 110°F, use thermometer to measure temperature. If water is too hot, it will kill the yeast. If water is too cold, it won't activate yeast.
2. In a big bowl or 4 quart pot, measure active dry yeast, sugar and salt. Pour in warm water and stir to dissolve dry ingredients. Let stand for a few minutes until yeast starts blooming to the surface and appears bubbly. This means the yeast is activated.
3. Add the soymilk, canola oil and honey. Then stir in whole wheat flour and unbleached bread flour, one cup at a time. Mix by hand with a big metal spoon, or use a food processor with a dough hook. Keep mixing until the dough forms a ball and becomes elastic.
4. Cover bowl or pot with a plate or lid so dough does not dry out and form a skin. Let stand in a warm spot, out of cold drafts, for about an hour or until dough doubles in size.
5. Clean a work surface using vinegar. Pour vinegar on the work surface, spread around with your hands, then wipe off with a clean dry cloth or paper towel. Vinegar is used because it is a non toxic acidic cleaner.
6. Once work surface is completely dry, liberally flour it so dough won't stick. Turn dough out onto floured surface. Dust the top of dough with some more flour so it won't stick to your hands.
7. Knead dough for a few minutes. Fold edges toward center, press down, and give dough ball a quarter turn. Repeat this step 3-4 more times.
8. Divide dough into 2 equal pieces. Keep dough pieces floured. If dough begins to stick to your hands or surface, sprinkle with more flour.
9. Form dough pieces into loaves. Fold dough pieces into thirds, press down and give a quarter turn. Repeat this step 2 more times. Then pinch bottom seam using thumb and pointer.
10. Oil pans with canola or extra virgin olive oil. For a lighter crust use canola oil, for a flavorful hearty crust use extra virgin olive oil.

11. Lightly flour pans so bread won't stick to pan. This light dusting also ensures thorough coverage of oil, because flour only sticks to the oiled surface of pan. Any spot where there is no oil is where the bread will stick to the pan, making it difficult to get the loaf out of the pan.
12. Sprinkle sesame seeds on the bottom of the oiled and floured pans. Then place loaves seam side down into pans. Press each loaf into pan from center to edges using a fist. Let sit and rest for 15-20 minutes.
13. Then score the top of loaves with 3 diagonal cuts about 1/8 inch deep using a sharp knife or pair of scissors. Don't score too close to the edge of pan, leave a 1 inch margin from sides. When bread rises, its surface will tear, scoring is controlled tears. You can put any pattern you want on the loaves, just make sure the score is not deeper than 1/4 to 1/8 inch. Let loaves rise for another 40-45 minutes, or until dough doubles in size.
14. Preheat oven to 400°. Bake breads for 30-35 minutes. When breads are a golden brown, remove breads from oven. Breads are done when they easily come out of the pan and have a hollow sound when you thump the bottom of the loaves.
15. Place loaves on a cooling rack. Cool 10-15 minutes before cutting.
Makes 2 loaves

PIZZA

Super Soy Veggie Pizza

> **2 large or 4 small super soy pizza crusts**
> **3-1/4 cups pizza sauce**
> **2-1/4 cups cheesy tofu pizza topping**
> **2 teaspoons dry parsley flakes**
> **2 teaspoons oregano flakes**
> **2 teaspoons marjoram**
> **2 teaspoons basil**
> **1 teaspoon garlic powder**
> **1 teaspoon onion powder**
> **veggie toppings: sliced tomatoes, roasted bell peppers (p. 131), sauteed mushrooms, sauteed onions and/or black olives**

Super Soy Crust: *This will make a light and airy crust of traditional pizza with the wholesomeness of soy.*

2 cups warm water - approximately 110°F
2-1/2 tablespoons sugar
2-1/4 teaspoons active dry yeast (1 package)
2 teaspoons salt

1. Put dry ingredients into a 4 quart pot or a large bowl with a lid. (A plate can be used as a lid). Heat water to about 110°F, use a thermometer to measure temperature. If water is too hot, it will kill the yeast. If it's too cold, yeast won't activate. Stir in warm water and let sit for 5 minutes, or until yeast begins to rise up to the water's surface. Then add:

1/2 cup water - room temperature
1 cup soymilk
2/3 cup soy flour
5-1/3 cups unbleached bread flour

2. Mix until all the flour is absorbed and you begin to feel a little bit of elasticity, this is the gluten forming. This will be a moist dough rather than a stiff one. Don't mix too much, just enough to form the gluten. You want this to be a light airy crust, not a tough heavy one.
3. After mixing the dough for about 1-2 minutes, cover with a lid so dough doesn't dry out on top and form a skin. Let it sit for about one hour or until it doubles in size.

Pizza Sauce:

26.5 ounces (750 grams) of chopped tomatoes (1 container)
1 tablespoon of sugar
3/4 teaspoon salt

1. Mix together chopped tomatoes, sugar and salt. Set aside.

Cheesy Tofu Pizza Topping: *This will simulate cheese. It will have a nice flavorful taste and look of cheese, but won't be stringy like cheese.*

5.3 ounces of tofu (1/3 of a 16-ounce block firm tofu)
1 large clove garlic

2 tablespoons nutritional yeast
1 tablespoon extra virgin olive oil
1/2 teaspoon salt
1/2 cup soymilk

1. Mix tofu, garlic, nutritional yeast, extra virgin olive oil and salt in a food processor for 1-2 minutes or until smooth and fully blended. Then add soymilk and blend for another minute. Set aside.

Assembly:
1. Use a thick oil like extra virgin olive oil, and a light dusting of flour on pans to simulate the crust from a high temperature pizza parlor oven. This recipe makes enough for two 11 x 17 inch pans, two 16 inch round pans, four 8 to 9 inch round pans, or any combination of these size pans. Thoroughly coat pans with extra virgin olive oil. Then flour pans so dough does not stick. This flouring also ensures proper oil coverage because the flour will not stick to any unoiled surface.
2. Wash, slice and prepare any veggie toppings, like sliced tomato, roasted bell peppers, sauteed mushrooms, sauteed onions and/or black olives (see p. 131 for instructions on roasting bell peppers). Set aside.
3. Preheat oven to 400°. Using a big spoon, scoop out dough onto pans and distribute evenly. Before touching dough with your hands, liberally flour the top surface.
4. Gently press down at center of pan and work your way to the edges, spreading dough to an even thickness. Create a rim by making an impression line around the crust about 3/4 inch from the edge.
5. Distribute pizza sauce amongst pans and spread on dough from center out to the impression line. Don't go past this line or the sauce will spill over the edge of the crust and cause the pizza to stick to the pan. Also, make sure sauce is evenly spread and does not pool in the center.
6. Add Italian herbs and spices. (When using fresh herbs double measurements.) Adjust spicing to your particular taste.
7. *Optional*-Drizzle some olive oil and sprinkle a little salt on top to enhance the pizza's flavor. Remember, cheese has a lot of fat and salt.
8. Add your veggie toppings of choice at this point.
9. Then add the Cheesy Tofu Topping. Using a fork, drizzle topping on pizza to create the look of melted cheese. Take a fork full of Cheesy Tofu Topping and drizzle on surface in a random pattern.
10. Bake at 400° for 20-30 minutes, until bottom of crust is a golden brown. Remove from oven and use either a pizza cutter or a pair of scissors to make slices. Serve with a Mixed Green Salad.

Makes 2 large, 3 medium or 4 small pizzas (6-8 servings)

Veggie Wheat Pizza

2 large or 4 small soymilk wheat pizza crusts
3-1/4 cups pizza sauce
2-1/4 cups cheesy tofu pizza topping
2 teaspoons dry parsley flakes
2 teaspoons oregano flakes
2 teaspoons marjoram
1 teaspoon garlic powder
1 teaspoon onion powder
veggie toppings: sliced tomatoes, roasted bell peppers (p. 131), sauteed mushrooms, sauteed onions and/or black olives

Soymilk Wheat Crust: This will make a light and airy crust of traditional pizza with the wholesomeness of whole wheat.

2 cups warm water - approximately 110°F
2-1/2 tablespoons sugar
2-1/4 teaspoons active dry yeast (1 package)
2 teaspoons salt

1. Put dry ingredients into a 4 quart pot or a large bowl with a lid. (A plate can be used as a lid). Heat water to approximately 110°F, use a thermometer to measure temperature. If water is too hot, it will kill the yeast. If it is too cold, yeast won't activate. Stir in warm water and let sit for about 5 minutes, or until yeast rises up to the water's surface. Then add:

1/2 cup water - room temperature
1 cup soymilk
1 cup whole wheat flour
5 cups unbleached bread flour

2. Mix together until all the flour is absorbed and you begin to feel a little bit of elasticity, this is the gluten forming. This will be a moist dough rather than a stiff one. It will be thinner and wetter than a bread dough. Do not mix too much, just enough to form the gluten. You want this to be a light airy crust, not a tough heavy dough crust.
3. After you mix the dough for about 1-2 minutes, put on a lid so dough does not dry out on top and form a skin. Let it sit for about one hour or until it doubles in size.

Pizza Sauce:

26.5 ounces (750 grams) of chopped tomatoes (1 container)
1 tablespoon of sugar
3/4 teaspoon salt

1. Mix together chopped tomatoes, sugar and salt. Set aside.

Cheesy Tofu Pizza Topping: This will simulate cheese. It will have a nice flavorful taste and look of cheese, but won't be stringy like cheese.

5.3 ounces of tofu (1/3 of a 16-ounce block firm tofu)
1 large clove garlic
2 tablespoons nutritional yeast
1 tablespoon extra virgin olive oil
1/2 teaspoon salt
1/2 cup soymilk

1. Mix tofu, garlic, nutritional yeast, extra virgin olive oil and salt in a food processor for 1-2 minutes or until smooth and fully blended. Then add soymilk and blend for another minute. Set aside.

Assembly:
1. Use a thick oil like extra virgin olive oil and a light dusting of flour on pans to simulate the crust from a high temperature pizza parlor oven. This recipe makes enough for two 11 x 17 inch pans, two 16 inch round pans, four 8 to 9 inch round pans, or any combination of these size pans. Thoroughly coat pans with extra virgin olive oil. Then flour pans so dough does not stick. This flouring also ensures proper oil coverage because the flour will not stick to any unoiled surface.
2. Wash, slice and prepare any veggie toppings, like sliced tomato, roasted bell peppers, sauteed mushrooms, sauteed onions and/or black olives (see p. 131 for instructions on roasting bell peppers). Set aside.
3. Preheat oven to 400°. Using a big spoon, scoop out dough onto pans. Before touching dough with your hands, liberally dust the surface of dough with flour.
4. Gently press down at center of pan and work your way to the edges, spreading dough to an even thickness. Create a rim by making an impression line around the crust about 3/4 inch from the edge.
5. Distribute pizza sauce amongst pans and spread on dough from the center to the impression line. Don't go past this line or the sauce will

spill over the edge of the crust and cause the pizza to stick to the pan. Also, make sure sauce is evenly spread and does not pool in the center.
6. Add Italian herbs and spices. (When using fresh herbs double measurements.) Adjust spicing to your particular taste.
7. *Optional*-Sprinkle some extra virgin olive oil and a little salt on top to enhance the pizza's flavor. Remember, cheese has a lot of fat and salt.
8. Add your veggie toppings of choice at this point.
9. Then add the Cheesy Tofu Topping. Using a fork, drizzle topping on pizza to create the look of melted cheese. Take a fork full of Cheesy Tofu Topping and drizzle on surface in a random pattern.
10. Bake at 400° for 20-30 minutes, until bottom of crust is golden brown. Remove from oven and use either a pizza cutter or a pair of scissors to make slices. Serve with a Mixed Green Salad.

Makes 2 large, 3 medium or 4 small pizzas (6-8 servings)

BURGERS

Earth Burgers

    3 cups cooked beans - any kind
5.3 ounces tofu (1/3 of a 16-ounce block firm tofu)
2 cloves garlic
5 tablespoons ketchup
6 tablespoons applesauce - unsweetened
1 teaspoon soy sauce
2 cups grated carrots (4 large)
1 cup dry textured soy protein
1 cup diced onion (1 large)
2 tablespoons virgin olive oil
1 cup water
1 teaspoon salt
1 teaspoon dry oregano
1 teaspoon dry parsley flakes
1 teaspoon dry marjoram
1/4 teaspoon black ground pepper
3/4 cup uncooked old fashioned rolled oats
1/4 cup bread crumbs
1/4 cup soy flour
2 tablespoons sesame seeds

1. In a food processor add 2 cups beans, garlic cloves, tofu, ketchup,

applesauce and soy sauce. Blend to form a thick paste. Transfer to a big bowl and set aside.

2. Grate carrots and add to the bean-tofu mixture. Set aside.
3. Heat skillet and toast textured soy protein to a golden brown, set aside.
4. Heat 1 tablespoon virgin olive oil in a skillet and add diced onions. Saute until onions become slightly translucent. Add the toasted textured soy protein and 1 tablespoon olive oil, turn off heat and mix well. Stir in salt, oregano, parsley, and marjoram. Then pour water over the seasoned textured soy protein and let stand for 10 minutes, or until most of the liquid is absorbed and the textured soy protein is soft.
5. Mix together the seasoned textured soy protein, grated carrots, bean-tofu mixture, and 1 cup of whole beans. Add the uncooked oats, bread crumbs and soy flour. Mix well and let stand for 10 minutes.
6. Preheat oven to 400°. Grease a baking sheet with virgin olive oil.
7. Form mixture into 12 patties using a big spoon or spatula. Patties should be about 3-1/2 to 4 inches round. Sprinkle about 1/2 teaspoon sesame seeds on top of each burger. Gently press seeds onto each patty.
8. Bake at 375° for 20 minutes. Flip burgers over, and bake another 20 minutes, or until they're nicely browned. Cool 5 minutes before serving. Serve on a bun like a traditional burger with lettuce, tomato and onions; or like a Salisbury steak with mashed potatoes, brown mushroom gravy and peas, broccoli or spinach. These burgers freeze very well. To thaw, either microwave for 1-2 minutes or place in toaster-oven for 3-4 minutes on medium heat.

Makes 12 burgers (12 servings)

Millet Black Bean Burgers

Millet:
  1/2 cup dry millet
  1 cup water
  1/2 teaspoon salt
Burger Mix:
  1 cup dry textured soy protein
  1-1/2 cups grated carrots (3-4 medium)
  1-1/2 cups diced onions (2 medium)
  2 cloves minced garlic
  1 tablespoon dry oregano
  1 tablespoon parsley flakes
  1/2 teaspoon summer savory
  1/2 teaspoon sage

1/2 teaspoon salt
1/4 teaspoon black ground pepper
1/8 teaspoon cayenne pepper
1 tablespoon virgin olive oil
2 cups cooked black beans
6 tablespoons applesauce - unsweetened
6 tablespoons tomato ketchup
1/2 teaspoon soy sauce
1 cup bean broth or water
1/2 cup bread crumbs
1/4 cup soy flour
3 tablespoons sesame seeds

1. Bring 1 cup of water to a boil, add 1/2 teaspoon salt and millet. Cook for 15-20 minutes or until soft and all liquid has been absorbed.
2. While millet is cooking, grate carrots, dice onions, and mince garlic. Set aside. Measure out salt and spices, set aside.
3. Heat skillet and toast textured soy protein until lightly browned, stirring constantly. Add onions, dry spices, garlic and 1 tablespoon virgin olive oil to textured soy protein. Mix well and saute for 1-2 minutes, to allow textured soy protein to absorb oil and flavorings. Turn heat off, pour in water, cover with lid and let sit for 5-10 minutes.
4. Meanwhile, in a food processor combine 1-1/2 cups beans, applesauce, ketchup and soy sauce until thoroughly mixed yet still chunky.
5. In a large mixing bowl, stir together cooked millet, grated carrots, 1/2 cup whole beans, bean mixture, textured soy protein mix, bread crumbs and soy flour. Let sit for 10 minutes.
6. While burger mix is sitting, preheat oven to 375°, and oil a baking sheet with virgin olive oil. Sprinkle pan with half the sesame seeds. Using a large spoon, make 12 patties on baking sheet. Form into 4 inch round burgers and sprinkle the rest of the sesame seeds on top of burgers. Gently press sesame seeds into burgers.
7. Bake for 20 minutes. Flip burgers over and bake another 20 minutes, or until burgers are nicely browned. Let cool for 5 minutes before serving. Serve as a Salisbury steak with mashed potatoes, brown gravy and peas, spinach or turnup greens; or as a traditional burger on a bun with lettuce and tomato. Burgers freeze very well and just need to be reheated for 1-2 minutes in microwave, or 3-4 minutes in a toaster-oven to warm.

Makes 12 burgers (12 servings)

Pinto Bean Tofu Burgers

3 cups cooked pinto beans
5.3 ounces tofu (1/3 of a 16-ounce block tofu firm tofu)
2 cloves garlic
6 tablespoons ketchup
1 cup applesauce - unsweetened
2 teaspoons soy sauce
2 teaspoons liquid hickory smoke seasoning
2 teaspoons virgin olive oil
2 cups grated carrots (4 large)
1 cup finely diced onion (1 large)
1/2 teaspoon salt
1 teaspoon dry oregano
1 teaspoon dry parsley flakes
1 teaspoon dry marjoram
1/8 teaspoon cayenne pepper
1-1/2 cups bread crumbs
2/3 cup soy flour
2 tablespoons sesame seeds

1. In a food processor add 2 cups beans, tofu, garlic cloves, ketchup, applesauce, soy sauce, liquid hickory smoke seasoning and extra virgin olive oil. Blend to form a thick paste. Transfer to a big bowl, set aside.
2. Grate carrots and finely dice onions. Add these and 1 cup whole beans to tofu-bean mixture.
3. Then add salt, oregano, parsley, marjoram, cayenne pepper, bread crumbs and soy flour. Mix well and let stand for 10 minutes to allow mix to absorb moisture.
4. Preheat oven to 400°. Oil a baking sheet with virgin olive oil.
5. Form mixture into 12 patties using a big spoon or spatula. Patties should be about 3-1/2 to 4 inches round. Sprinkle about 1/2 teaspoon sesame seeds on top of each burger. Gently press seeds onto each patty.
6. Bake at 400° for 15-20 minutes. Flip burgers over with a spatula, and bake another 15-20 minutes. Let cool for 5 minutes before serving. Serve on a bun like a traditional burger with lettuce and tomato; or as a Salisbury steak with mashed potatoes, brown mushroom gravy and peas, turnup greens, broccoli, Brussels sprouts or spinach. These burgers freeze very well. To thaw, either microwave for 1-2 minutes or place in toaster oven for 3-4 minutes on medium heat.

Makes 12 burgers (12 servings)

Pumpkin Oat Burgers

2 cups cooked beans (garbanzo, white or soybeans)
2 cups cooked pumpkin (fresh cooked or canned)
5.3 ounces tofu (1/3 of a 16-ounce block firm tofu)
6 tablespoons tomato ketchup
6 tablespoons applesauce - unsweetened
2 cloves garlic
3/4 cup dry textured soy protein
1-1/2 cups diced onions (2 medium)
2 tablespoons extra virgin olive oil
2 teaspoons parsley
1-1/2 teaspoons salt
1 teaspoon oregano
1 teaspoon marjoram
1/4 teaspoon black ground pepper
1/4 teaspoon ground coriander
3/4 cup water
2 cups uncooked old fashioned oats
2/3 cup bread crumbs
4 tablespoons sesame seeds

1. In a food processor add 1 cup cooked beans, tofu, garlic cloves, ketchup, applesauce and 1/2 teaspoon salt. Blend to form a thick paste. Transfer into a big bowl and set aside.
2. Mash fresh cooked pumpkin, or measure out canned pumpkin, and add to tofu-bean mixture. Set aside.
3. Heat skillet and toast textured soy protein to a golden brown, set aside.
4. Heat 1 tablespoon extra virgin olive oil in a skillet and add diced onions. Saute until onions become slightly translucent. Add toasted textured soy protein and 1 tablespoon extra virgin olive oil, turn off heat and mix well. Stir in parsley, oregano, marjoram and 1 teaspoon salt. Then pour in water and let stand for 10 minutes, until most of the liquid is absorbed and textured soy protein is soft.
5. Combine seasoned textured soy protein, pumpkin-tofu-bean mixture and 1 cup whole beans. Add uncooked oats and bread crumbs. Mix well and let stand for 10 minutes to allow oats to absorb moisture.
6. Preheat oven to 375°. Oil a baking sheet with virgin olive oil and sprinkle it with 2 tablespoons of sesame seeds.
7. Form 12 burger patties using a big spoon or spatula. Patties should be about 3-1/2 to 4 inches round. Sprinkle about 1/2 teaspoon of sesame seeds on top of each burger. Gently press seeds onto each patty.

8. Bake at 375° for 20 minutes. Flip burgers over and bake another 20 minutes, until nicely browned. Let cool for 5-10 minutes before serving. Serve on a bun like a traditional burger with lettuce and tomato; or with mashed potatoes, brown mushroom gravy and a green vegetable. These burgers freeze very well. To thaw, microwave for 1-2 minutes or place in toaster-oven for 3-4 minutes on medium heat. *Makes 12 burgers*

Soybean Burgers

3 cups cooked soybeans
1-1/2 cups grated carrots (3 medium)
1 cup finely diced onion (1 large)
1 cup dry textured soy protein
1-1/2 tablespoons extra virgin olive oil
1 cup water
1/2 cup applesauce - unsweetened
6 tablespoons ketchup
1 teaspoon soy sauce
1 teaspoon liquid hickory smoke seasoning
1 teaspoon salt
1 teaspoon dry oregano
1 teaspoon dry basil
1 teaspoon dry marjoram
1 teaspoon dry parsley flakes
1/2 teaspoon sage
1/2 teaspoon black ground pepper
1/4 teaspoon coriander
1/8 teaspoon nutmeg
1 cup bread crumbs
1 cup uncooked old fashioned oats
2 tablespoons sesame seeds

1. Grate carrots and place in a big mixing bowl. Set aside.
2. In a food processor add 2 cups soybeans, ketchup, soy sauce, liquid hickory smoke seasoning and applesauce. Blend to a paste like consistency. Add this mixture to grated carrots. Set aside.
3. Heat skillet and toast textured soy protein to a golden brown. Set aside.
4. In a heated skillet add 1/2 tablespoon extra virgin olive oil, onions and 1/4 teaspoon salt. Saute for 2-3 minutes or until onions become slightly translucent. Then add toasted textured soy protein, 1 tablespoon extra virgin olive oil, 3/4 teaspoon salt, oregano, basil,

marjoram, parsley, sage and black ground pepper. Mix well. Pour in water and let stand for 5 minutes or until the liquid is absorbed and textured soy protein is soft.

5. Add onions and seasoned textured soy protein to carrots and bean mixture. Mix well. Add bread crumbs, uncooked oats, and 1 cup whole soybeans. Mix well and let stand for 10 minutes.

6. Preheat oven to 375°. Oil a baking sheet with extra virgin olive oil.

7. Form mixture into 12 patties using a big spoon or spatula. Patties should be about 3-1/2 to 4 inches round. Sprinkle about 1/2 teaspoon sesame seeds on top of each burger. Gently press seeds onto each patty.

8. Bake at 375° for 20 minutes. Flip burgers over and bake another 20 minutes, or until nicely browned. Let cool for 5 minutes before serving. Serve on a bun like a traditional burger or as a Salisbury steak with mashed potatoes, brown mushroom gravy and peas. These burgers freeze very well. To thaw, either microwave for 1-2 minutes or place in toaster-oven for 8-10 minutes on medium heat.

Makes 12 burgers (12 servings)

SAUSAGE PATTIES

Country Soy Sausage Patties

2 cups dry textured soy protein
3-1/2 teaspoons salt
1 teaspoon black ground pepper
1/2 teaspoon sage
1/2 teaspoon marjoram
1/2 teaspoon thyme
1/2 teaspoon summer savory
1/2 teaspoon coriander
1/4 teaspoon ground nutmeg
5 tablespoons extra virgin olive oil
1-3/4 cups water
5.3 ounces tofu (1/3 of a 16-ounce block firm tofu)
2 teaspoons liquid hickory smoke seasoning
1 cup applesauce - unsweetened
1 cup unbleached bread flour
1/2 cup soy flour

1. Mix together 3 teaspoons salt with black ground pepper, sage, marjoram, thyme, summer savory, coriander and nutmeg. Set aside.

2. Heat a skillet and toast textured soy protein until golden brown. Stir

constantly to promote an even toasting and prevent burning.

3. When textured soy protein is golden brown, turn heat off but keep skillet on burner. Stir in extra virgin olive oil and spice mix. Then add water and let sit for 10 minutes, until textured soy protein hydrates.

4. Meanwhile, in a food processor blend tofu, liquid hickory smoke seasoning, applesauce and 1/2 teaspoon salt. Blend to a smooth paste.

5. In a big bowl, mix together seasoned textured soy protein, tofu mixture, unbleached bread flour and soy flour. Let sit for 10 minutes.

6. Preheat oven to 375°. Oil a baking sheet with extra virgin olive oil. Using a large spoon, scoop out 16 portions onto baking sheet. Form into 3 inch round patties.

7. Bake patties at 375° for 20 minutes. Flip patties over, and bake another 15-20 minutes or until patties are nicely browned. Serve with pancakes, waffles or any other breakfast entree; or with mashed potatoes, peas and applesauce for dinner. Patties freeze very well and reheat fast. Freeze patties in a plastic freezer bag. To heat, just place in a microwave for a minute or in a warm skillet until thawed. No need to cook patties, they just need to be heated.

Makes 16 patties (8-16 servings)

Spicy Country Soy Sausage Patties

2 cups dry textured soy protein
3-1/2 teaspoons salt
1-1/2 teaspoons black ground pepper
1 teaspoon sage
1 teaspoon marjoram
1 teaspoon summer savory
1 teaspoon coriander
1/2 teaspoon thyme
1/2 teaspoon ground nutmeg
1/2 teaspoon cayenne pepper
5 tablespoons virgin olive oil
1-3/4 cups water
5.3 ounces tofu (1/3 of a 16-ounce block firm tofu)
2 teaspoons liquid hickory smoke seasoning
1 cup applesauce - unsweetened
1 cup unbleached bread flour
1/2 cup soy flour

1. Mix together 3 teaspoons salt with black ground pepper, sage, marjoram, thyme, summer savory, coriander, and nutmeg. Set aside.

2. Heat a skillet and toast textured soy protein until golden brown. Stir constantly to prevent burning and promote an even toasting.
3. When textured soy protein is golden brown, turn off heat but keep skillet on burner. Add virgin olive oil and spice mix. Stir well. Then pour in water and let sit for 10 minutes, until textured soy protein has absorbed liquid and becomes soft.
4. Meanwhile, in a food processor blend tofu, liquid hickory smoke seasoning, applesauce and 1/2 teaspoon salt. Blend to a smooth paste.
5. In a big bowl, mix together seasoned textured soy protein, tofu mixture, bread flour and soy flour. Let sit for 10 minutes.
6. Preheat oven to 375°. Oil a baking sheet with virgin olive oil. Using a large spoon, scoop out 16 portions onto baking sheet. Form into 3 inch round patties.
7. Bake patties at 375° for 20 minutes. Flip patties over, and bake another 15 minutes or until patties are nicely browned. Serve with mashed potatoes, peas and applesauce for dinner; or with pancakes, French Toast or eggs for breakfast. Patties freeze very well and thaw fast. Freeze patties in a freezer bag. Reheat in a microwave for a 1 minute, or in a warm skillet until thawed. Don't over cook patties, they just need to be heated.

Makes 16 patties (8-16 servings)

CHAPTER 11: DIPS, SPREADS, DRESSINGS & VINAIGRETTES

DIPS

Baba Ganoujh

> **1 medium baked eggplant**
> **4 ounces silken tofu (1/3 of a 12-ounce block)**
> **3 tablespoons soymilk**
> **2 tablespoons tahini (sesame seed paste)**
> **1 tablespoon lemon juice**
> **2 teaspoons dry parsley flakes**
> **2 cloves garlic**
> **1/2 teaspoon salt**

1. Broil a whole eggplant for about 20 minutes, turning it about every 5 minutes until it is charred all over. This creates the wonderful smokey flavor characteristic of this Middle Eastern dish.
2. Carefully remove the eggplant from the oven and let cool for 5-10 minutes. Then cut the eggplant in half and scoop out the insides. Try to scoop as close to the skin as possible, and discard the skin.
3. In a food processor blend silken tofu, tahini, lemon juice, parsley, garlic and salt to form a paste. Then add eggplant and soymilk, blend until it's smooth and creamy (about 1 minute).
4. Transfer into a container and chill. Use as a dip or spread. Serve with crackers, pita bread wedges or fresh cut up vegetables.

Makes about 2 cups (4 servings)

Cheesy Herb Dip

> **5.3 ounces tofu (1/3 of a 16-ounce block firm tofu)**
> **4 tablespoons soymilk (1/4 cup)**
> **1 tablespoon tahini (sesame seed paste)**
> **1 tablespoon nutritional yeast flakes**
> **1 tablespoon extra virgin olive oil**
> **1 teaspoon Dijon mustard**
> **1 teaspoon dry parsley flakes**
> **1/2 teaspoon dry oregano**
> **1/2 teaspoon dry marjoram**
> **1/2 teaspoon salt**
> **1 clove garlic (medium clove)**

1. Put above ingredients into a food processor. Blend for a full 1-2

minutes to form a smooth and creamy dip.
2. Transfer dip to a bowl and chill before serving. Serve with fresh cut up vegetables, chips or wholesome crackers.
Makes about 1 cup (2-4 servings)

Creamy Garlic and Chive Dip

5.3 ounces tofu (1/3 of a 16-ounce block firm tofu)
3 tablespoons soymilk
2 tablespoons canola oil
2 cloves garlic
1 teaspoon sugar
1 teaspoon lemon juice
1/2 teaspoon salt
2 tablespoons chives

1. Place tofu, canola oil, soymilk and garlic cloves in a food processor. Blend for a full 1-2 minutes or until a paste is formed.
2. Add lemon juice, sugar and salt. Blend until it's smooth and creamy.
3. Transfer to a container and mix in chives. Refrigerate to chill. Serve as a dip with crackers, pita bread wedges or cut up vegetables.
Makes about 1 cup (2-4 servings)

Garlic Herb Dip

5.3 ounces tofu (1/3 of a 16-ounce block firm tofu)
4 tablespoons soymilk (1/4 cup)
2 tablespoons extra virgin olive oil
1/2 tablespoon dry parsley flakes
1 teaspoon Dijon mustard
1/2 teaspoon dry oregano
1/2 teaspoon dry basil
1/2 teaspoon salt
2 cloves garlic (medium cloves)

1. Blend ingredients in a food processor for a full 1-2 minutes, until it's smooth and creamy.
2. Transfer dip to a bowl and chill before serving. Serve with fresh cut up vegetables, chips or wholesome crackers.
Makes about 1 cup (2-4 servings)

Guacamole

1 ripe avocado (1 large or 2 small)
1 tablespoon lemon juice
4 ounces silken tofu (1/3 of a 12-ounce block)
3/4 teaspoon salt
3/4 teaspoon onion powder
3/4 teaspoon garlic powder

1. Blend ingredients in a food processor for 1 full minute, until it's creamy smooth.
2. Transfer into a container and refrigerate to chill. Serve as a dip with chips, crackers or fresh cut up vegetables; as a spread with tortillas, shredded lettuce, diced tomatoes and salsa; or with burritos.

Makes about 1-3/4 to 2 cups (4 servings)

Hummus - Black Bean

2 cups cooked black beans
2 tablespoons tahini (sesame seed paste)
2-1/2 tablespoons lemon juice
1 clove garlic
1/3 cup soymilk
1/2 teaspoon salt

1. Place beans, tahini, lemon juice, and garlic clove in a food processor. Blend for a full 1-2 minutes or until a paste is formed.
2. Add soymilk and salt. Blend until it's smooth and creamy.
3. Transfer to a container and refrigerate to chill. Serve as a dip with crackers, pita bread wedges or fresh cut up vegetables; or as a spread with pita bread or tortillas.

Makes 2-2/3 cups (4-6 servings)

Hummus - Classic

2 cups cooked garbanzo beans or white beans
2 tablespoons tahini (sesame seed paste)
2-1/2 tablespoons lemon juice
1 clove garlic
1/3 cup soymilk
1/2 teaspoon salt

1. Place beans, tahini, lemon juice, and garlic in a food processor. Blend for a full 1-2 minutes, until a paste is formed.
2. Add soymilk and salt. Blend until it's smooth and creamy.
3. Transfer to a container and refrigerate to chill. Serve as a dip with crackers, pita bread wedges or fresh cut up vegetables; or as a spread with pita bread or tortillas.

Makes 2-2/3 cups (4-6 servings)

SPREADS

Honey Mustard Tahini Spread

5.3 ounces tofu (1/3 of a 16-ounce block firm tofu)
2 tablespoons soymilk
2 tablespoons tahini (sesame seed paste)
1 tablespoon Dijon mustard
1 teaspoon lemon juice
1 teaspoon honey
1/2 teaspoon salt

1. Blend ingredients in a food processor for a full 1-2 minutes, or until it's smooth and creamy.
2. Transfer spread into a jar and chill. Use in place of mayonnaise.

Makes about 1 cup (8 ounces)

Russian Sandwich Spread

5.3 ounces firm tofu (1/3 of a 16-ounce block)
2 tablespoons canola oil
4 tablespoons tomato ketchup (1/4 cup)
1/2 teaspoon salt
1 tablespoon soymilk
1/2 teaspoon onion powder
2 teaspoons sugar
1/2 tablespoon lemon juice

1. Place all the above ingredients into a food processor. Blend for a full 1-2 minutes, or until a smooth and creamy spread is formed.
2. Transfer into a container and chill. Use in place of mayonnaise.

Makes about 1-1/4 cups (9.5 ounces)

Smokey Honey Tofu Spread

5.3 ounces tofu (1/3 of a 16-ounce block firm tofu)
2 tablespoons Dijon mustard
2 tablespoon canola oil
1 tablespoon soymilk
1 tablespoon tahini (sesame seed paste)
1 tablespoon honey
1 tablespoon liquid hickory smoke seasoning
1/2 teaspoon salt

1. Put all of the above ingredients into a food processor. Blend for a full 1-2 minutes, or until it becomes smooth and creamy.
2. Transfer spread into a jar and chill. Use in place of mayonnaise.
Makes about 1-1/4 cups (9.5 ounces)

Tahini Tofu Spread

5.3 ounces tofu (1/3 of a 16-ounce block firm tofu)
2 tablespoons soymilk
2 tablespoons tahini (sesame seed paste)
2 teaspoons canola oil
2 teaspoons Dijon mustard
1/2 teaspoon salt

1. Put all of the above ingredients into a food processor. Blend for a full 1-2 minutes, or until it becomes smooth and creamy.
2. Transfer spread into a jar and chill. Use in place of mayonnaise.
Makes about 1 cup (8 ounces)

Tofu Cream Cheese

5.3 ounces tofu (1/3 of a 16-ounce block firm tofu)
1 tablespoon soymilk
2 tablespoons canola oil
1 teaspoon sugar
1/2 teaspoon salt
1/2 teaspoon lemon juice

1. In a food processor, blend tofu, soymilk and canola oil until it forms a paste. Then add salt, sugar and lemon juice. Blend for a full 1-2

minutes, or until it's creamy smooth.
2. Transfer to a container and chill. Use instead of regular cream cheese.
Makes about 3/4 cup (7 ounces)

Tofu Mayo

5.3 ounces tofu (1/3 of a 16-ounce block firm tofu)
3 tablespoons soymilk
3 tablespoons canola oil
1 tablespoon Dijon mustard
1/2 teaspoon salt

1. Blend ingredients in a food processor for a full 1-2 minutes, or until it's smooth and creamy.
2. Transfer spread into a jar and chill. Use in place of mayonnaise.
Makes about 1 cup (8 ounces)

DRESSINGS

Creamy Garlic Salad Dressing

4 ounces silken tofu (1/3 of a 12-ounce block)
4 tablespoons soymilk (1/4 cup)
1 clove garlic
1-1/2 tablespoons extra virgin olive oil
2-1/4 teaspoons vinegar
1 teaspoon Dijon mustard
1 teaspoon sugar
1 teaspoon parsley flakes
1/2 teaspoon salt
1/4 teaspoon garlic powder

1. Blend ingredients in a food processor until it's creamy smooth.
2. Transfer to a jar or bottle and completely chill. Refrigerate at least 20 minutes to allow dressing to thicken, and flavors to meld. The longer it chills the better it tastes. Serve over a Mixed Green Salad.
Makes about 1 cup (4-6 servings)

Creamy Italian Salad Dressing

    4 ounces silken tofu (1/3 of a 12-ounce package)
    4 tablespoons soymilk (1/4 cup)
    2 tablespoons extra virgin olive oil
    1 tablespoon vinegar
    1/2 tablespoon honey
    2 teaspoons nutritional yeast
    1 teaspoon dry parsley flakes
    1/2 teaspoon dry oregano
    1/2 teaspoon dry marjoram
    1/2 teaspoon salt
    1/2 teaspoon onion powder
    1/2 teaspoon garlic powder
    1/4 teaspoon dry basil
    1/4 teaspoon summer savory

1. In a food processor, blend together above ingredients until it's smooth and creamy.
2. Transfer into a container, and chill. Serve over a Mixed Green Salad.

Makes about 1 cup (4-6 servings)

French Salad Dressing

    4 tablespoons soymilk (1/4 cup)
    2 tablespoons extra virgin olive oil
    2 tablespoons tomato ketchup
    2 teaspoons vinegar
    2 teaspoons sugar
    1 teaspoon lemon juice
    1/4 teaspoon salt
    1/4 teaspoon onion powder
    1/4 teaspoon garlic powder
    1/8 teaspoon paprika
    1/8 teaspoon black ground pepper

1. Mix together above ingredients, using a whisk, fork or food processor.
2. Transfer into a container, and chill. Serve over a Mixed Green Salad.

Makes approximately 2/3 cup (2-4 servings)

Russian Salad Dressing

4 ounces silken tofu (1/3 of a 12-ounce block)
4 tablespoons tomato ketchup (1/4 cup)
2 tablespoons soymilk
2 tablespoons canola oil
1 tablespoon sugar
1/2 teaspoon salt
1/2 teaspoon onion powder
2 teaspoons vinegar
2 teaspoons lemon juice
1 teaspoon honey

1. Blend ingredients in a food processor until it's creamy smooth.
2. Transfer into a container, and chill. Serve over a Mixed Green Salad.

Makes about 1 cup (4-6 servings)

Tofu Sour Cream

5.3 ounces tofu (1/3 of a 16-ounce block, soft or firm)
3 tablespoons soymilk
2 tablespoons canola oil
2 teaspoons vinegar
2 teaspoons lemon juice
1/2 teaspoon salt
1/2 teaspoon sugar

1. In a food processor, blend tofu and soymilk first, to form a paste. Then add canola oil, vinegar, lemon juice, salt, and sugar. Continue to blend for a full 1-2 minutes, or until it's silky smooth and creamy.
2. Transfer into a container and chill. Use instead of regular sour cream. Serve with baked potatoes, potato pancakes, borscht, burritos, or any recipe that calls for sour cream.

Makes about 1 cup (8.5 ounces)

VINAIGRETTES

Cesar Vinaigrette

> 4 tablespoons soymilk (1/4 cup)
> 2 tablespoons extra virgin olive oil
> 1 tablespoon vinegar
> 1 tablespoon nutritional yeast
> 1/2 teaspoon salt
> 1/2 teaspoon onion powder
> 1/2 teaspoon garlic powder
> 1/2 teaspoon dry parsley flakes
> 1/2 teaspoon dry oregano
> 1/8 teaspoon black ground pepper

1. Whisk together above ingredients.
2. Transfer into a container, and chill. Serve over a Mixed Green Salad.

Makes about 2/3 cup (2-4 servings)

Honey Mustard Vinaigrette

> 4 tablespoons soymilk (1/4 cup)
> 2 tablespoons extra virgin olive oil
> 2 tablespoons Dijon mustard
> 2 tablespoons honey
> 2 teaspoons vinegar
> 1/2 teaspoon salt
> 1/8 teaspoon black ground pepper

1. Whisk together above ingredients until smooth.
2. Transfer into a container, and chill. Serve over a Mixed Green Salad.

Makes approximately 2/3 cup (2-4 servings)

Italian Vinaigrette

4 tablespoons soymilk (1/4 cup)
2 tablespoons extra virgin olive oil
1 tablespoon vinegar
1/2 tablespoon honey
2 teaspoons nutritional yeast
1 teaspoon dry parsley flakes
1/2 teaspoon dry oregano
1/2 teaspoon dry marjoram
1/2 teaspoon salt
1/2 teaspoon onion powder
1/2 teaspoon garlic powder
1/4 teaspoon dry basil
1/4 teaspoon summer savory
1/8 teaspoon black ground pepper

1. Whisk together above ingredients.
2. Transfer into a container, and chill. Serve over a Mixed Green Salad.
Makes about 2/3 cup (2-4 servings)

Low-Fat Roman Vinaigrette

1/3 cup soymilk
2 tablespoons nutritional yeast
2 teaspoons vinegar
1 teaspoon onion powder
1 teaspoon garlic powder
1 teaspoon dry oregano
1 teaspoon dry parsley flakes
1 teaspoon sugar
1/2 teaspoon salt
1/8 teaspoon black ground pepper

1. Whisk together above ingredients.
2. Transfer into a container and chill. Serve over a mixed green salad.
Makes almost 3/4 cup (2-4 servings)

CHAPTER 12: SALADS, SANDWICHES & WRAPS

SALADS

Broccoli Carrot Cole Slaw

> 1-1/2 cups green cabbage - shredded
> 3/4 cups fresh broccoli stems - grated (1-2 stems)
> 1/2 cup carrots - grated (1 small)
> 3-4 tablespoons Tofu Mayo (p. 89)
> 2 teaspoons vinegar
> 2 teaspoons sugar
> 1/4 teaspoon Dijon mustard
> 1/8 teaspoon salt
> dash black ground pepper

1. Wash and shred green cabbage. Peel and grate broccoli stems and carrots.
2. Mix together Tofu Mayo, vinegar, sugar, Dijon mustard, salt and pepper.
3. Add Tofu Mayo mixture to cabbage, broccoli and carrots. Mix thoroughly and chill before serving.

Makes about 3 cups (4 servings)

Carrot Cole Slaw

> 2 cups green cabbage - shredded
> 3/4 cups carrots - grated (1 medium)
> 3-4 tablespoons Tofu Mayo (p. 89)
> 2 teaspoons vinegar
> 2 teaspoons sugar
> 1/8 teaspoon salt
> dash black ground pepper

1. Wash and shred green cabbage. Peel and grate carrots.
2. Mix together Tofu Mayo, vinegar, sugar, salt and pepper.
3. Add Tofu Mayo mixture to cabbage and carrots. Mix well and chill before serving.

Makes about 3 cups (4 servings)

Cole Slaw

2-3/4 cups green cabbage
3-4 tablespoons Tofu Mayo (p. 89)
2 teaspoons vinegar
2 teaspoons sugar
1/8 teaspoon salt
dash black ground pepper

1. Wash and shred green cabbage.
2. Mix together Tofu Mayo, vinegar, sugar, salt and pepper.
3. Add Tofu Mayo mixture to cabbage. Mix thoroughly and chill before serving.

Makes about 3 cups (4 servings)

Mixed Green Salad

4-6 leaves romaine lettuce
1-2 leaves red cabbage
1 medium carrot
1 medium tomato
1/3 cup cooked garbanzo beans
4-6 tablespoons soynuts
2 tablespoons raisins
1/3-1/2 cup salad dressing or vinaigrette (pp. 89-93)

1. Wash lettuce and either cut or rip lettuce leaves into bite sized bits. Divide in half and place on 2 plates or bowls. Wash and shred red cabbage. Divide in half and place on top of lettuce.
2. Peel carrot. Either grate carrot or make ultra thin carrot ribbons using a peeler. To make carrot ribbons, lay carrot on its side, hold green top end with one hand and run peeler along the length of the carrot with other hand. Continue until most of the carrot has been ribbon peeled. Divide carrots in half and place on top of lettuce and red cabbage.
3. Wash tomato and cut into wedges. Place half on top of each salad.
4. Place half of the garbanzo beans, soynuts and raisins on top of each salad. Serve with your choice of salad dressing or vinaigrette.

Makes 2 servings

Potato Salad

4 cups potatoes - cooked and diced (4-5 medium potatoes)
1 cup onion - finely diced (1 large onion)
6-8 tablespoons Tofu Mayo (p. 89)
1/4 cup soymilk
4 teaspoons vinegar
4 teaspoons sugar
1-1/2 teaspoons Dijon mustard
2 teaspoons dry dill weed
1/2 teaspoon salt
1/8 teaspoon black ground pepper

1. Peel and dice potatoes. Bring some salted water to a boil. Add potatoes and let cook for 15 minutes, or until they can easily be poked with a fork.
2. Drain potatoes. Finely dice onion and toss in with potatoes. Let cool.
3. Combine Tofu Mayo, soymilk, salt, vinegar, Dijon mustard, dill weed and black pepper. Add this mixture to potatoes and onions. Mix thoroughly and chill before serving.

Makes about 5-1/2 cups (6 servings)

Tri-Color Cole Slaw

1-3/4 cups green cabbage - shredded
1/2 cup red cabbage - shredded
1/2 cup carrots - grated (1 small)
3-4 tablespoons Tofu Mayo (p. 89)
2 teaspoons vinegar
2 teaspoons sugar
1/8 teaspoon salt
dash black ground pepper

1. Wash and shred green and red cabbage. Peel and grate carrots.
2. Mix together Tofu Mayo, vinegar, sugar, salt and pepper.
3. Add Tofu Mayo mixture to cabbage and carrots. Mix well and chill before serving.

Makes about 3 cups (4 servings)

Waldorf Carrot Salad

1 cup diced apple (1 medium)
2/3 cup grated carrots (2 small)
1/3 cup chopped walnuts
1/4 cup chopped celery (1 stalk)
4-5 tablespoons Tofu Mayo (p. 89)
2 teaspoons lemon juice
1/2 tablespoon sugar

1. Core and dice an apple, place in a large mixing bowl and sprinkle with 1 teaspoon lemon juice. Grate carrots, place in bowl with apples. Chop walnuts and celery, place in bowl with apples and carrots.
2. In a second bowl, mix together Tofu Mayo, sugar and 1 teaspoon lemon juice. Add this dressing to apple mix, toss well, cover and chill. Serve this salad heaped in the center of a bed of lettuce leaves.

Makes about 2 cups (2-4 servings)

SANDWICHES

BLT - Baconless, Lettuce and Tomato Sandwich

4 ounces of tempeh (1/2 of an 8-ounce package)
1 tablespoon liquid hickory smoke seasoning
1/8 teaspoon salt
1 teaspoon canola oil
4 slices Light Wheat Soymilk Bread (p. 62)
4-6 tablespoons Smokey Honey Tofu Spread (p. 88)
4 large leaves romaine lettuce
1 large ripe tomato (or 2 ripe plum tomatoes) - sliced

1. Cut tempeh into 20 thin strips about 1/8 to 1/4 inch thick. Place strips on a plate. Sprinkle liquid hickory smoke seasoning and salt over strips. Turn strips over to coat both sides, let sit for 1-2 minutes.
2. Heat 1 teaspoon canola oil. Saute tempeh strips until both sides are browned, about 4-5 minutes. Turn strips over often to ensure even browning on both sides. When done, let strips cool completely.
3. Wash lettuce leaves and cut in half. Wash and thinly slice tomato.
4. Lightly toast bread. Spread 1 to 1-1/2 tablespoons of Smokey Honey Tofu Spread on each slice of toast. Place 10 tempeh strips and 1/2 of sliced tomato on 2 slices of toast. Put lettuce leaf halves on top of tomato slices. Then put the other 2 slices of toast on top and serve.

Makes 2 sandwiches (2 servings)

Cucumber Sandwich

1 medium cucumber thinly sliced
4-6 tablespoons Tofu Cream Cheese (p. 88)
4 slices Seeded Soy Rye Bread - toasted (p. 63)
salt and pepper to taste

1. Lightly toast Seeded Soy Rye Bread. Spread 1 to 1-1/2 tablespoons of Tofu Cream Cheese on each toasted bread slice.
2. Peel and thinly slice cucumber and place 1/4 of it on each slice of bread. Salt and pepper to taste. Serve with soup or a salad.

Makes 4 open-faced sandwiches (2 servings)

Deluxe Hickory Burger

2 Millet Black Bean Burgers (p. 76)
4-6 tablespoons Smokey Honey Tofu Spread (p. 88)
2-4 leaves romaine lettuce
1 medium tomato - sliced
3/4 cup onion - sliced (1 medium)
1/2 tablespoon extra virgin olive oil
1/4 teaspoon salt
2 Sesame Seed Soy Wheat Buns (p. 64)

1. Wash lettuce and cut leaves in half. Thinly slice tomatoes and onions.
2. Heat extra virgin olive oil in a skillet. Add onions and salt, saute for 2-3 minutes or until onions become translucent. Set aside.
3. Slice buns in half and spread 1 to 1-1/2 tablespoons of Smokey Honey Tofu Spread on each half of the buns.
4. For each bun, place a warm Millet Black Bean Burger, and half of the sauteed onions, tomato slices, and lettuce leaves on next.

Makes 2 burgers (2 servings)

Egg Salad Sandwich

2 hard-boiled eggs - from all-natural grain fed, cage free hens
5-6 tablespoons of Tofu Mayo spread (p. 89)
1 teaspoon Dijon mustard
2-4 leaves of romaine lettuce
2 Soymilk Poppy Seed Rolls (p. 66) or 4 slices Whole Wheat Soymilk Bread (p. 69)

salt and pepper to taste

---

1. Mix together Tofu Mayo and Dijon mustard. Mash in egg yolks. Chop up egg whites and mix in egg yolk mixture. Salt and pepper to taste.
2. Lightly toast 2 Soymilk Poppy Seed Rolls cut in half, or 4 slices of Whole Wheat Soymilk Bread.
3. Evenly spread egg salad, place lettuce leaves on next and serve.

Makes 2 sandwiches (2 servings)

Grilled Tempeh Sandwich

    4 ounces tempeh (1/2 of an 8-ounce package)
    1 tablespoon soy sauce
    1 cup sliced onion (1 large)
    4-6 tablespoons Russian Sandwich Spread (p. 87)
    1 tablespoon extra virgin olive oil
    4 slices Light Wheat Soymilk Bread (p. 62) or 4 slices Honey Oat
    Soy Bread (p. 60)

---

1. Peel and slice an onion, set aside. Cut tempeh into 4 slabs that are about 2 inches wide, 3 inches long and 1/4 inch thick. (Cut an 8-ounce tempeh block in half. Take one half and slice it down the middle to make 2 slabs 1/4 inch thick. Then cut these slabs in half.)
2. Set tempeh slabs on a plate. Sprinkle 1/2 tablespoon soy sauce over one side of the slabs. Flip slabs over and sprinkle another 1/2 tablespoon soy sauce over other side of the slabs. Let sit.
3. Heat 1 teaspoon extra virgin olive oil in a skillet. Add sliced onion and saute for 3-4 minutes. When onions become translucent, set aside.
4. Heat 1 teaspoon extra virgin olive oil in the skillet. Add tempeh slabs and saute for about 1-2 minutes. When tempeh is golden brown, flip slabs over and saute other side for another 1-2 minutes. When both sides are golden brown, remove from skillet and set aside.
5. Spread 1 to 1-1/2 tablespoons of Russian Sandwich Spread on each slice of bread. Heat 1 teaspoon extra virgin olive oil. Place 2 slices of bread, spread side up, in skillet. Put sauteed onions on top of slices, and the sauteed tempeh slabs on next. Then place the other 2 slices of bread on top, spread side down. When bottom bread slices become golden brown, carefully flip sandwiches over and brown second side. When both sides are nicely browned, remove from skillet, slice in half and serve.

Makes 2 grilled sandwiches (2 servings)

Honey Mustard Earth Burger

>2 Earth Burgers (p. 75)
>4-6 tablespoons Honey Mustard Tahini Spread (p. 87)
>4 leaves romaine lettuce
>1 medium tomato - sliced
>2 Sesame Seed Soy Wheat Buns (p. 64) or 2 Soymilk Poppy Seed Rolls (p. 66)

1. Wash lettuce and cut leaves in half. Wash and slice tomato.
2. Slice buns (rolls) in half and spread 1 to 1-1/2 tablespoons of Honey Mustard Tahini Spread on each half.
3. On each bun (roll), place a warm Earth Burger, half of the sliced tomato, and half of the lettuce. Salt and pepper to taste, and serve.

Makes 2 burgers (2 servings)

Lentil Loaf Sandwich

>2 slices Lentil Rice Tofu Loaf (p. 147)
>4 leaves romaine lettuce
>1 large tomato - sliced
>4 slices Super Soy Honey Wheat Bread (p. 67)
>4-6 tablespoons Tofu Mayo (p. 89)

1. Wash lettuce and cut leaves in half. Wash and slice tomato.
2. Lightly toast bread. Spread 1 to 1-1/2 tablespoons of Tofu Mayo on each slice of toast.
3. For each sandwich, place a slice of Lentil Rice Tofu Loaf, half of the lettuce leaves and half of the sliced tomato between the 2 slices of toasted bread.

Makes 2 sandwiches (2 servings)

Pinto Bean Bistro Burger

>2 Pinto Bean Tofu Burgers (p. 78)
>4-6 tablespoons Tofu Mayo (p. 89)
>1 tablespoon nutritional yeast
>1/2 small onion - thinly sliced
>4 leaves romaine lettuce
>1 medium tomato - sliced

2 Soymilk Poppy Seed Rolls (p. 66)

1. Wash and cut lettuce leaves in half. Thinly slice tomato and onion.
2. Slice rolls in half and spread 1 to 1-1/2 tablespoons of Tofu Mayo on each half. Sprinkle 1/2 tablespoon nutritional yeast on bottom halves.
3. Place a warm Pinto Bean Tofu Burger on bottom half of each roll. Put half of the sliced onion, tomato and lettuce on top of each burger. Then place top half of the rolls on next and serve.

Makes 2 burgers (2 servings)

Ruben Burger

2 Soybean Burgers (p. 80)
1 cup sliced onion (1 large)
1/2 tablespoon extra virgin olive oil
1/4 teaspoon salt
2/3 cup sauerkraut
4-6 tablespoons Russian Sandwich Spread (p. 87)
1 tablespoon nutritional yeast
2 Sesame Seed Soy Wheat Buns (p. 64) or 2 Soymilk Poppy Seed Rolls (p. 66)

1. Peel and slice onions. Heat extra virgin olive oil in a skillet. Add onions and salt. Saute 2-3 minutes, until onions become translucent. Set aside.
2. Slice buns (rolls) in half. Spread 1 to 1-1/2 tablespoons of Russian Sandwich Spread on each half of the buns (rolls). Then sprinkle 1/2 tablespoon nutritional yeast on bottom halves of the buns (rolls).
3. For each bun (roll), place a warm Soybean Burger, half of the sauteed onions, and 1/3 cup sauerkraut.

Makes 2 burgers (2 servings)

Soy Sausage Biscuit

2 large Soymilk Biscuits (p. 55)
2 Country Soy Sausage Patties (regular p. 81 or spicy p. 82)
4 tablespoons ketchup (1/4 cup)
1 tablespoon nutritional yeast

1. Cut Soymilk Biscuits in half. Spread 1 tablespoon ketchup on each

half of the biscuit. Then sprinkle 1/2 tablespoon nutritional yeast on each bottom biscuit half.

2. Place a warm Country Soy Sausage Pattie on the bottom half of each biscuit. Then place top half of biscuits on next and serve.

Makes 2 biscuits (2 servings)

Soy Sloppy Joe's

1/2 cup dry textured soy protein
1/2 cup cooked mashed beans (red, pink, roman or pinto beans)
1 small clove garlic
3 ounces tomato paste
1 cup water
1/4 cup applesauce - unsweetened
1/2 cup diced roasted green bell pepper (1 small)
1/2 cup finely diced onions (1 small)
1/2 cup grated carrots (1 medium)
1-1/2 tablespoons extra virgin olive oil
3/4 teaspoon sugar
1/2 teaspoon salt
1/2 teaspoon paprika
1/4 teaspoon cayenne pepper
1/4 teaspoon vinegar
4 Sesame Seed Soymilk Buns (p. 64) or 4-8 slices of bread (pp. 60-69)

1. Toast textured soy protein in a skillet until lightly browned. Set aside.
2. In a food processor, blend beans and garlic clove to form a thick paste. Add tomato paste, sugar and applesauce. Blend well and set aside.
3. Roast a green bell pepper. Cut bell pepper in half. Remove seeds and inner membrane. Place peppers in oven and broil until the skin has blistered and starts to blacken. Put in a covered dish and let steam for 10 minutes. Carefully peel away skin and dice. Set peppers aside.
4. Finely dice onions and grate carrots. Heat 1/2 tablespoon of extra virgin olive oil. Add onions, carrots and 1/4 teaspoon salt. Saute until onions are translucent and carrots are soft. Add diced roasted green bell peppers. Saute for another 1-2 minutes.
5. Add toasted textured soy protein, paprika, cayenne pepper, 1/4 teaspoon salt and 1 tablespoon extra virgin olive oil. Mix thoroughly.
6. Add tomato-bean mixture and water, reduce heat to low. Cook for 10 minutes or until textured soy protein is soft. Serve on fresh or lightly

102

toasted buns or bread, opened-faced or sandwich-like. Use 1/2 cup of the Soy Sloppy Joe's mix per sandwich. Soy Sloppy Joe's freezes very well, place in 1 cup containers (2 serving size) and freeze until ready to use. To thaw, microwave for 3-4 minutes or until warm, or put in a sauce pan and heat on stove top at low until warm.

Makes 2 cups (4 servings)

Tempeh Ruben Sandwich

4 ounces tempeh (1/2 of an 8-ounce package)
1 tablespoon soy sauce
3/4 cup sliced onion (1 medium)
2/3 cup sauerkraut
4-6 tablespoons Russian Sandwich Spread (p. 87)
1 tablespoon extra virgin olive oil
1 tablespoon nutritional yeast
4 slices of Seeded Soy Rye Bread (p. 63) or Whole Wheat Soymilk Bread (p. 69)

1. Peel and slice an onion, set aside. Cut tempeh into 4 slabs that are 2 inches wide, 3 inches long and 1/4 inch thick. (Cut an 8-ounce tempeh block in half. Take one half and slice it down the middle to make slabs 1/4 inch thick. Then cut slabs in half to make them 2 x 3 inches).
2. Set tempeh slabs on a plate. Sprinkle 1/2 tablespoon soy sauce over one side of the slabs. Flip slabs over and sprinkle another 1/2 tablespoon soy sauce over other side of the slabs. Let sit.
3. Heat 1 teaspoon extra virgin olive oil in a skillet. Add sliced onion and saute for 3-4 minutes. When onions become translucent, set aside.
4. Heat 1 teaspoon extra virgin olive oil in the skillet. Add tempeh slabs and saute for about 1-2 minutes. When tempeh is golden brown, flip slabs over and saute other side for another 1-2 minutes. When both sides are golden brown, remove from skillet and set aside.
5. Lightly toast bread slices. Spread 1 to 1-1/2 tablespoons Russian Sandwich Spread over each slice. Then sprinkle 1/2 tablespoon nutritional yeast on 2 of the toasted bread slices.
6. Place these 2 slices of toast, spread side up, on a plate. Put half of the sauteed tempeh slabs, sauteed onions and sauerkraut on each slice of toast. Then place the other 2 slices of toast on top, spread side down. Cut in half and serve.

Makes 2 sandwiches (2 servings)

Avocado Wraps

1 ripe avocado - peeled and sliced
1 cup romaine lettuce - shredded (about 4-6 leaves)
1/2 cup chopped tomato (1 large)
4 tablespoons Honey Mustard Tahini Spread (p. 87)
2 tablespoons ketchup
4 Whole Wheat Soymilk Tortillas (p. 56)

1. Cut avocado in half. Remove pit and peel. Slice avocado length ways and divide into 4 portions. Shred lettuce and chop tomato.
2. For each wrap, arrange in center of tortilla, 1 tablespoon Honey Mustard Tahini Spread, 1/2 tablespoon ketchup, 1 portion of sliced avocado, 2 tablespoons chopped tomato and 1/4 cup shredded lettuce.
3. Wrap tortilla like a burrito. Fold bottom of tortilla up a third and fold both sides of tortilla toward the center, leaving the top of tortilla open.

Makes 4 wraps (2-4 servings)

Baba Wraps

4 Whole Wheat Soymilk Tortillas (p. 56)
2 cups Baba Ganoujh (p. 84)
6-8 leaves romaine lettuce - shredded
1 large tomato - chopped

1. Wash and shred lettuce. Wash and chop tomato.
2. Spread 1/2 cup Baba Ganoujh on the center of each tortilla. Then put 1/4 of the shredded lettuce and 1/4 of the chopped tomato on next.
3. Wrap tortillas like a burrito. Fold bottom of tortilla up a third and fold both sides toward the center, leaving the top of tortilla open.

Makes 4 wraps (2-4 servings)

Bean Burritos

1-1/3 cups Red Bean Chili (or any other chili pp. 107-109)
2/3 cup cooked brown rice
4-6 leaves romaine lettuce - shredded
1 large tomato - chopped

4 tablespoons Tofu Sour Cream (p. 91)
4 teaspoons nutritional yeast
4 tablespoons salsa
4 Whole Wheat Soymilk Tortillas (p. 56)

1. Wash and shred lettuce. Wash and chop tomato.
2. Spread 1 tablespoon Tofu Sour Cream (or Tofu Cream Cheese p. 88) on each Whole Wheat Soymilk Tortilla. Sprinkle 1 teaspoon nutritional yeast on each tortilla. Put 1/3 cup of Red Bean Chili (or any other chili) and about 2-1/2 tablespoons cooked brown rice on the center of each tortilla. Place 1/4 of the shredded lettuce and 1/4 of the chopped tomato on top. Drizzle 1 tablespoon salsa over each tortilla.
3. Wrap up tortillas like a burrito. Fold bottom of tortilla up a third and fold both sides toward the center, leaving the top of tortilla open.

Makes 4 burritos (2-4 servings)

Falafels

2 Pumpkin Oat Burgers (p. 79)
4-6 leaves romaine lettuce - shredded
5 tablespoons Tahini Tofu Spread (p. 88)
2 Whole Wheat Soymilk Tortillas (p. 56)

1. Wash and shred lettuce.
2. Spread 2-1/2 tablespoons Tahini Tofu Spread on each Whole Wheat Soymilk Tortilla.
3. Place a Pumpkin Oat burger on each tortilla. Then place half of the shredded lettuce on next. Fold each tortilla in half and serve.

Makes 2 Falafels (2 servings)

Hummus Wraps

4 Whole Wheat Soymilk Tortillas (p. 56)
1-1/3 cups Hummus (classic or black bean p. 86)
1 cup cooked brown rice or millet
8 leaves romaine lettuce - shredded
1 large tomato - chopped
1 large carrot - grated

1. Spread 1/3 cup of Hummus on each tortilla. Then mound in the center

of each tortilla 1/4 cup cooked brown rice or millet, 1/4 of the shredded romaine lettuce, 1/4 of the chopped tomato and 1/4 of the grated carrot.
2. Wrap each tortilla like a burrito or an egg roll.
    For a burrito style wrap: fold bottom of tortilla in towards the center. Then fold both sides in toward center leaving top of wrap open.
    For egg roll style wrap: fold top and bottom of tortilla in towards the center. Then fold both sides in towards center. Serve seam side down.
Makes 4 wraps (2-4 servings)

Smokey Tempeh Wraps

4 ounces of tempeh (1/2 of an 8-ounce package)
1 tablespoon liquid hickory smoke seasoning
1/8 teaspoon salt
1 teaspoon canola oil
6-8 leaves romaine lettuce - shredded
1 large tomato - sliced
4-6 tablespoons Smokey Honey Tofu Spread (p. 88)
4 Whole Wheat Soymilk Tortillas (p. 56)

1. Cut tempeh into 20 thin strips about 1/8 to 1/4 inch thick and 2 inches long. Place strips on a plate. Sprinkle liquid hickory smoke seasoning and salt over strips. Turn strips over so both sides get coated and let them sit for 1-2 minutes.
2. Heat 1 teaspoon canola oil. Saute the seasoned tempeh strips until both sides are browned, about 4-5 minutes. Turn strips over often to ensure even browning on both sides. When done remove from heat and let the smokey tempeh strips cool completely.
3. Wash and shred lettuce. Wash and slice tomato.
4. For each tortilla, spread 1 to 1-1/2 tablespoons Smokey Honey Tofu Spread over whole tortilla, put 5 smokey tempeh strips across center, then place 1/4 of the sliced tomato and 1/4 of the shredded lettuce on top.
5. Wrap each tortilla like a burrito. Fold bottom of tortilla up a third and fold both sides toward center, leaving top of tortilla open.
Makes 4 wraps (2-4 servings)

CHILI

Hot Pepper Harvest Chili (Very Hot)

3-1/2 cups cooked pinto beans (or 2 - 15 ounce cans)
1-1/2 cups diced onions (3 medium)
1 cup cooked mashed pumpkin (or an 8-ounce can)
3/4 cup dry toasted textured soy protein
1/2 cup diced green bell pepper (1 small)
6 tablespoons minced long hot peppers or jalapeno peppers
1 tablespoon minced garlic (2 cloves)
1 tablespoon virgin olive oil
6 ounces of tomato paste
1 teaspoon sugar
1/2 tablespoon ground cumin
1/2 tablespoon salt
1/2 teaspoon paprika
1/2 teaspoon cayenne pepper
1/4 teaspoon dried crushed red pepper
1/4 teaspoon onion powder
1/4 teaspoon garlic powder
2 cups bean broth or water
1 teaspoon hot pepper sauce (about 10 dashes)

1. Mix together sugar, cumin, salt, paprika, cayenne pepper, crushed red pepper, onion powder and garlic powder; set aside. Dice onions and bell peppers, mince hot peppers and garlic, and set aside.
2. Heat a skillet, add dry textured soy protein. Stir and toast until golden brown. Remove from heat and set aside.
3. Heat 1/2 tablespoon virgin olive oil in a 3 quart pot. Add diced onions and green bell pepper, stir to coat with oil. Stir in long hot peppers or jalapeno peppers. When onions become slightly transparent, stir in pumpkin and garlic. Cook for 2-3 minutes then add spices, textured soy protein, and 1/2 tablespoon virgin olive oil. Mix well.
4. Then add tomato paste, bean broth or water, and hot pepper sauce. Mix well and reduce heat. Let simmer for 20 minutes, stirring occasionally. Serve with brown rice and a salad. This chili freezes very well, place in 2 cup (2 servings) containers for future use. To thaw, place in a sauce pan on low, or microwave in a covered dish on high until thoroughly defrosted. Stirring frequently.

Makes 2 quarts (6-8 servings)

Pinto Bean Chili with Roasted Green Peppers

3 cups cooked pinto beans
1-1/2 cups diced onion (2 medium)
1-1/4 cups grated carrots (4 large)
1/3 cup minced long hot peppers or jalapeno peppers
1/2 cup diced roasted green bell pepper (1 medium)
2 cloves garlic - minced
3/4 cup dry textured soy protein
1 tablespoon extra virgin olive oil
2-1/4 teaspoons sugar
1-1/2 teaspoons salt
1-1/2 teaspoons ground cumin
1/2 teaspoon onion powder
1/2 teaspoon paprika
1/2 teaspoon ground cayenne pepper
1/4 teaspoon garlic powder
1/8 teaspoon oregano
6 ounces of tomato paste (canned)
1 teaspoon hot pepper sauce (10 dashes)
2 cups bean broth or water

1. Roast a green bell pepper. Cut pepper in half, remove seeds and inner membrane. Place on a baking sheet skin side up. Broil in a toaster-oven until skin begins to char and blister. Transfer to a bowl and cover with a lid to steam for 10 minutes. Then carefully remove the skin, dice and set aside.
2. Mix together sugar, salt, cumin, onion powder, paprika, cayenne pepper, garlic powder and oregano. Set spices aside. Grate carrots, dice onions, mince hot peppers and garlic, and set aside.
3. Heat a skillet, add dry textured soy protein. Stir and toast until golden brown. Remove from heat and set aside.
4. Heat 1/2 tablespoon extra virgin olive oil in a 3 quart pot. Add diced onions, stir to coat with oil. Stir in hot peppers. Cook until onions become slightly transparent, about 5 minutes. Add carrots, roasted bell peppers, and garlic. Cook for 3-4 minutes. Then add spices, textured soy protein and 1/2 tablespoon extra virgin olive oil. Mix well.
5. Add tomato paste, hot pepper sauce and bean broth or water. Mix well and reduce heat. Let simmer for 20 minutes. Serve with brown rice. This chili freezes very well, freeze in 2 cup (2 servings) containers. To thaw, place in a sauce pan on low, or microwave in a covered dish on high until thoroughly defrosted. Stirring frequently.

Makes 2 quarts (6-8 servings)

Red Bean Chili

3 cups cooked red beans
1-1/2 cups diced onion (2 medium)
1-1/4 cups grated carrots (4 large)
1/4 cup minced jalapeno peppers (1-2 large)
2 cloves garlic - minced
3/4 cup dry textured soy protein
1 tablespoon virgin olive oil
2 teaspoons sugar
1-1/2 teaspoons salt
1-1/4 teaspoons ground cumin
1/2 teaspoon crushed red pepper - dry
1/4 teaspoon ground cayenne pepper
1/4 teaspoon onion powder
1/4 teaspoon garlic powder
1/4 teaspoon paprika
1/8 teaspoon oregano - dry
6 ounces of tomato paste
3/4 teaspoon hot pepper sauce (7-8 dashes)
2 cups bean broth or water

1. Mix together sugar, salt, cumin, crushed red pepper, cayenne pepper, onion powder, garlic powder, paprika and oregano. Set spices aside. Grate carrots, dice onions, mince peppers and garlic, set aside.
2. Heat a skillet, add dry textured soy protein. Stir and toast until golden brown. Remove from heat and set aside.
3. Heat 1/2 tablespoon virgin olive oil in a 3 quart pot. Add onions, stir to coat with oil. Stir in jalapeno peppers. When onions become slightly transparent, stir in carrots and garlic. Cook for 3-4 minutes. Then add spices, textured soy protein, and 1/2 tablespoon virgin olive oil. Mix well.
4. Add tomato paste, hot pepper sauce and bean broth or water. Mix well and reduce heat. Let simmer for 20 minutes, stirring occasionally. Serve with brown rice and a Mixed Green Salad. This chili freezes very well, freeze in 2 cup (2 servings) containers for future use. To thaw, place in a sauce pan on low, or microwave in a covered dish on high until thoroughly defrosted. Stirring frequently.

Makes 2 quarts (6-8 servings)

Asparagus Noodle Soup

4-1/2 cups water
2 cups asparagus - sliced
1 tablespoon extra virgin olive oil
1 clove garlic - crushed
2 teaspoons salt
1 tablespoon dry parsley (2 tablespoons fresh)
1/4 pound ribbon noodles (4 ounces)
1/3 cup unbleached bread flour
1/4 teaspoon turmeric
1/4 teaspoon nutmeg
1/8 teaspoon sage
1/8 teaspoon onion powder
1/8 teaspoon garlic powder
1/8 teaspoon white ground pepper
1-1/2 cups soymilk

1. Wash and slice asparagus, set aside. Peel and crush garlic.
2. In a 3 quart soup pot, heat extra virgin olive oil. Add crushed garlic and saute for 1-2 minutes. Then stir in parsley and 1/2 teaspoon salt.
3. Add water and asparagus slices. Cover with a lid and bring to a boil.
4. Add ribbon noodles (or any noodle of your choice) and 1 teaspoon salt, stir until it comes back to a boil. Then cover with a lid, turn heat down to medium-low and let simmer 15-20 minutes, stir occasionally.
5. Mix together flour, turmeric, nutmeg, sage, onion powder, garlic powder, white ground pepper and 1/2 teaspoon salt. Slowly add soymilk, stirring vigorously until there are no lumps.
6. Turn heat up again. Stir soup and slowly pour in soymilk mixture. Continue stirring until soup thickens. Then turn heat down to low and let simmer for 5 minutes before serving. Salt and pepper to taste.

Makes 2-1/2 quarts (5-7 servings)

Cannellini Bean Cabbage Soup

4 cups water
3 cups cooked cannellini beans (or white beans)
2 cups shredded cabbage
1/2 cup finely diced onion (1 small)
1/2 cup finely diced carrot (1 small)

1/2 teaspoon rosemary (1 fresh sprig)
2 teaspoons salt
1/4 teaspoon nutmeg
1/8 teaspoon white ground pepper
1-1/2 cups soymilk

1. Wash and shred cabbage. Peel and finely dice onion and carrot.
2. Bring water to a boil in a 3-4 quart pot. Add cooked cannellini beans, shredded cabbage, diced onion, diced carrot, rosemary, salt, nutmeg and white ground pepper. Bring back to a boil. Then reduce heat and let simmer for 15-20 minutes.
3. Once cannellini beans begin to breakdown and soup begins to thicken, pour in soymilk, turn heat to low and let simmer for another 5-10 minutes. Salt and pepper to taste.

Makes about 3 quarts (6-8 servings)

Corn Chowder

4-1/2 cups water
3 cups diced potatoes
3/4 cup diced onion (1 medium onion)
1 tablespoon canola oil
2 teaspoons thyme
2/3 cup unbleached bread flour
2-1/2 teaspoons salt
1/8 teaspoon white ground pepper
1-3/4 cups (14 ounces) of corn - frozen, fresh or canned
1-1/2 cups soymilk

1. Peel and dice onions and potatoes.
2. In a 3-4 quart soup pot, heat canola oil. Add diced onions and thyme. Saute until onions are almost translucent.
3. Pour in water and 2 teaspoons of salt. Bring to a boil. Add diced potatoes, reduce heat and let simmer about 20 minutes or until potatoes become soft.
4. When potatoes are done, mix together flour and 1/2 teaspoon salt. Slowly add soymilk, mix to a smooth consistency. Turn up heat and stir this mixture into soup, stirring constantly until soup thickens.
5. Then add the corn and white ground pepper. Stir well, turn heat down to low, and let simmer for about 10 minutes. Stir occasionally to prevent flour and potatoes from settling and sticking to bottom of pot.

Makes about 3 quarts (6-8 servings)

Creamy Asparagus Soup

> 5 cups water
> 3 cups diagonally sliced asparagus
> 1 cup diced onion (1 large onion)
> 1/2 cup unbleached bread flour
> 2 tablespoons soy flour
> 2 tablespoons extra virgin olive oil
> 2-1/2 teaspoons salt
> 1/2 teaspoon sugar
> 1/4 teaspoon ground nutmeg (preferably fresh ground)
> 1/8 teaspoon black ground pepper
> 1-1/2 cups soymilk

1. Wash and diagonally slice asparagus, leaving tip whole. Set aside. Peel and dice onions.
2. Heat extra virgin olive oil in a 3 quart soup pot. Add onions and saute 2-3 minutes, until slightly translucent. Add water, 2 teaspoons salt and bring to a boil. Then add asparagus slices to soup and bring back to a boil. Turn heat to medium-high and let soup cook for 5-10 minutes.
3. Mix together bread flour, soy flour, sugar, nutmeg, pepper and 1/2 teaspoon salt. Slowly stir in soymilk, mix until there are no lumps.
4. Add the soymilk mixture to the boiling soup. Stir constantly until liquid begins to thicken. Then turn down heat to medium-low and simmer for 10 minutes, stirring occasionally. Salt and pepper to taste.

Makes about 2-1/2 quarts (5-7 servings)

Creamy Broccoli Soup

> 5 cups water
> 3 stalks fresh broccoli or 16 ounces frozen broccoli (1 package)
> 1 cup diced onion (1 large onion)
> 1/2 cup unbleached bread flour
> 2 tablespoons soy flour
> 2 tablespoons extra virgin olive oil
> 2-1/2 teaspoons salt
> 3/4 teaspoon sugar
> 1/4 teaspoon ground nutmeg (preferably fresh ground)
> 1/8 teaspoon black ground pepper
> 1-1/2 cups soymilk

1. If using fresh broccoli, peel and dice stalks, chop flowerets into bite

sized bits, and chop up any broccoli leaves. Peel and dice onion.
2. Heat extra virgin olive oil in a 3 quart soup pot. Add onions and saute until slightly translucent.
3. Add water and 2 teaspoons salt, bring to a boil. Then add broccoli cuts. Bring back to a boil and cook for about 15 minutes.
4. Mix together bread flour, soy flour, sugar, nutmeg, pepper and 1/2 teaspoon salt. Slowly stir in soymilk, mix until there are no lumps. Stir this mixture into the boiling soup. Stir constantly until liquid begins to thicken.
5. Then turn down heat to medium-low and simmer about 10 minutes, stirring occasionally. Salt and pepper to taste.
Makes about 2-1/2 quarts (5-7 servings)

Creamy Mushroom Soup

5 cups water
3 cups sliced button mushrooms
1 cup diced onion (1 large onion)
1/2 cup unbleached bread flour
2 tablespoons soy flour
2 tablespoons extra virgin olive oil
2-1/2 teaspoons salt
1/2 teaspoon sugar
1/4 teaspoon ground nutmeg (preferably fresh ground)
1/8 teaspoon black ground pepper
1-1/2 cups soymilk

1. Wash and slice mushrooms. Peel and dice an onion.
2. Heat extra virgin olive oil in a 3 quart soup pot. Add onions and saute until they become slightly translucent.
3. Add water, 2 teaspoons salt and sliced mushrooms. Bring to a boil and let cook for about 10-15 minutes.
4. Mix together bread flour, soy flour, sugar, nutmeg, black ground pepper and 1/2 teaspoon salt. Add soymilk and stir to a smooth consistency. Stir this mixture into the boiling soup. Stir constantly until liquid begins to thicken.
5. Then turn down heat to medium-low and simmer about 10 minutes, stirring occasionally. Salt and pepper to taste.
Makes about 2-1/2 quarts (5-7 servings)

Creamy Tomato Soup

    12 ounces of tomato paste
    3 cups water
    2 tablespoons unbleached bread flour
    1 tablespoon soy flour
    1 tablespoon sugar
    1 teaspoon salt
    1 teaspoon onion powder
    1/4 teaspoon garlic powder
    1-1/2 cups soymilk

1. Combine tomato paste and water. Bring to a boil in a 2 quart pot. Add sugar, salt, onion powder and garlic powder. Simmer 4-5 minutes.
2. Mix together bread flour and soy flour. Slowly add soymilk, mix well to eliminate lumps. Pour this mixture into soup, stirring constantly.
3. When soup begins to thicken, reduce heat to low and cook another 2-3 minutes before serving. Stir occasionally. Salt and pepper to taste.

Makes about 1-1/2 quarts (3-5 servings)

Creamy Vegetable Miso Soup

    3 cups water
    1-1/4 teaspoons salt
    1 cup sliced carrots (2 large fresh carrots)
    1 cup diced potatoes (2-3 medium potatoes)
    1/2 cup diced onion (1 small onion)
    1-1/2 cups fresh diced cabbage or 1 cup frozen turnip greens
    3/4 cup peas - fresh or frozen
    3/4 cup sliced button mushrooms
    3/4 cup bean sprouts (mung or soy)
    1 clove minced garlic
    1 teaspoon dry parsley flakes
    1/4 teaspoon turmeric
    1/4 teaspoon ground sage
    1/8 teaspoon cayenne pepper
    1-1/2 cups soymilk
    2 tablespoons soy flour
    2 tablespoons miso

1. Peel and slice carrots. Peel and dice onions and potatoes. Wash and dice cabbage. Wash and slice mushrooms. Rinse bean sprouts.

2. Bring water to a boil in a 3 quart soup pot. Add carrots, onions, potatoes, cabbage or turnip greens, peas, mushrooms and salt. Bring back to a boil. Add garlic, parsley, turmeric, sage and cayenne pepper. Then turn down heat, cover with a lid, and simmer for about 20 minutes.
3. Mix together soymilk and soy flour. Turn heat up to medium and add bean sprouts. Stir well. Then stir in soymilk mixture. Continue stirring until broth thickens.
4. Turn heat down to low and add miso. Let soup simmer until miso completely dissolves. Then turn heat off, and serve. Season with soy sauce and pepper to taste.

Makes about 2-1/2 quarts (5-7 servings)

Miso Noodle Soup

4 cups water
4 dry large shiitake mushrooms (or 6-8 small)
4 leaves cabbage, shredded
1/4 cup carrot, thinly sliced (1 small)
1/2 cup onion, thinly sliced (1 small)
1 tablespoon hijiki seaweed
4 ounces extra firm silken tofu (1/3 of a 12-ounce block)
4 ounces of cellophane noodles (two 2-ounce bundles/packages)
4 teaspoons miso
4 teaspoons soy sauce
1/8 teaspoon salt
2 tablespoons thinly sliced scallions

1. Rinse off dry shiitake mushrooms. Using a pair of scissors, cut mushrooms into thin strips. Wash and shred cabbage. Peel and thinly slice carrots and onions. Thinly slice a scallion and set aside.
2. In a 2 quart soup pot, add water, shiitake mushroom strips, cabbage, carrots, onions, seaweed, soy sauce and salt. Bring to a rapid boil, then turn heat down to medium and continue boiling soup for 3-4 minutes.
3. Carefully dip cellophane noodles in boiling soup to soften them enough to cut. Then using a pair of scissors, cut noodles to 1-2 inch lengths, noodles will expand lengthwise considerably. Add noodles to boiling soup and cook for 3-4 minutes.
4. Cut silken tofu into 1/4 inch cubes and add to soup. Stir in miso and turn heat down to low. Let simmer for 2-3 minutes. Serve in bowls with scallions sprinkled on top. Soy sauce to taste.

Makes about 1-1/2 quarts (3-5 servings)

4 cups water
4 dry large shiitake mushrooms (or 6-8 small)
1 tablespoon hijiki seaweed
4 ounces extra firm silken tofu (1/3 of a 12-ounce block)
4 teaspoons miso
4 teaspoons soy sauce
2 tablespoons thinly sliced scallions

1. Rinse off dry shiitake mushrooms. Using a pair of scissors, cut mushrooms into thin strips. Thinly slice a scallion, set aside.
2. In a 1-1/2 quart soup pot add water, shiitake mushroom strips and hijiki seaweed. Bring to a rapid boil. Turn heat down to medium and let boil for 2-3 minutes.
3. Cut silken tofu into 1/4 inch cubes and add to broth. Stir in miso and soy sauce. Turn heat down to low and simmer for 2-3 minutes. Serve in bowls with scallions sprinkled on top. Soy sauce to taste.

Makes about 4-1/2 cups (2-4 servings)

New England Chowder

4-1/2 cups water
2-3 tablespoons wakame seaweed
2-1/2 teaspoons salt
4 cups potatoes - diced
1-1/2 cups onions - diced (2 medium)
1 tablespoon canola oil
2 teaspoons thyme
2/3 cup unbleached bread flour
1-1/2 cups soymilk
1/8 teaspoon white ground pepper

1. In a 3-4 quart soup pot, bring water, wakame seaweed and 2 teaspoons salt to a rapid boil. (Kombu or alegra seaweed can be used as a substitute for wakame). Reduce heat and let simmer for 15 minutes.
2. While seaweed water is cooking, peel and dice the potatoes and onions. Set aside. After seaweed water has cooked for 15 minutes, strain liquid to remove seaweed bits.
3. Place soup pot back on heating element and heat canola oil. Add onions and thyme, saute for 2-3 minutes or until onions begin to sweat.

4. Pour seaweed flavored water back into soup pot and add diced potatoes. Bring back to a rapid boil. Then reduce heat to medium and simmer for about 20 minutes or until potatoes become soft.
5. Mix together bread flour, 1/2 teaspoon salt and soymilk until there are no lumps. When potatoes are done, turn heat up again and stir this mixture into soup. Continue stirring until soup begins to thicken.
6. Then turn heat down to low, add white ground pepper and let simmer for 10 minutes. Stir occasionally to prevent flour and potatoes from settling and sticking to the bottom of the pot. Salt and pepper to taste.

Makes about 3 quarts (6-8 servings)

Potato Cabbage Soup

4-1/2 cups water
3 cups shredded cabbage
3 cups diced potatoes (3 medium)
2-1/2 teaspoons salt
1 tablespoon extra virgin olive oil
1/2 teaspoon rosemary (1 fresh sprig)
1/2 cup unbleached bread flour
2 tablespoons soy flour
1 teaspoon sugar
1/4 teaspoon onion powder
1/8 teaspoon white ground pepper
1-1/2 cups soymilk

1. Shred cabbage. Heat extra virgin olive oil over medium heat in a 3-4 quart soup pot. Add shredded cabbage and rosemary. Saute for 4-5 minutes. While cabbage is cooking, peel and dice potatoes.
2. Add diced potatoes, water and 2 teaspoons salt to the cabbage. Turn up heat to high and bring to a rapid boil. Then reduce heat, cover and let simmer for about 20 minutes.
3. While soup is simmering, mix together bread flour, soy flour, sugar, onion powder, white ground pepper and 1/2 teaspoon salt. Slowly stir in soymilk and mix to a smooth consistency. Turn up heat again and stir this mixture into soup. Stir constantly until soup begins to thicken.
4. Turn heat to low and simmer 5-10 minutes, stirring occasionally. Cover with a lid until ready to serve. Salt and pepper to taste.

Makes about 3 quarts (6-8 servings)

Potato Leek Soup

> 4 cups water
> 3 cups diced potatoes (3 medium)
> 3 cups thinly sliced leeks (2 medium)
> 1/2 cup thinly sliced onion (1 small)
> 2-1/2 teaspoons salt
> 1 tablespoon extra virgin olive oil
> 1/2 teaspoon rosemary (1 fresh sprig)
> 1/2 cup unbleached bread flour
> 2 tablespoons soy flour
> 1 teaspoon sugar
> 1/4 teaspoon onion powder
> 1/8 teaspoon white ground pepper
> 1-1/2 cups soymilk

1. Thoroughly wash and thinly slice leeks, set aside. Thinly slice onions. Heat extra virgin olive oil over medium heat in a 3-4 quart soup pot. Add leek, onions and rosemary. Saute for 3-4 minutes. While leeks and onions are cooking, peel and dice potatoes.
2. Add diced potatoes, water and 2 teaspoons salt to the leeks and onions. Turn up heat to high and bring to a boil. Then reduce heat, cover and let simmer for about 20 minutes.
3. While soup is simmering, mix together bread flour, soy flour, sugar, onion powder, white ground pepper and 1/2 teaspoon salt. Slowly stir in soymilk and mix to a smooth consistency. Turn up heat again and stir this mixture into soup. Stir constantly until soup begins to thicken.
4. Turn heat to low and simmer 5-10 minutes, stirring occasionally. Cover with a lid until ready to serve. Salt and pepper to taste.

Makes about 3 quarts (6-8 servings)

Potato Turnup Greens Soup

> 2 cups finely diced potatoes (2 medium)
> 8 ounces frozen turnup greens (or 2 cups fresh)
> 3 cups water
> 1/2 tablespoon salt
> 1 teaspoon rosemary (1 fresh sprig)
> 2 tablespoons unbleached bread flour
> 1 tablespoon soy flour
> 1 teaspoon sugar
> 1/2 teaspoon onion powder

1/2 teaspoon garlic powder
1/8 teaspoon sage
1/8 teaspoon nutmeg
1/8 teaspoon white ground pepper
1-1/2 cups soymilk

1. Peel and finely dice potatoes. In a 2-3 quart soup pot, add water potatoes, turnup greens, salt and rosemary. Cover with lid and bring to a boil. Then turn heat down and let simmer for about 20 minutes.
2. Mix together bread flour, soy flour, sugar, onion powder, garlic powder, sage, nutmeg and white ground pepper. Slowly stir in soymilk. Mix to a smooth consistency. Turn heat up again and pour this mixture into soup, stir constantly until soup begins to thicken.
3. Then turn heat down again, and let soup simmer for another 5-10 minutes, stirring occasionally. Salt and pepper to taste.

Makes about 2 quarts (4-6 servings)

Pumpkin Cabbage Miso Soup

2 cups cooked mashed pumpkin (fresh cooked or canned)
2 cups diced raw cabbage
3-1/2 cups water
1 teaspoon salt
1 cup diced onion (1 large)
1 cup diced potato (1 large or 2 small)
1/2 tablespoon dry parsley
1 teaspoon dry oregano
1 teaspoon sugar
1/4 teaspoon rosemary (or 1 fresh sprig)
1/4 teaspoon sage
1/8 teaspoon turmeric
1 clove crushed garlic
2 tablespoons miso
2 tablespoons unbleached bread flour
1 tablespoon soy flour
1-1/2 cups soymilk

1. Bring water and salt to a boil. Add diced cabbage, mashed or canned pumpkin, diced onions and diced potatoes. Bring back to a boil.
2. Add parsley, oregano, sugar, rosemary, sage, turmeric and crushed garlic. Stir, reduce heat to medium-low, cover with lid and let simmer for about 20 minutes.

3. Add miso, stir well, cover with lid and let simmer 10-15 minutes.
4. Mix together bread flour, soy flour and soymilk. Turn heat up and stir this mixture into soup. Stir constantly until soup begins to thicken.
5. Then turn heat to low and cook another 5-10 minutes, stirring occasionally. Salt and pepper to taste.

Makes about 2-3/4 quarts (5-7 servings)

Pumpkin Chowder

3-1/2 cups water
2 cups cooked pumpkin (fresh cooked or a 15-ounce can)
2 cups diced potatoes (3 medium or 2 large)
1 cup diced onion (1 large)
1/2 tablespoon salt
1/2 tablespoon thyme
1/2 teaspoon sugar
1/4 teaspoon onion powder
1/8 teaspoon ground nutmeg
1/8 teaspoon black ground pepper
1/4 cup unbleached bread flour
2 tablespoons soy flour
1-1/2 cups soymilk

1. Peel and dice potatoes and onions.
2. In a 3 quart pot, add water, cooked and mashed pumpkin (or canned pumpkin), potatoes and onions. Bring to a boil. Add salt, thyme, sugar, onion powder, nutmeg and black ground pepper. Bring back to a boil, stirring occasionally. Then once soup begins to rapidly boil, reduce heat. Cover with lid and simmer for about 20 minutes.
3. Mix together bread flour and soy flour. Slowly add soymilk, stirring constantly to eliminate lumps. Turn heat up to medium and stir this mixture into soup. Continue stirring until soup begins to thicken.
4. Then reduce heat to low, cover with lid and simmer for another 5-10 minutes, stirring occasionally. Salt and pepper to taste.

Makes about 2-1/2 quarts (5-7 servings)

CHAPTER 14: STIR-FRY, SAUTE, PASTA & BAKED ENTREES

STIR-FRY ENTREES

Chinese Vegetable Stir-Fry with Baked Sesame Tofu

Baked Sesame Tofu Cubes:
  16 ounces of extra firm tofu (1 block)
  2 tablespoons soy sauce
  1 teaspoon canola oil
  1 teaspoon sesame oil
  1 teaspoon garlic powder
  1 teaspoon onion powder
  2 tablespoons sesame seeds
Chinese Vegetables:
  6 cups bok choy - diagonally sliced (1 medium head)
  1-1/2 cups sliced onions (2 medium)
  1 cup carrots - diagonally sliced
  1 cup snow peas - diagonally cut in half
  1-1/2 cups bean sprouts (mung or soy)
  1-1/2 teaspoons fresh ginger - minced
  3 teaspoons canola oil
  1/4 teaspoon salt
Sauce:
  2 tablespoons corn starch
  1 tablespoon soy flour
  1/2 teaspoon sugar
  1/2 teaspoon garlic powder
  1/4 teaspoon salt
  1/8 teaspoon cayenne pepper
  2 tablespoons soy sauce
  2 teaspoons sesame oil
  1 cup water

1. Cut tofu into 6-8 slices about 1/2 inch thick. Place slices on a plate and pour 2 tablespoons of soy sauce over slices. Make sure all sides have been coated with soy sauce, let sit for 1 minute. Then turn slices over and let sit in soy sauce for another minute.
2. Sprinkle tofu slices with 1/2 teaspoon onion powder, 1/2 teaspoon garlic powder and 1 tablespoon sesame seeds. Gently press seeds down into tofu. Oil a 8 x 10 inch baking sheet with 1 teaspoon canola oil and 1 teaspoon sesame oil.
3. Place tofu slices, seeded side down onto oiled baking sheet. Sprinkle

the rest of the onion powder, garlic powder and sesame seeds on top of tofu slices. Gently press sesame seeds down into tofu.
4. Preheat oven to 350°. Carefully cut tofu slices on baking sheet into 1/2 inch cubes. Separate pieces so edges do not touch. Bake for 25-30 minutes or until nicely browned.
5. While tofu is baking, wash and diagonally slice bok choy. Peel and diagonally slice carrots. Slice onions and diagonally cut snow peas in half. Rinse bean sprouts and mince ginger. Set all vegetables aside.
6. Prepare sauce mixture. Combine corn starch, soy flour, sugar, garlic powder, salt and cayenne pepper. Stir in soy sauce and sesame oil. Then slowly stir in water, mix well to eliminate any lumps. Set aside.
7. Heat 1 teaspoon canola oil in a wok or large skillet. Add bok choy and 1/4 teaspoon salt. Stir-fry for 3-4 minutes or until bok choy begins to shrink. Set aside.
8. Heat 1 teaspoon canola oil and add carrots. Stir-fry for 3-4 minutes. Add snow peas, stir-fry for 1-2 minutes. Then add bean sprouts. Stir-fry for another 1-2 minutes. Set aside.
9. Heat 1 teaspoon canola oil and add onions. Stir-fry for 2-3 minutes. Add ginger, stir well. Pour in sauce mixture. Stir constantly until sauce begins to thicken. Then add back the stir-fried vegetables. Mix well to coat everything with sauce. Turn heat off. Serve over brown rice and top with Baked Sesame Tofu Cubes.
Makes 4 servings

Fried Rice with Golden Tofu Strips

Golden Tofu Strips:
5.3 ounces of firm tofu (1/3 of a 16-ounce block)
1/4 teaspoon salt
1/4 teaspoon turmeric
1/2 tablespoon canola oil
Fried Rice:
1 cup diced onions (1 large)
1-1/2 cups shredded cabbage
1 cup frozen peas
1/2 cup finely diced carrots (1 medium)
1 cup mung bean or soybean sprouts
3 cups cooked brown rice (refrigerated day old preferred)
2 tablespoons soy sauce
3-1/2 teaspoons canola oil

1. Cut tofu into strips 1/4 inch wide and 2 inches long. Heat 1/2

tablespoon canola oil. Add tofu strips, 1/4 teaspoon salt and 1/4 teaspoon turmeric. Stir to thoroughly coat all sides of tofu. Cook tofu strips about 5 minutes or until golden brown. Set aside.

2. Heat 1 teaspoon canola oil. Add carrots, cabbage and peas. Stir-fry for 2-3 minutes. Add onions, stir-fry until they become slightly transparent. Then add bean sprouts and 1/2 tablespoon soy sauce, mix well with vegetables and stir-fry for about 1 minute. Set all the vegetables aside.

3. Heat 2-1/2 teaspoons canola oil. Add cooked brown rice and 1-1/2 tablespoons soy sauce. Stir to thoroughly coat rice.

4. Add vegetables and golden tofu strips. Mix well and serve, add more soy sauce at the table if needed.

Makes 4-6 servings

Fried Rice with Smokey Tempeh Strips

Smokey Tempeh Strips:
4 ounces of tempeh (1/2 of an 8-ounce package)
1/2 tablespoon liquid hickory smoke seasoning
1/2 tablespoon soy sauce
1 teaspoon honey
1 teaspoon canola oil
Fried Rice:
1 cup diced onion (1 large)
1-1/2 cups shredded cabbage
1 cup frozen peas
1/2 cup finely diced carrots (1 medium)
1 cup mung bean sprouts or soybean sprouts
3 cups cooked brown rice (refrigerated day old preferred)
2 tablespoons soy sauce
3-1/2 teaspoon canola oil

1. Cut tempeh into strips 1/4 inch thick and 2 inches long. Mix together liquid hickory smoke seasoning, honey, and soy sauce. Coat both sides of the tempeh strips with this sauce mix and let sit for 1-2 minutes.

2. Heat 1 teaspoon canola oil. Saute the seasoned tempeh strips until lightly browned on both sides, about 4-6 minutes. Then set aside.

3. Heat 1 teaspoon canola oil. Stir-fry carrots, cabbage and peas for 2 minutes. Add onions and sir-fry until they become slightly transparent. Then add bean sprouts and 1/2 tablespoon soy sauce, mix well with vegetables, and stir-fry for about 1 minute. Set all the vegetables aside.

4. Heat 2-1/2 teaspoons canola oil. Add cooked brown rice and 1-1/2

tablespoons soy sauce. Stir to thoroughly coat rice.
5. Add the stir-fried vegetables and smokey tempeh strips. Mix well and serve, add more soy sauce at the table if needed.

Makes 4-6 servings

Honey-Mustard Veggie Stir-Fry with Golden Tofu Cubes

Golden Tofu Cubes:
    5.3 ounces tofu - diced (1/3 of a 16-ounce block firm tofu)
    1/2 tablespoon canola oil
    1/4 teaspoon salt
    1/4 teaspoon turmeric
    1/8 teaspoon black ground pepper
Veggie Stir-Fry:
    1-1/2 cups carrots - diagonally sliced (2 large carrots)
    1-1/2 cups cabbage - shredded
    1 stalk fresh broccoli - peeled diagonally slice stems & flowerets
    1 cup onion - diced (1 large onion)
    1 cup bean sprouts (mung or soy)
    4 teaspoons canola oil
    1/2 teaspoon salt
Honey-Mustard Sauce:
    1 tablespoon Dijon mustard
    2 teaspoons honey
    2 teaspoons corn starch
    1 teaspoon pure sesame oil
    1/4 teaspoon salt
    1/3 cup soymilk
    1/3 cup water

---

1. Cut tofu into 1/2 inch cubes. Heat 1/2 tablespoon canola oil, add tofu cubes, 1/4 teaspoon salt, 1/4 teaspoon turmeric and 1/8 teaspoon black ground pepper. Saute until golden brown, remove from heat, set aside.
2. Begin vegetable stir-fry, starting with the hardest and most dense vegetables. Heat 1 teaspoon of canola oil, add carrots and broccoli stems, and 1/8 teaspoon salt. Stir constantly. When carrots and broccoli stems are tender remove heat and set aside on a plate.
3. Heat 1 teaspoon canola oil, add shredded cabbage and 1/8 teaspoon salt. Stir constantly until cabbage begins to wilt and become tender. Remove from heat and set aside on a plate.
4. Heat 1 teaspoon canola oil, add diced onion and 1/8 teaspoon salt. Stir constantly. When onions become slightly translucent, add bean sprouts

and stir-fry 1-2 minutes, then remove from heat and set aside.
5. Heat 1 teaspoon canola oil, add broccoli flowerets and 1/8 teaspoon salt. Stir to coat flowerets with oil, then put a cover on pan or wok to allow flowerets to steam. Steam for about 2 minutes. This will make flowerets bright green and tender. When flowerets are done they should be firm yet tender enough to easily poke a fork through it, remove from heat and set aside on a plate.
6. While broccoli flowerets are steaming, prepare sauce. Combine Dijon mustard, sesame oil, honey, salt and corn starch. Add soymilk and water, stir well. Set aside until broccoli flowerets are done.
7. Then pour the honey-mustard sauce mixture into pan, stir constantly. When sauce begins to thicken, turn off heat. Add all the stir-fried vegetables back to pan. Stir well to thoroughly coat all vegetables with sauce. Then add the golden tofu cubes, mix well. Serve over brown rice or udon noodles.

Makes 4 servings

Indonesian Stir-Fry with Baked Sesame Tofu

Baked Sesame Tofu Cubes:
8 ounces of extra firm tofu (1/2 of a 16-ounce block)
1 tablespoon soy sauce
1/2 teaspoon canola oil
1/2 teaspoon sesame oil
1/2 teaspoon garlic powder
1/2 teaspoon onion powder
1 tablespoon sesame seeds
Indonesian Stir-Fry:
2 cups sliced button mushrooms (12-16 medium)
1-1/2 cups diced green bell pepper (1 large)
1 cup diagonally sliced carrots (4 small)
1 cup snow peas
2 cups mung bean or soybean sprouts
1/2 cup sliced scallions
1 tablespoon canola oil
1/2 teaspoon salt
Indonesian Peanut Sauce:
1-1/2 tablespoons crunchy peanut butter - natural or old fashioned
2 tablespoons soy sauce
1 teaspoon vinegar
2 teaspoons sugar
1/8 teaspoon salt

1/2 teaspoon cayenne pepper
1/4 teaspoon hot pepper sauce (about 2-3 dashes)
1 tablespoon soy flour
1 tablespoon corn starch
1/2 teaspoon sesame oil
1/2 cup water
1/2 cup soymilk

---

1. Cut tofu into 3-4 slices about 1/2 inch thick. Place slices on a plate and pour 1 tablespoon of soy sauce over slices. Make sure all sides have been coated with soy sauce, let sit for 1 minute. Then turn slices over and let sit in soy sauce for another minute.
2. Sprinkle tofu slices with 1/4 teaspoon onion powder, 1/4 teaspoon garlic powder and 1/2 tablespoon sesame seeds. Gently press seeds down into tofu. Oil a 8 x 10 inch baking sheet with 1/2 teaspoon canola oil and 1/2 teaspoon sesame oil.
3. Place tofu slices, seeded side down onto oiled baking sheet. Sprinkle the rest of the onion powder, garlic powder and sesame seeds on top of tofu slices. Gently press sesame seeds down into tofu.
4. Preheat oven to 350°. Cut tofu slices into 1/2 inch cubes. Separate pieces so edges don't touch. Bake for 30-35 minutes or until browned.
5. While tofu is baking, slice mushrooms and diagonally cube green bell peppers, set aside on a plate. Peel and diagonally slice carrots, set aside. Diagonally cut snow peas in half, set aside. Diagonally slice scallions and rinse mung bean or soybean sprouts, set aside.
6. Prepare peanut sauce. Combine peanut butter, soy sauce, vinegar, sugar, salt, cayenne pepper, soy flour, corn starch, hot pepper sauce and sesame oil. Then add water and soymilk. Mix well and set aside.
7. Heat 1 teaspoon canola oil in a wok or large skillet. Add carrots and 1/8 teaspoon salt. Stir-fry for 3-4 minutes or until carrots become tender. Then set aside on a plate.
8. Heat 1 teaspoon canola oil, add peppers and 1/8 teaspoon salt. Stir-fry for 2-3 minutes, or until tender. Set aside.
9. Heat 1 teaspoon canola oil, add mushrooms, snow peas and 1/8 teaspoon salt. Stir-fry for 2-3 minutes, until mushrooms begin to release their juices. Then add bean sprouts, scallions and 1/8 teaspoon salt. Stir-fry for another 2-3 minutes. Set aside.
10. Pour peanut sauce mixture into the wok or skillet. Stir for 3-4 minutes or until the peanut sauce begins to thicken. Then add back stir-fried vegetables and turn off heat. Toss to thoroughly coat vegetables with peanut sauce. Serve over brown rice or udon noodles, and top with the Baked Sesame Tofu Cubes.

Makes 2-4 servings

Japanese Broccoli Stir-Fry with Golden Tofu Cubes

Golden Tofu Cubes:
   5.3 ounces tofu - diced (1/3 of a 16-ounce block firm tofu)
   1/2 tablespoon canola oil
   1/4 teaspoon salt
   1/4 teaspoon turmeric
Broccoli Stir-Fry:
   2 stalks fresh broccoli - peeled diagonally slice stems & flowerets
   1 cup carrots - diagonally sliced (2 medium carrots)
   1 cup onion - diced (1 large onion)
   1 cup button mushrooms - sliced (8-10 medium mushrooms)
   1 tablespoon fresh ginger - minced
   2 teaspoons fresh garlic - crushed (1 large clove of garlic)
   1-1/2 tablespoons canola oil
   1/2 teaspoon salt
Japanese Sauce:
   1 teaspoon wasabi powder
   1 tablespoon soy sauce
   2 tablespoons water
   1/2 tablespoon pure sesame oil

1. Cut tofu into 1/2 inch cubes. Heat 1/2 tablespoon canola oil in a wok or skillet. Add tofu cubes, 1/4 teaspoon turmeric and 1/4 teaspoon salt. Saute until golden brown. When done set aside on a plate.
2. Begin vegetable stir-fry, starting with the hardest and most dense vegetables. Heat 1/2 tablespoon of canola oil. Add carrots, broccoli stems, and 1/8 teaspoon salt. Stir constantly. When carrots and broccoli stems are tender, remove from heat and set aside on a plate.
3. Heat another 1/2 tablespoon of canola oil, add broccoli flowerets and 1/8 teaspoon salt. Stir to coat flowerets with oil, then put a cover on pan or wok to allow flowerets to steam. Steam for about 3-4 minutes. This will make flowerets bright green and tender. When flowerets are done they should be firm yet tender enough to easily poke a fork through it, remove from heat and set aside on a plate.
4. While broccoli flowerets are steaming, prepare sauce. Mix together 1 teaspoon wasabi powder, 1 tablespoon soy sauce, 2 tablespoons water and 1/2 tablespoon pure sesame oil. Set aside.
5. Finally heat 1/2 tablespoon of canola oil. Add onions, mushrooms and 1/8 teaspoon salt, stir well. When onions become slightly translucent, add ginger, garlic and 1/8 teaspoon salt. Stir-fry for 1 minute.
6. Add sauce mixture to onions, mushrooms, ginger and garlic. Stir for about 1-2 minutes. Then add stir-fried vegetables back to pan. Stir

well to thoroughly coat all vegetables with the sauce. Turn heat off. Add the golden tofu cubes and mix well. Serve over brown rice or udon noodles.

Makes 4 servings

Japanese Mushroom Stir-Fry with Tamari Tofu Strips

5.3 ounces firm tofu (1/3 of a 16-ounce block)
2-1/2 cups sliced button mushrooms (12-16 medium)
2 cups mung bean or soybean sprouts
1-1/2 cups diced onions (2 medium)
2 tablespoons soy sauce (Tamari, Shoyu or All-Purpose)
1 tablespoon canola oil

1. Cut tofu into 1 inch by 1/4 inch strips. Place in a bowl and add 1 tablespoon soy sauce. Carefully toss to coat all the strips with soy sauce. Let marinate for 2-3 minutes.
2. While tofu is marinating, slice mushrooms and dice onions. Set aside. Rinse mung bean sprouts and set aside.
3. Remove tofu strips from soy sauce. Add 1 tablespoon soy sauce, plus the remaining soy sauce from the tofu, to mushrooms and onions. Let mushrooms and onions marinate in soy sauce for about 2-3 minutes.
4. Heat 1/2 tablespoon canola oil in a wok or skillet, add the marinated tofu strips and saute for 4-5 minutes, until lightly browned. Set aside.
5. Remove mushrooms and onions from soy sauce. Add the remaining soy sauce to the mung bean or soybean sprouts. Let sit while mushrooms and onions are cooking.
6. Heat 1/2 tablespoon canola oil. Add marinated mushrooms and onions. Stir-fry 3-4 minutes or until mushrooms release their juices and onions become slightly translucent.
7. Stir in bean sprouts and the remaining soy sauce. Stir-fry for 1-2 minutes. Then add the tamari tofu strips, stir well. Serve over brown rice, udon noodles or rice noodles.

Makes 2-4 servings

SAUTE ENTREES

Roasted Red Peppers, Golden Tofu Cubes, Couscous and Pepitas

2 roasted red bell peppers
1/4 cup toasted pumpkin seeds (pepitas)
1 cup sliced onions (1 large)
1 teaspoon extra virgin olive oil
1/4 teaspoon salt
Golden Tofu Cubes:
5.3 ounces tofu - cubed (1/3 of a 16-ounce block firm tofu)
1/4 teaspoon salt
1/2 tablespoon extra virgin olive oil
1/4 teaspoon turmeric
Couscous:
2/3 cup uncooked couscous
1 cup water
1/2 teaspoon salt
1 teaspoon extra virgin olive oil

1. Roast red bell peppers. Cut peppers in half, remove seeds and inner membrane. Place on a baking sheet and broil in a toaster-oven until skin is charred and blistered. Transfer peppers to a bowl and cover with a lid to steam for 10 minutes. Then carefully remove the skins and slice peppers into strips. Set aside.
2. Place 1/4 cup of raw pumpkin seeds on a broiler pan and toast in a toaster-oven, stir occasionally. When you hear a popping sound (similar to popcorn) turn oven off. Let seeds cool before handling.
3. Bring 1 cup of water to a boil. Add salt and stir in couscous. Bring back to a boil. Then cover and remove from heat. Let stand for about 5 minutes. Sprinkle 1 teaspoon extra virgin olive oil over top of couscous and fluff with a fork. Cut tofu into 1/2 inch cubes.
4. Heat skillet, add 1/2 tablespoon olive oil, cubed tofu, 1/4 teaspoon salt and 1/4 teaspoon turmeric. Mix well to thoroughly coat tofu cubes. When tofu cubes become golden brown, remove from pan and set aside.
5. Heat 1 teaspoon extra virgin olive oil. Add sliced onions and 1/4 teaspoon salt, saute for 2-3 minutes or until slightly translucent.
6. Mix in roasted red pepper strips and saute for 1-2 minutes. Then toss in golden tofu cubes. Saute for another 1-2 minutes, then turn off heat.
7. Spread couscous on plate. Put roasted red peppers, golden tofu cubes and sauteed onions on next. Then top with toasted pumpkin seeds (pepitas) and serve.

Makes 2-4 servings

129

Soy Sweet and Sour Peppers

1-1/2 cups green bell pepper - sliced (2 medium)
1-1/2 cups onion - sliced (2 medium)
1 cup dry textured soy protein - toasted
2 tablespoons extra virgin olive oil
3/4 teaspoon salt
6 ounces of tomato paste
1-3/4 cups water
3 tablespoons vinegar
1 tablespoon sugar
4 tablespoons applesauce - unsweetened (1/4 cup)
1/2 tablespoon paprika
1 teaspoon oregano
1 teaspoon basil
1/8 teaspoon cayenne pepper
1/8 teaspoon black ground pepper

1. Toast textured soy protein in a skillet, stirring constantly until lightly browned, set aside. Slice peppers and onions, set aside.
2. Heat 1 tablespoon extra virgin olive oil, add the sliced peppers and 1/4 teaspoon salt. Saute for 2-3 minutes. Then add the sliced onions and another 1/4 teaspoon salt. Saute for another 2-3 minutes.
3. While onions and peppers are cooking, mix together tomato paste, water, vinegar, sugar, applesauce and 1/4 teaspoon salt. Set aside.
4. Add toasted textured soy protein, 1 tablespoon extra virgin olive oil, paprika, oregano, basil, cayenne pepper and black ground pepper to the sauteed onions and peppers. Mix thoroughly, allowing textured soy protein to soak up olive oil and spices.
5. Add the sweet and sour tomato mixture. Stir well, turn down heat and cover with a lid. Let simmer for 10-15 minutes, stirring occasionally. Serve over pasta cooked el dante, brown rice, couscous or millet; along with garlic bread and a Mixed Green Salad or a steamed green vegetable. This dish freezes very well. Freeze any leftovers. To thaw, place in a sauce pan on low heat or microwave until warm.

Makes 4-6 servings

Tempeh Strips with Roasted Green Peppers and Sauteed Onions

Tempeh Strips:
4 ounces tempeh (1/2 of an 8-ounce package)
1 tablespoon soy sauce

1 teaspoon extra virgin olive oil
Roasted Green Peppers and Sauteed Onions:
   2 roasted green bell peppers cut into strips
   2 cups sliced onions (2 large)
   2 teaspoons extra virgin olive oil
   1/2 teaspoon salt
   1/2 teaspoon paprika

---

1. Roast the green peppers. Cut peppers in half and remove the seeds and inner membrane. Place peppers in a toaster-oven and broil until the skin begins to blister and starts to blacken. Place in a covered dish and let peppers steam for about 10 minutes. Then carefully peel away skin and slice into strips. Set peppers aside.
2. While peppers are roasting, cut tempeh into strips 1/4 inch thick and 2 inches long. Sprinkle soy sauce over strips, let sit for 1-2 minutes.
3. Heat 1 teaspoon extra virgin olive oil in a skillet. Add the seasoned tempeh strips and saute for 1-2 minutes. Flip strips over and saute for another 1-2 minutes or until all sides are lightly browned. Set aside.
4. Heat 2 teaspoons extra virgin olive oil. Add onions and salt. Saute until onions are slightly translucent. Stir in paprika and roasted pepper strips. Saute for 2 minutes. Then toss in tempeh strips and take off heat. Serve with pasta, couscous or brown rice.

Makes 2-4 servings

PASTA ENTREES

Cheesy Macaroni

   1/2 pound macaroni - cooked el dante
   2 tablespoons unbleached bread flour
   2 tablespoons nutritional yeast
   1/2 teaspoon salt
   1/2 teaspoon onion powder
   1/2 teaspoon turmeric
   1/2 teaspoon dry parsley flakes
   1/4 cup water
   1-1/2 cups soymilk
   1 tablespoon extra virgin olive oil
   1 clove garlic crushed

---

1. Boil macaroni pasta in salted water for 8-10 minutes, until firm yet done or el dante. When macaroni is done, drain in a colander.

2. While pasta is cooking, mix together flour, nutritional yeast, salt, onion powder, turmeric, and parsley. Stir in water and soymilk. Mix well, to a smooth consistency.
3. Heat extra virgin olive oil in pan, add crushed garlic. Saute for 1-2 minutes on low heat, stir constantly so garlic does not burn.
4. Add soymilk mixture and turn up heat. Stir constantly until mixture begins to boil and thicken. Add macaroni and turn off heat. Mix thoroughly. Let macaroni sit for 2-3 minutes to absorb sauce. Serve with broccoli, spinach, Brussels sprouts or a Mixed Green Salad.

Makes 2-4 servings

Linguine in a White Mock Clam Sauce

1/2 pound linguine pasta cooked el dante
1/2 cup chopped button mushrooms (4-6 large)
3 cloves garlic - minced
2 tablespoons extra virgin olive oil
1 tablespoon parsley flakes
1/2 teaspoon salt
1/2 teaspoon onion powder
1/2 teaspoon garlic powder
1-1/2 tablespoons unbleached bread flour
1-1/2 tablespoons soy flour
1-1/2 tablespoons nutritional yeast
1/3 cup water
1-1/2 cups soymilk

1. Boil linguini pasta in salted water for 8-10 minutes, until firm yet done or el dante. When pasta is done, drain in a colander.
2. While pasta is cooking, chop mushrooms and mince garlic, set aside. Measure out parsley, onion powder, garlic powder and 1/4 teaspoon salt. Set spices aside. Mix together bread flour, soy flour, nutritional yeast and 1/4 teaspoon salt. Slowly stir in water and soymilk, mix to a smooth consistency. Set aside.
3. Heat extra virgin olive oil in a skillet. Add mushrooms, onions, garlic and spices. Saute 4-5 minutes over medium heat, stirring frequently.
4. Turn heat up and add soymilk mixture. Stir constantly until sauce begins to thicken. Then turn heat off and add drained linguini. Mix thoroughly so all pasta is completely coated with sauce. Serve with broccoli, spinach, Brussels sprouts or a Mixed Green Salad.

Makes 2-4 servings

Pasta Primavera with Golden Tofu Strips

1/2 pound of pasta cooked el dante
Golden Tofu Strips:
5.3 ounces of tofu (1/3 of a 16-ounce block firm tofu)
1/2 tablespoon canola oil
1/4 teaspoon salt
1/4 teaspoon turmeric
Italian Vegetable Saute:
1 red bell pepper - sliced
1 cup onion - sliced (1 large)
1 stalk broccoli (large)
2 teaspoons canola oil
1/2 teaspoon salt
Creamy Italian Primavera Sauce:
1 cup soymilk
1/4 cup water
2 tablespoons unbleached bread flour
2 cloves garlic - crushed
1 teaspoon canola oil
1 teaspoon oregano
1 teaspoon parsley flakes
1/2 teaspoon basil
1/2 teaspoon marjoram
1/4 teaspoon summer savory
1/4 teaspoon onion powder
1/4 teaspoon garlic powder
1/4 teaspoon salt

1. Bring water to a boil, salt to taste. Cook pasta until firm or el dante, about 8-10 minutes. Drain in a colander when done.
2. While pasta is cooking, cut tofu into strips (1-1/2 inches long and 1/4 inch wide). Saute tofu strips in 1/2 tablespoon canola oil, 1/4 teaspoon salt and 1/4 teaspoon turmeric. Stir to thoroughly coat all sides of tofu. Saute until golden brown. Set aside.
3. Cut broccoli stems into long thin strips, and slice red peppers and onions. Heat 1 teaspoon canola oil. Add broccoli stems, sliced red peppers and 1/4 teaspoon salt, saute for 3-4 minutes. Then add sliced onions. Saute for 2 minutes or until onions become slightly transparent. Set aside.
4. Cut broccoli flowerets into small bite sized pieces. Heat 1 teaspoon canola oil. Add broccoli flowerets and 1/4 teaspoon salt. Stir to coat flowerets with oil, then cover with a lid to steam for 3-5 minutes.

133

When flowerets are tender, remove from pan and set aside.

5. While broccoli flowerets are steaming, mix together bread flour, onion powder, garlic powder and 1/4 teaspoon salt. Slowly add water and soymilk, stir well. Set aside.
6. Heat 1 teaspoon canola oil. Add crushed garlic cloves and saute for 1 minute. Stir constantly so not to burn garlic. Add oregano, parsley, marjoram, basil and summer savory.
7. Add soymilk mixture to garlic and spices. Stir until thick. Turn off heat. Mix in all the sauteed Italian vegetables. Then add pasta and golden tofu strips. Mix well and let sit for 1-2 minutes before serving. Serve with garlic bread and a Mixed Green Salad.

Makes 2-4 servings

Pasta Shells in a Mushroom-Pea Sauce

1/2 pound pasta shells - cooked el dante
2-1/2 cups sliced button mushrooms
1-1/2 cups peas (frozen or fresh)
1/2 cup finely diced onion (1 small)
2 tablespoons extra virgin olive oil
1 clove garlic - minced
1 tablespoon dry parsley (2 tablespoons fresh)
2-1/2 tablespoons unbleached bread flour
1 tablespoon soy flour
3/4 teaspoon salt
2 tablespoons nutritional yeast
1/3 cup water
1-1/2 cups soymilk

1. Boil pasta shells in salted water for 8-10 minutes or until el dante.
2. While pasta is cooking, slice mushrooms, dice onions and mince garlic.
3. Heat 2 tablespoons extra virgin olive oil in a skillet. Add mushrooms, peas, onions, garlic, parsley and 1/4 teaspoon salt. Saute vegetables over medium heat for 3-4 minutes, or until onions are slightly translucent and mushrooms begin to release their juices.
4. Mix together bread flour, soy flour, nutritional yeast and 1/2 teaspoon salt. Add water and soymilk, mix until there are no lumps.
5. Pour soymilk mixture over mushroom-pea mix. Turn up heat and stir constantly. When sauce begins to boil and thicken, turn heat to low.
6. Drain pasta shells and add to the mushroom-pea sauce. Mix to thoroughly coat all pasta shells with sauce. Turn heat off and let pasta

shells sit in sauce for 2-3 minutes. Serve with garlic bread and a Mixed Green Salad.

Makes 2-4 servings

Rigatoni in a Cheesy Mushroom Sauce

1/2 pound rigatoni pasta cooked el dante
2-1/2 cups sliced button mushrooms
1-1/2 tablespoons extra virgin olive oil
1 clove crushed garlic
1 teaspoon parsley
3/4 teaspoon salt
2 tablespoons unbleached bread flour
2 tablespoons nutritional yeast
1 tablespoon soy flour
1/4 teaspoon turmeric
1/4 teaspoon onion powder
1/4 teaspoon garlic powder
1/8 teaspoon sage
1/4 cup water
1-1/2 cups soymilk

1. Boil rigatoni pasta in salted water for 10 minutes or until el dante.
2. While pasta is cooking, measure out bread flour, nutritional yeast, soy flour, turmeric, onion powder, garlic powder, sage and 1/2 teaspoon salt. Slowly stir in water and soymilk. Set aside. Wash and slice mushrooms, and crush garlic.
3. Heat extra virgin olive oil in a sauce pan. Add sliced mushrooms and crushed garlic. Saute for 2-3 minutes over medium heat. Then add 1/4 teaspoon salt and 1 teaspoon parsley. Saute for another 2-3 minutes.
4. Pour in soymilk mixture, stirring constantly. When sauce begins to boil and thicken, turn off heat. Drain pasta and add to sauce. Mix well to thoroughly coat pasta with sauce. Turn heat off and let pasta sit in sauce for 1-2 minutes before serving. Serve with garlic bread and broccoli, spinach or Brussels sprouts.

Makes 2-4 servings

Rotini in a Creamy Garlic Sauce

1/2 pound rotini pasta (spirals) cooked el dante
2 cloves garlic - crushed
1-1/2 tablespoons extra virgin olive oil
1/2 tablespoon dry parsley flakes (1 tablespoon fresh parsley)
1/2 teaspoon salt
1-1/2 cups soymilk
1/4 cup water
2-1/2 tablespoons unbleached bread flour
1/2 teaspoon garlic powder
1/2 teaspoon onion powder

1. Bring water to a boil, salt to taste. Cook rotini pasta for 8-10 minutes, until firm yet done or el dante. Drain in a colander when done.
2. While pasta is cooking, combine bread flour, garlic powder and onion powder. Stir in water and soymilk, mix well, set aside. Crush garlic.
3. Heat extra virgin olive oil in a sauce pan. Add crushed garlic and saute for about 1-2 minutes over low heat. Then stir in salt and parsley.
4. Turn heat up to medium. Add soymilk mixture to the garlic, stirring constantly. When mixture begins to boil and thicken, turn heat to low and continue stirring for another minute.
5. Then turn heat off. Add drained pasta to sauce and mix all together. Serve with garlic toast and a Mixed Green Salad, broccoli or spinach.

Makes 2-4 servings

Soy Fettuccini Alfredo

1/2 pound fettuccini pasta - cooked el dante
2-1/2 tablespoons unbleached bread flour
1/2 teaspoon salt
1-1/2 cups soymilk
1/4 cup water
2 tablespoons nutritional yeast
1 tablespoon extra virgin olive oil
1 clove garlic - crushed or minced

1. Boil fettuccini pasta in salted water for 8-10 minutes or until el dante.
2. While pasta is cooking, combine flour, nutritional yeast and 1/4 teaspoon salt. Stir in water and soymilk, mix well and set aside.
3. Crush garlic. Heat extra virgin olive oil in a sauce pan. Add garlic and 1/4 teaspoon salt. Saute for 1-2 minutes over low heat. Stir

constantly and don't burn the garlic, or it will taste bitter.
4. Add soymilk mixture to the pan. Keep stirring this mixture until it begins to boil and thickens. Don't over boil soymilk or it will curdle. Toss drained pasta in with the sauce. Serve with garlic bread and a Mixed Green Salad, broccoli, Brussels sprouts, or spinach.

Makes 2-4 servings

Spaghetti Florentine

1/2 pound spaghetti - cooked el dante
8 ounces of frozen spinach (or 2 cups fresh)
2 large cloves garlic - crushed
2 tablespoons extra virgin olive oil
1 tablespoon dry parsley (or 2 tablespoons fresh)
1/2 teaspoon salt
1-1/2 cups soymilk
1/4 cup water
2-1/2 tablespoons unbleached bread flour
1/2 tablespoon nutritional yeast
1/2 teaspoon garlic powder

1. Bring water to a boil, salt to taste. Cook pasta for 8-10 minutes or until el dante. Drain in a colander when done.
2. While pasta is cooking, mix together flour, nutritional yeast and garlic powder. Stir in water and soymilk, mix well, set aside. Crush garlic.
3. Heat extra virgin olive oil. Saute crushed garlic for about 2 minutes over low heat. Then stir in salt, parsley and spinach. Saute for about 3-4 minutes, or until spinach is cooked.
4. Turn heat up to medium. Add soymilk mixture to sauteed spinach and garlic, stir constantly. When mixture begins to boil and thicken, turn heat to low, continue to stir for another minute.
5. Then turn heat off. Add drained pasta to sauce and mix all together. Serve with garlic toast and a Mixed Green Salad.

Makes 2-4 servings

Tofu Cheese Ravioli

1-1/4 cups tofu cheese ravioli filling (p. 138)
4 sheets soymilk pasta dough (p. 138)
2-3 cups spaghetti sauce (pp. 161-163 or store bought)

Tofu Cheese Ravioli Filling:
   5.3 ounces of firm tofu (1/3 of a 16-ounce block)
   3 tablespoons soymilk
   2 tablespoons nutritional yeast
   1 tablespoon extra virgin olive oil
   1 teaspoon dry parsley flakes
   1/2 teaspoon garlic powder
   1/2 teaspoon onion powder
   1/2 teaspoon salt

1. In a food processor blend together tofu, extra virgin olive oil, and soymilk. Then add garlic powder, onion powder, parsley, salt and nutritional yeast. Blend until a cheesy paste is formed. Set aside.

Soymilk Pasta Dough:
   2/3 cup unbleached bread flour
   1/3 cup whole wheat flour
   1/2 teaspoon salt
   2 teaspoons extra virgin olive oil
   1/4 cup soymilk
   3 tablespoons water

1. Mix together bread flour, whole wheat flour, and salt. Add extra virgin olive oil, soymilk and water. Mix until all the liquid is absorbed and a dough ball is formed.
2. Clean a work surface with vinegar. Flour work surface and turn out dough ball. Flour the top of dough ball and knead it for 2-3 minutes.
3. Divide dough ball into 4 equal portions. Flour each quarter piece thoroughly and form into balls.
4. Using a rolling pin, roll out balls. Make a 1/8 inch thick sheet of dough, like a big thin tortilla. Make sure to coat dough with flour during the roll out, or it will stick to the rolling pin.
5. To roll out, start in the center of dough and roll out to edges, turn over. Then roll again from center to edges and turn. Up to 1-1/2 cups of flour will be used during the kneading and rolling out phase.

Assembly:
1. Place a sheet of pasta dough on a lightly floured surface. Put about 1 teaspoon of filling for each ravioli. Place 12-14 mounds of filling on the pasta sheet. Space each filling mound 1/2 to 1 inch apart from each other and from the edge of the pasta sheet.
2. Place a second sheet of pasta dough on top. Press down around each filling mound to form a tight seal and remove any air pockets.

3. Using a pastry cutter or sharp knife, cut out ravioli. Leave a 1/4 to 1/2 inch border around each filling mound. Remove excess pasta dough strips. (Set aside these pasta scraps and make bow ties).
4. Sift flour on top of ravioli's. Using a spatula, carefully place ravioli's on a floured plate or cookie sheet. Set aside.
5. Repeat the above steps for the third and forth pasta sheets. When all ravioli's have been made, either cook them or store them in a freezer for later use. (Place ravioli's in freezer on cookie sheet until frozen. Then transfer to a freezer bag for storage and use later.)

Cooking Ravioli:
1. Half way fill a 4 quart pot with salted water, and bring to a boil. Gently drop ravioli one at a time into the rapidly boiling water.
2. Stir continuously to keep ravioli's from sticking to the bottom of the pot. Boil 3 minutes for fresh ravioli and 5 minutes for frozen ravioli.
3. Drain in a colander and rinse to prevent sticking. Place on plates and top with spaghetti sauce. Serve with garlic bread and a steamed green vegetable or a Mixed Green Salad.

Makes 24-28 ravioli's (4 servings)

Ziti with Sauteed Tofu in a Creamy Mushroom Sauce

1/2 pound ziti pasta - cooked el dante
Sauteed Tofu:
5.3 ounces tofu (1/3 of a 16-ounce block firm tofu)
1/2 tablespoon virgin olive oil
1/4 teaspoon salt
1/8 teaspoon black ground pepper
Creamy Mushroom Sauce:
2 cups sliced button mushrooms (12-14 medium)
1/2 cup finely chopped onion (1 small)
1 clove minced garlic
1 tablespoon virgin olive oil
2-1/2 tablespoons unbleached bread flour
3/4 teaspoon salt
1 teaspoon dry parsley flakes
1/2 teaspoon onion powder
1/2 teaspoon garlic powder
1/2 teaspoon sage
1/8 teaspoon ground nutmeg
1-1/2 cups soymilk
1/4 cup water

1. Boil pasta in salted water 8-10 minutes, until el dante.
2. While pasta is cooking, mix together flour, onion powder, garlic powder, sage, nutmeg, and 1/2 teaspoon salt. Slowly stir in water and soymilk. Mix to a smooth consistency. Set aside. Dice tofu, slice mushrooms, finely chop onions, and mince garlic.
3. Heat 1/2 tablespoon virgin olive oil in a skillet. Add tofu, 1/4 teaspoon salt and 1/8 teaspoon black pepper. Saute until lightly browned then set aside.
4. Heat 1 tablespoon of virgin olive oil. Add mushrooms, onions, garlic, parsley and 1/4 teaspoon salt. Saute 4 minutes over medium heat, or until onions become translucent and mushrooms produce a liquid.
5. Stir in soymilk mixture and cook until it begins to boil and thicken, about 3 minutes. Stir constantly and do not over boil. When sauce has thickened, turn off heat. Drain pasta and add to sauce, toss thoroughly. Serve with garlic bread and a Mixed Green Salad, broccoli or spinach.

Makes 2-4 servings

BAKED ENTREES

Baked Cheesy Macaroni with a Bread Crumb Crust

1/2 pound macaroni
2 tablespoons unbleached bread flour
2-1/2 tablespoons nutritional yeast
1/2 teaspoon salt
1/2 teaspoon onion powder
1/2 teaspoon turmeric
1/3 cup water
1-3/4 cup soymilk
1-1/2 tablespoons extra virgin olive oil
1 clove garlic - crushed
2/3 cup bread crumbs

1. Boil macaroni in salted water for 8-10 minutes or until el dante. When macaroni is done, drain in a colander.
2. While macaroni is cooking, mix together flour, salt, onion powder, turmeric and 2 tablespoons nutritional yeast. Stir in water and soymilk. Mix to a smooth consistency and set aside. Crush garlic.
3. Heat 1 tablespoon extra virgin olive oil in a pan. Add garlic and saute 1-2 minutes on low heat, stir constantly so garlic doesn't burn.
4. Add soymilk mixture and turn up heat. Stir constantly until mixture thickens. Then add macaroni, mix well and turn off heat.

5. Preheat oven to 375°. Oil a 8 x 8 inch baking dish with extra virgin olive oil, sprinkle 1/3 cup of bread crumbs over the bottom and sides.
6. Evenly spread out cheesy macaroni in dish. Sprinkle the rest of the bread crumbs over top of macaroni. Then sprinkle 1/2 tablespoon nutritional yeast and drizzle 1/2 tablespoon extra virgin olive oil over top. Cover with lid or aluminum foil.
7. Bake for 15 minutes. Uncover and bake another 5 minutes, until bread crumb topping is golden brown. Let cool a few minutes, then cut into 4 pieces. Serve with and a Mixed Green Salad, broccoli or spinach.

Makes 4 servings

Baked Lentils and Brown Rice Bechamel

2 cups cooked lentils
2 cups cooked brown rice
2 tablespoons unbleached bread flour
1/2 teaspoon salt
1/8 teaspoon ground nutmeg
pinch of white ground pepper
3/4 cup soymilk
1/4 cup water
1 tablespoon extra virgin olive oil
2/3 cup bread crumbs

1. Cook lentils and brown rice as directed on packages.
2. Mix together flour, salt, nutmeg and white pepper. Stir in water and soymilk, mix well until there are no lumps.
3. Heat 2 teaspoons extra virgin olive oil in a sauce pan. Pour in soymilk mixture and heat until it begins to boil and thicken, stir constantly. Turn heat to low, continue stirring 1- 2 minutes. Then turn heat off and cover with a lid.
4. Mix together cooked lentils and brown rice. Then mix in the bechamel sauce. Let sit for a minute or two.
5. Preheat oven to 350°. Oil a 8 x 8 inch baking dish with extra virgin olive oil, sprinkle 1/3 cup of bread crumbs over the bottom and sides.
6. Evenly spread out the lentils and brown rice mix. Sprinkle the rest of the bread crumbs and drizzle 1 teaspoon extra virgin olive oil over top.
7. Bake for 20 minutes. Remove from oven and let cool for 5 minutes. Serve with Brussels Sprouts, broccoli or a Mixed Green Salad.

Makes 2-4 servings

Baked Sesame Tofu with an Indonesian Peanut Sauce

Baked Sesame Tofu:
16 ounces of extra firm tofu (1 block)
2 tablespoons soy sauce
1 teaspoon canola oil
1 teaspoon sesame oil
1 teaspoon garlic powder
1 teaspoon onion powder
2 tablespoons sesame seeds
Indonesian Peanut Sauce:
1 tablespoon crunchy peanut butter - natural or old fashioned
1 tablespoon soy sauce
1/2 teaspoon vinegar
1 teaspoon sugar
1/4 teaspoon cayenne pepper
1/8 teaspoon hot pepper sauce (about 1-2 dashes)
1-1/2 tablespoons corn starch
1/4 teaspoon sesame oil
1/4 cup water
1/4 cup soymilk

---

1. Cut tofu into 6-8 slices about 1/2 inch thick. Place slices on a plate and pour 2 tablespoons of soy sauce over slices. Make sure all sides have been coated with soy sauce, let sit for 1-2 minutes. Then turn slices over and let sit in soy sauce for another 1-2 minutes.
2. Sprinkle tofu slices with 1/2 teaspoon onion powder, 1/2 teaspoon garlic powder and 1 tablespoon sesame seeds. Press seeds into tofu.
3. Oil a 8 x 10 inch baking sheet with 1 teaspoon canola oil and 1 teaspoon sesame oil. Place tofu slices, seeded side down onto oiled baking sheet. Sprinkle rest of the onion powder, garlic powder and sesame seeds on top of tofu slices. Gently press sesame seeds into tofu.
4. Preheat oven to 350°. Carefully cut tofu slices on baking sheet into cubes 1/2 inch wide or strips 1 inch long. Separate pieces so edges do not touch, or else they will stick together and not brown properly.
5. Bake at 350° for 25-30 minutes or until nicely browned.
6. Prepare peanut sauce. Mix together peanut butter, soy sauce, vinegar, sugar, cayenne pepper, corn starch and sesame oil. When this mixture forms a paste, add water and soymilk, mix thoroughly.
7. *Stove Top Method:* Heat peanut mixture in a sauce pan or skillet. Stir constantly and cook for 3-4 minutes, or until the peanut sauce begins to boil and thicken. Turn down heat and cover until ready to serve.
   Microwave Method: Pour mixture into a covered microwave proof

dish. Microwave for 4-5 minutes, stirring mixture every 15-20 seconds until it thickens and begins to boil. Remove from microwave and serve, or cover until ready to serve.
Serve Baked Sesame Tofu with this hot and spicy Indonesian Peanut Sauce as a dipping sauce on the side, a Mixed Green Salad and a nice crusty bread, which can also be dipped in the peanut sauce.
Makes 4-6 servings

Eggplant Lasagne

2 baked eggplants
1-2/3 cups tofu cheese filling
12 lasagne pasta strips (soymilk pasta p. 144 or store bought)
3-1/2 cups spaghetti sauce (pp. 161-163 or store bought)
3/4 cup cheesy tofu topping (p. 144)
1 tablespoon extra virgin olive oil

Baked Eggplant:
2 large eggplants
2 tablespoons extra virgin olive oil
2 teaspoons oregano
1/2 teaspoon salt

1. Peel and cut eggplant into 1 inch round slices. Salt both sides of each slice and place in a colander for 10 minutes. Then rinse off all the slices and let drain until dry, about 3-5 minutes.
2. Oil a baking sheet with 1 tablespoon extra virgin olive oil. Sprinkle half the salt and oregano onto the baking sheet and place the eggplant slices on top. Brush each eggplant slice with extra virgin olive oil, use about 1 tablespoon in total to brush the tops of all the eggplant slices. Then sprinkle the eggplant slices with the rest of the oregano and salt.
3. Bake eggplant at 400° for 15 minutes. Turn slices over and bake another 10-15 minutes, or until eggplant is tender. Remove from oven and let cool.

Tofu Cheese Filling:
8 ounces firm tofu (1/2 of a 16-ounce block)
4-1/2 tablespoons soymilk
1-1/2 tablespoons extra virgin olive oil
1 clove garlic
3 tablespoons nutritional yeast

1/2 tablespoon parsley
3/4 teaspoon garlic powder
3/4 teaspoon onion powder
3/4 teaspoon salt
1/2 teaspoon oregano

1. In a food processor, blend tofu, soymilk, extra virgin olive oil and garlic clove. Then add nutritional yeast, parsley, garlic powder, onion powder, salt and oregano. Blend to a cheesy consistency. Set aside.

Soymilk Pasta Dough:
2/3 cup unbleached bread flour
1/3 cup whole wheat flour
1/2 teaspoon salt
2 teaspoons extra virgin olive oil
3 tablespoons soymilk
4 tablespoons water

1. Mix together bread flour, whole wheat flour, and salt. Add extra virgin olive oil, soymilk and water. Mix until all the liquid is absorbed and a dough ball is formed.
2. Clean a work surface with vinegar. Flour work surface and turn out dough ball. Flour the top of dough ball and knead it for 2-3 minutes.
3. Divide dough in half, flour each piece and form into 2 balls.
4. Using a rolling pin, roll out each ball until it is about 1/8 inch thick, 12 inches wide and 10 inches long. Make sure to coat dough with flour during the roll out or it will stick to the rolling pin.
5. To roll out, start in the center of dough and roll out to edges, turn over. Then roll again from center to edges and turn. Up to 1-1/2 cups of flour will be used during the kneading and rolling out phase.
6. Cut pasta sheets into 12 strips, about 2 inches wide and 10 inches long.
7. Bring a 4 quart pot of salted water to a rapid boil. Carefully place pasta strips in rapidly boiling water one at a time, stirring constantly. Let pasta cook for 3-4 minutes or until all the pasta begins to float to surface. Continue stirring during the cooking phase.
8. Drain pasta strips and rinse in cold water. Fill pot with cold water and let pasta sit in it until ready to assemble lasagne.

Cheesy Tofu Topping:
2.6 ounces of tofu (1/6 of a 16-ounce block firm tofu)
1/4 cup soymilk
1 small clove garlic or 1/4 teaspoon garlic powder
1 tablespoon nutritional yeast

1/2 tablespoon extra virgin olive oil
1/4 teaspoon salt

---

1. In a food processor first blend together tofu, soymilk and garlic. Then add nutritional yeast, extra virgin olive oil and salt. Blend for a full 1-2 minutes, until it's smooth and creamy. Set aside.

Assembly:
1. Preheat oven to 375°. Thoroughly oil a 9 x 13 inch baking pan or lasagne dish with extra virgin olive oil. Spread about 1/2 cup of spaghetti sauce over the bottom.
2. Place 4 lasagne pasta strips on next. Overlap each strip by 1/2-1 inch.
3. Spread half of the tofu cheese filling on top of the pasta.
4. Place half of the baked eggplant on top of the tofu cheese filling.
5. Spread 1 cup of spaghetti sauce on top of baked eggplant.
6. Place the next 4 lasagne pasta strips on top of the spaghetti sauce. Be sure to overlap the pasta strips.
7. Spread the rest of the tofu cheese filling on top of the pasta.
8. Place the rest of the baked eggplant on top of tofu cheese filling.
9. Spread 1 cup of spaghetti sauce on top of the baked eggplant.
10. Finally add the last 4 lasagne pasta strips. Spread the rest of the spaghetti sauce on top, and add the Cheesy Tofu Topping. Take a fork full of Cheesy Tofu Topping and drizzle on surface in a random pattern to create the look of melted cheese.
11. Bake at 375° for 20 minutes. Let cool 10-15 minutes before cutting. Serve with garlic bread and a Mixed Green Salad.

Makes 6-8 servings

Garbanzo Bean Moussaka

1 large baked eggplant
1 tablespoon extra virgin olive oil
Garbanzo Bean Moussaka:
2 cups cooked garbanzo beans
1-1/2 cups sliced onions (2 medium)
1-1/2 cups chopped tomatoes (2 medium)
1 tablespoon extra virgin olive oil
1-1/2 tablespoons parsley flakes
1 teaspoon ground cinnamon
3/4 teaspoon salt
1/8 teaspoon black ground pepper
1 tablespoon nutritional yeast

Cheesy Moussaka Sauce:
   4 ounces silken tofu (1/3 of a 12-ounce block)
   1 tablespoon extra virgin olive oil
   3 tablespoons unbleached bread flour
   1 tablespoon soy flour
   1/4 cup water
   3/4 teaspoon salt
   2 tablespoons nutritional yeast
   1-1/2 cups soymilk
Topping:
   2/3 cup dry bread crumbs
   1/2 teaspoon ground cinnamon

---

1. Peel and cut eggplant into 1 inch round slices. Salt both sides of each slice and place in a colander for 10 minutes. Then rinse off all the slices and let drain until dry, about 3-5 minutes.
2. Thoroughly oil a baking sheet with extra virgin olive oil and place eggplant slices on top. Brush extra virgin olive oil on each slice. Use about 1 tablespoon of extra virgin olive oil in total to brush all the eggplant slices. Sprinkle eggplant slices with salt and black pepper.
3. Bake eggplant at 400° for 15 minutes. Turn slices over and bake for 15-20 minutes or until eggplant is tender. Set aside.
4. While eggplant is baking, slice onions, peel and chop tomatoes, and mash 1 cup of garbanzo beans. Keep 1 cup of garbanzo beans whole.
5. Heat 1 tablespoon extra virgin olive oil in a skillet. Add onions and saute until onions are translucent, about 3-5 minutes. Add whole garbanzo beans, parsley, ground cinnamon, salt and black ground pepper. Saute for 2-3 minutes, stirring frequently. Then add chopped tomatoes, mashed garbanzo beans and 1 tablespoon nutritional yeast. Mix well and then turn off heat. Set aside.
6. Make the cheesy moussaka sauce. In a food processor blend silken tofu and 1 tablespoon extra virgin olive oil to form a thick paste. Then add in bread flour, soy flour, water, 3/4 teaspoon salt and 2 tablespoons nutritional yeast. Blend until smooth and creamy.
7. Pour this tofu mixture and 1-1/2 cups soymilk into a sauce pan, stir constantly. Heat until it thickens and begins to boil. Reduce heat and cook another 1-2 minutes. Then turn off heat and set aside.
8. Preheat oven to 400°. Thoroughly oil a 9 x 13 inch baking pan with extra virgin olive oil. Mix together 2/3 cup bread crumbs and 1/2 teaspoon ground cinnamon. Sprinkle 3 tablespoons of the bread crumb mix on bottom and sides of baking pan. Place baked eggplant slices on top of bread crumbs. Add the garbanzo bean mixture for the next layer. Pour cheesy sauce on top of garbanzo layer. Then sprinkle the

rest of the bread crumb mix on top.
9. Bake at 400° for 15-20 minutes. Then turn oven down to 350° and bake another 35-40 minutes. Cool thoroughly before slicing. Serve with pasta or couscous, and a Mixed Green Salad.
Makes 6-8 servings

Lentil Rice Tofu Loaf

2 cups cooked lentils
2 cups cooked brown rice
1-1/2 cups grated carrots (3 medium)
1 cup finely diced onion (1 large)
8 ounces tofu (1/2 of a 16-ounce block of firm tofu)
2 cloves of garlic
1 tablespoon nutritional yeast
1 tablespoon dry parsley
1 teaspoon salt
2 teaspoons oregano
1 teaspoon summer savory
1/2 teaspoon onion powder
1/2 teaspoon garlic powder
1/4 teaspoon black ground pepper
1 cup applesauce - unsweetened
6 tablespoons tomato ketchup
3 tablespoons canola oil
2 tablespoons soy sauce
1 cup of uncooked old fashioned rolled oats
1/2 cup bread crumbs
1/2 cup soy flour

1. In a bowl, mix 1 cup cooked lentils with 2 cups cooked brown rice. Grate carrots, finely dice onions and mix with lentils and brown rice.
2. In a food processor, combine 1 cup cooked lentils, tofu, garlic cloves, nutritional yeast, parsley, salt, oregano, summer savory, onion powder, garlic powder, black pepper, applesauce, ketchup, canola oil and soy sauce. Blend until smooth and creamy.
3. Add tofu mixture to the lentils, brown rice, carrots and onions. Mix well. Then add oats, bread crumbs and soy flour. Mix thoroughly. Let sit for 10 minutes to allow oats to absorb moisture.
4. Preheat oven to 400°. Line a loaf pan with aluminum foil. Oil the loaf pan using canola oil. Spread loaf mix into pan and press down to eliminate any air pockets.

5. Bake at 400° for 50-60 minutes. Let loaf cool in pan for at least 15 minutes before serving. Serve with mashed potatoes and brown mushroom gravy; steamed broccoli, spinach or Brussels sprouts; and applesauce or cranberry sauce. Refrigerate or freeze any leftovers. This loaf makes excellent sandwiches.

Makes 1 loaf (8-12 servings)

Soy Moussaka

1 large baked eggplant
1 tablespoon extra virgin olive oil
Moussaka:
1 cup dry textured soy protein
1-1/2 cups sliced onions (2 medium)
1-1/2 cups chopped tomatoes (2 medium)
3 tablespoons extra virgin olive oil
1-1/2 tablespoons parsley flakes
1/2 tablespoon ground cinnamon
3/4 teaspoon salt
1/4 teaspoon black ground pepper
1-1/2 tablespoons nutritional yeast
3 tablespoons soy flour
1 cup water
Cheesy Moussaka Sauce:
4 ounces silken tofu (1/3 of a 12-ounce block)
1 tablespoon extra virgin olive oil
3 tablespoons unbleached bread flour
1 tablespoon soy flour
1/4 cup water
3/4 teaspoon salt
2 tablespoons nutritional yeast
1-1/2 cups soymilk
Topping:
2/3 cup dry bread crumbs
1/2 teaspoon ground cinnamon

1. Peel and cut eggplant into 1 inch round slices. Salt both sides of each slice and place in a colander for 10 minutes. Then rinse off all the slices and let drain until dry, about 3-5 minutes.
2. Thoroughly oil a baking sheet with extra virgin olive oil and place eggplant slices on top. Brush extra virgin olive oil on each slice. Use about 1 tablespoon of extra virgin olive oil in total to brush all the

148

eggplant slices. Sprinkle eggplant slices with salt and black pepper.
3. Bake eggplant at 400° for 15 minutes. Turn slices over and bake for
   15-20 minutes or until eggplant is tender. Set aside.
4. While eggplant is baking, toast textured soy protein in a skillet until
   lightly browned. Set aside. Peel and chop tomatoes, peel and slice
   onions. Set aside.
5. Heat 1 tablespoon of extra virgin olive oil in a skillet. Add onions and
   saute until onions are translucent, about 3-5 minutes. Add toasted
   textured soy protein, chopped tomatoes, parsley, ground cinnamon,
   salt, black ground pepper and 2 tablespoons extra virgin olive oil.
   Saute for 1-2 minutes, stirring frequently. Then mix in 1-1/2
   tablespoons nutritional yeast, 3 tablespoons soy flour and 1 cup water,
   turn off heat and let sit for 10 minutes. Set aside.
6. Make the cheesy moussaka sauce. In a food processor blend silken tofu
   and 1 tablespoon extra virgin olive oil to form a thick paste. Then add
   in bread flour, soy flour, water, 3/4 teaspoon salt and 2 tablespoons
   nutritional yeast. Blend until smooth and creamy.
7. Pour this tofu mixture and 1-1/2 cups soymilk into a sauce pan, stir
   constantly. Heat until it thickens and begins to boil. Reduce heat and
   cook 1-2 more minutes. Then turn off heat and set aside.
8. Preheat oven to 400°. Thoroughly oil a 9 x 13 inch baking pan with
   extra virgin olive oil. Mix together 2/3 bread crumbs and 1/2 teaspoon
   ground cinnamon. Sprinkle 3 tablespoons of the bread crumb mix on
   bottom and sides of pan. Place baked eggplant slices on top of bread
   crumbs. Add the textured soy protein mixture for the second layer.
   Pour the cheesy sauce on next. Then sprinkle the rest of the bread
   crumb mix on top.
9. Bake at 400° for 15-20 minutes. Then turn oven down to 350° and
   bake another 35-40 minutes. Cool thoroughly before slicing. Serve
   with pasta or couscous, and a Mixed Green Salad.
Makes 6-8 servings

Spinach Lasagne

2 cups spinach filling (p. 150)
1-2/3 cups tofu cheese filling (p. 150)
12 lasagne pasta strips (soymilk pasta p. 150 or store bought)
3-1/2 cups spaghetti sauce (pp. 161-163 or store bought)
3/4 cup cheesy tofu topping (p. 151)
1 tablespoon extra virgin olive oil

Spinach Filling:
   4 cups of fresh or 16 ounces of frozen spinach
   1 cup diced onions (1 large)
   2 tablespoons extra virgin olive oil
   1 tablespoon nutritional yeast
   1 teaspoon oregano
   1 teaspoon marjoram
   1/2 teaspoon salt
   pinch of black ground pepper (less than 1/8 teaspoon)

1. Heat extra virgin olive oil in a skillet. Add onions, oregano, marjoram and salt. Saute until onions are slightly translucent.
2. Add fresh washed or frozen spinach to onions. Saute for 10 minutes. Stir in nutritional yeast. Turn off heat. Cover with lid and set aside.

Tofu Cheese Filling:
   8 ounces firm tofu (1/2 of a 16-ounce block)
   4-1/2 tablespoons soymilk
   1-1/2 tablespoons extra virgin olive oil
   1 clove garlic
   3 tablespoons nutritional yeast
   1/2 tablespoon parsley
   3/4 teaspoon garlic powder
   3/4 teaspoon onion powder
   3/4 teaspoon salt

1. In a food processor blend together tofu, soymilk, extra virgin olive oil and garlic clove. Then add nutritional yeast, parsley, garlic powder, onion powder and salt. Blend until a cheesy paste is formed. Set aside.

Soymilk Pasta Dough:
   2/3 cup unbleached bread flour
   1/3 cup whole wheat flour
   1/2 teaspoon salt
   2 teaspoons extra virgin olive oil
   3 tablespoons soymilk
   4 tablespoons water

1. Mix together bread flour, whole wheat flour, and salt. Add extra virgin olive oil, soymilk and water. Mix until all the liquid is absorbed and a dough ball is formed.

2. Clean a work surface with vinegar. Flour work surface and turn out dough ball. Flour the top of dough ball and knead it for 2-3 minutes.
3. Divide dough in half, flour each piece and form into 2 balls.
4. Using a rolling pin, roll out each ball until it is about 1/8 inch thick, 12 inches wide and 10 inches long. Make sure to coat dough with flour during the roll out or it will stick to the rolling pin.
5. To roll out, start in the center of dough and roll out to edges, turn over. Then roll again from center to edges and turn. Up to 1-1/2 cups of flour will be used during the kneading and rolling out phase.
6. Cut pasta sheets into 12 strips, about 2 inches wide and 10 inches long.
7. Bring a 4 quart pot of salted water to a rapid boil. Carefully place pasta strips in rapidly boiling water one at a time, stirring constantly. Let pasta cook for 3-4 minutes or until all the pasta begins to float to surface. Continue stirring during the cooking phase.
8. Drain pasta strips and rinse in cold water. Fill pot with cold water and let pasta sit in it until ready to assemble lasagne.

Cheesy Tofu Topping:
2.6 ounces of tofu (1/6 of a 16-ounce block firm tofu)
1/4 cup soymilk
1 small clove garlic or 1/4 teaspoon garlic powder
1 tablespoon nutritional yeast
1/2 tablespoon extra virgin olive oil
1/4 teaspoon salt

1. In a food processor blend together tofu, soymilk and garlic. Then add nutritional yeast, extra virgin olive oil and salt. Blend for a full 1-2 minutes, until it's smooth and creamy. Set aside.

Assembly:
1. Preheat oven to 375˚. Thoroughly oil a 9 x 13 inch baking pan or lasagne dish with extra virgin olive oil. Spread about 1/2 cup of spaghetti sauce over the bottom.
2. Place 4 lasagne pasta strips on next. Overlap strips by 1/2 inch.
3. Spread half of the tofu cheese filling on top of the pasta.
4. Place half of the spinach filling on top of the tofu cheese filling.
5. Spread 1 cup of spaghetti sauce on top of spinach filling.
6. Place 4 lasagne pasta strips on top of the spaghetti sauce. Be sure to overlap the pasta strips by about 1/2 inch.
7. Spread the rest of the tofu cheese filling on top of the pasta.
8. Place the rest of the spinach filling on top of tofu cheese filling.
9. Spread 1 cup of the spaghetti sauce on top of the spinach filling.

10. Place last 4 lasagne pasta strips on top of spaghetti sauce. Spread 1 cup of spaghetti sauce on top of the pasta strips.
11. Finally add the Cheesy Tofu Topping. Take a fork full of Cheesy Tofu Topping and drizzle on surface in a random pattern.
12. Bake at 375° for 20-25 minutes. Let cool 10-15 minutes before cutting. Serve with garlic bread and a Mixed Green Salad.

Makes 6-8 servings

Stuffed Cabbage

12 large leaves of cabbage - boiled
Filling:
1 cup dry textured soy protein
1-1/2 cups diced onions (2 medium)
1 clove minced garlic
3 tablespoons extra virgin olive oil
1/2 tablespoon salt
1/2 teaspoon black ground pepper
1 tablespoon parsley
1 teaspoon basil
1 teaspoon oregano
1/2 teaspoon paprika
1/4 teaspoon sage
1/4 teaspoon summer savory
1/4 teaspoon marjoram
1/4 teaspoon coriander
1/8 teaspoon nutmeg (fresh ground)
1 cup water
1 cup applesauce - unsweetened
1 cup cooked brown rice
2/3 cup uncooked old fashioned rolled oats
2/3 cup bread crumbs
Tomato Sauce:
6 ounces of tomato paste
1-1/3 cups water
1-1/2 tablespoons sugar
1/2 teaspoon salt
1/2 tablespoon vinegar

1. Heat skillet, add dry textured soy protein and toast until lightly browned, stir constantly. Set aside.
2. Bring a pot of water to boil. Add 12 large leaves of cabbage that has

been carefully separated from the head. (Cut stem end to help loosen leaves and gently pull back to remove leaves). Boil cabbage leaves for about 5-10 minutes, or until tender. Remove from water and rinse under cold water in a colander to stop cabbage from cooking. Set aside on a plate. You can use the cooking water in filling and sauce, or keep for soup stock.

3. While cabbage is cooking, mix together salt, black pepper, parsley, basil, oregano, paprika, sage, summer savory, marjoram, coriander, and nutmeg. Set spices aside. Dice onions and mince garlic.

4. Heat skillet, add 1 tablespoon extra virgin olive oil and onions. Saute for 2-3 minutes or until onions are slightly translucent. Add minced garlic and spices. Saute for 1-2 minutes or until onions are translucent.

5. Add toasted textured soy protein and 2 tablespoons extra virgin olive oil. Stir a minute to allow textured soy protein to soak up oil. Then add water, applesauce and oats. Turn off heat and let sit for 10 minutes.

6. When textured soy protein has softened, mix together with the cooked brown rice and bread crumbs. Let sit for about 5 minutes.

7. Lay out cabbage leaves. Divide filling into 12 parts. Put one part of filling on center of each of the cabbage leaves.

8. Fold sides of leaf toward the center, over the filling. Then roll up leaf, starting from the stem end. Repeat this step for all the leaves.

9. Mix together tomato paste, salt, sugar, water and vinegar.

10. Preheat oven to 400°. Put some of the tomato sauce on the bottom of a 9 x 13 inch baking dish. Place the 12 cabbage rolls seem side down in the baking dish. Pour the rest of the tomato sauce on top of the cabbage rolls. Cover top of baking dish with lid or aluminum foil.

11. Bake covered at 400° for about 30 minutes. Then reduce heat to 350°, uncover and bake another 10 minutes. Remove from oven and let cool for 2-3 minutes before serving. Serve with Mashed Potatoes, peas and applesauce; or with a Mixed Green Salad.

Makes 12 cabbage rolls (4-6 servings)

CHAPTER 15: SIDE DISHES, GRAVIES & SAUCES

SIDE DISHES

Broccoli in a Cheesy Sauce

2 stalks fresh broccoli or 8 ounces frozen broccoli
1 tablespoon unbleached bread flour
1/4 teaspoon salt
1 tablespoon nutritional yeast
1/8 teaspoon turmeric
dash of black ground pepper
1/3 cup soymilk

1. Wash broccoli, peel stems and slice into 1/2 inch rounds. Cut flowerets into small bits sized bits.
2. Mix together flour, salt, nutritional yeast, turmeric and pepper. Stir in soymilk. Mix until there are no lumps.
3. *Microwave Method:* Place soymilk mixture in a microwave cooking dish. Microwave mixture until it thickens, stirring every 15-30 seconds to prevent lumping. When sauce has thickened, cover and set aside.
4. Place broccoli and 1 tablespoon water in a covered microwave cooking dish. Microwave for 2-3 minutes, stir and microwave another 2-3 minutes or until broccoli is tender. Add sauce, mix to coat broccoli. Cover, let sit 1-2 minutes, then serve.
3. *Steamer/Stove Top Method:* Put broccoli in a steamer basket and place in a sauce pan with water below basket. Bring water to a boil and steam broccoli until tender, about 5 minutes.
4. While broccoli is steaming, pour soymilk mixture into a sauce pan and bring mixture to a boil, stir constantly. When sauce begins to thicken, turn off heat. Mix steamed broccoli and sauce together, and serve.

Makes 2 servings

Brussel Sprouts in a Quick and Easy Cheesy Sauce

8 ounces of Brussel sprouts - cut in half (fresh or frozen)
3 tablespoons soymilk
2 tablespoons nutritional yeast
1 tablespoon extra virgin olive oil
1/8 teaspoon salt

1. Cut Brussel Sprouts in half. If using frozen sprouts, cook in

microwave oven for 1 minute then cut in half. Brussel Sprouts will be easier to cut if not completely frozen or cooked. If using fresh sprouts, wash, trim end and cut in half.

2. *Microwave Method:* Place Brussel sprouts in a covered microwave proof bowl. Microwave the halved sprouts on high for 2-3 minutes. Stir sprouts around and microwave another 2-3 minutes or until tender.
Steamer Method: Place Brussel sprouts in a steamer basket. Put steamer basket in a sauce pan with water below basket. Cover and bring to a full boil. Let Brussel sprouts steam for about 5 minutes or until tender. (Save water for soup stock.)
Stove Top Method: Put Brussel spouts into briskly boiling water that has been salted to taste. Boil for 2-5 minutes or until tender. Do not overcook. Remove from water and save water for soup stock.

3. When sprouts are done cooking by any of the above methods, add soymilk, nutritional yeast, extra virgin olive oil and salt. Toss to completely coat all the sprouts. Salt and pepper to taste, and serve.

Makes 2 servings

Golden Tofu Bread Stuffing

Golden Tofu Cubes:
    8 ounces firm tofu (1/2 of a 16-ounce block)
    1/2 tablespoon canola oil
    1/4 teaspoon salt
    1/4 teaspoon turmeric
Bread Stuffing:
    6 cups dry bread cubes
    3/4 cup chopped onion (1 medium)
    3/4 cup chopped celery (2-3 large stalks)
    1/2 cup chopped carrot (1 large)
    1/2 cup chopped cabbage (1-2 leaves)
    1/4 cup peas (fresh or frozen)
    1/2 teaspoon salt
    1/2 teaspoon sage
    1/4 teaspoon onion powder
    1/4 teaspoon garlic powder
    1/8 teaspoon turmeric
    1/8 teaspoon black ground pepper
    2 tablespoons canola oil
    1/2 cup applesauce - unsweetened
    3/4 cup vegetable broth (or salted water)
    1/2 cup chopped walnuts or soynuts

1. Cut tofu into 1/2 inch cubes. Heat 1/2 tablespoon canola oil in a saute pan. Add tofu cubes, 1/4 teaspoon salt and 1/4 teaspoon turmeric. Stir to thoroughly coat all sides of tofu. Saute 5-7 minutes or until golden brown. Set aside. Chop onion, celery, carrot and cabbage.
2. Heat 1 tablespoon canola oil in a saute pan. Add onions, celery, carrots, cabbage, peas and salt. Stir well and saute for 5 minutes, or until vegetables become tender but not browned. Add sage, onion powder, garlic powder, turmeric and black ground pepper. Stir well and turn off heat. Let sit for a minute.
3. In a large bowl add bread cubes, sauteed vegetables, unsweetened applesauce and 1/2 tablespoon canola oil. Toss lightly. Then add liquid, (vegetable broth or water mixed with 1/2 teaspoon salt). Toss again, then let sit for 10 minutes to allow bread cubes to absorb liquid.
4. Once bread stuffing has absorbed all the liquid and is slightly moist, mix in golden tofu cubes and chopped walnuts or soynuts.
5. Preheat oven to 350°. Oil a 9 x 12 baking pan with canola oil. Spread golden tofu bread stuffing evenly and sprinkle 1/2 tablespoon canola oil over top. Bake for 20 minutes or until top of stuffing is lightly browned. Let cool for a few minutes before serving. Serve plain or with gravy on top along with a burger or Lentil Rice Tofu Loaf; mashed potatoes or sweet potatoes; broccoli or peas; and cranberry sauce or applesauce. This stuffing freezes very well, freeze any leftovers. To thaw, microwave or place in a toaster-oven on low until warm.

Makes 8-10 servings

Mashed Potatoes

4-5 potatoes
1/2 cup soymilk
2 teaspoons canola oil

---

1. Heat and salt water to taste. Peel and cut potatoes into chunks, add to water. Boil for 15-20 minutes or until potatoes are tender. The potatoes are done when they can easily be poked with a fork.
2. Remove potatoes from water and place in a bowl. Add soymilk and canola oil.
3. Mash potatoes with a potato masher or electric hand mixer until smooth. If potatoes are over mashed, they will become pasty. If potatoes are under mashed, they become lumpy. Salt and pepper to taste. Serve plain or with gravy.

Makes 2-4 servings

Mashed Sweet Potatoes

1-2 sweet potatoes (1 large or 2 small)
1/3 cup soymilk
1 tablespoon applesauce - unsweetened

1. *Stove top method:* Heat and salt water to taste. Peel and cut sweet potatoes into chunks, add to water. Boil for 15 minutes, until potatoes are tender. Sweet potatoes are done when they can easily be poked with a fork. Remove sweet potatoes from water and place in a bowl. *Microwave method:* Peel sweet potatoes and place in a covered microwave dish. Microwave for 7-9 minutes, or until sweet potatoes become soft and a fork can easily poke them.
2. Add soymilk and applesauce. Mash with a potato masher or electric hand mixer until smooth. Salt and pepper to taste.

Makes 2 servings

Soy Cheesy Turnup Greens

8 ounces of frozen turnup greens (or 2 cups of fresh)
1/4 cup water
2 tablespoons unbleached bread flour
2 tablespoons nutritional yeast
2 tablespoons soy flour
1/2 teaspoon salt
1/4 teaspoon onion powder
1/4 teaspoon garlic powder
1 tablespoon extra virgin olive oil
1/2 teaspoon soy sauce
3/4 cup soymilk

1. In a 1-1/2 quart pot, cook turnup greens in 1/4 cup water and 1/4 teaspoon salt. Bring to a boil, stir, turn down heat and cover with a lid. Let cook for 10-15 minutes, stirring occasionally.
2. Mix together bread flour, nutritional yeast, soy flour, 1/4 teaspoon salt, onion powder and garlic powder. Then slowly stir in extra virgin olive oil, soy sauce and soymilk. Mix to a smooth consistency.
3. Turn up heat and pour soymilk mixture into turnup greens. Stir constantly until soymilk mixture begins to thicken. Then turn heat down to low and let simmer for 5 minutes, stirring occasionally. Serve with Mashed Potatoes and a burger or Lentil Rice Tofu Loaf.

Makes 2-3 servings

Brown Mushroom Gravy

> **2 cups of sliced button mushrooms**
> **1 teaspoon extra virgin olive oil**
> **1/2 teaspoon salt**
> **1/4 teaspoon sage**
> **1/4 teaspoon onion powder**
> **1/4 teaspoon garlic powder**
> **3 tablespoons unbleached bread flour**
> **2 tablespoons soy sauce**
> **1/2 cup water**
> **1 cup soymilk**

1. Mix together flour and 1/4 teaspoon salt. Then add soy sauce, water and soymilk. Mix to a smooth consistency and set aside. Slice button mushrooms.
2. Heat extra virgin olive oil in a sauce pan. Add sliced mushrooms and 1/4 teaspoon salt. Stir and cover with a lid. When mushrooms begin to produce a liquid stir in sage, onion powder and garlic powder.
3. Increase heat and pour soymilk mixture in with mushrooms. Bring to a boil stirring constantly. When gravy begins to thicken, reduce heat. Salt and pepper to taste. Cover with a lid until ready to serve. Serve with Mashed Potatoes, Golden Tofu Bread Stuffing, brown rice, a burger or Lentil Rice Tofu Loaf.

Makes about 2-1/2 cups (2-4 servings)

Low-Fat Soy-Rich Golden Brown Gravy

> **2 tablespoons unbleached bread flour**
> **1-1/2 tablespoons soy flour**
> **1/2 teaspoon salt**
> **1/2 teaspoon onion powder**
> **1/2 teaspoon garlic powder**
> **1/2 teaspoon turmeric**
> **1/4 teaspoon sage**
> **3/4 cup water**
> **1 teaspoon soy sauce**
> **1 cup soymilk**

1. Mix together bread flour, soy flour, salt, onion powder, garlic powder,

turmeric and sage. Stir in water, soy sauce and soymilk. Mix to a smooth consistency. (For a thicker gravy, use 2 tablespoons less water. For a thinner gravy, add 2 more tablespoons of water.)

2. Pour mixture into a sauce pan. Bring to a boil, stirring constantly. When gravy begins to thicken, reduce heat to low. Continue stirring for a minute. Then turn heat off and cover until ready to serve to prevent a skin from forming on top. Serve over Mashed Potatoes, Golden Tofu Bread Stuffing, brown rice, a burger or Lentil Rice Tofu Loaf.

Makes 2 cups (2-4 servings)

Shiitake Mushroom Gravy

2-3 large dried shiitake mushrooms (or 4-5 small)
1/2 teaspoon salt
3 tablespoons unbleached bread flour
1/4 teaspoon ground sage
1/4 teaspoon onion powder
1/4 teaspoon garlic powder
1/4 teaspoon ground turmeric
1 tablespoon soy sauce
3/4 cup water
1 cup soymilk

1. Rinse mushrooms, let sit in 1/2 cup water and set aside to soften.
2. Mix together flour, salt, sage, onion powder, garlic powder, and turmeric. Then add 1/4 cup water, soy sauce and soymilk. Mix until there are no lumps. When mushrooms are soft and pliable, cut into small pieces with a pair of scissors. Add mushroom pieces and soaking water to mixture.
3. Pour gravy mixture into a sauce pan and bring to a boil, stirring constantly. When gravy begins to thicken, reduce heat to low. Keep stirring for a minute, then turn heat off and cover. Gravy is done and ready to serve. Keep covered until served or a skin will form on top. Serve over Mashed Potatoes, brown rice, Golden Tofu Bread Stuffing, Lentil Rice Tofu Loaf or a burger.

Makes about 1-3/4 cups gravy (2-4 servings)

SAUCES

Bechamel Sauce (Creamy White Sauce)

2 tablespoons unbleached bread flour
1/2 teaspoon salt
1/8 teaspoon ground nutmeg
pinch of white ground pepper
3/4 cup soymilk
1/4 cup water
2 teaspoons extra virgin olive oil

1. Mix together flour, salt, nutmeg and white pepper. Add water, soymilk and extra virgin olive oil. Mix to a smooth consistency.
2. Pour mixture in a sauce pan and heat until it begins to boil and thicken, stir constantly. Then turn heat off and cover with lid until ready to serve. Sauce is excellent over cauliflower, rutabagas, or beans and rice.
Makes 1 cup (2-4 servings)

Golden Mushroom Sauce

2 cups of sliced button mushrooms
1-1/2 cups soymilk
1/3 cup water
2-1/2 tablespoons unbleached bread flour
1-1/2 tablespoons soy flour
1 tablespoon virgin olive oil
1 teaspoon parsley
1/2 teaspoon onion powder
1/2 teaspoon garlic powder
1/2 teaspoon salt
1/4 teaspoon turmeric
1/4 teaspoon ground sage

1. Mix together bread flour and soy flour. Stir in water and soymilk, mix to a smooth consistency. Set aside. Wash and slice button mushrooms.
2. Heat virgin olive oil in a sauce pan. Add sliced mushrooms and salt. Saute for 2-3 minutes or until mushrooms begin to produce a liquid.
3. Add parsley, onion powder, garlic powder, turmeric, and sage. Stir well. Slowly stir in the soymilk-flour mixture. Stir continuously until sauce begins to boil and starts to thicken. Then turn heat to low and cover until ready to serve, stir occasionally. Serve over beans and rice,

burgers, Mashed Potatoes, Golden Tofu Bread Stuffing or Lentil Rice Tofu Loaf.

Makes 2 cups (2-4 servings)

Original Thick and Chunky Spaghetti Sauce

3/4 cup dry textured soy protein
1-1/2 cups diced onions (2 medium)
1 cup grated carrots (2 medium)
1-1/2 tablespoons minced garlic (3 large cloves)
1 tablespoon virgin olive oil
26.5 ounces of chopped tomatoes (1 carton/container)
12 ounces of tomato paste
1 small bay leaf (or 1/2 large)
2-1/2 cups water
4 teaspoons sugar
2 teaspoons salt
1 tablespoon oregano
1 tablespoon marjoram
1 tablespoon parsley
1 tablespoon basil
1 teaspoon summer savory
1 teaspoon thyme
1/2 teaspoon onion powder
1/2 teaspoon garlic powder
1/8 teaspoon black ground pepper

1. Lightly toast textured soy protein to a golden brown, set aside.
2. Mix together oregano, marjoram, parsley, basil, summer savory, thyme, onion powder, garlic powder, and black ground pepper. Set aside.
3. Dice onions, grate carrots, and mince garlic cloves.
4. Heat 1/2 tablespoon of virgin olive oil in a 3 quart pot. Stir in onions and 1/4 teaspoon salt. Saute for 3-4 minutes, until onions are slightly transparent. Add grated carrots and 1/4 teaspoon salt. Saute for 2 minutes. Add minced garlic, saute for 1 minute. Then stir in toasted textured soy protein, spice mix and 1/2 tablespoon virgin olive oil.
5. Pour in chopped tomatoes, tomato paste, water, bay leaf, sugar and 1-1/2 teaspoons salt. Mix well, reduce heat and cover.
6. Simmer for 30 minutes, stirring occasionally. Serve with any pasta. This sauce freezes very well. Store in 2 cup (2 serving) containers. To thaw, put in sauce pan and heat on low until completely warm.

Makes 2 quarts (6-8 servings)

Thick and Chunky Harvest Spaghetti Sauce

3/4 cup roasted green bell pepper (1 medium)
3/4 cup dry toasted textured soy protein
1-1/2 cups diced onions (3 medium)
1 cup cooked mashed pumpkin (or an 8-ounce can)
1-1/2 tablespoons minced garlic (3 large cloves)
1-1/2 tablespoons olive oil
2 teaspoons salt
1 tablespoon basil
1 tablespoon oregano
1 tablespoon parsley
1 tablespoon marjoram
1 teaspoon summer savory
1 teaspoon thyme
1 teaspoon paprika
1/2 teaspoon onion powder
1/2 teaspoon garlic powder
1/2 teaspoon rosemary
1/8 teaspoon ground black pepper
1/8 teaspoon cayenne pepper
26.5 ounces chopped tomatoes (1 carton/container)
12 ounces of tomato paste
2 cups water
1 bay leaf
1 tablespoon sugar
1 teaspoon vinegar

1. Roast a green bell pepper. Cut pepper in half, remove seeds and inner membrane. Place on a baking sheet skin side up. Broil in a toaster-oven until skin begins to char and blister. Transfer to a bowl and cover with a lid to steam for 10 minutes. Then carefully remove the skin, dice and set aside.
2. Lightly toast textured soy protein to a golden brown, set aside.
3. Mix together basil, oregano, parsley, marjoram, summer savory, thyme, paprika, onion powder, garlic powder, rosemary, black pepper and cayenne pepper. Set aside.
4. Dice onions and mince garlic cloves. Heat 1/2 tablespoon of olive oil in a 3 quart pot. Stir in onions and 1/4 teaspoon salt. Saute for 3-4 minutes, until onions are slightly transparent. Add pumpkin, minced garlic and 1/2 teaspoon salt. Saute for 2-3 minutes.
5. Add toasted textured soy protein, 1 tablespoon olive oil, 1/2 teaspoon salt and spice mix, stir well. Add roasted green bell peppers, mix well.

6. Pour in chopped tomatoes, tomato paste, water, bay leaf, sugar, vinegar and 3/4 teaspoon salt. Mix thoroughly, reduce heat and cover.
7. Simmer for 30 minutes, stirring occasionally. Serve over any pasta. This sauce freezes very well. Store in 2 cup (2 serving) containers. To thaw, put in sauce pan and heat on low until completely warm.

Makes 2 quarts (6-8 servings)

Thick and Chunky Mushroom Spaghetti Sauce

3/4 cup dry textured soy protein
1 cup sliced button mushrooms (6 -9 medium)
1 cup diced onions (1 medium)
1 cup grated carrots (2 medium)
1-1/2 tablespoons minced garlic (3 large cloves)
1 tablespoon virgin olive oil
26.5 ounces of chopped tomatoes (1 carton/container)
12 ounces of tomato paste
1 small bay leaf (or 1/2 large)
2-1/2 cups water
1-1/2 tablespoons sugar
2-1/4 teaspoons salt
1 tablespoon oregano
1 tablespoon marjoram
1 tablespoon parsley
1 tablespoon basil
1 teaspoon summer savory
1 teaspoon thyme
1/2 teaspoon onion powder
1/2 teaspoon garlic powder
1/8 teaspoon black ground pepper

1. Lightly toast textured soy protein to a golden brown, set aside.
2. Mix together oregano, marjoram, parsley, basil, summer savory, thyme, onion powder, garlic powder, and black ground pepper. Set aside.
3. Slice mushrooms, dice onions, grate carrots, and mince garlic cloves.
4. Heat 1/2 tablespoon of virgin olive oil in a 3 quart pot, stir in mushrooms, onions and 1/2 teaspoon salt. Saute for 3-4 minutes, until mushrooms produce a liquid and onions are slightly transparent. Add grated carrots and 1/4 teaspoon salt. Saute for 2 minutes. Add minced garlic and saute for 1 minute. Add toasted textured soy protein, spice mix and 1/2 tablespoon virgin olive oil, stir well.

163

5. Pour in chopped tomatoes, tomato paste, water, bay leaf, sugar and 1-1/4 teaspoons salt. Mix well, reduce heat and cover.
6. Simmer for 30 minutes, stirring occasionally. Serve with any pasta. This sauce freezes very well. Store in 2 cup (2 serving) containers. To thaw, put in sauce pan and heat on low until completely warm.

Makes 2 quarts (6-8 servings)

CHAPTER 16: DESSERTS, SNACKS & DRINKS

BAKED DESSERTS

Oatmeal Raisin Spice Nut Cookies

1/2 cup raisins
2 tablespoons water
1/2 teaspoon lemon juice
6 ounces of silken tofu (1/2 package)
5 tablespoons canola oil
2 tablespoons soymilk
1 cup applesauce - unsweetened
1 teaspoon pure vanilla extract
2 cups uncooked old-fashioned rolled oats
1 cup unbleached bread flour
1 cup sugar
1 tablespoon baking powder
2 teaspoons ground cinnamon
1/2 teaspoon ground ginger
1/2 teaspoon ground allspice
1/2 teaspoon salt
1/2 cup chopped walnuts

1. Cut raisins in half and soak in water and lemon juice for 10 minutes.
2. While raisins are soaking, blend silken tofu, canola oil, soymilk, applesauce and vanilla extract in a food processor. Set aside.
3. Mix together unbleached bread flour, sugar, baking powder, ground cinnamon, ground ginger, ground allspice and salt. Add silken tofu mixture, soaked raisins, the remaining lemon water, and chopped walnuts. Mix until well combined.
4. Preheat oven to 350° and oil two cookie sheets with canola oil.
5. Using a big spoon, drop 24 mounds of cookie dough onto the oiled cookie sheets (12 cookies per sheet). Wet fingers and gently pat down on mounds to form 1/4 inch high and 3 inch round cookies.
6. Bake at 350° for 10-15 minutes or until nicely browned. Let cool on a rack before serving. Store in an air tight container or storage bag.

Makes 24 cookies

Pumpkin Spice Walnut Cookies

5.3 ounces tofu (1/3 of a 16-ounce block, soft or firm)
5 tablespoons canola oil
2 tablespoons soymilk
1 teaspoon pure vanilla extract
1/2 teaspoon salt
1/4 teaspoon lemon juice
1 cup sugar
1 cup pumpkin (fresh cooked or canned)
2 cups unbleached flour (bread or all-purpose)
2-1/2 teaspoons baking powder
1/2 tablespoon ground cinnamon
1/2 teaspoon baking soda
1 teaspoon ground allspice
1/2 teaspoon ginger
1/2 cup chopped walnuts

1. In a food processor combine tofu, canola oil, soymilk, pure vanilla extract, salt, lemon juice, and sugar. Blend until smooth and creamy.
2. Mash fresh cooked pumpkin or measure out canned pumpkin. Add to tofu mixture and transfer into a big mixing bowl.
3. Mix together flour, baking powder, cinnamon, baking soda, allspice, and ginger. Add to pumpkin-tofu mixture, mix well.
4. Add chopped walnuts, stir until well combined.
5. Preheat oven to 375° and oil 2 cookie sheets with canola oil.
6. Using a spoon, drop 24 mounds of cookie dough onto the cookie sheets (12 cookies on each sheet). Wet fingers with water and pat cookie dough down to form 1/4 inch high and 3 inch round cookies.
7. Bake at 375° for 9-12 minutes. Cool on a wire rack. These are wonderful soft batch cookies. To keep fresh tasting, store in an air tight container or storage bag.

Makes 24 cookies

Pumpkin Walnut Cake

2 cups cooked pumpkin (fresh cooked or canned)
5.3 ounces tofu (1/3 of a 16-ounce block, soft or firm)
1/2 cup soymilk
1/2 tablespoon vanilla
3 tablespoons canola oil
1-1/3 cups sugar

2 cups flour (unbleached bread or all purpose)
1 tablespoon baking powder
2-1/2 teaspoons ground cinnamon
1/2 teaspoon salt
1/2 teaspoon ground allspice
1/2 teaspoon ground clove
1/2 teaspoon ground ginger
1/3 cup chopped walnuts

1. In a big mixing bowl, mash up fresh cooked pumpkin or scoop out canned pumpkin. Set aside.
2. In a food processor combine tofu, soymilk, vanilla, and canola oil. Blend 1-2 minutes, until silky smooth and creamy.
3. Add tofu mixture to pumpkin, mix well. Then mix in sugar.
4. In another bowl, mix together flour, baking powder, cinnamon, salt, allspice, clove and ginger. Add this to pumpkin mixture.
5. Thoroughly mix all ingredients together, then stir in chopped walnuts.
6. Preheat oven to 375°. Oil a 13 x 9 inch baking pan with canola oil and lightly flour pan. Then spread pumpkin walnut batter evenly in pan.
7. Bake at 375° for 30-35 minutes. Pumpkin Walnut Cake is done when a tooth pick or stick inserted in the center comes out clean. Cool thoroughly in pan.
8. Leave plain or frost top with Tofu Cream Cheese Frosting and top with a few chopped walnuts for decoration (*optional*). Cut into 16 bars.

Makes 16 servings

Tofu Cream Cheese Frosting

2.5 ounces tofu (1/6 of a 16-ounce block, soft or firm)
1 tablespoon canola oil
1/2 teaspoon soymilk
1 teaspoon pure vanilla extract
1/4 teaspoon salt
1/4 teaspoon lemon juice
1 cup powdered sugar

1. In a food processor, blend tofu and canola oil until tofu is completely broken up. Add soymilk, vanilla, salt and lemon juice, blend until it forms a smooth paste. Add powdered sugar and blend until creamy.
2. Let frosting sit for a few minutes, then blend again.
3. Refrigerate an hour, then spread over cooled Pumpkin Walnut Cake.

Makes 1 cup

Walnut Brownies

> 4 tablespoons cocoa powder
> 1-1/3 cups sugar
> 3 tablespoons canola oil
> 1/2 cup soymilk
> 1 tablespoon water
> 1/2 tablespoon vanilla
> 1 cup unbleached flour (bread or all-purpose)
> 2 tablespoons soy flour
> 1 teaspoon baking powder
> 1/2 teaspoon salt
> 1/3 cup chopped walnuts

1. In a mixing bowl combine cocoa powder, sugar, and canola oil. Stir until smooth. Then add soymilk, water and vanilla.
2. In another bowl, combine unbleached bread flour, soy flour, baking powder and salt.
3. Add the flour mix to the cocoa mixture, stir until smooth and creamy. Then add chopped walnuts and mix well.
4. Preheat oven to 375°. Oil a 9 x 9 inch baking pan with canola oil. Spread brownie mixture evenly into pan.
5. Bake at 375° for 20-28 minutes or until a wooden pick (toothpick) inserted in center comes out somewhat clean. Cool in pan for at least 15 minutes before cutting or eating. Once brownies are completely cool, cut into 16 squares or 8 rectangles, and enjoy.

Makes 8 servings

FROZEN DESSERTS & SMOOTHIES

Banana Sorbet

> 1 frozen ripe banana
> 1/4 cup soymilk
> 1 tablespoon sugar

1. Blend in a food processor for 1-2 minutes or until smooth and creamy.

Makes about 1-1/4 cups (1-2 servings)

Strawberry Sorbet

1 cup frozen strawberries (8 ounces)
1/4 cup soymilk
1 tablespoon sugar

1. Blend in a food processor for 1-2 minutes or until smooth and creamy.
Makes about 1-1/4 cups (1-2 servings)

Banana Strawberry Smoothie

1 frozen ripe banana
1 cup fresh strawberries
3/4 cup soymilk
1 tablespoon sugar or honey (optional)

1. Blend in a food processor or blender for 1-2 minutes, until smooth and creamy. (Raspberries can be used instead of strawberries.)
Makes about 2-3/4 cups (2 servings)

Tropical Fruit Smoothie

1 frozen banana
1 cup fresh or canned pineapple
3/4 cup soymilk
1 tablespoon honey or sugar (optional)

1. Blend in a food processor or blender for 1-2 minutes, until smooth and creamy. (Mango can be used instead of pineapple.)
Makes about 2-3/4 cups (2 servings)

PUDDINGS

Chocolate Pudding

2 tablespoons cocoa powder
1/3 cup unbleached bread flour
1/2 cup sugar
1/4 teaspoon salt

2 cups soymilk
2 teaspoons pure vanilla extract

---

1. Mix together cocoa powder, flour, sugar, and salt. Slowly stir in soymilk. Mix until there are no lumps.
2. *Stove top method:* Pour this mixture into a sauce pan and heat until it boils and begins to thicken. Stir constantly. Don't over boil pudding or a burnt and bitter taste will develop. Remove from heat and continue stirring for 1-2 minutes. Then cover and let cool.
   Microwave method: Pour mixture into microwave-proof covered dish. Microwave for 4-5 minutes, stirring mixture every 30 seconds until it begins to thicken. Remove from microwave and let cool.
3. Once pudding cools, add pure vanilla extract. Whip pudding with a hand blender or a whisk. Transfer into 4 individual containers, cover and refrigerate for at least 1 hour before serving.

Makes about 3 cups (4 servings)

Low-Fat Chocolate Pudding

2 tablespoons cocoa powder
1/3 cup unbleached bread flour
1/2 cup sugar
1/4 teaspoon salt
1 cup soymilk
1 cup water
2 teaspoons pure vanilla extract

---

1. Mix together cocoa powder, flour, sugar, and salt. Slowly stir in water and soymilk. Mix until there are no lumps.
2. *Stove top method:* Pour this mixture into a sauce pan and heat until it boils and begins to thicken. Stir constantly. Don't over boil pudding or a burnt and bitter taste will develop. Remove from heat and continue stirring for 1-2 minutes. Then cover and let cool.
   Microwave method: Pour mixture into microwave-proof covered dish. Microwave for 4-5 minutes, stirring mixture every 30 seconds until it begins to thicken. Remove from microwave and let cool.
3. Once pudding cools, add pure vanilla extract. Whip pudding with a hand blender or a whisk. Transfer into 4 individual containers, cover and refrigerate for at least 1 hour before serving.

Makes about 3 cups (4 servings)

Quick Chocolate Silken Pudding

    12.3 ounces silken tofu (1 carton)
    1/2 cup sugar
    2 tablespoons cocoa powder
    2 teaspoons pure vanilla extract
    1/4 teaspoon salt

1. In a food processor blend together silken tofu, sugar, cocoa powder, vanilla extract and salt. Blend 1 minute, until silky smooth and creamy.
2. Transfer into 6-8 individual dishes and refrigerate for at least 1 hour before serving.

Makes about 2 cups (8 servings)

Quick Lemon Silken Pudding

    12.3 ounces silken tofu (1 carton)
    1/2 cup sugar
    2 tablespoons lemon juice
    1/8 teaspoon salt

1. In a food processor blend together silken tofu, sugar, lemon juice and salt. Blend 1 minute, until silky smooth and creamy.
2. Transfer into 6-8 individual dishes and refrigerate for at least 1 hour before serving.

Makes about 2 cups (6-8 servings)

SNACKS

Savory Shiitake Walnut Swirls

Dough:
    1 cup unbleached bread flour
    1 tablespoon baking powder
    1 teaspoon sugar
    1/2 teaspoon salt
    1/2 cup soymilk
    1/2 teaspoon lemon juice
    2 tablespoons extra virgin olive oil

Filling:
1/4 cup dry shiitake mushrooms (8-10 small or 4-6 large)
1/4 cup water
1/3 cup walnuts
1/2 tablespoon Dijon mustard
1 tablespoon ketchup
1 tablespoon nutritional yeast
1/8 teaspoon salt

1. Soak shiitake mushrooms in 1/4 cup water for 5-10 minutes.
2. While mushrooms are soaking, sift flour into a bowl. Mix in baking powder, sugar and 1/2 teaspoon salt.
3. Mix in 1 tablespoon extra virgin olive oil. Sprinkle oil into flour and stir. Then with your thumb and pointer, pinch oil lumps in flour to help distribute oil. Set aside.
4. Strain mushrooms, pouring any left over water into flour mix. Place soaked mushrooms in a food processor. Add walnuts, Dijon mustard, ketchup, nutritional yeast and 1/8 teaspoon salt. Grind until everything is minced and well combined. Let sit.
5. Mix together soymilk and lemon juice. Add 1/4 cup of the soymilk mix to the flour mix and fold. Add another 1/4 cup of the soymilk mix and fold again. Mix gently, just until dough begins to hold together.
6. Wipe down a work surface with vinegar. Dry off with a clean towel and lightly dust with flour.
7. Place dough on floured surface, lightly flour top and gently flatten out to 1/4 inch thick. Sprinkle 1/2 tablespoon extra virgin olive oil over top surface and fold dough into thirds. Flatten again to about 1/4 inch thick. Shape into a 5 x 10 inch rectangle. Coat top with another 1/2 tablespoon extra virgin olive oil.
8. Spread shiitake mushroom-walnut filling evenly over dough. Go all the way to the edge of three sides, but leave 1 inch uncovered at one of the 10 inch long ends. Roll dough up like a jelly roll - start at the 10 inch side that has the filling up to its edge and roll up the 5 inch width until you end at the 10 inch side that doesn't have filling to the edge.
9. Preheat oven to 350°. Lightly oil a baking sheet with extra virgin olive oil. Cut roll into 12 slices and place each slice on its side, so you can see the swirl.
10. Bake at 350° for about 10 minutes, or until lightly browned and swirls rise. Let cool for 3-5 minutes before serving. These swirls are excellent as an appetizer, as a midday snack, or as a tasty side dish with soup. Freeze any leftovers. To thaw, warm in a toaster-oven for 1-2 minutes.

Makes 12 swirls (3-6 servings)

Walnut Raisin Cinnamon Swirls

Dough:
> 1 cup unbleached bread flour
> 1 tablespoon baking powder
> 1/2 tablespoon sugar
> 1/2 teaspoon salt
> 1/2 teaspoon lemon juice
> 1/2 teaspoon ground cinnamon
> 1/8 teaspoon ginger powder
> 2 tablespoons canola oil
> 1/2 cup soymilk

Filling:
> 1/2 cup walnuts
> 1/4 cup raisins
> 1/4 cup water
> 1-1/2 tablespoons honey
> 1 tablespoon maple syrup
> 1/8 teaspoon salt
> 1 teaspoon ground cinnamon

1. Soak raisins in 1/4 cup water for 5-10 minutes.
2. While raisins are soaking, sift flour into a bowl. Mix in baking powder, sugar, 1/2 teaspoon salt, 1/2 teaspoon ground cinnamon, and 1/8 teaspoon ginger powder.
3. Mix in 1 tablespoon canola oil. Sprinkle oil into flour and stir. With your thumb and pointer, pinch oil lumps in flour to help distribute oil.
4. Strain raisins, pouring any left over water into flour mix. Place soaked raisins in a food processor. Add walnuts, honey, maple syrup, 1/8 teaspoon salt and 1 teaspoon ground cinnamon. Grind until everything is minced and well combined. Let sit.
5. Mix together soymilk and lemon juice. Add 1/4 cup of the soymilk mix to the flour mix and fold. Add another 1/4 cup of the soymilk mix and fold again. Mix gently, just until dough holds together.
6. Wipe down a work surface with vinegar. Dry off with a clean towel and lightly dust with flour.
7. Place dough on floured surface, lightly flour top and gently flatten out to 1/4 inch thick. Sprinkle 1/2 tablespoon canola oil over top surface and fold dough into thirds. Flatten again to about 1/4 inch thick. Shape into a 5 x 10 inch rectangle. Coat top with another 1/2 tablespoon canola oil.

8. Spread walnut-raisin-cinnamon filling evenly over dough. Go all the way to the edge of three sides, but leave 1 inch uncovered at one of the 10 inch long ends. Roll dough up like a jelly roll - start at the 10 inch side that has the filling up to its edge and roll up the 5 inch width until you end at the 10 inch side that doesn't have filling to the edge.
9. Preheat oven to 350°. Lightly oil a baking sheet with canola oil, make sure surface is well coated. Cut roll into 12 slices and place each slice on its side, so you can see the swirl.
10. Bake at 350° for about 10 minutes, or until lightly browned and swirls rise. Let cool for 3-5 minutes before serving. These swirls are excellent with coffee or tea in the morning, as a midday snack, or as a tasty dessert. Freeze any leftover swirls. To thaw, warm up in a toaster-over for 1-2 minutes.

Makes 12 swirls (3-6 servings)

DRINKS

Chocolate Soymilk

1/2 tablespoon cocoa powder
1 tablespoon sugar
1/8 teaspoon salt
1/2 cup water
2 ice cubes
1-1/2 cups soymilk

---

1. Mix together cocoa powder, sugar and salt. Make sure these dry ingredients are thoroughly mixed, so they will better incorporate with the wet ingredients. Otherwise the cocoa powder will bubble up to the surface and won't mix well.
2. Stir water in with mixed dry ingredients. Mix thoroughly. Add 2 ice cubes to cool the liquid. Stir well.
3. Stir in soymilk. Adjust salt and sugar to taste. Salt is needed to create the more full bodied taste like traditional low-fat chocolate milk.
   Quick mix alternative: Instead of stirring ingredients in a glass, use a 24 to 32 ounce jar with a lid to shake up ingredients. First add dry ingredients, cover with lid and shake. Add water, cover with lid again and shake vigorously until there are no chocolate lumps. Then add ice cubes and soymilk. Cover with lid once more, shake again and serve.

Makes 2 cups (1-2 servings)

Hot Cocoa

1 tablespoon cocoa powder
4 teaspoons sugar
1/8 teaspoon salt
1-1/4 cups soymilk
1 cup water

1. Mix together cocoa powder, sugar and salt.
2. Stir in water and soymilk.
3. Heat in microwave for 1-2 minutes, or on stove top until hot, and serve.

Makes 2-1/4 cups (1-2 servings)

Hot Green Tea and Soymilk

1 cup water
2 teaspoons loose leaf green tea or 2 tea bags of green tea
1 cup soymilk
1 tablespoon honey

1. Bring water to a rapid boil, either on a stove top or in a microwave oven. Pour over green tea and let steep for 5 minutes.
2. Warm soymilk and honey in a microwave or on stove top.
3. Add warm soymilk and honey to green tea, and serve. Makes a soothing and nutritious drink.

Makes 2 cups (1-2 servings)

Hot Mocha

1 tablespoon cocoa powder
4 teaspoons sugar
1/8 teaspoon salt
1-1/4 cups strong coffee
1 cup soymilk

1. Mix together cocoa powder, sugar and salt.
2. Stir in coffee and soymilk.
3. Heat in microwave for 1-2 minutes, or on stove top until hot, and serve.

Makes 2-1/4 cups (1-2 servings)

GLOSSARY

Canola Oil - (kan-OH-luh) the market name for the monounsaturated oil that comes from rapeseed. It has a mild flavor and light color. It can be used for stir-frying, sauteeing, baking, marinades and dressings. Expeller pressed canola oil is best because it uses no chemicals or solvents during extraction. It is available at natural health food stores. Solvent processed canola oil is the kind generally available at most supermarkets.

Cellophane Noodles - (SELL-uh-fayn) clear, transparent Asian noodles made from the starch of green mung beans, also known as bean thread vermicelli. They hold their shape and texture very well in soups and stews, and are an excellent alternative to wheat noodles. They are available at natural health food stores and Asian food markets.

Couscous - (KOOS-koos) a tiny pellet made from semolina flour. It is processed by steaming, drying and crushing durum wheat. Couscous is common in North African dishes. It is available at supermarkets, natural health food stores and gourmet stores.

Dijon mustard - (dee-ZHOHN) a smooth and zesty French-style mustard made with mustard seed, white wine and seasonings. Dijon mustard is well known for its clean, sharp distinctive taste. It is available at supermarkets, natural health food stores and gourmet stores.

Edamame - (eh-da-MAH-me) large soybeans which are harvested when the beans are still green and sweet tasting, also known as green vegetable soybeans. Edamame can be a snack or a main vegetable dish. Either steam or boil in salted water for 5 minutes. Sprinkle with salt, and serve. Just pop the sweet green soybeans out of their pods, and enjoy. You can also hold the pod by the stem, place between your teeth, strip the soybeans from the pod with your teeth and discard the empty pods. Edamame is high in protein, fiber and isoflavones, and contains no cholesterol. Edamame can be found at Asian food markets and natural health food stores, shelled or in the pod.

Hijiki - (hee-JEE-kee) a dark brown seaweed with a strong hearty taste. Used as a vegetable in, or to flavor, soups and other dishes. Available at natural health food stores and Asian food markets.

Hot Pepper Sauce - a fiery sauce made from very hot peppers, vinegar and salt. Hot pepper sauce adds zest to numerous dishes, and is popular in Mexican and Southwestern cuisines. There are many different kinds of hot pepper sauce, ranging in heat and price, available at supermarkets, natural health food stores, gourmet stores and Mexican food markets.

Isoflavone - (i-so-FLAY-voh-nh) a plant-based estrogen (phytoestrogen) found in significant quantities in soybeans and many soy-based products. Isoflavones have the ability to interrupt the function of hormonal estrogen produced in the body. Isoflavones also have antioxidant capabilities that help reduce the effects of LDL cholesterol. The two most studied isoflavones are genistein and daidzein.

Jalapeno Pepper - (ha-la-PEE-nyo) a smooth, dark-green chili pepper, about one to two inches in length with a rounded tip. These peppers are extremely hot, ideal for making chilli and salsa. They are available at supermarkets, gourmet stores, natural health food stores, Mexican food markets and produce markets.

Lecithin - (LESS-uh-thin) a compound extracted from soybean oil. It is a fat-like substance found in the cells of all living organisms. Lecithin is often used in food processing and manufacturing as an emulsifier in products with a high fat or oil content. It promotes stabilization, antioxidation, crystallization and spattering control. Powdered lecithins are also taken to help aid the transformation of fats in the body. Soy lecithin can be found at supermarkets and natural health food stores.

Liquid Hickory Smoke Seasoning - a bottled smokey flavoring, also available in mesquite flavor. It is added to food to give a pork-like, smoked or barbeque taste. Use it in marinades, sauces, sausages, burgers and soups. Various brands of bottled smoke flavoring are available at supermarkets, gourmet stores, and natural health food stores.

Legumes - (le-GYOOMS) refers to a large group of plants that produce seed pods that split along both sides when ripe. Legumes include beans, lentils, peanuts, peas and soybeans. They are available at supermarkets and natural health food stores.

Millet - a tiny, round golden grain that becomes light and fluffy when cooked. Millet surpasses whole wheat and brown rice as a source of protein, some B vitamins, copper, and iron. People allergic to wheat can usually tolerate millet. It is popular in Middle-Eastern, Indian, North African and Chinese cuisines. Millet is available at natural health food stores, Middle-Eastern food markets, Asian food markets and various other ethnic food stores.

Miso - (MEE-so) a paste made by fermenting soybeans cultured with a beneficial bacteria, called Aspergillus orzyae. Grain, like barley or rice, is usually added and the miso is aged in cedar vats for one to three years. It comes in dozens of varieties, with a wide range of colors, flavors and textures. It is highly digestible, but also high in sodium. It's strong flavor makes it an ideal condiment. Miso is most often used to flavor soups, dressings, marinades and gravies. Varieties of miso can be found at natural health food stores and Asian food markets.

Mung bean sprouts - sprouted whole mung beans. These small beans usually have yellow flesh and a green skin. Mung bean sprouts are the most common and popular kind of sprouts. It is used in Asian cooking for soups and stir-fry, and is also excellent in salads. These sprouts are available at supermarkets, natural health food stores, gourmet stores and Asian food markets.

Nutritional Yeast - a dietary supplement and condiment with a distinct yet pleasant aroma. Nutritional yeast is similar to brewer's yeast, but better tasting. Its flavor varies from nutty to cheesy, and is light yellow in color. Nutritional yeast can be used as a cheese substitute and sprinkled on toast, popcorn, spaghetti, or added to soups, spreads, dips, dressings, sauces and casseroles. It is a good source of the B-complex vitamins, trace minerals, and protein. Nutritional yeast is mainly sold at natural health food stores.

Olive Oil - a monounsaturated oil prized throughout the world for both cooking and salads. Generally, domestic olive oil comes from California and imported oils from France, Greece, Italy and Spain. The flavor, color and fragrance of olive oils can vary dramatically. Olive oils are graded by their degree of acidity. The best oils are cold pressed, a chemical-free process that involves only pressure and produces a natural level of low acidity. **Extra virgin olive oil**, the first cold-pressing of the olives, has only 1 percent acidity. It is considered the finest and fruitiest of the olive oils, and is also the most expensive. Extra virgin olive oil can range in color from gold to green. Usually, the deeper the color, the more intense the flavor. **Virgin olive oil** is also a first-press oil, with a slightly higher level of acidity of between 1 and 3 percent. Products labeled **olive oil** contain a combination of chemically refined olive oil and virgin or extra virgin oil. Olive oils are available at supermarkets, gourmet stores, natural health food stores, Italian and many other ethnic food markets.

Pumpkin Seeds - the seeds from the pumpkin, also known as pepitas. They are a popular ingredient in Mexican dishes, and are available with or without their shells. Pumpkin seeds are usually eaten as a nutty snack. When freed of their white hull, the seeds are dark green and have a delicate flavor. Toasting intensifies its flavor. Use toasted pumpkin seeds as a topping for sautes, salads and casseroles. Un-hulled pumpkin seeds are available at supermarkets and natural health food stores. Hulled pumpkin seeds are sold at natural health food stores and Mexican food markets.

Sesame seeds - (se-sah-MEE) tiny, flat seeds that come in shades of ivory, brown, red and black. These seeds are used in Middle Eastern and Asian cuisines. Both hulled and un-hulled sesame seeds are available at natural health food stores. Hulled sesame seeds are available at supermarkets, Middle-Eastern and Asian food markets.

Sesame oil - the oil expressed from sesame seeds. Sesame oil adds a distinct nutty flavor to dishes. It comes in two basic varieties, light and dark. Light sesame oil is good for salad dressing and sauteeing. Dark sesame oil, which burns easily, is drizzled on Asian dishes as a flavor accent after cooking. Both types of sesame oil are available at natural health food stores and Asian food markets.

Shiitake mushroom - (shee-TAH-kay) a rich, woodsy mushroom with an umbrella shaped brown cap, used in traditional Japanese cuisine. It has a very strong flavor, a little goes a long way. It is available fresh or dried at natural health food stores, gourmet stores and Asian food markets.

Snow peas - flat and edible green bean pods, popular in Chinese cuisine. They are usually stir-fried, steamed, or boiled in soups. Snow peas can also be eaten raw in salads. Snow peas can be purchased at supermarkets, natural health food stores, Asian food markets and produce markets.

Soybean Oil - an unsaturated oil, more commonly known as vegetable oil. It is the natural oil extracted from whole soybeans. It is the most widely used oil in the United States. Soybean oil is cholesterol-free and high in polyunsaturated fat. It is popular in Chinese cuisine. Because it is inexpensive, healthful and has a high smoke point, soybean oil is ideal for frying. Partially or fully hydrogenated soybean oil is used to make margarine and shortening. However, when soybean oil is made into these solid forms, it produces trans fatty acids (trans fat) which are just as bad, if not worse, than saturated fats. Soybean oil, under its generic name vegetable oil, can be found at supermarkets and natural health food stores.

Soybeans - the mature ripened beans from the soybean plant. There are more than 1,000 varieties of this nutritious legume, ranging in size from as small as a pea to as large as a grape. Most soybeans are yellow and green, but there are also brown and black varieties. Whole soybeans are an excellent source of protein, isoflavones and dietary fiber. They can be cooked and used in sauces, stews and soups like any other bean. However, mature whole soybeans are less flavorful than other beans. They can be sprouted like mung beans, and used in salads or as a cooked vegetable. Soybeans can also be soaked and roasted as a nutty snack. Soybeans are available at natural health food stores, Asian food markets, and some supermarkets.

Soybean Sprouts - spouted whole soybeans. While not as popular as mung bean sprouts, they are an excellent source of nutrition. Soybean sprouts are packed with protein and vitamin C. They can be used in salads, soups, stir-fry, sautes, and casseroles. Soybean sprouts should be cooked quickly to prevent them from getting too soft and mushy. Fresh soybean sprouts are available at natural health food stores and Asian food markets.

Soy Cheese - a cheese made from soymilk. Most soy cheese is made with caseinate (a chemical derived from cow milk protein) to help it melt more like real cheese. Its taste, texture and melting factor make it a good cheese substitute for those who want to eliminate dairy from their diet or are lactose intolerant. Soy cheese can be found in a variety of flavors at natural health foods stores and most supermarkets.

Soy Flour - finely ground soybeans. Usually, the soybeans are roasted and then ground into a fine powder. Soy flour is high in protein. It is mixed with other flour for baking and binding sauces, rather than used alone. Soy flour is sold at natural health foods stores and some supermarkets.

Soy Grits - similar to soy flour except that the soybeans have been toasted and cracked into coarse pieces, rather than ground into a fine powder. Soy grits are also high in protein. It can be cooked by itself as a side dish, or added to rice and other grains and cooked together. Soy grits can be found at natural health food stores.

Soymilk - the liquid filtered from soybeans that have been soaked, finely ground, cooked and strained. It is an excellent substitute for cows' milk. Soymilk is a great source of protein, isoflavones and B-vitamins. It can be used hot, cold, on cereal, or in cooking. Soymilk may curdle when mixed with acidic ingredients such as lemon juice, vinegar or wine. Soymilk comes in special containers that only require refrigeration after opening, and in containers that require refrigeration before and after opening. Both types of soymilk can be found at supermarkets, natural health food stores and Asian markets. Soymilk is also sold in powder form at Asian food markets and some health food stores.

Soynut Butter - made from roasted, whole soybeans, which are then crushed and blended with soy oil and other ingredients, to produce a creamy paste. Soynut butter has a distinct flavor that is nutty in taste, but with less fat than peanut butter. Soynut butter is available at natural health food stores and some supermarkets.

Soynuts - whole soybeans that have been soaked in water and then baked or roasted until browned. Soynuts can be found in a variety of flavors, including chocolate covered. They are high in protein, isoflavones, and soluble fiber. Soynuts have a nutty texture and flavor, somewhat similar to peanuts. Roasted soynuts are available at natural health food stores, Asian food markets and some supermarkets.

Soy Protein Concentrate - made from defatted soy flakes. It contains about 70 percent protein, while retaining most of the bean's dietary fiber. Soy protein concentrate can be found at natural health food stores.

Soy Protein Isolate - a highly refined powder that is 90 percent soy protein, produced when protein is removed from defatted soy flakes. The advantage of powdered soy protein isolates is that they possess the greatest amount of protein of all soy products. It is used to make soy burgers, soy shakes, baked goods and other foods. Soy protein isolate is available at natural health food stores.

Soy Sauce - a dark brown liquid made from soybeans that have undergone a fermentation process. Soy sauces have a salty taste, but are lower in sodium than traditional table salt. Specific types of soy sauce are: shoyu, tamari and teriyaki. **Shoyu** is a blend of soybeans and wheat. **Tamari** is made only from soybeans and is a by-product of making miso, it is the liquid let off by miso as it ages. **Teriyaki** sauce can be thicker than other types of soy sauce and includes other ingredients such as sugar, vinegar and spices. There are also many low-sodium or lite soy sauces available on the market. Soy sauce is used to flavor soups, sauces, marinades, meat, fish and vegetables, and is also used as a table condiment in place of salt. All-purpose soy sauce is available at supermarkets. Specific varieties are available at natural health food stores, gourmet stores and Asian food markets.

Soy Yogurt - made from soymilk and active beneficial yogurt cultures, much like traditional yogurt. It has a creamy texture and comes in a variety of flavors. Soy yogurt can be found at natural health food stores and some supermarkets.

Tahini - (tah-HEE-nee) a thick, smooth paste made from ground sesame seeds. It is a staple of Middle Eastern cuisine. Tahini has a mild nutty flavor and is light brown to tan in color. It is available at natural health food stores and Middle Eastern food markets.

Tempeh - (tem-PAY) a traditional fermented Indonesian soy food, made from cracked, cooked soybeans, mixed with a grain such as millet, brown rice or barley, and sometimes all three. It is inoculated with Rhizopus oligosporus bacteria to make it meaty-tasting and chewy. Tempeh has a pleasant yet distinctive nutty flavor. It can be marinated, grilled, stir-fried or sauteed, added to soups, casseroles or sandwiches. Tempeh is available in the refrigerated section at natural health food stores, Asian food markets and some supermarkets.

Textured Soy Protein (TSP) - made by compressing de-fatted soy flour, also known as textured vegetable protein or TVP. When hydrated it has a chewy texture, and is widely used as a meat substitute or extender. TSP contains about 70 percent protein. It retains most of the soybean's dietary fiber, and contains virtually no fat. TSP is mainly sold in dried form. It can be found at natural health food stores and some supermarkets.

Tofu - (TOE-foo) the white, easily digestible soft cheese-like food made from coagulated soymilk that has been formed into blocks. It is sometimes called bean curd. Tofu has a bland taste and easily absorbs the flavors of other ingredients with which it is cooked. It comes in two forms, Japanese-style silken tofu and regular Chinese-style. These two forms of tofu are available in various weights and degrees of firmness, from extra firm to soft. Silken tofu varieties are the softest and creamiest of the tofu products. They are richer in flavor than regular Chinese-style tofu. Some varieties of tofu can be found at supermarkets. All varieties of tofu are available at natural health food stores and Asian food markets. Tofu is also sold in powder form at many Asian food stores.

Turmeric - (TER-muh-rick) the ground root of a plant related to ginger. It has a strong, pungent flavor and an intense yellow-orange color. Turmeric is popular in Spanish, Indian and Asian cuisines. It is a main ingredient in curries and is what gives American mustard its bright yellow color. Turmeric is available at supermarkets, natural health food stores, Spanish, Indian and Asian food markets.

Udon Noodles - (OO-dohn) firm, flat traditional Japanese wheat noodles. They are almost the thickness of thin spaghetti, and about the width of fettuccini (but shorter in length). Udon noodles are typically served instead of rice with stir-fried and sauteed dished. These noodles are available at natural health food stores, Asian food markets, and some supermarkets and gourmet stores.

Wakame - (wah-KAH-meh) a deep green, edible seaweed popular in Japan and other Asian countries. It is used like a vegetable in soups and simmered dishes, and occasionally in salads. Wakame is available fresh or dried at natural health food stores and Asian food markets.

Wasabi - (wah-SAH-bee) the Japanese version of horseradish. Wasabi powder mixed with water is used to make the pungent, fiery, light-green paste that accompanies sushi. This condiment adds a distinct sharp flavor to Japanese cuisine. It is available at natural health food stores, gourmet stores and Asian food markets in powder and paste forms. Some specialty produce markets carry fresh wasabi, which may be grated like horseradish.

REFERENCES

CHAPTER 1: SOY CULINARY HISTORY AND DIETS
(Phyto website; redrival.com/phyto/soyfacts.html) (Soy and Osteoporosis: Studies Show Soy Protein May Help in Prevention and Treatment of Bone Loss; PR Newswire; June 30, 1997) (Epicurious Food; www.epicurious.com)

How can I know that soy foods are not just one of the latest health food fads, in the news today and forgotten by tomorrow?
(A 3,000 Year History of Our Most Modern Oilseed; by Peter Warshall and Dan Imhoff; Whole Earth issue #97; www.wholefoods.com; Summer 1999) (HomeArts online magazine; www.homearts.com) (The Soy Queen Speaks!; by Polly Lanning; Whole Living Magazine; www.wholefoods.com; 1999) (Cook's century: Tea to Teflon; The Miami Herald, Tropical Life, 6K; December 26, 1999) (The Joys of Soy; www.hcf-nutrition.org) (USDA wants to allow soy products in school lunches; Soyfoods USA, Vol. 4, No. 12; January 17, 2000) (USDA Says All-Soy OK for School Lunch; by Adam Marcus; www.healthscout.com; March 10, 2000) (Dietary Guidelines for Americans, 2000; USDA Agricultural Research Service; www.ars.usda.gov/dgac; May 30, 2000) (Soy: Health claims for soy protein, questions about other components; by John Henkel; FDA Consumer Magazine, vol. 34 No. 3; www.fda.gov/fdac; May-June 2000)

What sparked so much interest in soy and soy-based products?
(Chinese researchers presented more evidence that the standard Western diet can cause heart disease; Reuters; www.cnn.com; November 10, 1999) (Soy may lower cholesterol levels; Reuters; www.msnbc.com; June 9,1999) (Ask the Nutrition Expert; by Sharon Howard; www.drkoop.com) (Soy Intake May Reduce Risk of Uterine Cancer, Says New Cancer Research Study in Hawaii; PR Newswire; www.talksoy.com; August 28, 1997) (A Serving of Soy a Day - Keeps Cancer at Bay?; by Kathleen McGarvey-Philippi, RN; www.webmd.com) (Osteoporosis and Soy Foods; www.hcf-nutrition.org) (Menopausal Symptoms and Soy Food; www.hcf-nutrition.org) (Eat Your Soy, Boy - Research says it may delay prostate cancer; by Neil Sherman; www.healthscout.com; October 6, 1999)

What exactly is the typical Asian diet, and how is it different from the standard American diet?
(Man to Man News: Summer 1998: Nutrition; American Cancer Society; www.cancer.org) (Soy to Prevent Breast Cancer?; by Nancy Snyderman, MD, FACS; www.drkoop.com; October 1998) (Chinese researchers presented more evidence that the standard Western diet can cause heart disease; Reuters; www.cnn.com; November 10, 1999)

What makes researchers believe that a soy rich diet is the cause of the health differences between Asian and Western populations?
(It's Official: Soy's a Joy - When eaten with a good diet, it can lower cholesterol; by Neil Sherman; www.healthscout.com; October 22, 1999) (Soy, disease prevention, and prostate cancer; by M.A. Moyad; Section of Urology, University of Michigan; Semin Urol Oncol, 17(2):97-102; www.oncolink.org; May 1999) (A Serving of Soy a Day - Keeps Cancer at Bay?; by Kathleen McGarvey-Philippi, RN; www.webmd.com) (Diet, Prostate Cancer Linked; www.abcnews.com; November 4, 1998) (Eat Your Soy, Boy - Research says it may delay prostate cancer; by Neil Sherman; www.healthscout.com; October 6, 1999) (Chinese researchers presented more evidence that the standard Western diet can cause heart disease; Reuters; www.cnn.com; November 10, 1999) (The Soy Queen Speaks!; by Polly Lanning; Whole Living Magazine; www.wholefoods.com; 1999) (Soy to Prevent Breast Cancer?; by Nancy Snyderman, MD, FACS; www.drkoop.com; October 1998)

What kind of diet do researchers recommend to promote and maintain good health?
(American Institute for Cancer Research; www.aicr.org) (Plant-based diet key to warding off cancer; by Karen Collins, RD; Nutrition Notes; www.msnbc.com; October 15, 1999) (Soybeans: A Secret to Good Health; by Sharon Howard, RD, MS, CDE; www.drkoop.com; December 1998) (United Soybean Board; www.talksoy.com) (Soy crazy: How much is enough? Nutrition Notes offers dietary advice; by Karen Collins, RD; www.msnbc.com) (Despite Promising Soy Research Results, Cancer Experts Urge Caution; www.aicr.org; October 29, 1999)

CHAPTER 2: NUTRITIONAL AND BENEFICIAL COMPOUNDS

(A Serving of Soy a Day - Keeps Cancer at Bay?; by Kathleen McGarvey-Philippi, RN; www.webmd.com) (Eating well, aging well; by Chris Parkhurst; WebMD; www.cnn.com; May 9, 1999) (15 Diet Weapons Against Cancer; by Sharon Howard, RD, MS, CDE; www.drkoop.com; December 1998)

Which particular vitamins and minerals are found in soy foods?
(Eating well, aging well; by Chris Parkhurst; WebMD; www.cnn.com; May 9, 1999) (United Soybean Board; www.talksoy.com) (A look at the newest in functional foods; www.cnn.com; January 1, 2000) (The Signet/Mosby Medical Encyclopedia; 1998) (The Energy Times; Vol. 1 No. 2, pp. 12-13; 1991) (The Energy Times; Vol. 2 No.1, p. 21; 1992)

I keep hearing how some fats are good for you and some are bad. I thought all fats were bad and should be eliminated from the diet. What makes a fat good or bad?
(The Signet/Mosby Medical Encyclopedia; 1998) (Hidden trans fats may kill thousands; by Robert Bazell; www.nbc.com; January 17, 2000) (15 Diet Weapons Against Cancer; by Sharon Howard, RD, MS, CDE; www.drkoop.com; December 1998) (American Heart Association; www.americanheart.org)

What kind of fat is found in soy foods? Are soy foods high in fat?
(American Heart Association; www.americanheart.org) (Ask Dr. Weil; www.drweil.com) (HomeArts online magazine; www.homearts.com) (Diet, Prostate Cancer Linked; www.abcnews.com; November 4, 1998) (15 Diet Weapons Against Cancer; by Sharon Howard, RD, MS, CDE; www.drkoop.com; December 1998)

Are soy foods a good source of fiber?
(American Heart Association; www.americanheart.org) (The Signet/Mosby Medical Encyclopedia; 1998) (United Soybean Board; www.talksoy.com) (HomeArts online magazine; www.homearts.com) (15 Diet Weapons Against Cancer; by Sharon Howard, RD, MS, CDE; www.drkoop.com; December 1998)

I keep hearing so much about the benefits of soy protein. What makes soy protein so good?
(American Heart Association; www.americanheart.org) (The Signet/Mosby Medical Encyclopedia; 1998) (United Soybean Board; www.talksoy.com) (Soy and Osteoporosis: Studies Show Soy Protein May Help in Prevention and Treatment of Bone Loss; PR Newswire; June 30, 1997) (HomeArts online magazine; www.homearts.com) (Soy Calms Cell Circuits; by Janice Billingsley; www.healthscout.com; February 17, 2000)

What are phytochemicals? Are isoflavones the only phytochemical contained in soy?
(Ask the Mayo Dietitian - Isoflavones; www.cnn.com; December 22, 1999) (Conference Reveals Details of Promising Phytochemical Research; www.aicr.org; September 2, 1999) (United Soybean Board; www.talksoy.com) (Legumes and soybeans: overview of their nutritional profiles and health effects; by M.J. Messina; Am J Clin Nutr, 70(3 Suppl):439S-450S; www.oncolink.org; September 1999) (Soy Calms Cell Circuits; by Janice Billingsley; www.healthscout.com; February 17, 2000) (Despite Promising Soy Research Results, Cancer Experts Urge Caution; www.aicr.org; October 29, 1999)

How do isoflavones offer protection against major health problems?
(Katrina Claghorn, RD; Section Editor of OncoLink's "Nutrition During Cancer Treatment" and "Diet and Cancer" menus; www.oncolink.org; August 26, 1999) (Eating well, aging well; by Chris Parkhurst; WebMD; www.cnn.com; May 9, 1999) (Soy Protein and Risk for Coronary Heart Disease; American Dietetic Association 80th Annual Meeting and Exhibition; www.soyfoods.com; October 27-30, 1997) (Soy Foods Decrease Risk for Heart Disease; www.hcf-nutrition.org) (It's Official: Soy's a Joy - When eaten with a good diet, it can lower cholesterol; by Neil Sherman; www.healthscout.com; October 22, 1999) (Soy to Prevent Breast Cancer?; by Nancy Snyderman, MD, FACS; www.drkoop.com; October 1998) (A Serving of Soy a Day - Keeps Cancer at Bay?; by Kathleen McGarvey-Philippi, RN; www.webmd.com) (Osteoporosis and Soy Foods; www.hcf-nutrition.org) (United Soybean Board; www.talksoy.com) (Soy, disease prevention, and prostate cancer; by M.A. Moyad; Section of Urology, University of Michigan; Semin Urol Oncol, 17(2):97-102; www.oncolink.org; May 1999) (Soybeans: A Secret

183

to Good Health; by Sharon Howard, RD, MS, CDE; www.drkoop.com; December 1998) (Soy Calms Cell Circuits; by Janice Billingsley; www.healthscout.com; February 17, 2000) (Database of Phytonutrients in Soy Foods; USDA Agricultural Research Service; www.ars.usda.gov)

How do isoflavones act as antioxidants?
(Plant-based diet key to warding off cancer; by Karen Collins, RD; Nutrition Notes; www.msnbc.com; October 15, 1999) (Natural Health, Natural Medicine online; Antioxidant Supplements; www.drweil.com; January 1, 1995) (Soy may lower cholesterol levels; Reuters; www.msnbc.com; June 9,1999) (Soy Foods Decrease Risk for Heart Disease; www.hcf-nutrition.org) (Third International Symposium on the Role of Soy in Preventing and Treating Chronic Disease; Session 7, Plenary Session: Hypertension, Renal Disease, and LDL Oxidation, Effects of Soy, as Tofu Vs. Meat on Coronary Heart Disease Risk Factors; by E.L. Ashton, J.E. Foster, M.J. Ball, and F.S. Dalais; October 31 - November 3, 1999) (Third International Symposium on the Role of Soy in Preventing and Treating Chronic Disease; Session 3, Cancer: In Vitro, Animal, and Human Studies Effect of Soy Supplementation on Levels of Oxidative Damage in Blood of Women; by Zora Djuric, Olga Mekhovich, Gang Chen, Fazlul Sarkar, Michael Tainsky, Omer Kucuk; October 31 - November 3, 1999)

Which soy foods are the best sources of soy protein and isoflavones?
(U.S. Soyfoods Directory; www.soyfoods.com) (Katrina Claghorn, RD; Section Editor of OncoLink's "Nutrition During Cancer Treatment" and "Diet and Cancer" menus; www.oncolink.org; August 26, 1999) (Soy Protein and Risk for Coronary Heart Disease; American Dietetic Association 80th Annual Meeting and Exhibition; www.soyfoods.com; October 27-30, 1997) (United Soybean Board; www.talksoy.com) (Soy crazy: How much is enough? Nutrition Notes offers dietary advice; by Karen Collins, RD; www.msnbc.com) (It's Official: Soy's a Joy - When eaten with a good diet, it can lower cholesterol; by Neil Sherman; www.healthscout.com; October 22, 1999) (Can Soy Help Menopause; by Michele Simon, JD, MPH; www.wholefoods.com) (Researchers Cautious About Calling Soy a Cancer Preventive; by Joel B. Finkelstein, www.oncology.com; November 10, 1999)

How much soy protein and isoflavones do researchers recommend consuming per day?
(FDA approves new health claim for soy protein and coronary heart disease; FDA Talk Papers; www.fda.gov; October 20, 1999) (FDA: Soy foods can be labeled 'good for you'; Associated Press; www.cnn.com; October 26, 1999) (Katrina Claghorn, RD; Section Editor of OncoLink's "Nutrition During Cancer Treatment" and "Diet and Cancer" menus; www.oncolink.org; August 26, 1999) (Prevention online magazine; www.healthyideas.com) (Third International Symposium on the Role of Soy in Preventing and Treating Chronic Disease; Session 2, Osteoporosis: In Vitro, Animal and Human Studies, Dietary Soy Isoflavones Favorably Influence Lipids and Bone Turnover in Healthy Postmenopausal Women; by Michael D. Scheiber, James H. Liu1, M.T.R. Subbiah, Robert W. Rebar, and Kenneth D.R. Setchell; October 31 - November 3, 1999) (Soyfoods USA, Vol. 4, No. 11; www.soyfoods.com; December 19, 1999) (United Soybean Board; www.talksoy.com)

What is the best way to consume soy products to get the most health benefits?
(Third International Symposium on the Role of Soy in Preventing and Treating Chronic, Session 1, Isoflavone Absorption/Metabolism and Effects of Processing, Absorption and Metabolism of Soy Isoflavones-from Food to Dietary Supplements and Adults to Infants; by Kenneth D.R. Setchell; Disease; October 31 - November 3, 1999) (Soy crazy: How much is enough? Nutrition Notes offers dietary advice; by Karen Collins, RD; www.msnbc.com) (Soyfoods USA, Vol. 4, No. 11; www.soyfoods.com; December 19, 1999) (OncoLink News In Focus: Soy foods get a boost - Are they good for you?; by Marilynn Larkin, MA; www.oncolink.org; November 7, 1999) (Soy isoflavones improve lipid levels in dose-dependent manner; Reuters Health; www.webmd.com; September 29, 1999) (The Soy Queen Speaks!; by Polly Lanning; Whole Living Magazine; www.wholefoods.com; 1999)

CHAPTER 3: HEART DISEASE, STROKE & CHOLESTEROL
(American Heart Association; www.americanheart.org) (It's Official: Soy's a Joy - When eaten with a good diet, it can lower cholesterol; by Neil Sherman; www.healthscout.com; October 22, 1999) (Soy Protein and Risk for Coronary Heart Disease; American Dietetic Association 80th Annual Meeting and Exhibition; www.soyfoods.com; October 27-30, 1997) (FDA Approves New

Health Claim for Soy Protein and Coronary Heart Disease; FDA Talk Papers; www.fda.gov; October 20, 1999)

What exactly is cholesterol and how does it contribute to coronary heart disease and stroke?
(Soy Protein and Risk for Coronary Heart Disease; American Dietetic Association 80th Annual Meeting and Exhibition; www.soyfoods.com; October 27-30, 1997) (American Heart Association; www.americanheart.org) (The Signet/Mosby Medical Encyclopedia; 1998)

How does soy and soy-based products effect cholesterol?
(Soy isoflavones improve lipid levels in dose-dependent manner; Reuters Health; www.webmd.com; September 29, 1999) (Soy may lower cholesterol levels; Reuters; www.msnbc.com; June 9,1999) (Third International Symposium on the Role of Soy in Preventing and Treating Chronic Disease; Session 7, Plenary Session: Hypertension, Renal Disease, and LDL Oxidation, Effects of Soy, as Tofu Vs. Meat on Coronary Heart Disease Risk Factors; by E.L. Ashton, J.E. Foster, M.J. Ball, and F.S. Dalais; October 31 - November 3, 1999) (Mens Health: The Joys of Soy; by Debra Wein; www.abcnews.com; July 2, 1999) (United Soybean Board; www.talksoy.com) (It's Official: Soy's a Joy - When eaten with a good diet, it can lower cholesterol; by Neil Sherman; www.healthscout.com; October 22, 1999) (FDA approves new health claim for soy protein and coronary heart disease; FDA Talk Papers; www.fda.gov; October 20, 1999) (Soybeans: A Secret to Good Health; by Sharon Howard, RD, MS, CDE; www.drkoop.com; December 1998) (Misunderstood soy may actually lower cholesterol; by Elizabeth Schwartz; www.cnn.com; August 2, 1996) (Soy crazy: How much is enough? Nutrition Notes offers dietary advice; by Karen Collins, RD; www.msnbc.com; 1999) (Soy: Health claims for soy protein, questions about other components; by John Henkel; FDA Consumer Magazine, vol. 34 No. 3; www.fda.gov/fdac; May-June 2000)

Are there any other positive effects that soy has on the cardiovascular system?
(Soy Protein and Risk for Coronary Heart Disease; American Dietetic Association 80th Annual Meeting and Exibition; www.soyfoods.com; October 27-30, 1997) (Third International Symposium on the Role of Soy in Preventing and Treating Chronic Disease; Session 7, Plenary Session: Hypertension, Renal Disease, and LDL Oxidation Soy Protein Dietary Supplementation Improves Lipid Profiles and Blood Pressure: A Double-Blind, Randomized, Placebo-Controlled Study in Men and Postmenopausal Women; by H.J. Teede, F.S. Dalais, D. Kotsopoulos, Y.L. Liang, S.R. Davis, and B.P. McGrath; October 31 - November 3, 1999) (United Soybean Board; www.talksoy.com) (American Heart Association; www.americanheart.org) (Soy Foods Decrease Risk for Heart Disease; www.hcf-nutrition.org)

CHAPTER 4: CANCER
(National Cancer Institute; www.cancer.org/statistis) (American Institute of Cancer Research; www.aicr.org) (The Signet/Mosby Medical Encyclopedia; 1998) (United Soybean Board; www.talksoy.com)

Can eating soy and soy-based products help reduce the risk of getting cancer?
(Diet and Cancer Risk; www.drkoop.com) (American Institute of Cancer Research; www.aicr.org) (15 Diet Weapons Against Cancer; by Sharon Howard, RD, MS, CDE; www.drkoop.com; December 1998) (United Soybean Board; www.talksoy.com) (A Serving of Soy a Day - Keeps Cancer at Bay?; by Kathleen McGarvey-Philippi, RN; www.webmd.com) (American Institute for Cancer Research Cites Soy Products for Fighting Cancer, Heart Disease; Taste-Tests for Soy Burgers; PR Newswire; September 17, 1997) (Researcher seeks anti-cancer agents in soybean leftovers; www.cnn.com; September 22, 1999) (Soybeans: A Secret to Good Health; by Sharon Howard, RD, MS, CDE; www.drkoop.com; December 1998) (Researchers Cautious About Calling Soy a Cancer Preventive; by Joel B. Finkelstein; www.oncology.com; Nov. 10, 1999) (Ask the Nutrition Expert; by Sharon Howard; Www.drkoop.com)

What types of cancer has soy been most effective in preventing?
(15 Diet Weapons Against Cancer; by Sharon Howard, RD, MS, CDE; www.drkoop.com; December 1998) (A Serving of Soy a Day - Keeps Cancer at Bay?; by Kathleen McGarvey-Philippi, RN; www.webmd.com) (Cancer and Soy; www.hcf-nutrition.org) (OncoLink News In Focus: Soy foods get a boost - Are they good for you?; by Marilynn Larkin, MA;

www.oncolink.org; November 7, 1999) (Researchers Cautious About Calling Soy a Cancer Preventive; by Joel B. Finkelstein; www.oncology.com; November 10, 1999) (Dietary Soy Seen Reducing Colon Cancer Risk; by Jeff Nesmith; New York Times Syndicate; www.drkoop.com; November 3, 1999) (Third International Symposium on the Role of Soy in Preventing and Treating Chronic Disease; Session 3, Cancer: In Vitro, Animal, and Human Studies Dietary Soy Is Associated with Decreased Cell Proliferation Rate and Zone in Colon Mucosa of Subjects at Risk for Colon Cancer; by M.R. Bennink, D. Thiagarajan, L.D. Bourquin, and J.E. Mayle; October 31 - November 3, 1999) (Soy Intake May Reduce Risk of Uterine Cancer, Says New Cancer Research Study in Hawaii; PR Newswire; www.talksoy.com; August 28, 1997) (Soy to Prevent Breast Cancer?; by Nancy Snyderman, MD, FACS; www.drkoop.com; October 1998)

How does soy effect breast cancer?
(The American Cancer Society; www.cancer.org/cancerinfo) (Ask the Nutrition Expert; by Sharon Howard; www.drkoop.com) (A Serving of Soy a Day - Keeps Cancer at Bay?; by Kathleen McGarvey-Philippi, RN; www.webmd.com) (Legumes and soybeans: overview of their nutritional profiles and health effects; by M.J. Messina; Am J Clin Nutr, 70(3 Suppl):439S-450S; www.oncolink.org; September 1999) (What Are Estrogen Receptors?; by Nancy Snyderman, MD, FACS; www.drkoop.com; November 1998) (Claims and Actualties About the "Breast Cancer Prevention Diet"; by Jack Raso; www.drkoop.com; June 4, 1999) (Miss Muffet Was on Right Track: Whey, Soy Proteins Seem to Stave Off Breast Cancer in Rats; by Janice Billingsley; www.drkoop.com; January 27, 2000) (Soy to Prevent Breast Cancer?; by Nancy Snyderman, MD, FACS; www.drkoop.com; October 1998)

Will a soy rich diet reduce the risk of breast cancer in every woman?
(Katrina Claghorn, RD; Section Editor of OncoLink's "Nutrition During Cancer Treatment" and "Diet and Cancer" menus; www.oncolink.org; August 26 and 27, 1999) (A Serving of Soy a Day - Keeps Cancer at Bay?; by Kathleen McGarvey-Philippi, RN; www.webmd.com) (OncoLink News In Focus: Soy foods get a boost - Are they good for you?; by Marilynn Larkin, MA; www.oncolink.org; November 7, 1999)

Does soy have an effect on male hormone-related cancers, like prostate cancer?
(Eat Your Soy, Boy - Research says it may delay prostate cancer; by Neil Sherman; www.healthscout.com; October 6, 1999) (NCI/PDQ Patient Statement: Prostate cancer; www.oncolink.org; July 1999) (The American Cancer Society; www.cancer.org/cancerinfo) (Testing time for prostate cancer; www.drweil.com; October 12, 1998) (Making a Prostate Cancer Diagnosis; www.drkoop.com, 1998) (Third International Symposium on the Role of Soy in Preventing and Treating Chronic Disease; Session 3, Cancer: In Vitro, Animal, and Human Studies, The Effect of Two Soy Preparations on Prostate-Specific Antigen Levels in Patients with Prostate Cancer and the Correlation of Prostate-Specific Antigen Changes with Plasma Genistein; by Israel Barken, Issacs Eliaz, I.E. Baranov, and Jack Geller; October 31 - November 3, 1999) (Diet, Prostate Cancer Linked; www.abcnews.com; November 4, 1998) (Third International Symposium on the Role of Soy in Preventing and Treating Chronic Disease; Session 3, Cancer: In Vitro, Animal, and Human Studies, Phytoestrogens and Prostate Cancer; by H. Adlercreutz, W. Mazur, and G. Hallmans; October 31 - November 3, 1999) (Man to Man News: Summer 1998: Nutrition; www.cancer.org) (Dietary Soy Seen Reducing Colon Cancer Risk; by Jeff Nesmith; New York Times Syndicate; www.drkoop.com; November 3, 1999) (Soy, disease prevention, and prostate cancer; by M.A. Moyad; Section of Urology, University of Michigan; Semin Urol Oncol, 17(2):97-102; May 1999)

CHAPTER 5: OSTEOPOROSIS
(What is osteoporosis?; Mayo Clinic Health Education; HealthOasis; www.mayohealth.org) (National Institutes of Health, National Institute on Aging; www.nih.gov/nia) (Osteoporosis and Soy Foods; www.hcf-nutrition.org) (Boning up on Osteoporosis; FDA Consumer; www.fda.gov; August 1997) (Attention men: 'Bone up' on eating and exercise tips; by Daniel Hayes, MD; WebMD; www.cnn.com; August 31, 1999) (Eating well, aging well; by Chris Parkhurst; WebMD; www.cnn.com; May 9, 1999)

How does soy reduce the risk of getting osteoporosis? Can it reverse the devastating effects of this disease in people who already have it?
(Soybeans: A Secret to Good Health; by Sharon Howard, RD, MS, CDE; www.drkoop.com;

December 1998) (Osteoporosis and Soy Foods; www.hcf-nutrition.org) (Boning up on Osteoporosis; FDA Consumer; www.fda.gov; August 1997) (Soy and Osteoporosis: Studies Show Soy Protein May Help in Prevention and Treatment of Bone Loss; PR Newswire; June 30, 1997) (Soy Isoflavones Strengthen Bone Mass in Women, Chinese Study Reports; 'Encouraging News' on Fractures; PR Newswire; www.doctordirectory.com; December 10, 1999) (Third International Symposium on the Role of Soy in Preventing and Treating Chronic Disease; Session 2, Osteoporosis: In Vitro, Animal and Human Studies, Dietary Soy Isoflavones Favorably Influence Lipids and Bone Turnover in Healthy Postmenopausal Women; by Michael D. Scheiber, James H. Liu1, M.T.R. Subbiah, Robert W. Rebar, and Kenneth D.R. Setchell; October 31 - November 3, 1999)

CHAPTER 6: MENOPAUSE & OTHER FEMALE CONCERNS
(The National Institutes of Health, National Institute on Aging; www.nih.gov/nia) (American Heart Association; www.americanheart.org) (Taking charge of menopause; by Lynne L. Hall; FDA Consumer; www.britannica.com; November-December 1999)

Can soy help relieve the symptoms associated with menopause?
(National Institutes of Health, National Institute on Aging; ww.nih.gov/nia) (American Heart Association; www.americanheart.org) (Can Soy Help Menopause; by Michele Simon, JD, MPH; www.wholefoods.com) (Taking charge of menopause; by Lynne L. Hall; FDA Consumer; www.britannica.com; November-December 1999) (New hope for easing menopause; by Dr. Bob Arnot; NBC News; www.msnbc.com; December 5, 1999) (Third International Symposium on the Role of Soy in Preventing and Treating Chronic Disease; Session 3, Cancer: In Vitro, Animal, and Human Studies Effects of Dietary Soy on the Uterus and Breast of Macaques; by J.M. Cline, M. Anthony, S.M. Mathes, and T. Clarkson; October 31 - November 3, 1999) (Ask the Mayo Dietitian - Isoflavones; www.cnn.com; December 22, 1999) (Diet and menopause: A change for the better; by Elizabeth Somer, RD; WebMD; www.cnn.com; September 6, 1999) (Answers to your menopause queries: Dr. Bob Arnot discusses soy, hormone replacement; by Dr. Bob Arnot; MSNBC's Crosstalk Monday; www.msnbc.com; December 6, 1999)

Which soy products work best at relieving menopausal symptoms, and how much is needed to produce any effect?
(Answers to your menopause queries: Dr. Bob Arnot discusses soy, hormone replacement; by Dr. Bob Arnot; MSNBC's Crosstalk Monday; www.msnbc.com; December 6, 1999) (The Today Show; www.msnbc.com; July 27, 1999) (Soybeans: A Secret to Good Health; by Sharon Howard, RD, MS, CDE; www.drkoop.com; December 1998) (Soy crazy: How much is enough? Nutrition Notes offers dietary advice; by Karen Collins, RD; www.msnbc.com) (United Soybean Board; www.talksoy.com) (Diet and menopause: A change for the better; by Elizabeth Somer, RD; WebMD; www.cnn.com; September 6, 1999) (Can Soy Help Menopause; by Michele Simon, JD, MPH; www.wholefoods.com) (Ask the Mayo Dietitian - Isoflavones; www.cnn.com; December 22, 1999) (North American Menopause Society; www.menopause.org/aboutm/faq.html)

Can soy also help relieve symptoms of PMS?
(Ask the Nutrition Expert; by Sharon Howard; www.drkoop.com) (Diet and menopause: A change for the better; by Elizabeth Somer, RD; WebMD; www.cnn.com; September 6, 1999) (Premenstrual Syndrom: The period before your period; HealthOasis; Mayo Clinic Women's Healthsource; www.mayohealth.org; May 1999)

Can soy cause problems during pregnancy or interfere with fertility?
(Studies Suggest a High Soy Diet for Pregnant Women; by Rebecca Jerman; Medical Tribune News Service; www.drkoop.com; November 5, 1999) (Soy to Prevent Breast Cancer?; by Nancy Snyderman, MD, FACS; www.drkoop.com; October 1998) (Researchers Cautious About Calling Soy a Cancer Preventive; by Joel B. Finkelstein; www.oncology.com; November 10, 1999) (Supplements: What does your body need?; by Jack Challem; Natural Health, p.128; July-August 1997)

CHAPTER 7: DIABETES & KIDNEY DISEASE
(American Diabetes Association; www.diabetes.org) (Soy Protein in Diabetes; www.hcf-nutrition.org) (Soy Foods and Kidney Health; www.hcf-nutrition.org) (We all could benefit from

following diabetic diet; by Jennifer Lowe; The Miami Herald, Tropical Life, 1K & 5K; February, 6, 2000)

Can soy help prevent diabetes, or treat any of the symptoms and conditions that develop as a result of having diabetes?
(Soy Protein in Diabetes; www.hcf-nutrition.org) (Soybeans: A Secret to Good Health; by Sharon Howard, RD, MS, CDE; www.drkoop.com; December 1998) (United Soybean Board; www.talksoy.com)

How can a soy-protein rich diet help diabetics maintain their kidney health?
(Soybeans: A Secret to Good Health; by Sharon Howard, RD, MS, CDE; www.drkoop.com; December 1998) (American Diabetes Association; www.diabetes.org) (Soy Protein in Diabetes; www.hcf-nutrition.org) (Soy Foods and Kidney Health; www.hcf-nutrition.org)

CHAPTER 8: OVERVIEW OF SOY FOODS
(Soy: Health claims for soy protein, questions about other components; by John Henkel; FDA Consumer Magazine, vol. 34 No. 3; www.fda.gov/fdac; May-June 2000)

I thought there was only one type of tofu. However, when I go to a health food store or an Asian store, I see so many varieties I don't know which one to choose. What is the difference between them all?
(Soyfoods Descriptions, U.S. Soyfoods directory; www.soyfoods.com, 1999) (HomeArts online magazine; www.homearts.com) (Epicurious Food; www.epicurious.com) (Vegetarian Times online magazine; www.vegetariantimes.com)

What is the difference between the various forms of soymilk?
(Soyfoods Descriptions, U.S. Soyfoods directory; www.soyfoods.com, 1999) (Epicurious Food; www.epicurious.com) (Vegetarian Times online magazine; www.vegetariantimes.com)

What is the difference between textured soy protein (TSP) and textured vegetable protein (TVP)?
(Soyfoods Descriptions, U.S. Soyfoods directory; www.soyfoods.com, 1999)

Can I use soy flour the same way I use wheat flour?
(HomeArts online magazine; www.homearts.com) (Soy: Health claims for soy protein, questions about other components; by John Henkel; FDA Consumer Magazine, vol. 34 No. 3; www.fda.gov/fdac; May-June 2000) (Soyfoods Descriptions, U.S. Soyfoods directory; www.soyfoods.com, 1999) (Epicurious Food; www.epicurious.com)

I keep hearing that miso is so healthy, how should I use it?
(Soyfoods Descriptions, U.S. Soyfoods directory; www.soyfoods.com, 1999) (HomeArts online magazine; www.homearts.com) (Vegetarian Times online magazine; www.vegetariantimes.com)

What exactly is tempeh, and what is the difference between the many varieties available?
(HomeArts online magazine; www.homearts.com) (Soyfoods Descriptions, U.S. Soyfoods directory; www.soyfoods.com, 1999)

GLOSSARY
(Soyfoods Descriptions, U.S. Soyfoods directory; www.soyfoods.com, 1999) (HomeArts online magazine; www.homearts.com) (Vegetarian Times online magazine; www.vegetariantimes.com) (Epicurious Food; www.epicurious.com) (Natural Health, Natural Medicine online, Miscellaneous Supplements; www.drweil.com)

INDEX

WEIGHTS & MEASUREMENTS CHART

A pinch or a dash . . . . less than 1/8 teaspoon
1-1/2 teaspoons . . . . 1/2 tablespoon
3 teaspoons . . . . 1 tablespoon
2 tablespoons . . . . 1/8 cup
4 tablespoons . . . . 1/4 cup
5 tablespoons + 1 teaspoon . . . . 1/3 cup
8 tablespoons . . . . 1/2 cup
10 tablespoon + 2 teaspoons . . . . 2/3 cup
12 tablespoons . . . . 3/4 cup
16 tablespoons . . . . 1 cup
1 tablespoon . . . . 1/2 ounce
2 tablespoons or 1/8 cup . . . . 1 ounce
1/4 cup . . . . 2 ounces
1/2 cup . . . . 4 ounces
3/4 cup . . . . 6 ounces
1 cup . . . . 8 ounces
1-1/4 cups . . . . 10 ounces
1-1/2 cups . . . . 12 ounces
1-3/4 cups . . . . 14 ounces
2 cups . . . . 16 ounces
8 fluid ounces or 1 cup . . . . 1/2 pint
16 fluid ounces or 2 cups . . . . 1 pint
24 fluid ounces or 3 cups . . . . 1-1/2 pints
32 fluid ounces or 4 cups . . . . 2 pints or 1 quart
48 fluid ounces or 6 cups . . . . 3 pints or 1-1/2 quarts
64 fluid ounces or 8 cups . . . . 4 pints or 2 quarts
80 fluid ounces or 10 cups . . . . 5 pints or 2-1/2 quarts
96 fluid ounces or 12 cups . . . . 6 pints or 3 quarts
112 fluid ounces or 14 cups . . . . 7 pints or 3-1/2 quarts
128 fluid ounces or 16 cups . . . . 8 pints or 4 quarts
4 quarts . . . . 1 gallon
1 jigger . . . . 1-1/2 fluid ounces or 3 tablespoons
1/2 cup or 4 ounces (oil or liquid) . . . . 1/4 pound
1 cup or 8 ounces (oil or liquid) . . . . 1/2 pound
2 cups or 16 ounces (oil or liquid) . . . . 1 pound
8 ounces (dry ingredients) . . . . 1/2 pound
16 ounces (dry ingredients) . . . . 1 pound
2-1/4 cups (granulated sugar) . . . . 1 pound
3-1/3 cups (unbleached bread flour) . . . . 1 pound

Printed in the United States
1100100002B/261